BRIGHT
WE BURN

BRIGHT WE BURN

KIERSTEN WHITE

CORGI BOOKS

CORGI BOOKS

UK | USA | Canada | Ireland | Australia
India | New Zealand | South Africa

Corgi Books is part of the Penguin Random House group of companies
whose addresses can be found at global.penguinrandomhouse.com.

www.penguin.co.uk
www.puffin.co.uk
www.ladybird.co.uk

First published in the USA by Delacorte Press, an imprint of Random House
Children's Books, and in Great Britain by Corgi Books 2018

001

Text copyright © Kiersten Brazier, 2018
Map illustration copyright © Isaac Stewart, 2018
Cover art by Alessandro Taini

The moral right of the author and illustrator has been asserted

Set in 11.74/15.1 pt Centaur MT by Jouve (UK), Milton Keynes
Printed in Great Britain by Clays Ltd, St Ives plc

A CIP catalogue record for this book is available from the British Library

ISBN: 978–0–552–57376–4

All correspondence to:
Corgi Books
Penguin Random House Children's
80 Strand, London WC2R 0RL

To Wendy Loggia, darling sunshine
in human form, who saw what these books
would be from the very beginning and
helped me every step of the way

MOLDAVIA

Chilia

Tirgoviste
Night Attack
Snagov

C H I A

Bucharest

A Arges River

Giurgiu

Danube River

VASSAL STATE OF
BULGARIA

BLACK SEA

1

1454, Wallachia

Lada Dracul had cut through blood and bones to get the castle.

That did not mean she wanted to spend time in it. It was a relief to escape the capital. She understood the need for a seat of power, but she hated that it was Tirgoviste. She could not sleep in those stone rooms, empty and yet still crowded with the ghosts of all the princes who had come before her.

With too far to go before reaching Nicolae, Lada planned to camp for the night. Solitude was increasingly precious—and yet another resource she was sorely lacking. But a tiny village tucked away from the frosted road beckoned her. During one of the last summers before she and Radu were traded to the Ottomans, they had traveled this same path with their father. It had been one of the happiest seasons of her life. Though it was winter now, nostalgia and melancholy slowed her until she decided to stay.

Outside the village, she spent a few frigid minutes changing into clothes more standard than her usual selection of black trousers and tunics. They were noteworthy enough that she risked being recognized. She put on skirts and a blouse—but with mail underneath. Always that. To the untrained eye, there was nothing to mark her as prince.

She found lodging in a stone cottage. Because there was not enough planting land for boyars to bother with here, the peasants could own small patches of it. Not enough to prosper, but enough to survive. An older woman seated Lada by the fire with bread and stew as soon as coins had exchanged hands. The woman had a daughter, a small thing wearing much-patched and too-large clothes.

They also had a cat, who, in spite of Lada's utter indifference to the creature, insisted on rubbing against her leg and purring. The little girl sat almost as close. "Her name is Prince," the girl said, reaching down to scratch the cat's ears.

Lada raised an eyebrow. "That is an odd name for a female cat."

The girl grinned, showing all the childhood gaps among her teeth. "But princes can be girls now, too."

"Ah, yes." Lada tried not to smile. "Tell me, what do you think of our new prince?"

"I have never seen her. But I want to! I think she must be the prettiest girl alive."

Lada snorted at the same time as the girl's mother. The woman sat down in a chair across from Lada. "I have heard she is nothing to look at. A blessing. Perhaps it can keep her out of a marriage."

"Oh?" Lada stirred her stew. "You do not think she should get married?"

The woman leaned forward intently. "You came here by

yourself. A woman? Traveling alone? A year ago such a thing would have been impossible. This last harvest we were able to take our crops to Tirgoviste without paying robbers' fees every league along the road. We made two times again as much money as we ever have. And my sister no longer has to teach her boys to pretend to be stupid to avoid being taken for the sultan's accursed Janissary troops."

Lada nodded as though hesitant to agree. "But the prince killed all those boyars. I hear she is depraved."

The woman huffed, waving a hand. "What did the boyars ever do for us? She had her reasons. I heard—" She leaned forward so quickly and with such animation half her stew spilled, unnoticed. "I heard she is giving land to anyone. Can you imagine? No family name, no boyar line. She gives it to those who deserve it. So I hope she never marries. I hope she lives to be a hundred years old, breathing fire and drinking the blood of our enemies."

The little girl grabbed the cat, settling it on her lap. "Did you hear the story of the golden goblet?" she asked, eyes bright and shining.

Lada smiled. "Tell me."

And so Lada heard new stories about herself, from her own people. They were exaggerated and stretched, but they were based on things she had actually done. The ways she had improved *her* country for *her* people.

Lada slept well that night.

<hr />

"Did you know," Lada said, scanning the parchment in her hand, "that to settle a dispute between two women who were fighting over an infant, I cut the infant in half and gave them both a piece?"

"That was very pragmatic of you." Nicolae had ridden out to the road to meet her. Now they were side by side, their horses meandering through the ice-glazed trees. This winter was preferable to last, though, oddly, she found herself missing the camaraderie of camping as a fugitive alongside her men. Now they were scattered. All doing important work for Wallachia, but any chance she had to reunite with them, she took. She had been looking forward to this time with Nicolae.

He guided them toward the estate that had formerly belonged to her advisor, Toma Basarab. Before Lada's rule, Toma had been alive and well, and these roads had been nearly impassable without an armed guard for protection. Now, Toma was dead and the roads were safe. Both of those—death of boyars and safety for everyone else—were patterns of Lada's rule so far.

The frigid air stung her nostrils in a way she found bracing and pleasant. The sun shone clear, but it was no match for the blanket of ice that Wallachia slept under. Perhaps that also contributed to the safety of the roads. No one wanted to be out in this.

Lada preferred it to the castle with a fierceness that was as sharp and pointed as the icicles she passed beneath.

She waved the parchment with the story of her unusual methods of solving family disputes. "The most offensive part," she said, "is that the story is unoriginal. The Transylvanians got that one from the Bible. The least they could do is make up *new* stories about me, rather than stealing from Solomon." She should print the stories the woman and her daughter had told last night. Spread *those* rumors instead.

Nicolae gestured to the bundle of reports he had given her. "Did you see the new woodcut? Very skilled artist. It is the next page."

She was sorting through as best she could while riding, dropping each page to the road as she finished. None had been anything but slander. Nothing important. Nothing true. Her thick gloves were not suited to manipulating thin sheets, but she shuffled until she found the illustration. "I am dining on human flesh amid a forest of impaled bodies."

"You are! Meals in Tirgoviste have changed since you sent me out here."

Lada adjusted her red satin hat, a jeweled star in the middle representing the falling star that had accompanied her ascension to the throne. "He got my hair wrong."

Nicolae reached out and tugged one of her long, curling locks. "It is difficult to capture such majesty with simple tools."

"I have missed you, Nicolae." Her tone was acidic but her sentiment sincere. She needed him where he was, but she missed him at her side.

He gestured to the star in the center of her hat, beaming. "Of course you have. I dare say I am one of the brightest— nay, the very brightest—point of your existence. How have you scrambled in the dark these long six months without me?"

"Peacefully, now that you mention it. Such blessed quiet."

"Well, Bogdan's strength never has been conversation." Nicolae's smile twisted, puckering his long scar. "But you do not keep him around for talking."

Lada gritted her teeth. "I *can* kill you. Very quickly. Or very, very slowly."

"As long as the Saxons make a woodcut of my demise, I will accept it with grace." He stroked his chin. "Please ask them to get my face right. A face such as this should never be poorly represented."

Nicolae was not wrong about Bogdan, though. Bogdan, her childhood companion and now most stalwart soldier and supporter, did not speak often. But lately even that had been too much. A break from him had been one of her motivations in making this trip alone. She was meeting him in Arges, but she had deliberately given him a task that took him from her before then.

Bogdan was like sleep. Necessary, sometimes enjoyable. She needed him. And when he was unobtainable, she missed him. But she liked that she could take him for granted most of the time.

Mehmed would never have tolerated such treatment. She scowled, pushing him from her mind. Mehmed deserved no place among her thoughts. He was a usurper there, just as he was everywhere.

They passed a frozen pond, patterns of frost telling a story she could not read. The trees opened up ahead to rolling farmland softened with snow. "Why did Stefan not stay after delivering these letters? He knew I was due here soon."

"He wanted to get back to Daciana and the children. And he was probably worried if he saw you before that, you would send him away again and he would not get a chance to stop in Tirgoviste."

Lada grunted. That was true. She wanted him in Bulgaria, or maybe Serbia. Both were active vassal states of the Ottoman Empire, and likely staging areas for any attacks. She did not *expect* an attack. But she would be prepared, and for that, she needed Stefan. He had spent the last couple of months scouting in Transylvania and Hungary to get a feel for their political climates, whether there were any active threats toward Lada's rule. She wanted to speak with him in person. Daciana should not take priority over that. Nothing should.

Daciana ran the day-to-day business at the castle, all the details and mundanity that Lada could not begin to care about. Lada was grateful for her work. It had been a stroke of luck, finding her during their campaigning last year. But there was nothing at the castle that required Stefan's attention. Daciana was safe and busy. He should know better than to waste all their time.

Lada scanned the neatly ordered reports impatiently. Stefan had written his own observations and coupled them with the woodcut printings. In Hungary, Matthias was king. He did not go by Hunyadi, as his father did, but had styled himself Matthias Corvinus. Lada was not surprised. Matthias's relationship with his soldier father had been fraught. Of course he would not honor the man who had cut the path to the crown for him. And Lada had helped, in the end. She had betrayed Hunyadi's legacy and committed murder for Matthias.

And then she had had to do everything by herself anyway, because the aid of men was never what they promised. It always came with hooks, invisible barbs to tug her back when she got close to her goals.

Matthias was not having an easy time of being king, at least. According to Stefan's report, he spent all his time and money flattering nobles and trying to buy back his crown from Poland. The Polish king had taken it for *safekeeping* years before when the previous king had been killed in battle. It was an important symbol, and Matthias was desperate for the legitimacy it would give his questionable claim to the throne.

Lada skimmed that information. Matthias was a fool if he thought a piece of metal would give him what he wanted, and she did not particularly care about any of his machinations as long as they were directed toward other countries. It also served the benefit of keeping him distracted. As far as Stefan could tell, he had no designs on Lada despite her refusal to defer to his authority.

The woodcut printings demonstrated Transylvania's continued opposition to her rule, but aside from the artistic flair, they had no organized opposition. There did not seem to be any attempt to destabilize her militarily. Stefan mentioned the downside to losing them as allies—they had long served as a buffer between Wallachia and Hungary—but there was nothing to be done. She had, after all, spent much of the previous year burning their cities. But if they had not wanted her to do that, they should have allied with her sooner.

All things considered, it was as good of news as she could have hoped for. But she had questions for Stefan. And concerns, now. Daciana was hers. Stefan was hers. She did not like them being each other's before that.

She tucked the papers into her saddlebag. "And how have you managed?"

"I sleep well at night, and my appetite remains consistent. Some days I feel a touch of melancholy, but I combat it through long walks and deep barrels of wine." He grinned at Lada's exasperated look. "Oh, were you not asking about me, personally? I was born to be a lord. This much authority suits me nicely. My crops flourished, the fields are ready for the thaw, and the people on my land are happy. Revenues should be robust this year. Good news for the royal treasury, which is—"

"Still empty. And the men?" Along with the farmland, they had set aside a portion of Toma Basarab's estate for training Lada's soldiers. Princes had never been allowed to have a standing army. They were expected to depend entirely on the boyars and their individual forces. It was a disorganized, messy system. And a system that saw prince after prince dead before their time.

But Lada was like no prince before.

Nicolae tugged down his hat. In the cold, his nose had gone bright red, and his scar almost purple. "You were right to send us out here. It is easier to control the men and instill discipline when there are no city temptations. And everything I learned from the Janissaries is being put to use. This will be the greatest group of fighting men Wallachia has ever had."

Lada was not surprised, but she was pleased. She knew her methods were better than what had always been done. Power was not split among meddling, selfish boyars. It flowed in a direct line of command to her. She rewarded merit, and she punished disloyalty and crime. Both with very public efficiency. And she knew from her stay the night before that word was spreading. Her people were motivated.

They passed two frozen bodies hanging from a tree. One had a sign that said DESERTER. The other, THIEF. Nicolae grimaced and looked away. Lada reached up and straightened one of the signs.

She had been focusing on making the roads safe and preparing for the spring planting. She had also been pruning the boyars. But Nicolae's work was just as important for the future of Wallachia, and she would invest whatever she had to. It was a different type of seed to nurture.

Nicolae stretched, holding his long arms above his head and yawning. "How are things in the capital? Any problems with the boyars? I heard rumors that Lucian Basarab was angry." Nicolae's casual tone was as artfully constructed as a Transylvanian woodcut. Lada knew he had not forgotten nor forgiven her choices at the bloody banquet.

Though she had mostly killed Danesti boyars, the family most directly responsible for the death of her father and older brother, Toma Basarab had also been eliminated. It did not go over well with the Basarab family, including his wealthy and influential brother, Lucian. She was not sorry. The fewer boyars alive to betray her, the better. They had outlived far too many princes. This had made them comfortable and lazy, assured of their own importance. If boyars now lived in constant fear for their lives? She did not think that was a problem. They needed to know they were the same as all Lada's citizens: they served Wallachia, or they died.

But Nicolae always wanted more delicacy. More mercy. It was part of the reason she had sent him out here, even though he was one of her best. She had no use for his counsel on moderation and placation. Neither of those were skills she had any interest in cultivating. If boyars served a purpose, they could remain. But they so very rarely did.

Mercy was a luxury Lada's rule was not yet stable enough to afford. Perhaps someday. Until then, she knew what she was doing was both necessary and *working*.

She breathed in the sharp, cold air, the scent of woodsmoke beckoning them toward warmth and food. They rode across the fields, through the Wallachia she had carved free from the failure of the past. "I addressed Lucian Basarab's concerns. It is all taken care of. I am a very good prince."

Nicolae laughed. "When you are not busy cutting babies in half."

"Oh, that takes almost no time. They are such small things, after all."

—————•————

A few days later, satisfied that Nicolae had her troops well under control, Lada rode along the same banks she had traveled twice before. Once, as a girl with her father discovering her country. And then with her men in an attempt to take that country back.

This time she rode alone. She paused at a bend in the river where a hidden cave contained a secret passage down from the ruins of the mountain fortress.

But they were ruins no longer. There was no solitude to be found here today. Lada listened to the chisels, the shouts of men, the clinking of metal chains. Here, at last, a promise fulfilled: she had come back to rebuild her fortress.

She rode slowly along the narrow switchbacks leading up

the steep mountainside. This morning, she had dressed in her full uniform, complete with her red satin hat marking her as the prince. Where she passed, her soldiers bowed. And the men and women working cowered, ducking out of the way.

Near the top, as the new walls of her fortress loomed gray and glorious from the peak, Bogdan came out to meet her. She let him help her down from her horse, his hands lingering at her waist.

"How is it?" She devoured the walls with her eyes. Her silver locket, given to her by Radu and filled with the flower and tree clipping she had kept with her all their long years away, felt heavy around her neck, as though relieved to be home, too.

"Nearly finished."

A man in chains staggered past, pushing a cart filled with stones. His clothes were ragged and stained, only a hint of their former finery showing through. She much preferred Lucian Basarab this way. Behind him, his wife and their two children pushed more carts. The children were dead-eyed, trudging numbly along. Lucian Basarab looked up, but did not seem to see her. He collapsed on the side of the path.

One of her soldiers hurried forward, a club in his hand. Lada did not know whether Lucian Basarab was dead. It did not matter. There were more to take his place. Just like the rest of her Wallachia, the fortress was being remade at remarkable speed thanks to the unwilling efforts of those who opposed her.

At last she had found something that boyars were good for.

"Show me my fortress," Lada said, striding past her foes and into her triumph.

2

Constantinople

SOMEDAY RADU WOULD NOT long for a time when he was certain things were terrible but had no idea just how much worse they were about to get.

This day, however, he was plagued with memories of riding this same road to Constantinople with Nazira and Cyprian at his side. He had been so nervous, so frightened, so determined to make something of his time there. To prove himself to Mehmed.

He pitied the man he had been on that ride. And he missed him. Riding toward the city today, all he felt was the absence of Nazira and Cyprian. The absence of his assurance that he was doing the right thing. The absence of his faith in Mehmed. The absence of his faith in faith itself.

It was a very lonely road.

He had not planned to return to Constantinople. The city was haunted for him, and forever would be. After Mehmed took it, Radu had returned to Edirne at the first possible opportunity. Both to escape, and to be with Fatima. The guilt he carried was nothing compared to the debt he owed her for losing her wife, and so, to ease some of Fatima's suffering, he endured his anguish at being around her. There was nothing else he could do for Nazira.

All his letters—joined by Kumal's and even Mehmed's efforts—had yielded no news. Nazira, Cyprian, and the servant boy Valentin had disappeared. He had watched them sail away from the burning city, swallowed up by smoke and distance. He had sent them away so they could live, but he feared he had simply found another way for them to die. Every day Radu prayed that they had not joined the thousands sent to anonymous graves. He could not bear the idea that the people he longed for might not exist anymore.

And so he sent more letters, and waited at their home in Edirne, where he would be easy to find.

But then Mehmed had written. A request from the sultan was never a request—it was a command. Though Radu considered rejecting Mehmed's invitation to join him in Constantinople, in the end he did what he always did: he returned to Mehmed.

Fatima had enough faith for both of them that all would be well. She waited at the window of their house in Edirne every day. Radu imagined her there now, in the same place she had been when he left. Would she wait there fruitlessly for the rest of her life?

A passing cart startled him from his gloomy reverie. The road to Constantinople had been empty last time, cleared by the specter of war hanging over the countryside. Now traffic flowed to and from the city like blood through a vein. Carrying life in and out in a constant pulse. The city was no longer a dying thing.

Like arms reaching out to welcome—or drag—him in, the gates were open. Radu tamped down the panic that arose at seeing them that way. He had spent so long both defending them and praying they would fall, his body did not know how to respond to seeing them function as city gates should.

Much had been done to repair the walls he had fought on. Shiny new rocks re-formed sections that had fallen during the long siege. It was as though the events of last spring had never occurred. The city healed, the past erased. Rebuilt. Buried.

Radu looked at the land in front of the wall and wondered what had been done with the bodies.

So many bodies.

". . . Radu Bey!"

Radu crawled out of his memories of darkness, thrust back into brilliant day. "Yes?"

It took a few confused moments for Radu to realize that the young man who had addressed him had been only a boy a few months ago. Amal had grown so much he was nearly unrecognizable. "I was told you would be arriving sometime today. I am to escort you to the palace."

Radu reached out his hands to clasp Amal's. His heart swelled to see the young man here, alive, healthy. He was one of three boys Radu had been able to save from the horrors of the siege.

"Come," Amal said, grinning. "They are waiting. We will ride between the walls and go straight there."

Radu did not know whether to be relieved or disappointed.

He had thought about riding through the city, but he knew where his heart would take him. An empty house where no one waited for him. Better to go straight to Mehmed.

"Thank you," Radu said. Amal took the reins of Radu's horse and led him through the space between the city's two defensive walls. Radu did not want to be here. He would have preferred to visit ghosts that were, if melancholy, at least tinged with sweetness. Here at the walls there were only the ghosts of steel and bone, blood and betrayal.

Radu shuddered, dragging his eyes from the top of the wall and toward the gate they were heading for. The gate Radu had unlocked in the midst of the final battle, sealing Constantine's fate and bringing the city down around himself.

Amal gestured to the walls on either side. "They finished repairs only last month."

Radu glanced up at the nearest Janissaries. He wondered if these men had been part of the siege. If they had flooded the wall, spilling over it. What had they done when they got into the city after so many endless days of anticipation fueled with frustration and hatred?

Radu swallowed a bitter, acidic taste, unable to look at the walls any longer. "I would like to go the rest of the way alone." Radu took the reins back.

"But I am to—"

"I know the path." Radu ignored Amal's panicked expression and turned his horse around. He entered at the main gate amid the press of humans, the crush of life. It was something, at least.

Once inside, he let his horse meander, guided by the crowds.

He was desperate not to be alone. There was much to be distracted by. This portion of the city had been nearly abandoned before. Now windows were thrown open, walls repainted, early flowers planted in tiny pots. A woman beat a rug, humming to herself, as a child toddled on unsteady legs after a dog.

Where the spring had been unseasonably cold, the winter was moderate and pleasant. It did not feel like the same desperate, starving, suspicious city. Everywhere Radu looked, things were being built and repaired. There was no evidence of fire, no hint that any tragedy other than age had ever befallen this city.

Radu was so distracted that he missed the road he was supposed to follow and ended up in the Jewish sector. He had not spent any time there before. It, too, was humming with activity. He paused in front of a building under construction.

"What is this?" Radu asked a man carrying several large wooden beams.

"New synagogue," the man said. He wore a turban and robes. He passed the beams to a man wearing a kippah on his head and ringlets at his ears.

Radu rode through the sector, then found himself in a more familiar area. Boys surrounded a giant building that had been a derelict library. They lounged on the steps, talking or playing. A bell clanged, and the boys jumped up and rushed inside. Radu wondered what their lives were like. Where they had come from. What they knew of what had happened to create a city where they could play on the steps of their school, safe. At peace.

Radu stared down the street. If he went farther this way, he would reach the Hagia Sophia.

He turned and headed for the palace instead. The ride had been enough to clear his head a bit. He had anticipated how difficult it would be to see the walls again. But seeing the vitality of the city was a balm to his senses. He would not risk that by revisiting the Hagia Sophia so soon.

Amal was waiting near the palace entrance, nervously wringing his hands. Doubtless Radu had complicated his day by taking a detour. It was not Amal's fault Radu felt the way he did, and Radu really was glad to see Amal alive and well. He dismounted and passed his reins to his former aide. "Forgive me," Radu said. "Coming back has been . . . emotional."

"I understand." Amal smiled, and suddenly he looked even older than the young man he had grown into. Radu had shielded Constantine's two young heirs from the horrors of the city's fall, but Amal had been in the thick of it before Radu pulled him free. "I will see to your horse. And, if you do not mind, I have asked to be assigned as your personal servant while you are here."

"I would like nothing more." Radu watched as Amal led the horse away, putting off his own entrance into the palace.

A small bundle of motion rushed toward him. Radu barely had a chance to hold out his arms before a boy threw himself into them.

"Radu! He said you were here!"

Radu pulled back, looking into the saintly face of Manuel, one of the two heirs to the fallen emperor Constantine. Radu had stayed behind when Nazira, Cyprian, and Valentin left so that he could save Constantine's child heirs. They were his attempt at redemption for all he had done during the siege and everyone he had betrayed. He had fallen far short of redemption, but holding Manuel—alive, healthy, happy Manuel—in his arms, Radu felt joy for the first time in months. Laughing, Radu pulled him close, pressing a kiss to the top of his head.

Of all the life he had seen return to the city, this little life was the best he could possibly have hoped for. "Where is your brother?"

Manuel squirmed free, adjusting his clothes. He wore silk robes in the style of the Ottomans. It was a far cry from the stiff and structured Byzantine clothes he had worn before. "Murad is inside, waiting. He is too old now to run, he says."

"Murad?" Radu asked, puzzled. It had been Mehmed's father's name.

Manuel beamed. "Yes. And I am Mesih. The sultan let me choose it myself."

"You have new names." Radu frowned.

"We thought it was best. It is a new empire! A new start. A rebirth, we decided."

"We?" Radu asked.

"Yes, Murad and me. And the sultan."

Mehmed had meant what he said, then—that he would make the boys part of his court. Radu was glad to hear that this promise had been kept. And he supposed renaming them made sense. He himself had finally been able to adjust and accept his new life when he felt like he truly belonged. It was probably best for the boys to remove themselves from who they had been, to forget the trauma and loss of the past. Manuel—Mesih—certainly seemed happy enough.

If only Radu Bey's new name had had the same effect.

Mesih took Radu's hand and pulled him deeper into the palace. He kept up a steady stream of chatter, telling Radu what they could expect for dinner and asking whether Radu would join them for evening prayer at the Hagia Sophia or if he would be praying somewhere else. Then he went on to speak of his lessons, which tutors he liked best, how his writing was much better than his brother's. "And you have noticed how good my Turkish is, I am sure."

Radu laughed. "I have. I could listen to it all day." And he suspected he would, until they were separated. Something nagged at Radu, though, as Mesih continued describing his lessons.

He realized with a pain both happy and sad what was different: This boy was receiving a true education with no cruelty. There were no visits to the head gardener, no instructional trips to the prisons and torture chambers, no beatings. This was not the same childhood Radu and Lada had experienced under a sultan.

Mehmed was not his father. He had taken the city and made something better. He had taken the heirs of his enemy and made them his family. The dread Radu had felt about seeing his oldest friend dissipated. There was still much distance between them, but at least Radu had not been wrong to believe in Mehmed's ability to do great things.

"Are you well, Radu Bey?" Mesih asked.

Radu sniffed, clearing his throat. "Yes, I am well. Or at least, I think I will be."

3

Tirgoviste

IF LADA HAD KNOWN the sheer volume of parchment she would be buried under, she might have taken a title other than prince. She had returned revitalized from her visit to her fortress, only to find mounds of letters waiting for her.

Lada groaned, leaning her head forward. The brush Oana was working through her hair caught on a snarl.

"Sit up straight," Oana snapped.

"I do not want to do this." Lada gestured weakly toward the table covered with demands for her time and attention.

"Well, I would help, but I cannot read."

"Count yourself fortunate." Lada sat on the floor next to the table, sweeping a pile of missives onto her lap. "Go find Stefan. I want to speak with him if any of these prove interesting." Lada began sorting.

Boyar asking for redress for the loss of life of a relative—tossed in a pile in the corner.

Boyar asking for a meeting to address the conscription of land for Lada's own purposes—same pile.

Letter from her cousin Steven, the king of Moldavia. This, she read carefully. She had never met him, but he had a fierce reputation. He wrote to congratulate her on taking the throne, and to commend her on the reports of order and peace in her country. He said nothing of her mother. It gave Lada a dark thrill of vindictive pleasure. Her mother had talked almost obsessively of his yearly visits. He was one of the highlights of Vasilissa's sad, solitary life, and she did not so much as register in his own.

But then the end of the letter soured some of her pleasure. *Please take care to avoid antagonizing our neighbors. Let me know when you have new terms with the sultan. I am most curious to hear them.*

Glowering, she threw his letter in with the boyar demands.

"From Matthias Corvinus," Stefan said, passing her a slender letter.

Lada did not know when he had entered the room, but would not give him the pleasure of reacting to his stealth. She was still cross with him for failing to meet her at Nicolae's estate. "Read it. I do not care to." She picked up another letter, more nonsense from a wheedling boyar.

"Matthias wants to meet. He says you have much to discuss."

"I have nothing to say to him. We both got what we bargained for. As far as I am concerned, our relationship is over."

Stefan held out the letter to her. "We want him as an ally."

" 'We'? *I* do not want him as anything."

Stefan did not lower his hand or change his impassive expression. Growling in frustration, Lada snatched the letter and set it next to herself, but not in the pile for burning. "Very well."

Stefan picked up another letter. "This one is from Mara Brankovic. She is——" He paused, eyes scanning the air as he retrieved one of the thousands of bits of stored information he carried at all times. "The daughter of the Serbian king. Widow of Sultan Murad."

Lada opened this letter with more curiosity than she had felt about any so far. Mara's handwriting was perfect and elegant. There was not so much as an ink spot out of place. Lada read the letter twice to make certain she understood it. "Mara has gone to Constantinople and joined Mehmed's court as one of his *advisors*. Have you ever heard of such a thing? She was so eager to escape Edirne, and now she goes back to the empire of her own free will?"

"I have never heard of a foreign woman advising a sultan."

Lada frowned, looking over the words. "It is smart of him, though. She is brilliant. And, as Serbian royalty, she has connections and can deal with Europeans better than he could. She is a perfect choice for soothing relations." Lada leaned back, tapping the letter against her leg. Mehmed obviously benefited, but Mara was not the type to get into any situation she did not want to. Her marriage to Murad had been forced, but she had made of it what she could. And she had gotten out, to return to her family.

Ah. There was her motivation. She was still young enough to be enticing for a political marriage. This move and position put her entirely out of her father's power. She was, for all intents and purposes, free forever now. Clever woman!

"What does she want from you?" Stefan asked.

"Hmm?" Lada looked up, stirred from her memories of

meals with Mara, during which the older woman advised her how to use society's demands to create a position of stability. Lada did not care for her methods, but she could not deny that Mara knew what she was doing. "Oh, she asks me to visit Constantinople. She makes it sound like a social call. 'Come and visit the palace! We will eat, take a walk around the gardens, discuss the ways in which you should let Mehmed and his horrible empire continue to dictate your life!' I wonder if she thought of this on her own, or if Mehmed asked her to write, thinking our past connection would sway me." Lada did not know which she preferred to believe: that Mara was trying to manipulate her—she would not doubt it, or be bothered by it—or that Mehmed was trying to get to her through any means possible.

But if that were the case, surely Radu would have been sent. Or at least written. She had not heard from him since his letter telling her of the fall of Constantinople and his new title of Radu Bey.

Maybe his absence meant that Radu was finally out of Mehmed's control. Because Mehmed would never neglect an advantage like Radu—not if he had a choice.

"We should write my brother," Lada said, picking up another letter.

"To ask him to come back and help?"

"No." She threw the letter aside without looking at it. "I have learned how to handle the boyars on my own. I do not *need* him for anything. But he may be a useful source of information about Mehmed." Lada could accept that as the reason. The other, smaller reason was that she missed him. She had feared for his life in Constantinople, and wondered what had happened to him there. She did not like feeling this way. Radu was the one who missed, who mourned.

"From the pope," Stefan said, passing her another letter. "He curses the infidels and calls down destruction from heaven on their empire. And then he urges peace."

"He should make up his mind." Lada tossed the pope's letter into the pile for burning. "Would that I had a country without borders. Would that I had an island." She stood and looked at the rest of the letters. Demands and requests, alliances and enemies, the subtleties of politics of a dozen countries and an encroaching empire screaming for her attention.

She gathered them all and threw them in the fire. The remains of parchment dust and sealing wax were easily wiped away on her breeches. "I am going to the stables. It is a lovely afternoon for a ride."

Two weeks later, the Turkish ambassadors showed up unannounced and uninvited, complete with a Janissary escort. Lada had her own men line the room for a show of power. They outnumbered the Janissaries three to one. Her men, several of them former Janissaries, looked on coldly.

Lada lounged on her throne, one leg draped over its arm. She tapped her foot impatiently, bouncing it through the air. She could see in the puzzled looks and shuffling posture of the ambassadors that her lack of decorum made them nervous.

She smiled.

"This is Wallachia. Remove your hats out of respect."

Neither the Janissaries in their cylindrical caps with white flaps, nor the ambassadors in their turbans, made any move to follow her order.

The lead ambassador, an older man with a silver beard and shrewd eyes, raised an eyebrow dismissively. "We bring terms of your vassalage from our sultan, the Hand of God on Earth, Caesar of Rome, Mehmed the Conqueror."

Lada tapped her chin thoughtfully. "What a burden, to be the hand of God! Which hand is it, I wonder? God's right hand, or God's left? If Mehmed cleaned his ass with the hand that is the hand of God instead of his own hand, would he be struck down for blasphemy?"

Many of her men in the room laughed raucously, and Lada flushed with pleasure. But Bogdan had his eyes averted. He hated it when she spoke this way about God. It was a good reminder. She had no use for God, but most of her people did, and anything that held faith and belief was a source of power. She had seen what Mehmed had accomplished because of his steadfast faith. She had seen that same faith steal her own brother from her. Faith was power. She knew she should not dismiss anything that gave her power over others. She sat up straight. "Our god, the true God of Christianity, is without form and thus without hands. We reject your sultan's title and his authority. You have no purpose here. Leave."

"There is something else." The Janissary captain stepped forward. He was compact and broad, years of training evident in every move. She had almost forgotten how perfect the Janissaries were. It made her uneasy, thinking back on the men she led now. They were nothing compared to these soldiers, who were trained from childhood to be weapons of the sultan. The captain continued, "On our journey here we passed through Bulgaria. It appears there have been some conflicts along your border. Several Wallachian villages were burned."

Lada could not believe she was hearing about this now, from an enemy instead of her own people. She hated that he was showing her he had more information than she did. "I have not had reports of this yet."

He did not change his expression, which was as sharp and unyielding as steel. "All the Wallachians were dead. It is unfortunate. Most likely due to a misunderstanding. But once your terms of vassalage are secure, Bulgaria will be a powerful ally and such conflicts will cease. The sultan protects his vassals."

This man, this Ottoman, thought he could come here and tell her about attacks on her own country—slaughter of her own people—as a method of forcing her to agree to Ottoman rule? As though dead Wallachians somehow argued in favor of allying with those who killed them? And it did not make sense that he would have news of this before her.

Unless he had come directly from doing it himself. Lada leaned forward, her voice cold. "You killed my people."

The Janissary captain flashed a smile that did not touch his eyes. "No. Bulgarians killed your people along a chaotic border. The sultan's terms eliminate such chaos. A solid treaty, respectfully followed, will protect your people."

Lada bared her small white teeth. It was not a smile. "*I* protect my people. I avenge them, too. And you have nothing to teach me about respect. After all, none of you showed me the respect of removing your hats." She stood. "Bind them."

Her men sprang into action. The Janissary captain and his soldiers put up a fight, but they had not been allowed to bring weapons into the throne room. Everyone was subdued, though not without a struggle and several broken noses.

The lead ambassador glared murderously at Lada. "You cannot harm us. You do not want to risk what it will bring."

"You did not worry about what risk killing my own people would bring." Lada seethed with rage. They had come into her land. Slaughtered Wallachians under her protection. Unlike letters, such a thing as this could not go unanswered. She would send a message the likes of which would echo through Mehmed's empire and all of Europe.

She prowled in a circle around the ambassador, then tugged on the edges of his turban. "I am going to help you. If it was so important to you to leave your heads covered in my presence, so important that it was worth disrespecting a *prince*, then I will make certain you never have to uncover your heads again." Lada turned to Bogdan. "Bring me nails and a hammer."

Finally, the lead ambassador trembled. Finally, he saw how Lada answered disrespect and the deaths of her own people.

Lada stood in the corner of the throne room as her men drove nails into the heads of the Ottomans. As always, she made herself watch. It would have been easier to do in private. In some hidden dungeon. But no. She would bear witness to the things that had to be done for Wallachia to be secure. This was her burden, her responsibility.

Their screams were loud. In a bright, bloody flash, she remembered one of her many childhood trips to watch the sultan's torturers' brutal work. The price of stability was always paid with blood and flesh and pain.

She watched, but as though from a great distance.

They were not men. They were goals accomplished. They were not men.

A sudden wave of relief that Radu was not here washed over her. She did not like to imagine the look on his face if he were. She had always tried to protect him because he was her responsibility. Now all of Wallachia was. She would do whatever it took to protect her people.

The screams stopped. Which was good. She had other things to do.

"Send them back to their Hand of God," she said, glancing over the bodies. Some were still alive. It was unfortunate for them but would not last long. "Tell him I *will* have his respect."

She turned to Bogdan, whose hands were slick with blood. His mother, Oana, would be the one to clean it up. Some things never changed. "Send for Nicolae and our forces. We have business to attend to in Bulgaria."

4

Constantinople

RADU WAS NOT SITTING as far from Mehmed as he had in Edirne, when they had pretended Radu was out of favor. But no one sat next to Mehmed here. He lounged at a table on a dais, at the head of the room and separate from everyone.

Radu was grateful he had not spent much time in the palace under Constantine, so this room was new to him. Dazzling blue and gold tile covered the walls in floral patterns growing up to the ceiling, which was ringed with gold leaf. A heavy chandelier hung overhead. It, at least, looked original. But Radu suspected that beneath the tile were the more Byzantine-favored religious murals. Mehmed was claiming every inch of the city, one mosaic at a time.

Radu had come in late—his detour into the city had made him miss the beginning of the meal—so after washing, he took a spot next to his old friend Urbana and a woman he vaguely recognized from Murad's court. It was unusual for this many women to be at a formal dinner. Murad had excluded them entirely. But Radu was comforted and pleased to sit by Urbana. She had not been changed by the siege, other than the shiny burn scar that disfigured half her face. She smelled faintly of gunpowder and had black scorch marks on all her fingers.

Unchanged also was Urbana's distaste for Ottoman food. She kept up a steady stream of complaints in Hungarian to the other woman. Radu stared determinedly at his plates, avoiding looking at Mehmed. Why had Mehmed called him back to the city? What would it feel like to talk to him again? When Radu had left six months before, Mehmed had been so busy with planning and rebuilding that they had scarcely seen each other. Had Mehmed missed him?

Had Radu missed Mehmed?

Glancing up, his stomach clenched and his pulse raced to see the other man. Yes, he had missed him. But it was not the same easy longing he had experienced before.

Mehmed was swathed in purple. His turban, gold and fastened with an elaborate gold-and-ruby pin, haloed his head. He was twenty-one now, and his features had settled into adulthood. His eyes were sharp with intelligence, his eyebrows finely shaped, his full lips static and expressionless. Radu longed for them to curve in a smile, for Mehmed's solemn eyes to wrinkle in delight.

But Mehmed his friend had become Mehmed the sultan. It was like looking at a drawing of someone beloved. He both recognized Mehmed and felt that something was disturbingly altered and lost in the process of being captured on paper.

A servant knelt beside Radu. "Allow me to deliver the sultan's welcome. After the meal, I will show you to his reception room, where you can await your audience." The servant bowed, then backed away. Radu was startled. He had never had *audiences* with Mehmed. Particularly ones scheduled by servants.

This was nothing like how Murad had run his court. Favorites had always been allowed to swirl around him, to sit next to him. He had been at the center of everything, reveling in parties and close relationships. But even this meal was evidence that Mehmed ruled in a much more formal capacity. No absconding to the countryside to dream with philosophers. No allowing advisors like Halil Pasha—publicly executed months ago in a demonstration Radu had not attended—and his ilk to gain favor and therefore power.

Radu wondered whether the distance Mehmed had created in public would continue even in private. Or would he simply communicate with Radu through messengers, remaining forever separate?

"How is your sister, Radu Bey?"

Radu looked up, surprised. The woman who had been part of Murad's court had spoken. She was a paradox of harsh elegance. Everything about her was precisely fashionable by European standards, her elaborate dress and hair acting as a barrier between herself and the world. She sat up straight, her skirts awkwardly pooled around her, rather than leaning on an elbow like many of the other diners.

"I am sorry, I do not remember your name." Radu smiled in apology.

"Mara Brankovic. I was one of Murad's wives."

"Ah, yes! You negotiated the new terms of Serbia's vassalage." It had been her parting move, using an offer of marriage from Constantine to negotiate her own freedom and better rights for her country. Mehmed had admired her for it.

Without conscious thought, Radu found himself staring again at Mehmed. He dragged his eyes back to Mara. "What brings you to the empire?"

She turned her gaze toward Mehmed. Her look was affectionate. "A leader who recognizes my value. I am here as an advisor on European issues. I help with handling the Venetians. The Serbians, obviously. And a troublesome little country you are quite familiar with. And familial with." She laughed lightly at her own joke.

"So you are not asking after my sister as a social courtesy."

"Oh, I am! Social courtesy is the heart of my role here." Her tone was pleasantly wry. "It is amazing what one can accomplish through polite inquiry. Besides, I quite liked Lada. Though she was foolish to pass up a marital alliance with Mehmed. She would have done quite well."

Radu looked at his plate, now filled with tiny pieces of flatbread he had torn apart. "*Quite well* would never have been enough for her."

Mara laughed. Urbana snagged her attention to point out how much worse unleavened bread was, and Radu was again left to his own thoughts. Which, to his surprise, did not linger on the person on the dais. "Mara," he interrupted. "Do you have any contacts in Cyprus?"

She frowned thoughtfully. "Not personally, but I am certain I know someone who will. Why?"

"I am looking for news of my wife and my . . . friends. They fled during the fall of the city, and I have had no word of them since."

Mara put a hand on his. Her dark eyes were sympathetic and serious. "Write down their names and any details that matter. I will set all my resources on it."

"Thank you," Radu said. "I have been searching, along with Kumal Pasha, and—"

"He is very handsome." Urbana said it in the same tone she would use for talking about the quality of metal for casting cannons, or remarking on the weather. "He does not seem like he would ever be violent. And he has been a widower for some time."

Radu could not quite follow the change in conversation. "Are you . . . courting him?"

Urbana gave him the same glare of disgust she directed at the spiced meat. "I meant for Mara. I have neither use nor time for a husband."

Mara shared a long-suffering look with Radu. "Urbana worries that my childbearing years are dwindling quickly. She speaks of it often." She sighed heavily. "Very often."

Radu nearly laughed but was hit with a pang, remembering Urbana prying into his own private life—and lack of babies—with Nazira. Nazira should be here, at his side. No. She should be at Fatima's side. It was his fault she was not.

"You could marry Radu," Urbana said, thoughtful. "He is quite young for you. Eighteen, now? But he married his first wife very young, so he does not mind. He is very kind and does not have a temper. I used to hear girls gossiping about how handsome he is, with his large dark eyes and his prominent jaw." She peered at Radu in a way that made him intensely uncomfortable. "I suppose I understand what they meant. He is tall and healthy, at least. And with his wife missing, he is lacking for company."

Radu choked on the piece of bread in his mouth. He stood, unable to sit for a meal in this place that had taken so much from him. If Mehmed wanted him here, he would be here. But he could not pretend everything was normal. He could not have conversations about his future as though his past were not looped around his neck like a noose, choking him with regret and sorrow.

Just then, the banquet hall doors opened. A procession of unarmed men, roughly dressed under fine black cloaks, entered, dragging and pushing large wooden boxes. Mehmed's Janissaries stood at the ready, eyes narrowed in observation. A servant hurried past them and bowed at the base of Mehmed's dais. "They would not wait," he said, trembling.

The leader of the men bowed as well, sweeping one arm out in exaggeration. His boots were filthy and his clothes dusty. They must have just arrived. Radu looked closer, and realized all the men wore cloaks with the Dracul family seal on them. It was a dragon and a cross, taken from the Order of the Dragon. It felt wrong, seeing it here. Radu's already fragile emotions recoiled at the symbol of his family. Of his past.

The man spoke Wallachian, not Turkish, as would have been appropriate. "We bring a gift from Lada Dracul, vaivode of Wallachia, to his honor the sultan. She sends her respects, and asks that, in the future, you make certain your men offer her the level of respect she deserves as prince."

With that, the man turned on his heel and left the room. The other Wallachians followed him out. They walked quickly. Radu looked up at Mehmed, who met his gaze, raising an eyebrow. Mehmed did not speak much Wallachian.

"He said it is a gift. From Lada. She sends her respects and asks that your men respect her as a prince in the future."

"What is it?" Mehmed asked.

Radu shook his head in a small motion. "He did not say."

Mehmed had gotten even better at keeping his expressions guarded. Radu did not know how Mehmed felt about the surprise, or how he felt about Lada. The sultan gave away nothing. He gestured, and a servant ran forward with a lever to pry open the lid of the first box. As soon as it was lifted, he cried out in shock and dismay. He covered his nose and mouth with one arm and backed away.

Mehmed moved to get off the dais, but Radu held up a hand in warning. "Let me." He stopped a few paces from the boxes. The smell released with the lid gone was enough to tell him he did not want to see what his sister had sent.

He leaned over to peer inside anyway.

A corpse stared up at him, dried blood in lines of agony down its sunken face. As far as Radu could see from his vantage point, a metal spike had been driven through the turban, right into the head.

Radu leaned away to hide the horror from his sight once more. Keeping his eyes on the far wall, he replaced the lid. "Clear the room," he said.

No one moved.

Mehmed stood, gesturing sharply. The room emptied rapidly, only his Janissary guards and one personal servant remaining. He stepped down from the dais and joined Radu next to the first box. There were ten more. Mehmed reached out.

"No," Radu said. "You do not need to see it."

"My ambassadors?" Mehmed asked.

"Yes."

Mehmed stared down at the box, then swept his eyes over the rest of them. "And there is no letter with them."

"No."

Mehmed pointed to one of his guards. "Catch the men who delivered these. I want a full account of what happened." The guard sprinted from the room.

Mehmed turned, his purple silk robes swishing through the air. "Come with me." He glided through a separate, private door. Radu followed. They entered a sitting room with high ceilings. Tiny jeweled windows let in light but were too small for anyone to break in through. As soon as Radu was inside, Mehmed bolted the door behind them. There were no other exits.

Radu faced a wall bearing Mehmed's elaborate, beautiful tughra, the sultan's own seal and signature. Around it in gold Arabic script were verses from the Koran. Without turning around, Radu said, "This is why you called me back, then. Because of her."

Mehmed hesitated. Radu could feel the other man just behind him, close enough to touch. Then Mehmed sat with a sigh on one of the low sofas. "I did not know this was coming."

"You should not be surprised."

"She always surprises me."

Radu clenched his teeth so hard his jaw ached. "I cannot help you with her. I cannot—I will not—go between you and my sister. You will have to find someone else."

Radu turned to leave. Mehmed stood and grabbed his arm. Radu looked down at Mehmed's hand, each finger weighted with a jeweled ring. Mehmed was heavy with privilege and power. Radu remembered the lightness of their shared childhood. If the two boys who had met at a fountain in Edirne, who had clung to each other against the cruelty of the world, saw themselves now, they would see strangers. All the years had built a wall of silk and gold and power and pain between them.

Mehmed dropped his hand from Radu's arm. "I did not ask you here to help me with Lada!"

"Then why did you?" Radu turned to face him.

"Because!" Mehmed wrapped his own arms around himself, shrinking. "Because I am building an empire, and turning this city into the jewel of the world, and becoming the sultan my people need. And it is so lonely." His voice broke on the last word.

Gone was the cold assurance of the sultan, the calculating intelligence that last year had sent Radu away as a spy. The untouchable Hand of God was replaced by the boy at the fountain. The friend of Radu's youth. The foundation of his heart. Radu opened his arms, and Mehmed fell into him, burying his face in Radu's shoulder.

Radu held him close, taking his own deep, shuddering breaths.

"I need you," Mehmed whispered.

"I am here," Radu answered.

"Halil amassed too much power." Mehmed was on the floor of his private chamber, lying on his back and staring up at the ceiling. Radu lay next to him, shoulder to shoulder. No sultan and bey. Just Mehmed and Radu. "My father was too permissive, too willing to let others take over much of the business of running the empire. It led to corruption and waste and weakness. So I keep myself separate, let no one think they have a greater portion of my ear or my confidence. Soon I will have a palace complex made, all the rooms and walls circling out in rings from the center. I will be there, and everyone else will revolve around me. Just as I am at the center of the empire, and everyone else exists to serve the empire through me."

"It does sound lonely," Radu said softly.

"It is. And it will be. But I cannot put my own needs ahead of the needs of my people. They need a strong sultan. They need me to be the Hand of God, not a mere man. And so I must set aside the things that I want, my own comforts and relationships, to be what my people deserve."

Radu thought of his own life, of the things he had sacrificed to be the person others needed him to be. Most often to be the person Mehmed needed him to be. Could he do the same as Mehmed? Set aside the things he wanted—the things of his heart—for the good of the empire?

He closed his eyes. He did not know where his heart was anymore. He could not set aside something he could not find.

"I want you to stay here with me," Mehmed said, his voice tugging Radu back. "Be my friend in the midst of the madness."

Radu knew he should say yes. He should not ruin this

closeness. But he had spent so much of his life pretending. He did not wish to any longer. "You know what people will say. What they already thought. If I am back at your side, Halil's old rumors will resurface." Radu felt Mehmed's head turn toward him, felt Mehmed's dark gaze heavy on his cheek. Swallowing against the emotion pounding in his chest, Radu turned his own head toward Mehmed's, their lips a breath apart. Mehmed was watching him, his dark eyes careful and searching.

"Let them say what they will. They cannot harm me, and I will not let them harm you."

"And Lada?" Radu asked, dragging his sister into the space between them, where she always was.

Mehmed frowned. He looked back up at the ceiling, but linked his arm with Radu's. The move felt very deliberate, like a step in a dance. "We three were always meant to be together. I have you. She will come back to us."

"You want her to? Even after that?"

Mehmed's silence was answer enough. He would forgive her this murder of his envoy. Radu should have been surprised. He was not.

"And if she does not come back to us?"

"Well." Mehmed let the word hang heavy in the air above them. "At least I will always have you."

"I am the prettier one, after all."

Mehmed's laugh filled the room. It used to fill Radu, too, until he could feel it in his veins. But the feelings he had now were echoes of the ones he had before. He did not know if they would grow again.

Mehmed laced his fingers through Radu's and Radu lay still

beside him, thinking of how often he had imagined what that would feel like.

He had been wrong. Time had taken even this from him, because with Mehmed's fingers tangled in his own, he remembered another finger tracing wounds on his hands. Gray eyes in place of dark ones. The love he had found when his first love had been lost.

Now Cyprian was lost. Would his feelings for Mehmed return?

Did he want them to?

5

Bulgaria

THE ASHES OF THE village were as cold as the dawn around them. Everywhere the ground was dusted black instead of white, like some hellish snow had fallen.

Lada, wrapped in furs, crouched down. She took off her gloves and ran her hand through the ashes that remained of the village. Her village. Wallachia's village. Her hand came away stained with dull black.

"How many people were killed?" she asked. They had ridden here immediately after seeing Mehmed's envoy off. She had come straight down the border to make certain no other villages had been attacked. Along the way, she had picked up witnesses.

A peasant from the next village scratched his head, eyes wandering as he mentally calculated. "Three hundred?"

"Who is the boyar in charge of this region?" She should know. But she had never been able to care about the boyars unless they were giving her trouble.

He shrugged. "Never met him."

Lada looked at Stefan. He nodded, slipping away. He would find out. And there would be consequences for the boyar, both for failing to protect the people in his care and for failing to report this attack to Lada. She should not have heard about it from Mehmed's people. She closed her eyes, letting herself imagine Mehmed's reaction to her message. It filled her with something sharp and hot, like anticipation.

"What are you smiling about?" Bogdan asked.

Her eyes snapped open. "Nothing." Standing, she brushed her hands off on her trousers, the ash that had looked black against the snow now showing up gray against the black cloth. A shift in perspective changed everything. "When will Nicolae be here?"

"Within the hour."

Nicolae had been gathering all her soldiers. When he arrived, it would be with over three thousand men. And the special supplies she had been stockpiling.

Lada squinted at the rising sun, let its brightness warm her face. "Three hundred. Very well. We will kill three thousand of them. Every Wallachian death will be answered tenfold."

"We will have to go deep into Bulgaria to kill that many," Bogdan said.

"Then we will go deep." No one would be able to doubt her ferocity, her commitment to her people. And no one would attack Wallachia without thinking very carefully about the consequences from now on. It would be a lot of bodies, but she looked at them as an investment. Kill thousands to save thousands.

———————

Two days later, the boyar who had failed his people clutched his chest with his torn and bleeding hands. The hole he had dug—

one of hundreds since Stefan brought him to their camp—was ready. Two men took the stake and leveraged it into the hole, tipping it up. The body slumped at the top, a gruesome coat of arms for Lada's push into Bulgaria.

Lada looked down the road lined with a forest of bloody reminders.

"How many is that?" she asked Bogdan, who rode next to her.

"Fifteen, sixteen hundred."

They had broken through the border villages as swiftly as a river smashing through a dam. Everyone was swept up in their wake, no one spared. But it was not quite right. So few of them had been her actual enemies. She spared no love for Bulgars— they were too weak to break from Ottoman rule, and were thus as culpable as anyone—but they were not Turks. Her point that her borders were inviolable had been made. But . . . she wondered if she could make another point, too.

A point that the protection of the Ottomans was no protection at all.

A point that her way was better.

Nicolae eyed the stakes with weary distaste. "Only a handful of casualties among our men."

"Good. And does word spread?"

He shook his head. "No one is left to send out warnings. My scouts report no mobilization of the Turkish forces at any of the nearby fortresses."

Lada rubbed her eyes. They were irritated from the smoke of burning cottages and fields. "This is all the protection their loyalty to the sultan buys them. How can they not see it? How can they not see that all their bowing and scraping to Mehmed benefits them nothing?"

"Onto the next village?" Bogdan asked.

Lada shook her head. "Where are the Turkish troops?"

"There is a stronghold two hours' ride from here. Perhaps a thousand men are stationed there for easy deployment around the region. Another one, with five hundred men, is half a day's ride from there."

Lada nodded, turning her horse from the corpse-lined road. "No more Bulgar deaths. I want the rest of my stakes baptized in the blood of Mehmed's men."

Taking their first fortress was easier than Lada had expected. The Ottoman troops here were lazy, unused to resistance or fighting. She had sent her Janissary-trained men on ahead. By the time they reached the fortress, the guards at the gate had been slaughtered and everything was wide open, waiting for them.

She lost one hundred and twenty-seven men, and added their deaths to the count required in vengeance.

Before they impaled the Ottoman troops, they stripped them. The guards at the next fortress opened their gates without question when they saw the uniforms of their fellow Ottoman soldiers coming toward them in the night. Lada rode at the front and killed both gate guards herself. Most of the Ottomans were sleeping, slaughtered in the chaos and tangle of their sheets. Those who were awake fought well.

Her men fought better.

The next day they reached a small city. It was made almost entirely of wooden structures, with a high fence encircling them. Two gates, one at the front and one at the back, let people in and out.

Word had preceded them. Hundreds of Bulgars were outside the city gates, prostrate. "Please," a man said as Lada rode up. He did not look up at her. "Please, do not kill us."

"Who protects you?" she asked, looking from side to side with her arms extended, palms up. "I thought this country was under the protection of the sultan."

The man trembled. "No one protects us."

Lada dismounted. She gestured impatiently for him to stand. He did, shoulders stooped, balding head respectfully lowered. "Are you Christians?"

He nodded.

"Would you like protection?"

He nodded again, shivering though the day was warm enough to hint at spring.

Lada lifted her voice. "Any Christians this close to Wallachia are close enough to be my people. I have farms and land and safety for any who go back with me. Which is more than the sultan can offer you."

"But our city . . . our homes."

"Your city and homes were sold by your prince to the sultan. Just as your lives were." Again Lada looked around. "I see neither your prince nor your sultan here. There is only me."

The man nodded rapidly. "Yes. Yes. Come in with me, for food and wine, and I will—"

A woman nearby stood up. She was gaunt but had a strong

46

face, and a stronger spirit than the man, indicated by the lift of her chin and unflinching gaze. "Do not go into the city," she said. "Infidel soldiers are waiting to ambush you. I saw them on my way out."

The bald man let out a low moan of despair. The air suddenly smelled of piss.

Lada smiled at the strong woman. "Thank you. I will see to it that you have home, land, and animals to start your new life as a Wallachian."

The woman smiled grimly, bobbing her head in a bow.

Lada examined the wall. There was no one watching that she could see. They were probably all hiding. The city did not have a tower where she could be observed. "Nicolae, secure the back gate. Quietly."

He rode away with several hundred men to circle the city. Lada raised her voice. "The offer remains for those who wish to take it."

The Bulgars pushed themselves up off the ground. Many carried children. Eyeing Lada's men warily, they walked past them and onto the road toward Wallachia. She could be generous, too, and word of that would spread. Not as quickly as word of her violence, but both had merit.

Lada turned back to the man. "Go inside."

"I—I am sorry, I—"

"Go back to your city."

He let out a quick, terrified sob, then turned and walked slowly back through the gate. "Close it behind you," Lada called.

He did as he was asked, a flash of his eyes, wide with terror, the last thing she saw before the gate shut. Lada gestured toward it. "Let us help them keep it secure." A dozen of her men hurried forward with hammers, nails, and a few solid planks. Nicolae would be doing the same at the other gate.

"Send them a warm greeting."

As the burning arrows arced overhead into the wooden city, Lada turned to watch the peasants making their long walk toward a new home. One she had given them.

———•———

"How many dead?" Lada asked Bogdan five nights later, after hitting every major Turkish stronghold along the Wallachian border. Around her campfire sat Nicolae, Stefan, Bogdan, Iskra—the woman from the wooden city who had warned them and been taken on as a regional advisor—and some of her higher-ranked men.

Bogdan shrugged. "Two thousand Bulgars. A thousand Ottomans from the first fortress. Five hundred at the second. Anyone's guess how many were in the city we burned. We shot at least a thousand as they tried to climb the walls to escape."

Iskra grunted. "They came from all the garrisons around the city. Probably two thousand, two thousand five hundred."

Bogdan nodded, ticking cities off on his fingers. "So in addition to that, we have hit Oblucitza and Novoselo, Rahova, Samovit, and Ghighen. The entire region around Chilia. All told, twenty-five thousand dead? Mostly Turks, though many Bulgars as well."

Lada laughed in surprise. Such a number was unfathomable. At least to leaders like Matthias of Hungary, who wanted to play politics, to rule behind walls, to fight with letters instead of weapons. But she had known what she could accomplish with a few thousand men.

The Ottoman forces were scattered and lazy. Too used to being unchallenged. If the Ottomans had been prepared, Lada's forces would have been slaughtered. But it had been easy enough to quickly cut their way up and down the border between Wallachia and Bulgaria. She had been lucky.

No. She had been smart. She knew she would not face such easy odds again, but she would be smarter than her enemy. Do the unexpected at every turn. This had worked once; it would not work again.

"Is it enough?" Bogdan asked, fingers still extended in calculating the volume of terror they had accomplished.

It would never be enough.

It was enough for now.

"Yes." She heard Nicolae sigh in relief.

He dropped his head from shoulder to shoulder, rubbing his neck. "Do you want me to leave men behind?" he asked. "Are we expanding?"

"No, we are deterring. I have no interest in conquering. Only in letting others know the borders of Wallachia are inviolable. No one will attack my villages again. Not unless they want war."

Nicolae grinned wearily. "I think that message has been sent."

"Good. I have new messages to send now." Lada stared into the fire, watching it devour the darkness around it.

6

Constantinople

RADU STILL FOUND PEACE in prayer. During the siege, he had missed mosques, missed praying in unison with his brothers all around him. It was a comfort returning to that routine.

He could not bring himself to go to the Hagia Sophia, though, even now that it was a mosque. He had too many memories there to truly lose himself to praying. Instead, he visited other mosques through the city. They were mostly converted Orthodox churches, though a few new mosques were being built. His brother-in-law, Kumal, joined him for most prayers, and, as promised, Radu also joined little Murad and Mesih in prayer.

Coming back with them from afternoon prayer, Radu was surprised to meet Mehmed. The sultan was so rarely in the streets. Radu bowed low. Mehmed gestured for him to join them. One of his Janissary guards dismounted, offering Radu the horse.

"Where are we going?" Radu asked, careful to keep his horse

a step behind Mehmed's for appearance's sake. He had been in Constantinople for a week, and while in private they were as close as ever—when Mehmed had time to see him—in public Radu knew the importance of maintaining distance. Mehmed needed to be apart, needed to stand above. Radu would not disrupt that.

"Urbana has some new hand cannon designs she wishes to show me. I am certain she would be happy to see you, too."

Radu snorted a laugh. "You do not know her very well, do you?"

Mehmed turned his head, smiling at Radu over his shoulder. "I cannot imagine anyone would ever be unhappy to see you." His gaze lingered on Radu's face. It felt almost as though he was watching for Radu's reaction more than wishing to continue to look at Radu.

Mehmed did that more and more often lately. He would say some little shining thing, or touch Radu on the shoulder or the hand or even the cheek, always watching, studying. Cataloging what actions or words triggered which reactions. Radu did not know what to make of it. He offered Mehmed a smile now, which seemed to satisfy him.

Over their past week together, though, Mehmed had not spoken again of Lada. Whether he had discussed her "message" in private with other advisors, Radu did not know. But it seemed as though, for the time being, Mehmed was content to let the issue be buried alongside the bodies of the men Lada had sent back.

Envoys were often casualties of aggression between countries—Mehmed had killed Emperor Constantine's envoy a year ago, Cyprian spared only because he had taken Radu and Nazira out of Edirne—but Mehmed had to be bothered by the loss and the intent behind it. Maybe he was planning something and thought Radu would object. Or maybe, with Constantinople so recently settled, Mehmed did not want to antagonize Lada until he absolutely had to.

Either way, the memory of what Radu had seen in the box stayed with him, wriggling beneath the surface of his skin. The spike. The face frozen in agonized death. His *sister* had done that. And she would have to be answered. When she was, Radu did not know how he would feel, or what he would want to happen.

He had chosen Mehmed's side the year before when Lada asked for his help. He would, it seemed, have to make that choice over and over again for the rest of their lives. He had changed his faith, his life, even his name, but he could not change or escape his sister.

Radu was still thinking about the problem of Lada when they arrived at their destination. The world swirled around him. Frozen atop his horse, he stared at the foundry where he and Cyprian had spent a long night melting down silver and making coins.

"Radu?"

Startled, Radu blinked rapidly and turned toward Mehmed.

The other man stared expectantly at him. "You look as though you have just woken up." Mehmed gestured to the foundry. "Do you know this place?"

Radu nodded silently, hoping Mehmed would not inquire further.

"What did you do here?" Mehmed leaned eagerly toward Radu. "You have told me so little of what you did in the city during the siege! You were a stranger to me those months. I want to hear all of it. Did you sabotage their attempts at building an arsenal?"

Radu rubbed his eyes, leaving his fingers covering them for a few seconds too long for the gesture to appear casual. "No. They never had a hope of amassing enough cannons to meet you that way."

"Then what did you do here?"

Radu straightened his shoulders, staring at the door behind which he had spent a deliriously hot and confusing night with Cyprian. He remembered the shape of the other man's shoulders, the lines where his torso dipped down to his trousers. The feelings in Radu's own body that he had hidden behind the table between them. But before that, the laughter, the pure devious fun of it all, sneaking around with his beloved false wife and the friend they were already betraying.

"We stole silver from the churches and melted it down to make coins."

"You and Nazira?"

"And Cyprian."

Mehmed abruptly straightened in his saddle, no longer leaning toward Radu. The eagerness in his voice had shifted, just like his posture. "What were you making coins for?"

Radu sighed, letting the memory slip away. "To buy food. People were starving."

"How did that help our cause?"

Radu dismounted and paused, stroking his horse's flank.

He did not look to see if Mehmed was studying him. "It did not help. Not you, and in the end, not them. But it felt right at the time." Radu walked inside the foundry, blinking at the sudden dimness. His conflicted past, confusing present, and unknown future were all harsher and more difficult to breathe through than the blistering air inside.

Just like silver melted down, its impurities burned away, Radu felt himself as molten and unformed. He could pour himself into any shape. He could fill a mold as Mehmed's dearest friend and confidant. He could fill one as Radu Bey, powerful force in the Ottoman Empire. He could probably even return to Lada and fill one as the lesser Dracul once again.

But the mold he found himself longing for, the shape that felt truest, could not be formed. Because the people he wanted to form it around were lost to him. Maybe forever.

Lada had always known exactly what shape she would take. She had never let it be determined by the people around her. But Radu could not escape the need for love, the need for people in his life to help him see what he should—and could—be. Lada shaped herself in spite of her environment. Radu shaped himself because of it.

He would stay in the city because Mehmed still shaped some part of him. But he could not become what Mehmed wanted or even needed him to. And he feared that a refining fire would reveal he had never been silver to begin with; he was simply dirt and impurities, burned away to ash while desperate to become something worth valuing.

7

Tirgoviste

LADA ENTERED HER RECEPTION room with Bogdan at her back and Nicolae at her side. Two men were waiting for her. One, the king she knew. And the other, her cousin.

Matthias Corvinus stood and threw a sheaf of parchment on the stone floor. "You monstrous little fool," he snarled.

Lada smiled.

"Now, now," said the other man, Stephen, King of Moldavia. He leaned casually in his chair, one leg stretched in front of him, and eyed Lada with curiosity. "Cousin."

Lada acknowledged him with a dip of her head. "Cousin." She did not know much about him, other than his penchant for picking fights and winning them. She already liked him better than Matthias.

But as much as she would have preferred to meet only with Stephen, it was good that the two kings had arrived at the same time. It made things quicker.

Stephen sat up straight. "It is good to finally meet you. Your mother is—"

"I care nothing for my mother." She did not want to bring that woman—and her weakness—into this discussion. Stephen needed to see she was nothing like the woman who had given birth to her. Lada took the chair opposite the two men. She sat as a man did, back straight, legs apart, arms crossed over her chest.

Matthias sat back down, anger in his stiff posture. He had probably hoped for more of a reaction from her. She was determined to give him nothing that he hoped for. When they had last been together, he had been almost a king, and she, fighting for the chance to be prince. Now she was prince. She would not let him forget it.

"I assume you got the same letter I did," Matthias said to Stephen.

Raising an eyebrow, Stephen pulled out his own sheaf of parchment. He cleared his throat, then read aloud. *"I have killed peasants, men and women, old and young, who lived at Oblucitza and Novoselo, where the Danube flows into the sea, up to Rahova, which is located near Chilia. . . .'"* He paused, looking up. "How is Chilia this time of year?"

"Quite pleasant," Lada said, not failing to notice Stephen's pointed question. Nor had she forgotten that Moldavia had a vested interest in Chilia. She had mentioned it specifically for that exact reason. Over the years it had shifted between Bulgaria, Wallachia, and Moldavia. Now it was hers, because she had taken it.

Stephen lifted an eyebrow in amusement. "I am happy to hear it. Continuing, more locations, following the Danube, ah yes, this is my favorite part: *'We killed twenty-three thousand, eight hundred and eighty-four Turks without counting those whom we burned in homes or the Turks whose heads were cut off by our soldiers. Thus, your highness, you must know I have broken the peace with Mehmed.'"* Stephen lowered the letter, laughing. "I should say you have."

"Why would you do this?" Matthias demanded. "We cannot afford a war with the Ottomans!"

Lada met his intensity with a cool gaze. "We cannot afford *not* to have war with them. They take our fortresses, they take our villages, they take our land, they take our children. I, for one, cannot bear the cost of their stewardship any longer. I will have Wallachia free of them. And I have proved it is possible. They rule because we allow it. No more."

Stephen tapped the letter on his knee. "Your numbers are impressive."

"I did it all with only three thousand men of my own."

Matthias grunted in disbelief. "You exaggerate on one end or the other."

Lada pulled out a dagger and cleaned her fingernails with the tip. "We moved fast and surprised them, fortress by fortress. We never faced more than a thousand men at a time. So, no, I do not exaggerate, and you know it is the truth. Do not pretend you are not aware of precisely how many men I have at my disposal, Matthias. And do not do me the dishonor of implying I would falsify my accomplishments. Those of us who actually *do* things have no need of falsehoods."

Matthias rose like a storm once again. Stephen stood, too, holding out a hand. "Calm yourself. Think it through. She has handed a devastating loss to the Turks. And, as she pointed out, she has proved that such a thing, however surprising, is possible. So tell me, Cousin: Why are we here? What else do you have planned?"

"We are going to crusade," Lada said.

Matthias sat yet again. His chair groaned in protest of so much movement. "Constantinople has already fallen. Even you cannot be so delusional as to think you can take it back."

"I care nothing for the woes of Greeks and Italians. Let Mehmed have what he has taken from them. But let him never again take anything from us. We crusade for Europe. We crusade to prove our borders are our own, immovable, inviolable, that never again will he take Christian land from us."

Matthias was listening, his eyes narrowed. "I will not fight for Wallachian land."

"I am not asking you to fight for Wallachian land. I will fight for my own land. I am simply asking you to fight your own battles for once in your pathetic life."

Matthias's sword was half drawn before Bogdan was at his side with a knife pressed against the king's neck.

Lada let the knife stay there for the time being. "This is what we do. Antagonize Mehmed. Harass him. If Stephen does the same, we give Mehmed three fronts, three battles he does not want. His empire depends on stability. He will not risk everything for borders he does not need. We force him to withdraw from our lands." Lada waved one hand, and Bogdan moved the knife but did not back away from looming over Matthias.

"So you want to work together? Coordinate?" Stephen asked.

"No. If we give him a single front, it is that much easier for him to defeat us. I want us to do everything separately. No clear target, no attainable path for defeating us. I used a small, unexpected force to slaughter his men up and down the border. Our best plan is to defy plans."

Matthias rubbed his throat, his glare as sharp as Bogdan's blade. "But Mehmed is not *in* Hungary. I am not going to attack other countries. What good will I do you?"

"Deal with the Transylvanians. Convince them to work with me. I need their numbers."

Stephen laughed, idly spinning an empty wine goblet on the arm of his chair. "I have read some of their work on you, Lada Dracul. Very creative."

"Did you see the one about the picnic?" Nicolae asked.

Stephen nodded. "Oh, yes. Charming. King Matthias will have his work cut out for him."

"I am certain he is up to the task," Lada said. She was certain of no such thing. "And your other role is far more important, Matthias. We need money. The only person who can give us the funds we seek is the pope."

"The pope?" His threatened throat forgotten, Matthias leaned forward, eyes narrowed shrewdly as the conversation turned to something he was interested in. "What makes you think the pope will give us money?"

"He fears Islam invading Europe. I wrote him about my victories in Bulgaria, and he likes me very much."

Matthias laughed meanly. "That is because he does not know you."

"Exactly. I have neither the time nor the temperament to pursue that advantage. Will you?"

The Hungarian king steepled his fingers. "You will have to convert to Catholicism."

"No."

"He will not support you if you are still Orthodox."

Why were men always trying to claim different parts of her? Her body, her name, her soul. Why should they care where its allegiances lay? She waved a hand crossly. "Then I have converted. You can inform him."

"I think it is rather more complicated than that," Nicolae said.

"If the king of Hungary writes to the pope that I am Catholic, I am Catholic." Lada had converted to Islam in much the same way, thanks to Radu's political maneuverings. That had been to save their lives. This was to finance war.

Besides, they could not touch her soul in the end, despite all demands on its loyalties.

"Your people will not like your conversion." Stephen raised his eyebrows meaningfully. Lada followed his gaze to find Bogdan aghast. Bogdan held his Orthodox faith almost as dearly as he held Lada.

"My people," Lada said, glaring at Bogdan, "will like it because I choose it, and everything I choose is for the good of Wallachia." Bogdan looked down at the floor, chastised.

Matthias's eager hunger had not quite left his face, though he tried to smooth it away. Lada was struck with a sudden, powerful longing for Matthias's father, Hunyadi. An honest man. A true man. A man who would have been invaluable on the battlefields to come.

But all she had was Hunyadi's son, so she would use him if she could.

He smiled tightly. "It may work. With the loss of Constantinople so fresh, I think I can convince Rome to send us gold. Perhaps a lot of it."

"Good. We all know what our duties are, then."

Stephen grinned rakishly, holding his goblet out to Lada in a toast. "Disrupt stability. Petition for gold. Provoke the greatest empire on the face of the earth." He paused. "This is going to be fun."

8

Constantinople

OVER THE NEXT TWO weeks, Radu kept to the palace—
the least haunted part of the city for him. He spent his
time writing letters and consulting with Mara on where they
could look for Nazira. Mara's smiling patience nagged at him;
the calm and soothing way she spoke terrified him that there
was, in fact, no hope.

He would not give up hope. Not for Nazira. Not ever.

Radu was invited to sit in on all the meetings that involved
Europe. He wondered if it was to give some legitimacy to his
place in Mehmed's court, though he felt useless. Unlike Mara,
he had not kept up any of his ties with his home country aside
from Aron and Andrei Danesti, whom he met with occasion-
ally. Theirs was a relationship destined for discomfort. His sister had murdered their father; their father had murdered Radu's
father. And now his sister sat on the throne they had equal
claim to. He avoided them, and everyone else, as much as was
polite.

The only peace Radu found was in prayer, but even his

studies of Islam could not distract his itching, straining heart. Every time Radu thought he had found a place in the world, the world changed around him, and he was once again left alone.

Today, Mehmed was at the head of the room on an elevated platform. Along with several other of Mehmed's advisors, Radu sat nearest to him. But no one was allowed on the platform. Not even Radu, despite how close they were behind closed doors. Some things never changed.

He rubbed his eyes wearily. He did not know how much longer he could stand playacting. It had kept him alive through his cruel childhood, navigating the Sultan Murad's capricious court, and behind the walls of Constantinople during the siege. But when Nazira and Cyprian left, he had lost the one person who *truly* knew him. And he had lost the other person whom he would have liked to let try.

He tried to pay attention to the council going on around him, but he had a hard time focusing. Mara was detailing some nuance of diplomacy to give Mehmed more trading advantages with the Venetians. It felt deeply unimportant.

"What about Nazira?" Radu asked when there was a lull in the discussion.

"What about her?" Mehmed asked.

"Has there been any word? Can we send out more men to search? We know they left the city in a boat. Perhaps if we looked up and down the coastline . . ."

Mehmed shook his head. "It would be a waste of resources. She left with a nephew of the emperor. He knows what value Nazira has. If we go searching, they will only see our desperation and increase the eventual ransom demand. Our best course of action is to wait and see what they ask for." He noticed Radu's horrified expression and held up his hands in placation. "We will pay it, of course! Whatever they ask. But we have to be smart about how we portray her value."

"Cyprian would never do that."

Mehmed's face was carefully neutral. "Cyprian. Ah yes. I had forgotten his name."

Radu did not believe him. And he could not accept that this was Mehmed's solution. To simply *wait* and see what happened. Radu had been waiting for months. "If we have had no word of Nazira, they must have run into trouble. If you would give me the men, I can—"

The door burst open, and Kumal Pasha, Radu's beloved brother-in-law, hurried in. Radu wondered if he had somehow been drawn by discussion of his sister. Radu stood, grateful. Kumal would support his petition for more resources.

Kumal bowed. "I apologize for interrupting, but we have just received word from Bulgaria." He held out a sheaf of paper. A servant took it, then shuffled toward Mehmed, bowing and holding it out. Radu itched to keep pressing about Nazira, but Kumal was here on other business. Radu would speak with Mehmed later. And he would bring it up again when next they were alone. Mehmed had been so evasive about expanding the search that Radu wondered now if it was because of Cyprian. Could he be jealous?

Mehmed looked over the papers, his normally composed expression shifting as his eyes widened the more he read. When he looked up, it was directly at Radu.

"Lada. She has attacked Bulgaria and killed tens of thousands."

Radu's heart raced as though he were the one attacked. "Why?" She had murdered the envoy, and before they had even sent a response she had done *this*?

Mehmed stood. "Kumal Pasha, Mara Brankovic, Radu Bey, stay. Everyone else, get out."

There was a rush and flutter of robes, and soon the four of them were alone, save Mehmed's guards. "Come." He retreated into his private room.

Radu followed, the space feeling oddly larger with more people in it. Perhaps because Mehmed alone was so much more overwhelming than Mehmed with other people present. Radu leaned against a wall as Mehmed paced. Kumal and Mara both sat on a long, low bench.

"You cannot let this stand," Mara said, breaking the silence.

Mehmed looked as though he wanted to throw something. But everything in the room was expensive, exquisite, his own property. His fists clenched and unclenched at his sides. "I do not understand this. I *gave* her the throne."

Radu shifted uncomfortably. "But you did not. Not really. You never sent her men or aid. She took it on her own. You can see how she feels that she is not a vassal."

"Wallachia is a vassal state! She knows this."

"You did not respond to her murder of the envoy, either."

Mehmed gave Radu a pointed and wary look. "You think I invited this?"

"Of course not!"

Mara shook her head. "It does not matter. She has to be held accountable."

Radu ran his fingers along the edge of his turban. Normally the cloth felt soothing, but he found no comfort now. Tens of *thousands.* Bulgarians, no less. It made no sense. What was she trying to accomplish? "Did she take any land?"

Kumal had been whispering to Mara, filling her in on details. He looked up and shook his head. "Just a fortress at Chilia that has traditionally been Wallachian."

"So she is not expanding. But why would she attack Bulgaria? It destabilizes the entire region."

Mara snapped a fan open and waved it in front of her face even though the room was cool. "She swept through and attacked all the Ottoman fortresses. Our forces there must be in utter chaos. I do not think the Bulgarians will use it as an opportunity to rise up against us—Serbians would not, we would fight alongside you—but it will make everyone in the region bolder. Moldavia, especially. Does she have a relationship with King Stephen? He is your cousin, is he not?"

Radu shook his head, feeling worthless. "I do not know. I have not been home—" He stopped on the word, wondering how it had slipped out in relation to Wallachia. "I have not been there since I was a child. The relation is on my mother's side, and she left when we were very young. If Lada has contacted him, it is recent."

"How did she even accomplish this much damage?" Kumal asked. "It should not have been possible."

"You never really knew her. The impossible is where my sister excels," Radu said. "That, and never backing down."

Mara was still toying with her fan, opening and closing it. "What does she want? Can we buy her?"

Mehmed laughed darkly. "If being empress could not tempt Lada from Wallachia, nothing can."

Radu inhaled sharply. Empress? When had Mehmed offered that? He had not mentioned having seen or communicated directly with Lada since she left. Mehmed always kept her secret, kept her in a portion of his heart Radu had no access to. Radu lowered his head. All their hours in here alone. All the confidence and closeness. All the work Radu had done for him while Lada was far away and actively working *against* Mehmed. And still she held him. She always would.

Kumal stood, walking to a map displayed on the wall. "If she gets Hungary, Moldavia, and Transylvania on her side, they may be able to shift the whole region out of our control. We would lose the Danube as well. We can fight Wallachia without any real loss, but I do not like spreading so thin between more regions."

"Wallachia is not well liked. It will take her time to get traction within Europe. You should attack her," Mara said. "Immediately."

Radu opened his mouth to disagree, but then he paused. His own hesitation had cost so many lives in Constantinople, on both sides of the wall. He had not acted aggressively, and was haunted by what might have been if he had. If he had assassinated Constantine when he had the chance, perhaps he could have saved tens of thousands. He had not because he cared about the emperor, and because he cared about Cyprian. He still did not know whether he had made the right decision.

He suspected he had not. Could he stand idly by while more innocents died? It was not his fault this time, but—

Or was it? Lada had asked him to join her. Without him by her side, there was no one to temper her, no one to guide her from her first impulses. Without Radu to gently push her in new directions, she was turning into the most brutal version possible of herself.

He had chosen Mehmed over Lada, and this was the result. More death. Always death.

There had been no response to Mara's suggestion of attack. Radu looked up. Everyone was watching him. Kumal with compassion, Mara with expectation, and Mehmed with agitated turmoil. Finally, his fists relaxed and his shoulders slumped.

"I do not want to," Mehmed said, his voice soft. "I do not want to destroy her."

Radu nodded, his head leaden. "I will go speak with her, then."

Mara jumped in, still as poised and elegant as a painting, though a line had formed between her brows. "What good will speaking with her do? You cannot release Wallachia from vassalage. It sets a terrible precedent. If we can think of nothing short of total independence that she might be willing to bargain for, we have nothing to offer."

"If she continues to push on this, she will be killed." Kumal lifted his hands as though weighing two choices. "I do not mean that as a threat. I mean it as truth. You have said yourself that she will never back down. Her actions threaten everyone in our empire. Instability creates cracks through which death seeps in. Our responsibility is to keep our people safe, and to address threats to their well-being. Radu, I know she is your sister, but if she will not compromise, this necessarily ends in her death."

Radu felt a pressure behind his eyes like tears he would not release. Kumal was right. Lada was courting death, and would drag untold numbers down with her on her bloody journey. He had failed her before. He would not fail her this time. But to protect her, he would have to betray her. Betrayal was quickly becoming the only skill he had to offer anyone.

Radu nodded. "She will not compromise. When she comes to meet me—as she must, because I am *her* brother and it aggravates her that I have belonged to someone else these last years—I will bring her back here."

"She will never come back," Mara said.

"Not willingly." Radu waited as his meaning sank in.

"No," Mehmed said. "I cannot make her a prisoner. Not like my father did. It would ..." His voice broke as he trailed off.

"It would kill whatever love she has left for both of us." Radu crossed the room and took Mehmed by the shoulders. He saw his own sadness and exhaustion reflected in his friend's eyes. He hated this decision, even as he felt it was the right one. The only one. "Maybe, someday, we can fix it. But right now, people are dying because of her. Your people. Our people. Can we let them die because of our history with her?"

Mehmed's eyes tracked back and forth, as though tracing potential futures. Doubtless he searched for one in which he might have Lada the way he wanted her. The future he was seeing did not revolve around Radu. "Bring her back," Mehmed said. "Bring her home."

Whatever they had here, whatever they might possibly move toward, it would end if Lada was back, no matter how unwilling she was. She always came first. But it did not matter. Radu had not known what to hope for, but all hope had disappeared when Mehmed did not hesitate to send him away again if it meant getting Lada back.

It was the door, swinging shut. Radu knew the momentum had started the day he ran away from Edirne with Cyprian and discovered that some hearts were more worth breaking for. And very soon, he sensed, the door would close forever. He could still acknowledge his feelings for Mehmed while knowing they were nearly done.

Radu dropped his hands from Mehmed's shoulders, smiling because he did not know what else to do. He had held on to his love for Mehmed for so long. It had been his first, and he could not imagine anything ever taking its place. He had been wrong.

He would let this impossible love slowly end, then. Forever.

9

Tirgoviste

LADA WAS HIDING.

She preferred to think of it as a strategic retreat, but the truth was she needed a few minutes surrounded by the warm scent of baking bread and nothing else. She stuck her finger in a jar of fruit preserves, taking out a glob and licking it off.

"Have some manners," Oana chided, but her words had no sting. She hummed, bustling around the cavernous kitchen. Lada was transformed into a child again, and for once in her nineteen years, she did not mind. She crawled under a table and huddled close to the warm ovens, closed her eyes, and finished off the jar of preserves.

"Have you seen Lada?" Nicolae asked. He had stayed with her after Bulgaria, his presence needed more at the castle than at the training grounds. Lada froze. She could not see him, but that did not mean he could not see her. "There is a dispute between two landowners, and they are here demanding she settle it. We also have several petitioners asking to be granted land before the planting season starts, and a few dozen recruits for her forces to be approved, and we need to discuss how we will collect taxes from the regions without boyars. And we have had more letters."

Oana shifted so that her skirts were blocking Lada's nest. "Maybe she is out riding."

"In this cold?"

Oana harrumphed. "I am not her nurse anymore, as she is so fond of reminding me. I do not know where she is. Now get out of my kitchen or start helping. Damn castle cannot feed itself."

Nicolae beat a hasty retreat. Oana's hand appeared beneath the table, holding another jar of preserves and half a loaf of still-steaming bread.

Lada would be prince again in an hour. But for now, she allowed herself the luxury of letting her former nurse take care of her. "Thank you," she murmured. Oana's happy humming indicated Lada's presence was all the thanks she desired. Perhaps they never really grew out of their roles. Oana would always be a nursemaid. Lada, her charge. Bogdan, the loyal playmate. Radu...

She pressed the warm bread against her cheek and decided not to think about anything at all.

———————•———————

Her older brother, Mircea, had been buried alive in dirt. Sometimes Lada feared she would be buried alive in parchment.

She shuffled through a new mound, squinting against a headache, missing the warmth of the kitchens. Spring kept promising it was coming, only to be met with a frost icing the stones of the castle.

"The fortress at Bucharest is almost done," she said. Nicolae wrote it down, waiting for further information. "Poenari Fortress on the Arges is almost complete as well. I wish I were there right now." Lada rubbed the back of her neck, dreaming of the cold stone of the peak, the deep green of the trees, the sparkling ribbon of the river far below. Of anywhere in Wallachia, her mountaintop fortress felt the most like home. But Tirgoviste demanded her presence with the nagging insistence of a hundred daily petitioners and dozens of urgent letters.

"Do we need to focus on any other fortifications?" Nicolae asked. "The city walls here could use some attention."

"We will not win anything by barricading ourselves in."

"Defending a well-fortified location is easier than meeting in the open."

Lada put her feet up on the table. "Tell that to Constantinople. No. We will fight in ways no one has ever seen. That is how we will hold our land."

"*If* the sultan comes after us."

"He will come," Lada said, her voice dark with memories of the last time she had seen Mehmed in person.

The gentleness in Nicolae's voice was as false as a warm day in February. "Do you think maybe you are provoking him because you *want* him to come?"

Lada snarled, "Say what you mean, Nicolae."

"I mean you are going out of your way to antagonize him. Bulgaria was unnecessary."

Lada dropped her feet to the floor. "They killed my people!"

"In *one* village. You killed his envoy in response. I think that was more than enough of a message, but you keep stabbing deeper and harder. I am trying to understand why."

"I do what I do for Wallachia."

Nicolae smiled ruefully, his face twisting around its old scar. "Do you? Mehmed cares about you. You could leverage that, get him to agree to different terms of vassalage. Lower payments. No boys for his armies. He would do it. You could create the best, most powerful, most stable position for Wallachia in generations."

"As a vassal state to the Turks!"

"Then so be it!"

Lada burst out of her chair, throwing Nicolae from his own and pinning him to the floor with one forearm pressed against his throat. She bared her teeth, her heavy breaths mingling with his increasingly labored ones. He did not move, did not attempt to push her off.

"I will not be anyone's vassal," she hissed. "Wallachia is mine. *Mine.* Do you understand?"

Nicolae blinked, his dark lashes moving over his brown eyes. Something that had been there longer than his scar, as long as Lada had known him, had disappeared from his gaze. She did not know what it was, had never noticed its presence, only registered it now that it was gone.

"I understand," Nicolae said, his voice strained.

"Lada?" Daciana asked.

Lada stood and turned her back on Nicolae. Daciana stood in the doorway, hesitantly regarding the scene. She held several bundles in her arms.

"Yes?" Lada demanded.

"Your new clothes. We were going to make certain I cut everything correctly?"

"Very well. You may go, Nicolae. Speak to Bogdan before you leave. He has been scouring the prisons for likely new soldiers."

She expected Nicolae to argue—he always argued—but he bowed and exited.

Daciana took his place, wordlessly helping Lada disrobe. She was a better seamstress than Oana, whose eyes were not good anymore. So Oana had taken over the kitchens, and Daciana the clothing of Lada. When she had Lada stuck in place while she measured, Daciana finally spoke. "Is there a problem with Nicolae?"

"No."

"Good. I like him."

"I did not ask your opinion."

Daciana made a small noise, looking up at Lada from where she was marking cloth with chalk. The new coat would have a fur collar and cuffs. It was dyed deep red to match Lada's hat. "Then perhaps you do not want to hear my next opinion, which is that you should be careful not to let Bogdan get you alone any time soon."

"What do you mean?"

"He is going to ask you to marry him."

Lada jerked away in surprise, leaving a long trail of chalk along the hem of her would-be tunic. "What?"

"He talks to me sometimes, after church. This last time he looked around and mentioned how nice it would be to be married there. Asked whether I thought a girl would prefer to be married in that one, or the monastery on Snagov Island. And since I know he was not coyly trying to get *my* attention, I can safely assume he was thinking of the only woman he realizes exists."

Lada sat, ruining the shape of the unsewn tunic. "Why can none of the men in my life simply do what I ask them to?"

Daciana gathered up the fallen cloth, then gently unwrapped the rest from around Lada. "Have you asked Bogdan not to be in love with you?" Her tone was teasing.

"I cannot understand what possesses him to be in the first place. Or why he would imagine I am ever going to marry him."

"He is a little boy." Daciana set the cloth to the side, then pulled out a comb and began working on Lada's hair. She was much gentler than Oana had ever been. Lada did not mind it so much when Daciana groomed her. "He sees in you what he wants to see. Be kind when he asks you."

Lada looked up through her heavy lashes at Daciana and raised an eyebrow.

Daciana laughed. "Well, not kind, then. But do try not to be cruel. He is a fragile soul."

"He is twice your size. I have seen him break necks with his bare hands."

"Ah, but you will break his heart with yours."

"I never asked for his heart."

Daciana finished, stroking her hand through Lada's hair. "That is the thing with giving your heart. You never wait for someone to ask. You hold it out and hope they want it."

The door burst open and two small children toddled inside. Stefan followed, a brief flash of surprise disrupting his plain face upon seeing Lada. "I am sorry, I thought you were gone." He leaned down to scoop up the children, but they squirmed away.

"They want their mother," Daciana said, laughing. She held out her arms and both ran to her, collapsing against her.

Lada was confused. Given how often she was away from the castle, she did not see Daciana much. And she had not seen Daciana's baby—named for Lada herself—since she was an infant.

But Lada was absolutely certain there had been only one of them.

"Who is that?" she asked, pointing to the other child.

A furtive look passed between Daciana and Stefan. Lada only caught it because she was so used to Stefan being expressionless. That shared look cut straight through her confusion. Suspicion bled out instead.

"Our son." Daciana smiled pleasantly, as though such a thing went without saying.

"And where did he come from?"

Daciana pulled her hair free from the little boy's dimpled fist. "Where all babies come from, of course."

Lada would not play along. She stood. "Whose child is that?"

Stefan picked up the boy, holding him close. "Mine," he said. He took the little girl in his other arm and walked out of the room.

Daciana gathered her things, keeping her eyes anywhere but on Lada. "There are a lot of orphans," she said, shrugging. "We thought our little Lada would like a brother."

"Hmm." Lada watched as Daciana fumbled the comb, dropping it on the floor. She picked it up, then dipped her head and hurried from the room. She had not finished her work, which was unlike her.

Daciana had been a wet nurse to a boyar family after she had her own baby. A Danesti boyar family.

Lada had killed all the Danesti boyars. And ordered all their heirs killed as well.

She found Nicolae's sheet of carefully taken notes and added two of her own at the end.

Watch Nicolae.

Watch Stefan.

10

Constantinople

RADU AND HIS MEN rode out to the gates of Constantinople, accompanied by Mehmed. Mehmed rode in the center of a ring of guards. His turban gleamed and sparkled in the sun, woven through with pure gold threads. His horse stepped high, a head taller than the rest of the horses, white and gleaming. Mehmed's purple cloak cascaded behind them. Radu imagined he was a citizen on the side of the road, watching, dazzled. The sultan was certainly everything he should be. Power and glory personified.

They stopped just outside the city, and Mehmed allowed Radu to approach him. "Bring her home." The quiet urgency in his voice was in contrast to his confident posture.

Radu nodded, but he could not pretend at confidence. Lada was already home. And Radu did not feel at home in Constantinople. But he would get Lada, and he would bring her back. And then . . .

He did not know where he would go. But his duties to both Mehmed and Lada would be discharged, and he knew what he would *do:* spend the rest of his days looking for Nazira.

With a hollow pain in his body that was familiar and dull around the edges now, Radu spurred his horse forward. Away from Mehmed.

Kumal drew close to him a few miles outside the city. "Thank you for coming," Radu said with a more genuine smile than he had been able to muster for Mehmed.

"Of course. It will be good to get out of the city."

"Do you dislike it?" Radu had never heard a word of complaint from Kumal. But he had also never heard a word of remonstration for losing Kumal's only sister. Radu wondered if Kumal was capable of cruelty. He hoped so, actually. It gave him hope to think that men like Kumal were the same as everyone else—they simply chose to be better.

Kumal looked surprised, then shook his head. "No. I am happy with my position close to the sultan. He is a good man, and I respect him. It is an honor to serve our people. But it is difficult not to feel like we are doing nothing while waiting for word of Nazira."

Radu hunched his shoulders reflexively. He knew Kumal did not bring up Nazira to chastise him, but he could not escape his guilt over her continued absence.

Kumal noticed his discomfort and drew his horse even closer. "You made the best decision you could have at an impossible time. I know you did everything in your power to protect her. I meant that staying in one place waiting will drive a man insane. It is good to be going out, being active, defending the empire. We will continue to hope and pray for word of Nazira's safety. But that can be done just as well from the road."

Radu nodded, feeling slightly less burdened. "Thank you. You have always been a friend to me."

"You are my brother."

Radu laughed. "You are certainly the brother I chose. My own brother was never a friend."

"Speaking of your siblings, what is the plan for your sister? Will you try to negotiate first?"

"I am sending word ahead for her to meet us at our outpost in Giurgiu. She will come to see me, I think, even without specific promises. When she arrives, we separate her from her men and bring her back to Constantinople."

"How much force are you prepared to use?"

Radu shifted uneasily in his saddle, hunching deeper into his furs. It had seemed like a good plan when discussing it with Mehmed and Mara. But Radu had not thought through the specifics. Lada would not want to come. That much was obvious. Would he have to kill her men? What if Bogdan was with her? Radu had never liked Bogdan; he encouraged the worst in Lada through his dogged loyalty. But Radu did not want to kill him. Or Nicolae. He had always thought Nicolae superior to the rest of Lada's men. Funny and smart, even kind sometimes.

And then there was Lada herself. Radu imagined tying her up, bringing her back in one of their supply wagons. She would fight them the whole way, otherwise. And once they got her back, what then? A prison cell?

Radu sighed, rubbing his eyes. "As much force as it takes." He could not see a happy resolution to this plan, but he could not leave Lada to her continued aggressions.

"Is that the right thing to do? Bring her in under false pretenses of peace, and then kidnap her?" Kumal did not sound angry, but there was disapproval in his soft tone. He had not contributed much during their planning. He still deferred to Mehmed and would not disagree with him, but with Radu, he was more comfortable.

"It will save lives in the long run." Radu held out his hands, then dropped them helplessly to his sides. "And it will save her life, too. Mara was right. She cannot go on like this. Someone *will* kill her. I would rather her safe in Constantinople in prison than in an unmarked grave next to our father and brother."

Kumal nodded. "Very well, then. If you think this is the best course of action, I will do everything in my power to support you. Sometimes we must work in subterfuge. Though I must admit, it fits me like a too-small tunic. I have no skill or taste for it."

"That is because you are a good, honest man." Radu could not smile this time. He slipped into subterfuge as easily as sliding into a warm bath. It had always been his greatest skill, saying and doing whatever it took to survive.

Now he would say and do whatever it took to make sure his sister survived. Even if she never forgave him for it.

———◆———

Two days into their journey north toward the fortress at Giurgiu that marked the edge of Ottoman-controlled land, a messenger caught up with them.

"I was sent by Mara Brankovic," he said, covered in dust and holding out a letter.

Radu took it, puzzled. What would Mara need to communicate with him so desperately? He broke the seal and opened it. One of the sheets was a note from Mara. The elegant lines of her writing cut him apart. He could not catch his breath, could not manage to look at the next letter.

"What is it?" Kumal asked.

"Mara. She found word of Nazira. I cannot— Kumal, I cannot read it." Radu trembled, too terrified to learn what had happened to Nazira. Not knowing had been awful, but holding her fate in his hands was worse. He could not bear it if she was dead.

Kumal gently took the letters from Radu. Radu kept his eyes fixed on the ground. Watching Kumal for a reaction was the same as reading the letter. He wanted to pause time here, forever, where he did not have to know if his truest friend was dead and it was his fault.

Kumal let out a sharp, relieved breath and praised God. Radu was pierced through with hope and dared to look up. Tears shone in Kumal's eyes, and he smiled. "She is alive."

A gasp tore free from Radu's chest, loosing all the months of torment and fear. "She is alive?"

"She is." Kumal scanned the letter again. "They were shipwrecked on an island in the Sea of Marmara. Nazira was unharmed. Cyprian and the servant boy were badly injured. She had to stay to care for them and did not have a way to send word until she could travel to a more populated area."

Nazira was alive. Cyprian and Valentin were hurt. "Are they . . . ? Did Cyprian and Valentin recover?"

"It does not say. This is not written by Nazira herself. It

is from one of Mara's contacts. The writer says he can escort Nazira as far as the port city of Bursa, but that she will need someone to meet her there."

Radu was already turning his horse. He took a deep breath, closed his eyes, and lifted his face toward the heavens. Breathing in gratitude, breathing out fear. Breathing in hope, breathing out worry. Nazira was alive and well. He had not killed his truest, dearest friend. He would bring Fatima's wife home to her.

And Cyprian.

If Cyprian and Valentin were dead, the letter would have noted it. Surely they were well, which was all he could ask for. Anything more was too selfish on his part after everything he had done.

"You should go to her." Radu smiled at Kumal.

Kumal's warm eyes were filled with tears. He shook his head, a smile lighting his face. The same kind, gentle smile that had been a lifeline to Radu as a terrified and lost young boy in a foreign land. "You are her husband. Go and get her."

"But Lada . . ."

"I will see to everything. I promise I will treat her with respect and as much gentleness as I can. Let me take care of your sister while you go take care of mine."

Radu laughed, reaching out and clasping Kumal's hand. "Thank you, my brother. I will bring her home." Radu turned his horse toward the route that would take him to Bursa and Nazira. He paused. "Please be careful with my sister."

"I promise I will be kind."

"No, I mean, be cautious. For yourself."

Kumal's expression turned colder and decidedly grimmer. "I have read the reports. I will not underestimate her."

With another shared nod, Radu and Kumal parted ways to retrieve sisters who needed to return to the empire. One as a rescue, the other as a prisoner.

11

Tirgoviste

"WHAT DID THIS ONE do?" Lada asked, sharpening daggers while a motley group of prisoners waited in front of her throne, surrounded by her own soldiers.

"Rape," answered Bogdan.

"Kill him." Lada did not look up as the man was dragged away and the next was brought up. "And this one?"

"Theft." She felt Bogdan staring at her, willing her to look at him. She had avoided him since Daciana's warning. She did not have time to be careful with his feelings and resented having to accommodate them in any way.

"Why?" she asked.

"My family was starving," the prisoner growled. "I would do it again."

Lada paused, considering him. He was lanky and thin, but with the potential to be strong if well fed. "You may join my army. You will be on the front lines of any conflict and will most likely be killed. If you survive and distinguish yourself, your crimes will be forgiven and you will have the opportunity to get land for yourself and your family. If you steal again, or you disappoint me in any way, you will be killed. Otherwise you will go back to a cell. Do you agree?"

The man hesitated, his brow furrowed in thought. Lada appreciated that. The men who agreed without taking time to weigh the offer were lying either to themselves or, more likely, to her. She always had them put back in prison or had them killed, depending on their crimes.

Finally, the man bowed his head and dropped to one knee. "I agree, my prince."

"Very good." Lada waved him away. The soldiers directed him to the opposite exit, where he would join the ever-swelling ranks of her forces. She was approaching five thousand and hopeful for even more from Transylvania.

"Do we really want criminals for our army?" Nicolae asked. He sat nearby, though she had not asked him to join today's session.

"We have had criminals for our nobility for centuries. Why not let criminals actually accomplish something for us?"

Nicolae sighed. "But will you really give them land after?"

"I give land to whomever I see fit. If it comes from me, they owe me everything. If I fall, they lose all they have gained. Do you see a better way to encourage loyalty among my people?"

Nicolae shrugged, grinning. But the grin felt off, faded and worn like his scar. Things had not been the same since he had questioned her. She felt the distance between them like the edge of a serrated blade. Move a finger along it slowly and it was merely uncomfortable. But move too fast and there would be blood.

"Why are you here, Nicolae? You should be training our new recruits."

"There has been a letter."

"Oh, a letter. That is new. Is it a proposal of marriage? Perhaps a careful admonishment to keep to my own borders and stop antagonizing our enemies? Or would someone like to congratulate me on my actions but do nothing to actually help us? I do so love these letters." Lada sheathed a razor-sharp dagger at her wrist and pulled out the next one to be sharpened.

"It is from your brother."

Lada sat up. "Clear the room."

The soldiers pushed the remaining prisoners out, leaving only Bogdan and Nicolae.

"Where is Stefan?" Lada asked, holding out her hand.

"I do not know." Nicolae passed her the letter. Radu had a new seal, something in swirling and stylized Arabic script. She crumbled the red wax to pieces before opening the letter.

Beloved Sister,
I write on behalf of his magnificence, the Hand of God on Earth,
the emperor of Rome, the sultan of the glorious Ottoman Empire,
Mehmed the Conqueror.

Lada marveled at the sheer weight of titles Mehmed had attached to himself. How did he walk with all those words trailing from his shoulders?

Recent events require a renewing of terms of Wallachia's vassalage
to the Ottoman Empire. To avoid a conflict you cannot hope to win,

please attend to me at Giurgiu, where we can come to an agreement for how to go forward with friendship and peace. Preferably a friendship that includes significantly fewer impaled bodies.

Lada snorted a laugh, surprised by the flare of delight. There was her brother. There was the Radu hiding behind a new title, behind an empire that was not his own. She was hit with a pang of both melancholy and anger. She missed him. She had asked for his presence so long ago, but he was only coming now at the insistence of Mehmed, who correctly guessed that Radu was the *only* envoy not at risk of being sent back in a wooden box.

It was clever of him.

I will be awaiting your arrival. It has been too long, Sister. We have much to discuss, and I have missed you. Until we meet again soon,

Radu Bey

His handwriting, always elegant and meticulous, wobbled a bit around the words *I have missed you.* Was it because he was lying? Or because he was admitting a difficult truth?

Lada passed the letter to Nicolae and began pacing.

"Interesting," he said upon finishing. "Far more civil than I expected, to be honest. Perhaps the little zealot still holds some affection for you, even now."

Lada did not react, suspecting Nicolae was baiting her again.

"What are you going to do?" he asked.

"I will meet my brother."

"And will you accept new terms? Between your brother's

influence and the sultan's leniency, I think we can secure the greatest terms Wallachia has ever had." Nicolae sounded excited, his words rushing together. He had suggested the same thing in her rooms. This letter was proof that his ideas were correct. "Everything you have worked for will be rewarded. And all your people will benefit."

Lada smiled, twisting her dagger to catch the light. "I will meet Radu. And I will bring him home."

Nicolae sounded significantly less excited and far warier. "He said nothing about coming back to Tirgoviste."

"No, he will not wish to." Her grin spread. "We are going to kidnap my brother."

"What?" Bogdan asked. "Why?"

Because he should have been hers regardless.

Because she missed him, and she hated him for that.

Because Bogdan wanted more than she could ever give him. Because she mistrusted Stefan. Because Nicolae's questions festered under her skin. Because Petru, young and thickheaded but *hers*, was dead, killed by the boyars she had then eliminated in the dining room of this very castle. Because even after all this, she knew in the blood that flowed through her veins that she could trust Radu.

And because . . . Nicolae had been right. Lada *was* trying to pick a fight with Mehmed, even if she had not realized it before. She was not doing it for Wallachia. She did it for herself. For everything he had been to her. For all the ways he had failed her. She had Wallachia, and she would do everything she could to protect it, but she wanted to punish Mehmed. Kidnapping Radu—taking back the first, and the last, thing Mehmed had taken from her—might be enough to make him come to her when tens of thousands of bodies had not.

Just three bodies mattered. The same three that had always mattered.

Radu's.

Lada's.

And Mehmed's.

12

Bursa

RADU COULD NOT GET off the boat fast enough. For once it was not because he was sick, but because of who was waiting for him. He had been at the bow, searching the horizon since dawn. As soon as he saw Bursa in the distance, it was all he could do not to jump out and swim. Knowing he would be far slower than the boat kept him onboard.

They drew closer, alongside the city—one he had visited with Nazira, before Constantinople—and the wind whipped at Radu's face, as frenzied as his anticipation. Finally, they approached the dock.

Radu saw a familiar figure, as bright and welcome as spring.

He jumped over the side of the boat, landing hard on the dock. Nazira met him halfway. He threw his arms around her, lifting her off the ground and spinning her in a circle. He did not know whether he was laughing or crying. After a few minutes of embracing, Radu released her. He cupped her face in his hands and studied it. She was browner than she had been— evidence of more time in the sun than usual—and her clothes were in colors she would never have picked out for herself, but she looked healthy. There were no haunted hollows beneath her eyes, no suppressed terrors in the full sweet circle of her lips.

"Nazira, I—"

She put one hand over his mouth. "Please do not apologize. I know you. You have probably carried nothing but guilt all these months, tearing yourself apart. But you did it. You got us out safely. We survived, which means we are alive to heal and grow."

Radu sighed, hanging his head and shifting her hand so it rested on his cheek. "The whole time we were in Constantinople together, that was my only prayer. That whatever else happened, you would be safe."

"God is good," Nazira said, smiling.

Radu had not looked for anyone else but Nazira. Now, however, with his heart filled to bursting at the sight of her healthy and well and *alive*, he had room to wonder. "Valentin and Cyprian, did they—"

"They are not here. But they are alive, too."

A shudder passed through Radu. The release of the guilt and terror was a physical sensation, and he felt close to collapse. Nazira took his hand, as unwilling to let go of him as he was of her, and led him to a jumble of stones near the water where they could sit. They had last been here together watching Mehmed's armada. Back when Radu thought he knew what the future held, when Constantinople was simply a goal. Not a blood-soaked reality.

Touching his turban, Nazira searched his face. "It is good to see you back in this. It is good to leave behind pretending."

She looked down at her own clothes. "Sometimes when I dream, I am still wearing the styles of Constantinople. When I wake up, I cannot breathe."

She shook her head as though waking. "How is Fatima?"

Radu put an arm around her, drawing her close. He did not think he would ever let her go again. Except to give her to Fatima. "She is well," he said, gently. "I sent word to her that I was bringing you back, but I did not have time to go and get her."

Nazira wiped beneath her eyes. "I have missed her so much. But I knew that you would take care of her. It has made the missing bearable. It was simply sadness, not sadness and fear."

"She never lost hope. She is made from it, I think."

Nazira laughed and nodded, her head bobbing against Radu's shoulder. "She is. She is my light that never goes out. And you are the glass that protects our flame." Nazira kissed him on the cheek. "I have been in Bursa for three days. I waited here at the docks for each of them, knowing you would come. When Mara Brankovic's man arrived to bring me here, I parted ways with Cyprian and Valentin. I do not know where they are now. I was sorry to leave them. They have become family."

Radu knew they should go find horses to return to Fatima as fast as possible, but he was still unsteady and needed a few minutes for his body to accept the truth of Nazira's safety. "Tell me everything that happened since you left. Please."

"First, tell me: Did you save them? Constantine's nephews?"

Radu nodded, gazing at the cloud-strewn sky above. He had left Nazira with Cyprian to go back into the city and save the two boys. It had been a gamble for all of them. Radu risked his life for what could have been a futile mission, and he risked Nazira's by trusting Cyprian with her care even after Radu had revealed their treachery. But *that* had never felt like a risk. He had known then as he did now that Cyprian would never do anything to hurt them.

It was perhaps more than they deserved, and it made missing Cyprian hurt all the more. "I did. And they were spared the greater part of the carnage and terror. They are part of Mehmed's court now, renamed Murad and Mesih. They are happy."

Nazira squeezed his hand. She did not ask for details, and he would not offer them. She had seen enough during their flight to know better than to want more images from that nightmare. "I would say you did the right thing, but I think under those circumstances 'right' ceased to exist. You did a *good* thing, though. How is the city?"

"Flourishing. As we knew it would under Mehmed's careful care."

"And how is the sultan?"

Radu gently nudged her. "You do not have to speak as though you are a surgeon exploring a wound. I have had no one to talk to, no one who knows everything I am. Please let us drop all pretenses."

Nazira nudged him back with her elbow. "Very well. How has it been, being reunited with him?"

"Do you remember when you told me being as great as he is makes him both more and less than a man? I have thought of that often. He is so isolated, by necessity. He refuses to fall into the same errors his father did. And he depends on me, and loves me even, in his own way. But this—what I have with you—has fed me more in the past few minutes than months at Mehmed's side have."

"I am sorry, then."

"To be right?"

Nazira laughed. "It is a heavy burden, always being right. But some of us must bear it."

"I am grateful you bear it for me, as I am not qualified to carry it myself." Radu stood, holding out his hand. "Now come. We will get horses and supplies. And you still have told me nothing of what has transpired since I left you at the Golden Horn."

"Brace yourself," Nazira said. "It is a *very* good story. At least now that I know I have a happy ending, it is."

They navigated the windy streets of Bursa, purchasing what they needed. Having the purse of the sultan helped speed the process remarkably. Nazira told her tale between their errands.

"We swam out to one of the abandoned small galleys. Cyprian was able to turn the sails to catch the wind, and we slipped out unnoticed amid the chaos. We decided to head for Cyprus. Cyprian wanted to dock earlier, but I refused. I was afraid that if we were caught by Ottoman forces, Cyprian would be killed. I knew you would want us to go farther rather than risk his life."

Radu nodded, stroking the horse he had chosen as they waited for saddles and packs.

Nazira continued. "Our second day on the boat, things took a turn for the worse. We had no supplies, and in our exhausted state, we all fell asleep at the same time. A storm awakened us, and before we could direct the boat to shore, we capsized.

"Cyprian was hit hard. He went under. In the tempest I could not find him or Valentin. Then I saw the boy, clinging to the mast, his arms around Cyprian. Between the two of us, we managed to hang on long enough to drift to an island shore. But Valentin's leg had been badly broken, and I could not tell the extent of Cyprian's injuries."

Even knowing all three had survived, Radu found himself holding his breath.

"I dragged Cyprian onto dry ground, and then went back to help Valentin. We waited out the storm under the shelter of some trees. When it finally passed, with Cyprian still unconscious, I ventured out to find help.

"There was none. No one. We managed to land on the loneliest island in all of Europe, I think." She laughed lightly, but Radu knew it cost her to pretend it had not been terrifying. As they strapped the packs onto the horses, Nazira filled in details. The next few months she had taken care of Cyprian—he had wounded not only his head but also an ankle and a shoulder—and Valentin, while struggling to provide enough food and also cobble together a boat from the remnants of their old one.

"You never cease to astonish me," Radu said, halfway through buckling his pack. He could not take his eyes from Nazira. She blushed, smiling coyly.

"I hope I can cease immediately, as I never wish to do anything quite so astonishing again. We finally made it from the island to the mainland and found a lonely farmstead. But they mistrusted us and wanted money, and we had none. They put us to work. When they decided we had earned enough to pay them back for feeding and sheltering us, I was allowed to walk to the next closest town—a full day away—where I could ask for help and information. Imagine my surprise at finding that someone had left word and was already looking for us! At first I feared it was because of Cyprian, that there was a price on his head, so I did not write you. I am sorry. I could not risk him being found. After everything we have been through, he is family. I take care of my family."

"I know you do." Radu finished cinching up his pack and helped Nazira mount her horse, then mounted his own.

"So I set up a meeting with the man who had left word, and waited. When he told me that Mara Brankovic was the one looking so intently, I assumed we would be safe. Her agent gave us a ride as far as a port where I could get passage to Bursa. That was where Cyprian and Valentin parted ways with me. I tried to get them to come, but . . ."

Radu did not force her to tell the hard truth. "After all my deception and my role in the fall of Constantinople, I cannot imagine they were eager to see me again. We used Cyprian terribly. I do not blame him for anything."

"I told Cyprian everything."

"What do you mean by everything?"

"I mean *everything*. He deserved nothing less than total honesty. He was angry. But more than that, he was hurt. He wanted to understand why we did what we did. How we could have lied to him for that long. I told him of your childhood, how we met, what you did for me. I told him of Lada and your father. I told him what the empire offered you—safety, home, faith. Things you had never had. I told him why we were in the city as spies, what we actually did while we were there. I told him of Fatima and my own reasons for wanting security for both our empire and our faith. I told him what I thought the sultan would do with the city. And I told him of your relationship with Mehmed, both what it is and what it is not."

Radu flinched, closing his eyes. He had already told Cyprian the hardest truth, of course: the truth of his duplicity. But knowing that Cyprian knew everything felt more intimate, more humiliating. How Cyprian must hate him! Finally, Radu nodded. "You made the right choice. He saved you in spite of everything."

"He did not save me in *spite* of everything. He saved me *because* of everything. We may have entered Constantinople with false intentions, but our friendship was true. We saved his life several times over. And we did it because we loved him. I think he knows that."

Radu sighed. "It does not matter. It is in the past. I hope he can forgive us someday, but that is a selfish hope. It is for myself, not for him. So instead I will hope he finds happiness somehow."

"We can hope for nothing more and nothing less."

Radu felt both heavier and lighter for the information. At least he had given Cyprian another chance at life. Without Radu, Cyprian surely would have died at his uncle's side. Radu was glad knowing he was out there, somewhere. He tugged on the reins. "Come. There is a girl in Edirne who has been waiting a very long time."

"I am going to hold her for weeks. You will have to feed us both, because I will not let her go for anything."

Radu laughed. "It would be an honor."

"And my brother?"

"He would have come, but we were on our way to Wallachia to bring Lada back. By force, if necessary. Kumal volunteered to see it through so I could get you."

"You traded sisters."

Radu laughed, but more from guilt than happiness. "He said the same thing. I got by far the better end of the trade." Radu was enormously in Kumal's debt.

"And what will you do after we get back? Will you go to Constantinople again?"

Radu guided their horses past the outskirts of Bursa, to the roads that would take them to Fatima. "I do not know. And I do not care. I have you, and you have Fatima. I have fulfilled all my promises. I am tired. And I am happy." The clouds had cleared, and the sky was brilliantly blue, promising a gentle journey. It was not as cold as it had been heading toward Wallachia. Everything felt warmer with Nazira at his side, though.

The future was blank, and Radu did not mind. He had Nazira back, and soon Kumal would return and be reunited with them. Cyprian was safe. Mehmed would have Lada again, and for once Radu did not feel anything about that. If she was imprisoned, she would be less likely to be killed. And she would certainly be doing less killing. As far as Mehmed's feelings for her, Radu was numb. This last horrible chapter of his time in Constantinople was closed. Everyone he loved was safe. Radu was going home for good.

13

Near Giurgiu

"WHERE HAVE YOU BEEN?" The Janissary scout glowered at Lada's men, who were all wearing Janissary uniforms. The ones in front spoke Turkish. The ones in the back were silent. "We expected you yesterday."

"We had some complications," Bogdan growled. In fact, they *were* the complications. The previous day they had ambushed a group of Janissary reinforcements heading toward the Giurgiu fortress. Today, they had become those Janissaries. Lada stood, anonymous, in the middle of her men. The Wallachians who had not grown up as Janissaries were behind her so they could follow her cues. They did not know how to behave as Janissaries, but they knew how to mimic.

Nicolae rode in front as their leader. He stopped beside Bogdan to talk with the scout. They were still a few hours from the fortress, so the scout must have been sent to look for them. Lada worked her way closer so she could eavesdrop. Insects just beginning to reemerge from the deep freeze of winter flitted through the crisp air, landing on trees speckled with green hints of buds. Getting here had been a muddy, roundabout trek, but they had to make certain they had Janissary uniforms and arrived *after* Radu.

"What is the plan at the fortress?" Nicolae asked.

"You do not know?"

Nicolae shrugged, indifferent. "We go where they tell us. We were told to come here. That is all I know."

"You frontier forces are as bad as spahis sometimes."

Nicolae moved closer, toying with the hilt of his weapon. His pleasant voice took on a dangerous tone appropriate to that level of a Janissary insult. The spahis were the elite, landed men, not the lifetime soldiers Janissaries were. There was no small amount of rivalry between the two. Spahis had the privilege, but Janissaries had the prestige and often the preference of the sultan. "You should take that back," Nicolae said.

The man waved his hands. "Sorry. It can be frustrating, being stationed at an outpost. We get all the news but none of the action. We are here with some pasha. The bitch who declared herself prince of Wallachia is on her way to sign new terms of vassalage."

Nicolae picked idly at his teeth. "Why do you need so many extra men for that?"

The scout shrugged, scratching under his signature white-flapped cap. "You heard how many she killed in Bulgaria?"

Nicolae grunted. "We were in Serbia. Been marching ever since. I still cannot believe the numbers."

"Well"—the soldier leaned closer conspiratorially— "they gave me no specifics, but I have a feeling we are not really here to make a deal. Too many men, and a wagon with bars and shackles. I think we are here to take her back for punishment."

Lada bit back a smile. It was gratifying that Radu still knew not to underestimate her. He had laid a trap to accomplish her same goal. She almost laughed at the irony of going to kidnap her brother, who was here to kidnap her.

Nicolae actually laughed. "Easy enough to take one woman. I still do not understand why you requested so many extra men. I hate traveling during this time of year. Snowstorms just when you get comfortable. Rain otherwise. Mud everywhere. It takes forever to clean my uniform."

"After Bulgaria, I think the pasha is spooked. Wants extra protection."

"How many men already in the fortress?"

"A thousand."

"Hmm." Nicolae sounded mildly impressed. Lada was flattered. It was a significant investment of men for what they anticipated to be easy trickery. The Janissary troop they had ambushed and killed on the way here had been two hundred strong. So she had two hundred of her men with her, and another five hundred following at a distance.

"How many men do we expect her to bring?" Nicolae asked.

"No more than a personal guard. I like our chances." The Janissary laughed brightly. "You should be glad you got such an easy assignment."

Nicolae grunted. "Good thing it will be easy, since we will do all the work, as usual. I met Radu Bey once years ago, at the siege of Kruje. He had to wear brown pants to cover constantly shitting himself in fear. He still that way?"

"I would not know. He is not here."

Lada hissed in surprise. Bogdan coughed to cover the noise.

Nicolae rushed another question. "But I thought Radu Bey was the lure? He is her brother, is he not? Who would come but him?"

The scout paused, eyeing Nicolae with sudden scrutiny and doubtless regretting his loose tongue. "I thought you did not know much about this."

Nicolae grinned. "I am full of surprises."

Lada drew her knife, jumping in front of the scout and knocking him to the ground. She straddled him, her knife against his throat.

"Who are you?" he gasped.

"I am the bitch who butchered thousands. Tell me: How do you like your chances now?"

His face went white.

"Where is Radu?"

"I do not know," the scout said, rapid, shallow breaths betraying his panic. But he did not yet realize he was dead. He spoke fast, as though he could talk his way free. "Radu broke away from the group before they got here. I never met him."

"Who is in his place?"

"Kumal Pasha."

Lada's muscles clenched instinctively, recoiling from that name. Unfortunately for the scout, her twitch sliced through his jugular vein. Lada stood as he bled out onto the forest floor.

"He might have had more information," Nicolae said, frowning.

"Accident." Lada picked up the dying scout's cap and used the white flaps to clean her blade. Kumal, not Radu, was waiting for her.

All her old resentment flared to life, burning hot and hungry. Once again, Kumal Pasha had taken her brother from her. He was the reason Radu had willingly accepted their captivity among the Ottomans. Certainly, Radu had loved Mehmed. But Lada had loved him, too, and still been able to walk away. Radu, however, had been poisoned from his childhood by the god that Kumal gave to him. It was Radu's false faith that separated him from Lada, his false faith that joined him forever to their enemies. Kumal had even claimed him as a brother through marriage, further cutting Radu off from his true family and heritage.

Now Kumal had again taken her brother from her. Instead of riding back to the city with Radu at her side—willing or not—she was once again left bereft. Gritting her teeth, she sheathed her blade.

"What now?" Nicolae asked. "We do not know where Radu is."

"I will not go back to Tirgoviste empty-handed." Lada started marching toward the fortress. "The plan is the same. Infiltrate. Bring someone back."

But unlike the Ottoman plan for her, he would not be alive.

They waited until darkness obscured their ranks.

"Hey!" Nicolae called as they marched up to the gate. "Is she here yet?"

A man shouted back down, "You know women. They are always late."

"We are tired and hungry. Open the gate." Nicolae kicked it for good measure.

The gates opened, and Lada and her two hundred Janissary-uniformed men filed in. The rest were hidden and circling the fortress.

"Where is everyone?" Nicolae gestured at the empty courtyard. A few solitary torches threw more shadow than light. A handful of men were visible on the walls, black silhouettes against the night sky. But they all looked outward, not in, where the threat already was.

"In bed. You are too late for a cot. It is the floor for you as punishment."

"I curse every mile of this forsaken country for it." Nicolae put an arm around the guard. Then the guard slumped to the side.

"The barracks first," Lada said, keeping her voice low. "Kill them quietly. Then spread out and take the walls. I will find Kumal."

She stalked forward, trusting her men to follow Nicolae, Bogdan, and their other leaders. After entering the fortress, she killed the guards in the hallways, as silent as a shadow, until she came to a living area. She took a torch from several lining the wall. The first bedroom was empty. The second held her target.

She kicked the bed. "Wake up."

Kumal Pasha sat up, eyes wide and blinking in the flickering light. She had never seen him without a turban. He was mostly bald, his scalp paler than his face.

"Lada Dragwlya," he said, recognition of the situation settling his features from surprise to sadness.

"Lada Dracul," she corrected. "Prince."

He had the audacity to tip his head respectfully, as though he was not here to kidnap her. As though he had not stolen her treasured chance to get her brother and hurt Mehmed in one easy step.

"Where is Radu?"

"He went to get Nazira. She had been lost since the city fell, and—"

Lada waved the torch through the air, cutting him off. "I do not care what your sister was doing. Always the two of you have worked together to take my brother from me."

"He wanted to be here," Kumal said softly.

"Was this his idea? Kidnapping me?"

"Yes. We did not like the deceit, but he said it was necessary."

Lada laughed, and it flickered warmly in her chest. "Well, I was coming to kidnap him, so it appears we have more in common than we thought."

"Come back with me. The sultan cares for you. He will deal fairly. You cannot continue on this path."

"What path do you think I am on?" Lada wanted to strike him. His calm demeanor was infuriating.

"You have what you wanted, but you are not happy. You

lash out and make others suffer. Those are not the actions of a person at peace with their past and future."

Lada snarled. "You know nothing about me or my past."

"I know your brother's past. And I know that he can still find happiness even in the darkest of circumstances, because his faith sustains him. What sustains you?"

"The blood of my enemies," she said.

14

Edirne

NAZIRA HAD NOT EXAGGERATED her intentions. She let go of Fatima only when absolutely necessary. Radu leaned back on his cushion, smiling to himself as Nazira tried to navigate eating dinner while keeping hold of Fatima's hand at all times.

"When will you return to the country home?" Radu asked. He knew that was where the two women were happiest. They had been in Edirne to help him, and since the siege was over and everyone was finally safe, he no longer needed help. But he would miss them. Living without Nazira these past terrifying months had been torture. It would be different, knowing she was content, but he still anticipated her absence with tremendous sadness.

"We are not going back," Fatima said.

"What?"

Nazira let go of Fatima's hand, but only to twist a lock of Fatima's hair around her fingers and stroke it. "We talked about it last night. Fatima and I will stay wherever you are."

"But Fatima hates to be away from home!"

Fatima's smile was sweet and shy. "Our family is my home."

Nazira's smile was as firm and determined as anything she set her mind to. "We are settled on this. We are never being separated again."

Radu could not deny the wash of relief he felt. He did not want to ask this of them. But he had not asked—they had offered. And, having lived so long without honesty and without love, he would not reject it.

"Thank you." He hoped they felt how much those two words conveyed. "I will ask Mehmed to give me a position in the countryside, somewhere with fewer memories."

"We will make new ones." Fatima rested her head on Nazira's shoulder.

"Also," Nazira said, teasingly popping a grape into her wife's mouth, "we would like to have a baby."

Radu choked on his bread.

His choking was interrupted by a firm knock. He stood so fast he tripped over his cushion. "I will see who it is."

He could hear Nazira laughing as he hurried out of the room and through the hall. At the front door he found a messenger wearing Mehmed's seal.

"The sultan, his magnificence Mehmed the Second, Caesar of Rome and the Hand of God on Earth, requests your presence immediately in Constantinople." He gestured to direct Radu's attention to a team of horses waiting in the street.

Lada, Radu thought. It had worked, then. He wondered what Mehmed thought Radu could accomplish. She would never accept captivity, just as she had not before. And Radu could do nothing to help that. Still, he would go. He would do what Mehmed asked, because he did not know how to do anything else.

The idea of seeing Lada terrified him. He was not the same person she had left behind. He could not imagine her, though, as anyone but who she had always been. And he did not want to see how she would judge him and find him lacking.

But having Nazira and Fatima with him would give him the strength to remember things could—and should—be different. He would ask Mehmed for a new position immediately. These were no longer his problems to handle. It was not a betrayal of his friend or his sister to be honest about that. Lada and Mehmed had chosen power. Neither had chosen him.

Radu could walk away.

The messenger cleared his throat. Radu had been standing there, silent, lost in his own history.

"Give me a few minutes to gather my things." Radu closed the door gently. He turned to find Nazira and Fatima standing in the hallway. His smile felt like the first layer of ice on a river in winter. Cold and fragile. "I have been summoned to Constantinople. Your resolve is tested sooner than we thought."

Fatima surprised him by speaking first. "We have already packed for just such a scenario." She disappeared upstairs.

Nazira fixed a wry smile on Radu. "You cannot get away from this conversation by an urgent summons to the city. And think of all that time on the road we will have to talk about adding to our family!"

It turned out there was, in fact, something even more terrifying than Lada.

Radu had been saved on the long ride to Constantinople by the addition to their party of a minor bey, summoned on a matter of tax revenue. Though Radu had never met him before, he quickly became the man's best friend by encouraging him to tell them every detail of his entire life.

Nazira watched and waited, an amused twinkle in her eyes. Radu had not gotten out of the conversation about ... their family. He was only delaying the inevitable. But he would take every delay he could get.

As they passed through the walls and into Constantinople, Fatima gazed around in wonder. They had traveled all night—an urgency that had been demanded by Mehmed, apparently—and so entered Constantinople as a warm, golden dawn bathed it in softest light. Radu tried to see it as Fatima would: without ghosts, without blood, without the weight of memories heavier than the stones of the walls. Nazira reached across the space between them and squeezed his hand. "He has made it beautiful."

But she kept her eyes firmly on her own hands.

Though morning had barely broken, the sounds of hammers and construction already rang like music through the air as they reached the palace. A servant met them, directing the tax-busied bey elsewhere and bidding Radu's company to follow.

"We will help your sister," Nazira murmured at Radu's side. "However we can. We will see you through this."

Radu tried to smile his gratitude, but his jaw was clenched too tightly. Lada had never wanted his help growing up, and when she had finally asked for it, he had refused. And now he had trapped her. A pit of dread opened in his stomach as the servant gestured to a door and bowed. Radu was not familiar with this room, but the palace had numerous receiving areas.

Taking a deep breath, Radu strode forward, followed by Nazira and Fatima.

Mehmed stood from the sofa he had been sitting on. Radu swept his eyes over the room. Mehmed was alone. Was Lada so feral with rage, then, that she was already in a cell?

Mehmed looked behind Radu at Nazira and Fatima, who both bowed prettily. Radu remembered to do the same. When he straightened, Mehmed was still staring at Nazira. His imperious features would have revealed nothing to one who did not know him. But Radu knew him.

Mehmed did not want to utter whatever he had to say next.

"What is it?" Radu asked, the pit of dread growing ever deeper. "Where is Lada?"

Mehmed shook his head. "She is not here."

Radu's chest tightened. He closed his eyes, reassuring himself. She was not dead. She could not be dead. That was not what Mehmed meant! He meant she was in another building. Radu would get her nicer accommodations than the dank prison cells he had seen when interrogating a prisoner on behalf of Constantine. It was the absolute least he could do. "Where are you keeping her?"

"I mean, she is not here at all."

Radu frowned. "Is Kumal not back yet? What happened?"

Mehmed shook his head again, and the shift in his eyes from horror to sadness made Radu's heart race. He wanted to run away from whatever was coming next.

Radu glanced at Nazira, a pleasant and respectful look on

her face as she waited for news of her beloved brother. Radu's stomach contracted, a shudder running through his whole body. "What did she do?" he whispered, planting his eyes on the floral patterns of the thick carpet. He could not bear to look at anyone.

"I am so sorry," Mehmed said. "Apparently she went into the fortress with the intent of kidnapping you. But she found Kumal." He paused, as though searching for the next words. "She was not merciful."

Radu choked, somewhere between a laugh and a sob.

She was not merciful.

When had she ever been? Radu dropped to his knees, hanging his head. "This is my fault. I should have been there. I should have gone to her, and sent Kumal to . . . If I had, then—"

A light, trembling hand settled on his shoulder. Nazira spoke in a whisper. "What does he mean? Tell me what he means, Radu."

Radu shook his head. "I should have known. She is my sister. I of all people know that mercy is not in her nature. It should have been me." Being a Dracul had cost him so much. He had thought he was done paying for the blood that ran through his veins. But he would never be done. The price of being in his family was everything he held dear, taken from him over and over again. They were the dragons. The devils. There was no mercy in them or for them.

Nazira knelt next to him. "Tell me. Tell me exactly what he means."

Radu's punishment was having to say the words. Having to do this to Nazira. "She killed him."

An unearthly wail started, so low at first that Radu did not know what it was until it built to a scream. Nazira, who had always been so strong, was broken. Fatima dropped down next to her, taking her in her arms. Nazira screamed and sobbed, clawing at Fatima's arms as though she could burrow in there and hide herself from sorrow.

Radu did not know what to do. Could not do anything. "I am— Nazira, I am so sorry, I—"

"Please," Fatima said. She shook her head in warning. "Please stop talking." She held out one arm and Radu crawled to the two women.

Fatima held them both up.

Radu pictured Kumal as he had last seen him. Smiling. Waving. An unbidden image of his brother, his teacher, his friend sliced like a blade through his memory. Lada killing Kumal. How had she done it? With a knife? A sword? Had Kumal fought back? Radu did not want to imagine it, did not want to picture it. Could not stop.

He did not realize the guttural sobs were coming from himself until Fatima stroked his back, making a soft *shh* sound. Nazira grabbed his arm, her fingers digging in painfully as she dragged him closer and buried her face in his shoulder. She shook, silent now, her breath coming in shuddering gasps. They were all three a tangle, a mess of devastation.

It was not appropriate to behave this way with a servant, but Radu no longer cared to maintain that charade of Fatima's role. Not now. Not in front of Mehmed, who had not moved to comfort or even touch him. Let Mehmed see and know what he wanted to.

Radu cried with his family, for all they had lost.

For all he had cost them.

15

Tirgoviste

LADA SURVEYED THE BRIDGE mournfully. "Are we certain we do not have enough gunpowder to just blow it up?"

Nicolae put a hand on her shoulder and gave a grim nod. "I am afraid we have to dismantle it the old-fashioned way: by forcing other people to do it."

Lada and Nicolae stood on a hill overlooking the work. Below, her men supervised a group of criminals in tearing down the bridge. It was the first of several they had to visit that day. She wanted to oversee everything, to make certain the tasks were done. It was also a chance to take stock of the countryside.

"All that work to make the roads safe," she said, scuffing one boot through the dirt, "and now our job is to make the country impassable."

"We do not have to do this, you know." Nicolae was using that soft voice again, the one that slipped like a blade between her ribs. They had not spoken privately since the fight in her rooms. She had not wanted to. She did not want to now.

She delivered her words like angry blows. "And what should we do instead?"

Beneath the scar that bisected his face, Nicolae's expression was wistful. "I rather liked being bandits. We could do that again. Slip away in the night and never look back."

Lada leaned back in surprise. She had expected him to push for a new treaty again. "Why would we do that?"

"Because it would be easy. Because we can. We do not have to choose this."

"Are you afraid?"

Nicolae laughed. "Of course I am afraid. You are demanding the greatest military in the world come fight you. I have *been* in that military. I know what they can do. I dream about it every night. I am so scared I have had to cut back drinking simply to avoid pissing my pants as frequently." He paused, and that horrible soft tone came back. He stared at her as though committing her face to memory. "I am afraid to die, and I am afraid to watch you die, powerless to stop it. Every step we take in this direction feels like one step closer to your grave. I do not want to see that." He cleared his throat, looking away with an automatic smile. "Though we will not have graves, I suspect. Pikes for our heads, if we are very lucky."

Lada lifted her eyes to the sky. She had left Bogdan in Tirgoviste to avoid having conversations filled with emotions she did not want to address. Apparently she should have left Nicolae as well. But he was one of her oldest friends, her first supporter, the one who had gotten her into the Janissary ranks. Her father had given her a knife; Nicolae had given her a sword.

"You did it," he pressed. "You became prince. No one ever said you had to *stay* prince. We have so many other options."

"I cannot leave."

"Why?"

Like a melody she could not stop from ringing through her head, Mehmed arose in her memories. *He* knew why. He alone understood this drive, this ambition, this need to have her country. She could not abandon it, because Wallachia *was* her. If she could walk away from Wallachia, if she could leave it to others, she would not *be*. It was as simple as that.

"Will you stay with me?" This time she did not have an elbow to his throat. She held out a hand instead, staring at his hazel eyes, still trying to figure out how they had changed. As he put his hand on hers, she realized what it was that had been missing since the day she attacked him.

Nicolae no longer hoped.

His optimism, cloaked in dark and bloody humor, had been a constant in her life. He was a man who was staring at his own death. She had seen men look at her that way before, but always when she was holding a blade. Not when she was holding their hand.

"Nicolae, I—"

The bridge fell with a tremendous cracking splash into the river below. Nicolae and Lada shifted to look. "Oh," Nicolae said, stumbling into Lada's side. She staggered under his weight.

"What are you—"

Nicolae glanced over his shoulder, then shoved Lada to the ground. He flinched, dropping to his knees.

"What is the matter with you?" Lada demanded, sitting up. Nicolae fell forward.

Two crossbow bolts were embedded in his back. Dark circles of blood bloomed outward along his tunic. Lada scanned the tree line, where a man fumbled a third bolt. She leapt over Nicolae and sprinted, screaming. The assassin loaded the bolt.

Her knife found his neck before his finger found the trigger.

She slashed his throat, then followed him to the ground, stabbing again and again and again. Only when his glassy eyes stared up at the sky, lifeless, and her hand dripped with his blood did she stop.

Part of her wanted to run back. To help Nicolae up.

The other part of her knew exactly what it meant when blood spread that fast, when bolts hit those parts. Those bolts had been meant for her. The first he had taken by accident as they turned toward the falling bridge. But he had taken the second on purpose. Maybe there was still time to say thank you. To berate him for being so stupid. To say she was sorry. But she did not want to say any of those things.

Not when they were the same as saying goodbye.

She ran toward him anyway, each footstep a breath, each footstep a heartbeat, each footstep an eternity.

Dropping to his side, she lifted his head onto her lap. He gazed up at her, his ugly, beloved face pale. She pushed his hair back, stroking his forehead. The blood from her hands smeared across his skin and she panicked at the sight. She needed to clean him up, to get that blood off him. There was a tremendous pressure behind her eyes, a tightening of her throat that made it hard to speak.

"You would follow me to the ends of the earth, you said." She held his gaze, though his eyes were going unfocused. "I am holding you to that. We are very far from the ends of the earth."

Nicolae's grin spread slower than the blood pooling beneath him. "No, Lada. I am already there. I beat you, is all."

"Be careful, or I really will display your head on a pike."

Nicolae laughed.

And then he died.

"But who was the assassin working for?" Bogdan asked. He sat at a table in the corner of the kitchen along with Daciana, Oana, and Stefan. The scent of freshly turned dirt clung to them, as did the memory of lowering Nicolae's body into the ground only an hour before.

Lada kicked a chair. It skittered across the uneven stone floor before tipping and clattering to the ground. "It does not matter who he was working for!"

"It might have been better to take him alive and get information," Daciana said. "Then we would know who wanted you dead."

"Who does *not* want me dead? That would be a shorter list." Lada paced, prowling the length of the room, angry and devastated, wanting to do something, anything, to stop feeling this way. She rubbed at her arms to keep from tearing at her hair.

The last time she had lost one of her men, it had been Petru, killed in this very castle. That still hurt. But Nicolae. Nicolae she had depended on, had needed in a way she needed very few people. And even though she had doubted him, he remained loyal to her until the end. He had found his end *because* of his loyalty to her.

"If we—" Bogdan started, but Lada cut him off.

"It does not matter. The assassin failed." He had not failed entirely. A part of her had gone into the ground with Nicolae. She did not know how large a part. It was still too raw, too new to see how the scar would form. She wished it were written across her face the way Nicolae's scar had been. She wanted visual evidence of what she had lost.

Lada righted her chair, dragged it back to the table, and sat. "We have too much to do to worry about who sent an assassin. And now we are down one trusted ally, so there is more work for everyone. The first problem is that we do not have enough men. Even if we conscript convicts and vagrants, we are massively outnumbered. I am expecting Mehmed to come with at least twenty thousand, probably thirty or forty. Right now, at most, we have five."

"Lada." Daciana leaned across the table with a hand outstretched. "Let me help. Take some time."

Lada stared at Daciana's hand, then looked up into her face. Daciana was strong. All Wallachian women were—they could not be otherwise and still survive. Lada smiled. They *would* help. "The women can fight. This is their country as much as the men's."

Bogdan scoffed. "The women?"

His mother slapped his shoulder. "We are no delicate flowers. We break our backs with the washing and the tilling of soil and the bearing of children. We can beat an enemy as handily as we beat a rug."

Lada nodded. "Anyone strong enough will fight. Men, women, it does not matter. We have a lot of work to do before the actual fighting begins, and we only have until mid-spring. Mehmed will not come until then." Logistically it was impossible. He would wait until there was no risk of freezing to death, until there was scavenging of the land available to help feed his men. "We will start gathering and training women immediately. Children and the elderly will be sent into the mountains."

"What about the sick?" Daciana asked, her tone wry.

"Oh, I have other plans for them." Lada smiled at the woman's confused look.

Stefan sat motionless, always the last to attract attention. "We will still be outmanned and out-trained. What else do we have?"

"Matthias."

"You trust him?"

"Not at all. But I have word that he received money from the pope to fight the infidels. And he does not want to face an entire Ottoman army camped on his borders. It is in his best interest to keep Wallachia free. He will help."

Stefan looked troubled.

"What?" Lada said.

"I do not trust him to use the money for what it is intended. He has been trying to raise money for other purposes for a long time."

Stefan waited, placid and patient. He already had a conclusion, Lada could sense it. Frustrated, she sorted through what she knew of Matthias. What he would need money for. Then she threw her head back and glared at the ceiling. "The crown taken by Poland. The crown he could not afford to get back." She swore, grinding her teeth. "That stupid, pointless crown. He is still fixated on it, doubtless. But he took the money with the promise of fighting infidels. He cannot bring the ire of the entire Catholic Church on his head. He will *have* to come."

Stefan did not respond.

Lada shrugged against the cold prickling of fear on the back of her neck. "He will come, or he will pay for it, one way or another."

"I think he will come," Bogdan said, smiling encouragingly at her.

"I think you know nothing of Matthias, and therefore should not volunteer an opinion on this subject," Lada snapped. Bogdan flinched as though struck. Oana shifted in her seat, but Lada avoided looking at either of them. She was not fair to him. But she was prince; she did not have to be fair.

"Do we have any money?" Oana asked, neatly changing the subject.

"No." She should have waited another year or two, let the country settle, let tax revenue come in. But the idea of sitting in this castle, slowly gathering coins, eyeing a future where Wallachia would be free when it was already agonizingly close . . . She should have waited, but she never could have.

"Weapons?" Daciana asked.

"My cousin Stephen cannot send us troops, but he has sent some gunpowder and hand cannons. We will have to use them strategically. We have plenty of bows and crossbows."

"What are all those carpenters doing?" Bogdan asked. Lada had invited everyone with knowledge of carpentry and experience clearing forests to the capital. She had several of her men supervising the enormous task. It did not require a tremendous amount of skill, simply a tremendous amount of supplies and manpower.

Lada smiled again. "They are attending to a different project."

"So we have men and women. And sick people, apparently." Daciana watched as Stefan made notes, calculating roughly how many additional troops they would have if a significant portion of the country's women were conscripted. "Some gunpowder. Some hand cannons. Do we fortify the cities?"

"No," Lada said. "In any siege situation, we lose. We never let it come to that."

Stefan nodded in silent agreement.

Daciana watched him, fear forming new lines around her eyes. "Will what we have be enough?"

"No." Lada leaned forward, looking at Stefan's calculations. They would be outnumbered at least four to one. Probably more, depending on just how big an example Mehmed wanted to make of her. And she was missing so many things she needed. People, too. Nicolae. Petru. *And Radu.*

But she would do this in spite of what she lacked. She was strong enough. Her country was strong enough. She would show Mehmed exactly why he could never own Wallachia, why he could never own her.

"We have something else: our land. I will use every single league of it against the Ottomans." Out of habit, Lada's fingers touched the knives at her wrists. "The empire is coming for us, and I intend to win."

16

Constantinople

MEHMED RESTED A TENTATIVE hand on Radu's back. "At least Kumal died knowing his sister was safe."

Radu was leaning forward, head cradled in his hands. He had left Nazira and Fatima—finally asleep, thankfully, curled around each other with faces pale and hollowed out by grief— after a long, restless night. Radu had not slept. He had not eaten. He had no desire to do either.

"We could not have known—"

Radu sighed to stop Mehmed from talking. Mehmed moved the hand on his back but did not shift away. They sat, shoulder to shoulder, in Mehmed's private chamber.

Radu's voice was filled with the tiny fissures that ran through his whole soul now. "We could have known. We *should* have known. Of everyone in the world, we should have been the last to underestimate her. And I knew she hated Kumal. She has always hated him. I was so eager to see Nazira and to find out—" He stopped, holding back the next words. *To find out Cyprian's fate as well.* "And to find out what had happened to her that I did not think. Kumal paid the price I should have."

"If you had gone, we would have lost you."

"She would not kill me." Radu paused. In fact, Lada had promised to do just that one day. "Regardless, I was her target. Kumal took my place. It is my fault he is dead."

"It is Lada's fault."

"Well, then it is our fault. We are the ones who put her in that position."

Mehmed stood. There was a cold pride in his expression that Radu had never felt directed at himself when they were alone. It was a sultan look, not a Mehmed look.

"She made her own decisions. I did not ask her to attack Bulgaria. I have done everything I could to help her."

Radu lifted an eyebrow, too exhausted with grief and guilt to defer to Mehmed's needs. "Have you? Really?"

A flicker of guilt shifted behind Mehmed's eyes. Then he turned away, clasping his hands as he paced. "We cannot let this stand. She murdered my ambassadors, attacked one of my vassals, and murdered a pasha on a diplomatic mission."

"A *kidnapping* mission."

Mehmed stopped, startled by the correction. "Radu," he said, his voice a reprimand.

Radu shrugged. "Why must we pretend when it is only the two of us?"

Mehmed's eyebrows drew close, his mouth tightening into a line somewhere between a challenge and a smile. "Oh, are you done pretending? Is it time for honesty?"

Radu looked at the floor. His face burned brighter than the room's coal brazier.

Mehmed crouched before him, forcing Radu to meet his eyes. "I am sorry, my friend. But I cannot let this stand. It threatens everything I have built—everything *we* have built. It is too dangerous a precedent. I have to go after her."

"I understand. And I am not against it." Radu hated that the death of one man felt worse than the death of thousands in Bulgaria. But this was personal. Lada had made certain of that. He suspected she *wanted* them to attack, though he could not fathom why.

"Will you help me?"

"You know I always will."

Mehmed caressed Radu's cheek with the back of his fingers. They lingered there for a few breathless seconds, then Mehmed smiled. It was the smile that had been Radu's protection and torment for so many years.

Radu was cold with sadness at everything his desire for that smile had cost him and would continue to cost him. "We cannot underestimate her," he said.

"We will not. Not this time."

———◆———

Mara Brankovic sat straight-backed in her tightly structured dress. Radu could not sympathize with her reluctance to embrace the far more comfortable—and beautiful—flowing robes and layers of the Ottomans. Even Urbana, seated next to Mara at the table, had finally converted to entaris and slippers. Joining them were Aron and Andrei Danesti, who were still living in Constantinople as guests of Mehmed; Ishak Pasha and Mahmoud Pasha, older pashas who had distinguished themselves at the walls of Constantinople; and the Janissary leader Ali Bey. They all regarded Mara's and Urbana's presences with curious disapproval.

"It is *Wallachia*," Ali Bey said. Though a Janissary, he was also a bey, and had a carefully trimmed and styled beard appropriate to his status. He was younger than the pashas, in his mid-thirties. Sometimes Radu forgot he himself was not yet nineteen, Mehmed only twenty-one. Had they really lived so many lives in so few years?

Ali Bey crossed his arms and continued. "I hardly think we need worry."

"It is not Wallachia we are worried about," Radu said. "It is my sister. She trained with Ilyas Bey, and then with Hunyadi."

"Ilyas?" Ali Bey scoffed. "The traitor?"

"She killed him." Radu pushed away the memory of that night, when Ilyas Bey—their friend—had tried to assassinate Mehmed. Lada had killed Ilyas, but Radu had killed the co-conspirator, Lazar. His own friend. It had felt unavoidable at the time, but how many unavoidable choices of his had resulted in unforgivable consequences?

Ali Bey appeared slightly cowed. "Very well. The Janissaries will lead the assault, taking the Danube and securing the river passage. After that, we will scout and clear the roads. We should take Bucharest easily, as well as Snagov. That is less strategic and more to send a point. My scouts tell me she has paid patronage to the monastery on the island. We should make certain to take everything that matters."

Ishak Pasha leaned forward, tapping his notes. Radu mistrusted most of the pashas who had served under Murad, but Ishak Pasha had always been devout and committed to Mehmed's plans. Kumal had trusted him, too. Radu listened with a sharp stab of mourning, wishing Kumal were here instead.

"My spahis will be in charge of finding supplies," Ishak

Pasha said. "It is still early, but there is a good amount of farmland between the Danube and Tirgoviste, so the logistics of the campaign should not be too taxing on our resources. I would prefer late summer or early fall, but we can manage. We will plan for a short siege."

Mehmed nodded. He was seated in an elevated chair at the head of the room, separated from their table. "Radu Bey will be in charge of four thousand mounted troops. He knows his sister and the land."

Radu supposed he should be grateful for such a show of confidence. He did his best at faking it with a somber bow. This conflict felt so personal—like it was really between Mehmed, Lada, and Radu. It felt wrong to be planning it out on fields with tens of thousands of men. How had this happened?

"Get me a detailed schematic of Tirgoviste." Urbana ran her fingers idly along the smooth, shiny scar that covered half her face, a token of her time at the greatest siege in history. "I can have the walls down in a day."

Aron Danesti turned to Urbana. "We do not have a schematic, but we can draw one and fill you in on any details." Andrei pulled over a piece of parchment and started drawing, with Aron watching over his shoulder and whispering guidance.

Mara Brankovic was writing a list in an elegant hand. "Obviously we can count on the support of the Bulgars. Lada is known as the Lady Impaler there, and they are agitating for vengeance. Serbia will contribute men. I will write my Italian contacts with advice that they stay out of it, but I doubt even that will be necessary."

"The Saxons?" Mehmed asked.

"Oh, they loathe Lada. Have you seen any of their wood-cuts? Just horrible." Mara bit back an amused smile. "She will have no help from them. But neither will we. The only person they hate more than the Lady Impaler is Your Grace."

"What about Hungary?" Ali Bey asked. "If she trained with Hunyadi, surely they are allied."

Mara pursed her lips, tapping her quill against the sheet and leaving a series of dots. "Perhaps. But Matthias Corvinus is nothing like his father. He is a statesman, not a warrior. I am certain there are cracks that could be widened with the right amount of applied pressure." She paused in thought and drew a circle. "He recently received a large sum from the Catholic Church for crusading."

"I thought we were finished with the damn crusades," Mahmoud Pasha grumbled. He was the oldest in the room, black hair gone almost all gray. He, too, bore scars from the siege and decades of sieges before. "We already have their precious Christian capital. What will they crusade for now?"

"Lada has the support of the Catholics, then?" Ali Bey interrupted. "*Should* we worry about the Italians?"

Mara shook her head. "Her conversion is viewed with an appropriate amount of skepticism. The Catholic connection goes through Matthias. If we can get to him in any way, we should. But we cannot count him out of the fight yet. I will think of something."

"What about Moldavia?" Mehmed asked.

Mara consulted her list. Radu wondered if there was a single country in Europe she did not have connections to. "Their young king, Stephen, is a force to be reckoned with. And allegedly very charming and attractive, or so my sister receiving proposal offers is told." Mara paused, smiling benignly at Mehmed. "She will, of course, reject him as recommended by her most trusted older sister."

Radu stifled a laugh. Even sitting in a war council, Mara found ways to remind Mehmed how valuable she was and how important it was to keep her happy and close. The more Radu knew the women around him, the more he wondered if *any* of them were not secretly terrifying.

Mara continued. "I would recommend against trying to stage any attacks from Moldavia. We should aim to leave them out entirely."

Ali Bey pointed to the large map in the center of the table. "King Stephen will secure the borders. But if we send forces close, along here, it will keep him contained and under pressure to protect his own country rather than coming to Wallachia's aid."

"So she will have no help besides Hungary, and even that is in question." Mehmed sounded pleased.

"Ten thousand men should be more than enough," Mahmoud Pasha said.

Mehmed raised an eyebrow. "We go in with sixty thousand."

Ishak Pasha coughed, sputtering. He opened his mouth in outrage to argue, then remembered his place. He lowered his eyes to the table. "Whatever Your Grace thinks is best. It will be done."

The two pashas did not look pleased. Because they kept their own armies, they were not funded by the sultan like the

Janissaries were. Going to war was an expensive endeavor. In contrast, Ali Bey smiled as though anticipating an afternoon of sport. He was in charge of the best-trained fighting units in the world. Doubtless he saw this as a good time to remind Mehmed of their value.

The empire was settled on a course of action. But there were still three Wallachians present. And Radu wanted to make his intentions clear when it came to their throne. "When we take Tirgoviste, Aron will be crowned prince."

Aron inclined his head, and Andrei nodded. Radu knew, as they did, that his claim to the throne was as strong as theirs. The Draculesti and Danesti lines had violently traded the throne between them for decades, and neither family had more right to it than the other. In fact, Radu's claim was stronger, since he had the favor of the sultan. But he wanted their support and confidence. That would happen only if they did not view him as a threat. Perhaps that was why they had been cruel to him as a child. He had not yet understood the nature of their rivalry, but they had grasped it early on. The fights in the forest were a reflection of reality, played out on a child-sized scale.

Radu had not won those fights, but neither had Aron and Andrei. Lada had.

Still, the Danesti brothers had grown into intelligent adults. He had no qualms about giving them the country. He certainly did not want it.

"You should know," Mara said, her voice soft, "my reports indicate that Lada has killed nearly every Danesti left in Wallachia. Those still alive have fled to surrounding countries."

"We know." Aron did not sound angry or vengeful, just

tired and sad and a little frightened. Radu met his eyes and they shared a moment of understanding. They were not men driven by rage. Aron wore his family name as a mantle of responsibility, not a cloak of entitlement.

Mehmed stood. "We go in hard and we move fast. We give her no opportunities. We take the capital, secure the country, and show the rest of Europe we tolerate no offense or aggression toward—or from—our vassal states."

"And what about the girl prince?" Ali Bey asked.

"I want her alive," Mehmed said without explanation. "At all costs."

Radu told Nazira and Fatima the plans with a heavy heart. He was relieved that Lada would not be killed—even now—but he did not expect Nazira to feel the same. Regardless, he did not think he would be able to see his sister or speak with her again. He would leave that to Mehmed.

Radu glossed over the specifics of the campaign, focusing on the timeline. "I do not want to leave you again so soon, but this is my responsibility."

"We will come with you," Fatima said, already standing to pack their belongings.

Radu smiled affectionately. "You do realize I am going to war."

Nazira stood, too. She looked dazed, unable to focus. Fatima guided her gently back to sitting. "Then we will meet you there," Fatima said.

"Mehmed has asked me to stay for a while after we have set Aron up on the throne."

"Why Aron?" Nazira snapped. "I know another heir much more deserving."

Radu reached for the bundle of clothing that Nazira held. Nazira was staring at it as though she could not account for its being in her hands. She passed it to him. Rather than putting it in her trunk, he put it back down on the bed. "You know I do not want that. But it means I will stay in Tirgoviste for some time after the conflict is over. You two should go back to Edirne or to the countryside to wait for me. Unless you would rather stay here."

"I cannot wait to get out of this accursed city." Nazira's words were clouded with the memories they shared. And now this city had brought her news of the death of her brother.

Fatima took the clothes Radu had set down on the bed and moved them to the trunk. "We will meet you in Tirgoviste when the fighting is over. It will be nice to see where you came from." She said it so convincingly Radu almost believed she did not mind that much travel. He raised an eyebrow and she looked away, blushing at her lie.

"You do not have to," Radu said.

Nazira stood to join Fatima but then hovered next to the bed, swaying and directionless. Radu knew how hard she was trying to be brave. How hard she was trying to function through the overwhelming grief. It would be good for her to get out of this city. Radu would try to persuade them to go home, instead. Regardless, Nazira needed to be taken from Constantinople.

Fatima spoke for them both. "But we want to join you in Wallachia."

"You would not want to if you had ever been before."

"We will come and discover how much we would rather

not have come, then. Will your sister ... will she stay there, in Tirgoviste, when you are done?" Fatima asked. Nazira went stiff at the mention of Lada. Radu hated that his place in Nazira's life had also introduced Lada into it, and all the accompanying loss and bloodshed. He loved his sister, but ...

But *did* he? Knowing that she had finally become the worst of what she had always had the potential to be?

"No," Radu said. "They will bring her back here. She will never be free again." It was the cruelest fate for Lada. He knew she would rather die fighting. But she would not be allowed to. Radu felt something sharp and mean inside hardening as he anticipated how it would destroy his sister to be powerless and captive once more.

Good. Let it.

17

The Danube, Ottoman Territory

L ADA LAY ON HER stomach, peering over the cover of rocks at the wide expanse of the Danube. She could make out a flurry of activity on the other side, though she was too far to see specifics. But she was close enough. Close enough to know they were there. Close enough to know *he* was there.

Mehmed.

And probably Radu as well.

Lada scooted back, standing when she reached the trees that hid Stefan, Bogdan, and the men she had handpicked to lead her soldiers. "They are out in the open. Which means they do not expect trouble until they are within the borders of Wallachia. If they cannot cross the Danube, all the men in the world will not be enough for them to invade."

"Eventually they will make it across." Doru scratched the side of his nose with one blunt, dirty finger. He was smart and brutal and good at leading men, but every time Lada looked at him, she saw who was not there: Nicolae. She tried not to hate Doru for it. She did not always succeed.

"Not if it costs them too much. Mehmed values stability

over all else. He will not risk upsetting that just to punish us. If we hit them hard enough here, he will retreat."

Doru squinted doubtfully. "How do you know—"

"Do not question her." Bogdan's tone was flat. His eyes, however, were dangerous. Doru bowed his head contritely.

"We will set up a line along this bank." Lada had four hundred men here. The rest of her forces were deeper in the country, forming line after line of defense. But four hundred men well used on a river crossing could hold back thirty thousand men on the other side.

"Alert the archers to be ready to pick them off as they try to float across. And keep hidden at all costs. We would not want to ruin the surprise." Lada smiled in the direction of the Danube. It was the first of any number of surprises she had planned, but, if it worked, it would be the only one she needed.

That night, even though Lada was well hidden among the reeds on the bank, a man slipped in and got down next to her.

"How did you find me?" she asked.

Stefan shrugged.

"Well?" She waited for his report. He had crossed the river several leagues down to scout the enemy camp. Lada had not expected him back this soon.

"Sixty thousand."

Lada choked on her breath, muffling her cough with the dark-green hooded cloak she wore to blend in with the shadows. "Sixty thousand? How many fighting men?" Mehmed normally traveled with one person in support of every man actually fighting. So that meant thirty thousand. She had expected fewer than that, but—

"Sixty thousand *fighting* men."

"God's wounds," she exhaled, letting the number wash over her like the waves lapping at the shore in front of her. "Sixty thousand? Are you certain?"

"Another twenty thousand in support, but judging from the supply trains, they do not expect this to be a long campaign."

"Sixty thousand." Lada lowered her head. And then she started laughing. It was snorts and exhalations, her shoulders shaking with the effort of keeping silent.

"Are you . . . well?"

Lada shook her head. Sixty thousand! No one could have guessed Mehmed would bring that many. Not even she had guessed. She knew it was wrong, but something warm and pleasant licked to life deep inside her. It really was a tremendous show of respect on his part.

And a deeply inconvenient one. This was a fine time for someone to take her seriously at last.

"Well, sixty thousand or six hundred thousand, if he cannot ferry them across the water, he will either have to tack weeks onto the plans to find another passage or give up. And given how much he loves frugality for everything other than his wardrobe and personal tent, I am counting on the latter option."

Stefan nodded. "Where do you want me?"

"Back near the capital. When we know the outcome here, we will be able to determine our next best move. I want you out of harm's way, and as close to Hungary as possible."

Without another word, Stefan slipped into the darkness where he was most at home.

"Sixty thousand," Lada whispered to herself, giggling. Mehmed might as well have sent her another love letter.

It was two nights until the Ottoman crossing was attempted.

A broad, flat skiff launched, maneuvered with poles across the narrowest part of the river. A thick rope trailed behind it. Lada and her men watched as the skiff hit their side of the river. They waited as the Janissaries disembarked, then trudged through the mud and reeds up to the point directly across from where they had launched. The Ottomans had built a dock on their side, and several much larger skiffs were waiting to ferry men and wagons across.

Metal on metal rang through the night as huge spikes were driven into the soft ground and the rope was tied off for the skiffs to be pulled back and forth across the river.

Still, Lada and her men watched. They waited until the work was finished. They waited while the first three skiffs—packed shoulder to shoulder with two hundred men each, all Janissaries with their stupid white-flapped caps glowing like surrender in the moonlight—were filled to capacity and began the slow pull across the river.

When at long last they were halfway, Lada stood, stretching her agonized muscles. Then she fired her crossbow. All the crossbows around her went off, the bolts singing dark through the night. Men fell, the river accepting Lada's offerings with hungry splashes.

The skiff in back reversed direction, heading for the dock. The men in the first skiff pulled faster, evidently thinking reaching the closer shore was the best course of action. And the middle skiff simply let go, drifting aimlessly down the river as Lada's men decorated it with death.

Lada whistled sharply. Her cannons fired. Three of the shots went wide, but two found their mark on the skiff closest to Mehmed's shore. The skiff capsized, dumping all the men still onboard into the swift, unforgiving water. Their armor would be their end.

The skiff heading for Lada's bank slowed, and then stopped. There were no longer enough men to pull it. It drifted, one last Janissary heroically keeping hold of the rope until Lada planted a bolt in his back. Then the skiff joined its brother on a scenic trip down the Danube and away from Lada's land forever.

Mehmed's men had finally recovered their senses. Cannons wheeled into place to answer Lada's. But a few parting shots from hers made quick work of the temporary dock, and then Lada and her men slipped back down to the ground, giving Mehmed nothing to aim for.

Lada, elated, knew *exactly* what she was aiming for. She would not miss.

"If only we had more cannons," Lada said with a sigh, patting the heavy, cold metal side of one, "we could have bombarded his whole camp."

Nicolae's voice whispered in her ear: *Stop calling it his camp. You are not fighting Mehmed, you are fighting the Ottomans.*

Lada rested her cheek against the cannon. Her heart squeezed painfully. What she would not give for Nicolae to actually be here, making her angry with his always-too-insightful observations. Or Petru, eager and excited for whatever came next. She would never hear the two of them again, never listen to Nicolae mock Petru, and Petru threaten to kill him for doing so.

She wanted them back.

She wanted everything she had ever lost back. Her childhood. Her brother. Even her love and respect for her father. The Ottomans had taken them all.

A gentle hand came down on her shoulder. "Are you well?" Bogdan asked.

"Why does everyone ask me that? I am always well!" Lada stood straight, shaking off her feelings and, inadvertently, Bogdan's hand. He flinched, his face falling.

Lada reached out and took his hand. She had not lost him. She had not lost Wallachia. She would yet regain some of what she had lost, but she would give nothing else without a fight.

Bogdan's face lit up with quiet joy. He held perfectly still, as though afraid of spooking her. "What next?"

"We need to move the cannons. Fire them and then move them again. We will keep doing that, keep them guessing and pinned down and unable to attempt another crossing. Tell—"

A bolt bounced off the cannon, spinning in the air before coming to rest at Lada's feet. She frowned down at it. Bogdan tackled her, his body on top of hers as more bolts flew around them.

"Janissaries!" someone screamed.

Lada rolled out from under Bogdan—he was unhurt, she noticed with trembling relief, a flash of Nicolae's bloodied back rising unbidden—and drew her sword. Because they had chosen deep tree cover, it meant they could not form a line. They were not expecting hand-to-hand combat, not now.

"Where did they come from?" Bogdan whispered as they crawled away from the cannon and met up with a reserve of men that had been resting. They were not resting now.

"The second boat. The one that floated downstream. They must have made it to this shore and worked their way back up to us. Damn. Damn, damn, damn." That meant there were at least one hundred Janissaries, assuming half of them had been killed before their escape. Lada knew better than to question their skills. They were far deadlier than the bulk of her newly trained forces. One hundred Janissaries on the attack could easily wipe out her four hundred scattered men.

"We should pull back to the second line," Bogdan said.

"We will lose the cannons. We cannot afford that." Lada whistled sharply. "To the guns!" she shouted. "Protect the cannons!"

"She's over here!" a man shouted in Turkish. "Take her alive!"

The men around her hesitated. "They are here for you," Bogdan said.

"But the cannons!"

"Better the cannons than you." He drew his sword, then shouted the next commands. "Protect the prince! Form around us and spread word down the line to hold off pursuit. We get the prince to the second line! Abandon the cannons!"

Lada stood rooted to the ground, staring at the taunting river. They had come so close to victory, so close to winning without ever having to fight. So close to humiliating Mehmed as he had humiliated her. It was not fair. If she had half the resources Mehmed did—a quarter, a tenth, even—she would have beaten him here. All she had was Wallachia. And as much as she loved it, she was seized with a sudden fear that it would not be enough. It never had been. Who was she to defy all of history, which taught her that her country had never and could never be free?

"We can lose today and still win," Bogdan said, buzzing with urgency. "But if we lose you, we lose everything."

Who was she? She was the *dragon*. Her country had teeth and claws and fire, and she would use every last bit of them. Lada drew her own sword. "To the second line!" she shouted, each word causing her more pain than the crossbow bolt would have. As they cut their way through the Janissaries appearing in the dark to bar their path, all Lada's thoughts were on what they were leaving behind.

Mehmed. Radu. And a clear crossing for their journey into Wallachia.

She had failed at her first task. But she would make certain to send a strong welcome message.

18

Southern Border of Wallachia

RADU STOOD OUTSIDE WITH the other leaders, watching as their men set up a massive, neatly organized camp for the night. With this many men, they had to stop marching for the day by midafternoon to have everything settled before nightfall. It was a tremendous undertaking, and one they had to do every single day.

"We lost over three hundred Janissaries," Ali Bey said with a concerned frown. "And as far as we know, they lost only a few dozen men in the retreat. I do not like those numbers. If they continue . . ."

Mahmoud Pasha squinted at the forbidding clouds in the distance. It was not monsoon season, but spring brought heavy rains that would swell the rivers and muddy the roads, making their jobs more difficult. There was a reason attacks took place at the end of spring instead of at the beginning. Lada had pushed them too soon. "The numbers will not continue. We took all their cannons. She is running scared."

"My sister does not do anything scared." Radu looked ahead

toward Wallachia with a heavy heart and heavier worries. He was fairly certain they would face no attack here. Lada knew what her strengths were, and direct combat with the stronger Ottoman forces was not something she would risk. But she was out there, somewhere. Waiting.

Waving off further discussion, Radu entered Mehmed's tent. His had gone up first, in an easily defensible position, while the rest of the camp was staged. Radu expected to find his friend angry. Instead, he found Mehmed sitting on a pillow, staring up at the ceiling of the tent with a bemused smile.

"I think she missed us," he said.

Radu lowered himself to the carpeted floor, biting back a bitter reply. Mehmed's amusement neglected to take into account that men had died between them. But Mehmed probably needed a few moments to be a person instead of the sultan. All recent conversations about Lada had revolved around tactics, viewing her as a prince and a military leader. She was just Lada in this tent. Radu ignored the ghosts of the dead to speak with Mehmed on the level Mehmed wanted. "She is angry with us. And as fearsome as that was when she was young, facing it now that she is grown, armed, and surrounded by soldiers? I find myself longing for a stable to hide in until she finds another object to direct her ire toward."

Mehmed laughed. "Do you remember when we used to have footraces through the hills in Amasya?"

Radu cringed. He did his best imitation of Lada's voice, adding a slight growl to his own even as he projected it higher. "Are you proud of yourself for being able to run faster than me? It does not matter, because I will always catch you in the end. You may run faster, but I still hit harder." Radu rubbed his shoulder at the phantom pain. Most of his memories of Lada included that sensation.

Mehmed laughed even harder, laying back on the floor cushions. "Do you remember when she memorized more verses of the Koran than I did, just to prove she was better than I was at everything?"

"I remember all this. And it is making me question our judgment in chasing her. Do we really want to catch her? And what will we do once we have her?"

The easy happiness in Mehmed's face was replaced with familiar tension. "You know why I have to. You have not changed your mind."

"No. I agree that we cannot let her actions stand without a response. She threatens the stability of all our European borders. But I cannot help worrying where this ends. *How* it ends."

"I worry about that as well. I just want her back home, with us."

Radu spoke as gently as he could. "She is home, Mehmed."

Mehmed scowled, waving Radu's words away. "She cannot sustain this. We both know it. If she keeps fighting the whole world, eventually she will lose." He sat up, earnest and intense. "She needs to lose to *us*, Radu. Not because I hate her, or because I am angry with her. She needs to lose to us because we love her. Because we understand her."

"But losing Wallachia might break her."

"Better broken than dead."

Radu was not certain that he agreed with Mehmed. Not after what he had been through and seen himself. He was still healing, and was uncertain he would ever fully heal. And the things that meant the most to him—Nazira, his faith, protecting those most innocent—had not even been taken from him. If they had . . .

He was also uncomfortably uncertain whether the claim that they both loved Lada was true. Certainly their actions over the past year said otherwise.

"I know what Wallachia is to her," Mehmed continued. "I am not blind to her devotion to it. She has made it clear she will always choose it over me." There was a pause, then bitter longing in Mehmed's tone. "But we will take that choice away from her before it destroys her."

Radu looked up at the elegant silk ceiling of the tent. A gold chandelier hung from it, lit even though it was day. Only Mehmed could make taking an army against his sister sound like an act of love and friendship.

"Today we will reach the Arges," Aron Danesti said, riding beside Radu and Mehmed. Aron was shorter than both of them—Mehmed and Radu were tall and lean, though Mehmed was growing broader now that he had finally stopped growing taller—and it did not help that Aron's horse was smaller than theirs. He constantly adjusted in his saddle, trying to sit up straighter, but he still had to crane his neck to look up at them. "There is a good bridge we can use. And the land across is a fertile area. We should find early crops and livestock. We can rest there."

Mehmed did not respond. More and more often he chose not to speak to those around him unless he was correcting them.

Aron cleared his throat self-consciously, then continued.

"We should not leave Bucharest open behind us. It will cost several days, but it is worth it to take the fortress rather than leaving us exposed to a potential attack from the rear."

Ali Bey, on the other side of Radu and Mehmed, grunted. "I do not like it. We had to send men to retake Giurgiu as well. But it is a necessity. We will cross the Arges, and then send a force to take Bucharest."

Radu wanted it all to be over with. He wanted Tirgoviste taken, Lada in custody, this entire country and his history with it behind him. But he knew even after they took Tirgoviste it would not be simple.

They crested a hill and found the scouts waiting, all facing the same direction.

Where they had anticipated a bridge bordered by a large town, complete with livestock, supplies, and crops—not to mention people—lay only a smoldering ruin. Radu had a sudden flashback to his time in Albania fighting the Ottoman rebel Skanderberg. Radu had been at Murad's side then in an endless siege. It was his first taste of war, and he had never managed to cleanse his palate of the burning rot it had left behind. Skanderberg's men had waged the same type of campaign, destroying their own crops to prevent the Ottomans from getting to them.

Had Radu told Lada about that strategy? He could not remember. They had not been close anymore, not at that point. She had taken Mehmed, and he had joined Murad in an effort to prove himself the more useful sibling through political maneuvering. Surely he had not told her about it. This was not his fault. She could have learned it from her time with Hunyadi, though it did not seem like the old Hungarian military leader's style.

It was probably his sister's natural inclinations coming out. If she could not have it, no one could.

"So much for our bridge," Radu said. It would mean a delay, and one spent without extra provisions at that. Radu watched as a few mounted scouts explored the area around the bridge. One of them just . . . disappeared. There, and then gone. The others quickly turned their horses, shouting about pits and traps. Ali Bey began issuing instructions to avoid the entire area.

"Radu Bey?" a man interrupted, drawing Radu's attention. Several of his own scouts had approached. Though Ali Bey had the bulk of the forces, Radu's four thousand mounted men were independent of the main Janissary troops. Radu had sent them scouting the surrounding area rather than the path directly ahead.

The scouts had two people with them, peasants by the look of their clothing. The man and the woman regarded Radu with baleful expressions.

The lead scout bowed. "We caught them a few miles up, dumping rotten animal carcasses in the river. They have been doing it for weeks. It will have tainted the water this far down for at least a few days."

The woman grinned. "Thirsty? I hope you brought the Danube with you."

Radu massaged his forehead. "Where is the nearest source of clean water?"

The man snickered. He had facial hair, which was puzzling. Only boyars were allowed to have facial hair in Wallachia, just as Janissaries were required to be clean-shaven. It was a matter of status. "You are welcome to try any well you find. Please do."

"What family are you from?" Radu asked. The man had neither the speech nor the carriage of a boyar to account for the facial hair.

"No family you would know." He rubbed his jaw, eyes narrowing with a sly smile. "Did you think you would return and find things how you left them? We have a new prince. New rules. New freedom."

Aron Danesti had joined Radu. "This does not look like freedom to me. You have no crops. No people."

"They are in the mountains." The woman shrugged, grinning to reveal more gaps than teeth in her mouth. "I can tell you that, because you will never find them. You would all starve first, or look so long that winter will return and claim you blue and frozen as its own. Then our people will step over your bodies to reclaim our land. Look as long and as hard as you want, you will find only death here."

"We are coming to *help* you," Aron said, genuinely puzzled by their defiance. "Your false prince is provoking other countries. She has made you unsafe."

"She is everything." The woman spat at Aron. One of the scouts grabbed her arm, but she jerked toward them, eyes feverish. "Everything we have, we owe to her. The bastard boyars have been given the place they always wanted: they are above everything, looking down on us from their lofty stakes." She jutted out her chin. "I know you, Danesti son. You will join your father."

Another group of scouts came riding from the direction

of the road leading to Bucharest. "Take these two away," Radu said, waving. He did not want to order their deaths—they had not killed any of his men that he knew of—but he did not know what to do with them. He would worry about it later.

Radu recognized a short, stocky Janissary named Simion whom he had sent out as soon as they crossed the Danube. "What is it?" Radu asked, seeing the scouts' white faces and furrowed brows. "Is someone coming? You had more men when you left. Did you encounter resistance?"

"No," Simion said, dismounting and bowing. "Just traps. We lost three. No one is coming to fight us because they do not need to. Everything as far as we rode looks like this. The wells are poisoned. There are no animals or crops or even people. If we send men to Bucharest, we had better take the city, or we will starve."

Radu thanked Simion, then rode slowly back toward Mehmed, with Aron at his side.

"What has happened in our country?" Aron asked, horrified. Radu realized that aside from Constantinople, where Aron had only been outside the walls, the Danesti had never seen combat.

"Lada knows what it takes to lay siege. She wants it to cost Mehmed as much as possible. Losses of men and gold and morale."

"No, not that. I mean, yes, that is awful. But the way that man and woman spoke to us. I have never been thus addressed in my entire life. He wears a beard! She speaks as though she is our equal—or our better!"

Mara had not bothered getting reports out of Wallachia

itself. They had focused on who Lada's outside allies would be. But it was obvious now they should have focused more on whom she would have on her side *within* the country. Lada had always believed Wallachia was the greatest place in the world. Apparently her pride in her homeland had extended to her people. They had not factored this much sheer devotion into their plans.

Radu watched as the two Wallachians were hauled toward the camp. How many more like them were lying in wait? Radu needed to find support inside the country. "We will send out riders to search in secret for boyars. I cannot imagine many of them support her, not after the Danesti deaths."

Radu stopped his horse at a distance, a momentary thrill of pleasure coursing through him as he saw Mehmed shift with impatience on his own horse. Watching him. Waiting for him.

But still in pursuit of his sister. Radu smiled at himself, knowing how much this campaign would have bothered him even a year ago. Instead, he missed Nazira.

He missed Cyprian.

That one hurt more, because it was a missing with no purpose. As many times as he told himself he would think no more on Cyprian now that he knew the other man was alive and safe, those gray eyes and that soul-searing smile were never far from Radu's thoughts.

"Everything has changed," Aron said.

"Nothing ever changes," Radu answered, finally urging his horse toward his friend so they could worry about his sister together.

19

Outside Bucharest

LADA SAT, THE TEPID spring sun still too hot for her taste. It had been an arduous climb, getting all her soldiers and their remaining cannons up the steep, rocky hillsides. She stared down into the canyon beneath them. It was the only logical path for an army to take to reach Bucharest.

She had already tested this particular canyon strategy once before. Hunyadi continued to help her from beyond the grave. She had, the year before, rescued him during an ill-fated fight in a canyon by unexpectedly attacking from above and blocking the exits. It would be on a larger scale here, but she was confident. She had to be creative in avoiding direct combat with Mehmed's massively superior numbers; this was perfect.

And, as she kept reminding herself after their loss at the Danube, they did not need to *win*. Not outright. They simply needed to make this attempt cost more than Mehmed was willing to spend in every way possible. Men. Gold. Time. Pride.

She liked chipping away at that last one, especially.

"Are we certain they will come for Bucharest?" Bogdan

asked, clearing the top of a rock for Lada to sit on. After giving instructions, she had left the rest of the soldiers to set up at their various positions. They were all loyal and good at what they did, but increasingly they aggravated her. She could only see who they were not.

She clutched the locket she wore around her neck, as much a part of her now as her daggers. If lost, she knew she would constantly reach for them, and every time be surprised that they were gone. Just like mentally she kept reaching for Petru and Nicolae, only to remember they were forever out of her grasp.

How many more would she lose? How many could she afford to?

She dropped the locket beneath her tunic. "They have to come for Bucharest. It is too important to leave behind their lines. And it is the first major city past the Arges, with no more river crossings to bar their way to Tirgoviste. They will need to use it as a staging point."

"And if they take the city?"

Lada shrugged. "Then they take it. But we make them pay dearly. It will take time and supplies and give them nothing in return. We will not come back for it, so the men they leave here will be idle and wasted, fewer that we have to fight elsewhere."

Bogdan nodded, satisfied. He was playing with something, too. Lada peered closer. Prayer beads. She bit back her instinct to belittle him. She would take all the help she could get, and if Bogdan's god was interested in aiding them, he was welcome to help.

There was nothing to do now except wait for the Ottomans to arrive.

It was boring. Lada hated it.

Far too late, as usual, Lada noticed Stefan approaching them. She would be dead if he had been there to kill her. But he brought only information, not death.

He sat, folding his long legs beneath him. He was so dusty and dim he blended in with the rocks. "The Turks will be here within two hours. He sent ten thousand."

That was unfortunate. Lada had hoped Mehmed would detour his whole force here. He was making certain Bucharest did not threaten him with attacks from the rear without committing too many men. But that only altered things slightly. She could move through the country much faster than Mehmed's huge camp and supply trains could. He would stay with his main force, but Lada could—and would—be everywhere.

"Good," she said. "We will bog them down in this pass so they can go neither forward nor backward. We do not even have to kill them all for Mehmed to have lost a sixth of his forces."

"And after?" Stefan asked.

"I go to Tirgoviste to make certain everything there is prepared. Daciana should have overseen the evacuations into the mountains by now." Lada frowned. "I could have used her elsewhere, though."

Stefan frowned. It was incredibly demonstrative of him. He must have been truly upset. "She is with child, Lada. And she would not trust our children to someone else."

"She is with child? Another one?" This was a terrible time to be having children. And selfish, too. Lada did not want her followers' attentions divided any further than they already were. "Well, at least this one will be yours."

Stefan straightened, his face so carefully and deliberately blank that Lada got a chill. "They are *all* mine."

Something in his posture made Lada want to draw her knives defensively. Instead, she looked away in a show of confidence. She did not need to watch him for attack. He belonged to her, and he would do well to remember it. "I want you to go to Hungary. Make certain they are mobilizing their forces as promised."

"And if they are not?"

"Kill Matthias."

"That will not be easy. And how will it help you?"

"If Matthias cannot keep his word, I want him dead. *That* is how it will help me."

Stefan stood, brushing off his hands. "I will check on Daciana on my way, make certain they have everything they need. Where are they?"

Lada looked down into the canyon, tracing an imaginary trajectory with her eyes. Men would die here very soon. It was odd, looking at the peaceful and quiet and clean place, knowing what it would hold before the day's end. "Only I know their location. It is safer that way. If caught, no one can betray them." Lada turned to Stefan to gauge his reaction. She had put special weight on the word *betray.*

His face was as unknowable and unremarkable as ever. If he understood that Lada was threatening him, he did not acknowledge or respond to it. He inclined his head, then walked silently away.

"Lada." Bogdan's tentative tone was utterly incongruous with how physically intimidating he was. He was a bull of a man, made kitten around her. "I wanted to speak with you, but we have not had any time alone."

"I will not marry." Lada did not try to soften her tone or her words, but neither did she wish to wound him. Not with the loss of Nicolae still so fresh. His death had given her, perhaps, a new perspective on the men she did have. She had lost Bogdan when they were children. He had been taken by the Ottomans. She had found him and reclaimed him, and she would not relinquish that claim.

Bogdan nodded, his eyes on the rocky ground beneath them. "My mother said as much. And if you did marry, it would not make sense to marry me. I would bring you no advantage."

Lada tugged rather viciously on one of his stupid jug-handle ears. Those ears had listened to her all her life without question. She had taken those ears between her teeth, too. He served many purposes. "I never want you apart from me," she said. It was the truth. It did not mean as much as he wanted it to, but it was all she could offer him.

His face bloomed with joy like a field of new spring flowers, all tender and brilliant. "I will never leave you."

Lada nodded. Her work here was done. She owed him nothing else emotionally, which was good because even this much had exhausted her. She wanted to fight someone, to have that clarity of action and goal aligned. How considerate of Mehmed to provide her an entire army to do just that.

Bogdan twisted his foot through the pebbles beneath it with an aggravating scraping noise. "But if you were to decide to marry someone, and it did not matter whether or not they brought you any political advantage, would—"

"If you ever bring it up again, I will throw you off this canyon wall. Then I will find your body, drag it back up here, and do it a second time just to be certain that any spirit of you hanging about gets the message."

Bogdan ducked his head, rubbing the back of his neck, where a blush had formed. "Right. Well, we have an hour still. Do you want to . . . ?" He gestured inelegantly at her trousers.

It *had* been a long time, with all her avoidance of him. She was not gentle. He did not complain. All was back in place between them as it had ever been.

<hr />

"Keep them pinned down!" Lada pointed at a group of Janissaries attempting to skirt the edge of the line and climb up the canyon wall. It was not as good a scenario as the canyon with the Bulgars had been. There were too many boulders here, too many defensible areas for the troops to hide and return fire. But her men could keep them pinned for a long time. Days, perhaps. That was all the victory they needed.

Satisfied, Lada turned to the mean-spirited, brutal man she was leaving in charge. She had found Grigore in prison, where he was awaiting execution for beating the son of a boyar. He was perfectly suited to her needs.

"Make them pay for every step of progress with ten bodies. Once you finish off the gunpowder, no more is coming. Destroy the cannons so they do not take them. Then run to Bucharest and man the walls."

Grigore smiled, breathing deeply of the scent of burning flesh and blood. "It will be my pleasure."

Bogdan was waiting with their horses. While an army could not get through the land without tremendous planning and difficulty, two people on horseback could cover the distance with ease. Lada knew Mehmed's main force had not advanced far toward Tirgoviste yet. They would easily beat him to their target.

"I will go on to Tirgoviste alone," Lada said. "I need to make sure Oana is out safely, and that there is nothing for them to take. Also, I need to check the final logistics for their welcome. I want you to go to the hill camps and organize the soldiers. Some of them are being led by boyars"—Lada grimaced at the thought—"and I expect they will need a lot of help." It aggravated her that she had to use *any* of the boyars, but some had remained loyal to her and she simply did not have enough men trained to lead. After this was over, she would change that. Never again would she depend on anyone else. They all inevitably disappointed her, or left. Or chose someone over her.

Bogdan leaned close as if he would try to kiss her. She kicked her horse's flanks, quickly outpacing him.

She rode alone. It felt right.

20

Wallachian Countryside

RADU FINISHED PRAYING AND remained on his rug. The loss of Kumal weighed heavily on him at all times, but he felt it most strongly during prayer. Kumal was the man who had invited him in, who had given him Islam as a refuge for his soul when all else was in turmoil.

All else was in turmoil once again, and Radu had cost Kumal his life.

Radu could not help but wonder what his relationship to his God was. It had been sorely tested and tried during his time in Constantinople. But it had not broken. Sometimes Radu had feared it would, but he still found the same peace and solace in prayer he always had.

Radu wished he had been open with Kumal about what was in his own heart. He had worried that Kumal might say something that would separate them, or, worse, separate Radu from God. Molla Gurani, the scholar who had taught Mehmed and Radu and had witnessed his conversion, doubtless could have told Radu everything written about whether the love in his heart for other men condemned him. Radu had done some study on the subject, but it brought him no peace.

Perhaps Kumal could have talked about the heart of faith, and whether Radu could have a heart filled with God and still love as he needed to.

But Kumal was gone. Molla Gurani, too. All Radu had was himself and his God, the movement of prayer and the ritual of worship connecting them. He would not sever that connection. He felt Nazira was right: where God and love were concerned, he was happy to leave it unreconciled.

Wishing he could linger, Radu rolled up his rug and packed his tent. He made his way to Mehmed's tent. By the look of things, packing the sultan for the day's travel had not yet begun. Radu did not relish the idea of standing about idly. The progress of the camp was plodding, and Radu did not think he could handle the boredom today. It left too much room for thought. He saw a group of his scouts and mounted to join them.

The day had dawned bright and clear, the air warm and humid. "Do you know the land well?" one of the scouts asked. He was a quiet, thoughtful man, a Janissary named Kiril. Radu had ridden with him before and liked him.

"I remember it," Radu said, "though I have not been through here since I was a boy. We followed a road along the river, from Tirgoviste to Edirne."

"What brought you to the empire?"

Radu smiled wryly, remembering. "Politics. I was a hostage, actually."

"I did not know, Radu Bey."

Radu laughed to ease the other man's discomfort. Kiril was

older than him by only a year or two. Radu liked the younger Janissaries. It was easier to be in their company. He felt he had less to prove to them than he did to the older ones. "It was the best thing that ever happened to me."

"As being sent to train as a Janissary was for me. This must be an odd sort of homecoming for you, then."

"It is not my home. It never was, really."

A scout appeared from a bend between two tree-dense hills farther up the road. He rode to them, frowning, his freckled features twisted with confusion. "Is there another road? I think we have taken a wrong turn."

"No," Radu answered. According to both his memory and his maps, they were exactly where they were supposed to be. "This is the only road wide enough for the wagons to get through. There are no other major roads. It is all farmland until outside Tirgoviste."

"There is no farmland up there."

Radu shared an alarmed look with Kiril. He had not been here since he was a child, but things could not have changed that much. With a growing pit of dread in his stomach, Radu spurred his horse forward. He stopped abruptly as they crested a low hill. Instead of rolling acres of budding green fields lining the river, there were . . . marshes.

Leagues and leagues of marshes. The river, now low and sluggish, had soaked the land all around it. Radu knew that on occasion the river flooded and caused this type of damage, but they had had no such rainy season lately.

This was man-made.

No. This was Lada-made.

"See, there," Kiril said, pointing. "Trenches. Diverting the river into the fields. It must have taken forever to dig them."

"Find a way through, then return and report how far the marsh continues," Radu said to the freckled scout. He could not hide his own despair as he looked at yet more land for feeding both the Wallachians and the Ottoman troops completely destroyed. He turned to Kiril. "Go around and see how far we have to go to skirt it. It may be better to clear our own roads than to drag cannon-laden wagons through this mire." Radu stared at the ruin of the land. Lada had hurt them, yes. But she had also hurt her own people in the long run. How could she not see what she was doing? How could she justify this cost?

"Your *sister* did all this?" Kiril asked, surveying the damage as a group gathered to scout with him.

Radu took a deep breath, closing his eyes against the anger flaring toward Lada and her ever-growing damage to the world they both had to live in. "I cannot imagine this is the worst of what awaits us, either."

Radu had been wrong all this time. He had felt guilty for the way his heart yearned for other men. But it was not his own love that was poisonous and destructive. His love destroyed nothing, hurt no one. Lada loved Wallachia above all else, and this was the result. What Mehmed and Lada did—because of what they set their hearts on with both people *and* land—was far worse than anything Radu's love could ever lead him to do.

It was an odd sort of thing to take comfort in, but he accepted it. Nazira *was* right. His love had no evil in it.

He could not say the same for his sister's.

21

Tirgoviste

LADA HAD NOT BEEN able to take a deep breath since she hit the outskirts of Tirgoviste. Closing the castle door behind her, she pulled off the cloth over her mouth and nose and gasped for air.

"Yes, it is unpleasant out there," Oana remarked, eyeing her with something like humor, though far darker.

"They have not completed as much as I had hoped." Lada leaned against the door as though her weight would help keep the air outside from coming in. The smell had followed her, but it was merely overwhelming, not unbearable.

"They can only work in short shifts. We have to trade workers in and out more often than we had planned for."

"They can do more."

Oana laughed gruffly. "Not unconscious, they cannot. You will have to buy them a little more time."

"Fortunately that costs only effort and lives, not money. I can always give up more of the first two, but the third I am entirely lacking." Lada rubbed the small of her back. It had been a long, hard ride, and she did not have the luxury of resting. Not that she thought she could sleep *here*. "Why are you still here? I want you in the mountains. Go to my fortress at Poenari."

Oana patted the top of Lada's head in a way that made Lada wonder if it would be inappropriate to punch her old nurse in the stomach. "Child, are you worried about my safety?"

"The entire city could burn down and you would be standing in the center, entirely unharmed, holding a comb and telling me it was time to deal with my hair."

Oana squinted. "It *is* looking rather the worse for wear."

"Oh, go hide in the mountains, you monster." Before Lada could dodge, Oana wrapped her in a hug.

"Be careful. We need you." Oana squeezed too tightly, then released her and opened the door. The stench was so powerful that Lada staggered back as though struck. Oana did not even cover her face as she scuttled toward Lada's horse.

Lada slammed the door shut again. She needed to do one last sweep to make certain Mehmed would find nothing to his advantage here, should he manage to make it to the center of the city.

In the throne room she found tiles still stained with the blood of her predecessor. The faded outline of the sword that once hung over her father's head—now worn at her side— remained on the wall. In the halls she found ghostly whispers and memories of fear and rage. And in her chambers that had once belonged to her father, she found no memories at all worth taking.

"Lada," a man said behind her.

She shouted in surprise, turning around with one dagger already drawn. Stefan was standing in a shadowed corner of the room. How long he had been there, she had no idea. Either she was slipping, or he was better than ever. She hoped it was the latter.

"I am glad it is you." Her heart still raced as she replaced her dagger in its wrist sheath.

He remained as unmoving and still as his expression. His was such a forgettable face that when he was away, Lada had a hard time remembering what, exactly, he looked like. He tilted his head ever so slightly to the side as though Lada were a problem to be solved.

"I have been paid a tremendous amount of money to kill you." His voice was so emotionless it took Lada several seconds to process what he had said.

Her hand twitched toward her wrist, but she stopped. She knew how deadly Stefan was. She had taken great pride in it. It was rather less pleasant knowing that, if he wanted *her* dead, she already was. At first, anger and sadness bubbled to the surface. But they were replaced with a bleak sort of pleasure. Had she not hoped that someday someone would realize she was deserving of an assassin of Stefan's caliber?

She would have preferred that day never come. But it was validating in its own morbid way.

"How much?" she asked.

"More than you have left to fund this fight." He reached into his vest—his movements deliberate and slow—and pulled out a leather pouch. He tossed it onto the bed behind her. "That is not all of it. Or even most of it." This time a hint of a smile, like a quickly fading dream, brushed over his face. "But you can use it how you see fit."

"So you are not going to kill me."

"I considered it."

She appreciated his honesty. If she had to kill him, she would be very sorry. "Why?"

"Because if whoever wants you dead is willing to offer this much gold, someone will do the job sooner or later. I could do it in a manner befitting our long history."

"I think that is the most emotional sentiment I have ever heard you express about us."

This time his smile was real and lasting. She hoped she would remember it, even if she forgot his face. "I do not know who paid me to kill you. I suspect either Matthias Corvinus, because you are making him look weak in the fight against the infidels, or your Moldavian cousin, who is using your distraction to take back several border fortresses."

"God's wounds. I liked him!" Lada rubbed her forehead, then shrugged. "Though I would do the same in his position. We *are* blood, after all." She sat on the bed, tapping a foot against the worn carpet beneath it. "You do not think it was Mehmed?"

"He has proved several times over he wants you alive. If you die because of him, it will be in battle and against his wishes."

Lada agreed. She felt the same way about sending an anonymous assassin after Mehmed. If he died, she wanted it by her hand. Anything else would feel unfinished.

She did not know if she wanted him dead. All this maneuvering, all this horror and fighting and death between them, and still she did not think she preferred the world without him.

She looked back up, wishing more than ever she had time

to sleep. And when she awoke, Stefan would still be hers. So would Nicolae. And Petru. And Radu and Mehmed and everyone else she wished to have. "Where does this leave us?"

"I cannot stay at your side when this is over. And ... I do not wish to. You gave me something to fight for, and I am not ungrateful. But now I have something to live for. And long lives do not seem likely in your company."

Lada grinned at him. "I can see why Daciana fell for you, with a sweet tongue such as that."

Stefan cleared his throat, as though clearing away any emotion that had managed to work its way through.

Though his choice was not unexpected, it still stung. She hated that Stefan would not be hers for much longer. It was good that Daciana was far away from Lada's anger and resentment. Lada had liked her, too, but now that meant losing both of them. Her smile turned darker and sharper. "I have the family that you live for. You see this through to the end, whatever that may be, and I will give them back to you."

She expected anger, but Lada could swear something like affection disturbed Stefan's calm. He inclined his head respectfully. "I started this at your side. I will finish it there. And then you will never see me again."

"Fair enough. Go get me word of the men Matthias is sending, and where we stand with the pope."

Stefan turned toward the door.

"Stefan," Lada said. He paused, his back toward her. She could put a knife in it right now. But she did not reach for her blades. Perhaps she was tired, or just tired of seeing her friends bleed. Or perhaps it was because he had to know she could do it, and in spite of everything, he trusted her enough to turn his back on her anyway. "How *would* you have killed me?"

"With all the gentleness you never had in life." He walked out.

For a few brief, mean seconds Lada considered sending word to have Daciana and the children killed. Stefan would not find out until it was too late. But she did not wish any of them dead. They had been her friends. That they would betray that friendship did not threaten her life or her success.

She had been trying so hard not to lose anything or anyone. But she had been wrong to feel that way. They would all be gone one day, one way or another. She stood, striding from the room without bothering to look anywhere else in the castle. Nothing—and no one—was left inside that she could not afford to lose.

And that was why she would win in the end. Because she would offer up *everything* on the altar of sacrifice, so long as she kept her country.

22

Three Days South of Tirgoviste

"DOES IT MAKE ANYONE else nervous that the prince has not yet attacked us?" Ali Bey asked, staring down at their map—which had been altered with notations for the new bogs and swampland. All the existing wells and cities had been crossed out. The map sat in the center of a table set up in Mehmed's tent. Around it also stood Aron, Andrei, Radu, and the pashas, bleakly considering their options in ink and parchment.

Aron's face was as dour as the map. "She does not need to. It has taken us three weeks to get this far. We had planned for three days."

"How are we with supplies?" Radu asked.

"Between the delays and the lack of anything to scavenge or claim, we are not doing well." Ali Bey slammed his fist down on the table. "Why will she not just meet us out in the open?"

Mehmed laughed, startling them and drawing their attention to the other end of his sumptuous tent, where he sat, apparently engrossed in a book about the life of the Prophet, peace be upon him. "Why would she? We have all the men and force on our side. But on her side she has time. She will wield it against us in whatever ways she can."

Ali Bey frowned, his bushy eyebrows drawing so low Radu wondered whether they tickled his eyes. "It sounds as though you admire her."

"Should I not admire excellence wherever I find it? I am certainly not finding any to admire in my current company."

The other men flinched. Radu felt the sting of the words, but they did not wound him as deeply as they once might have. There was something to be said for having his heart broken so many times. Broken things healed thicker and stronger than they were before. Assuming one survived long enough to heal.

"The sultan is right," Radu said. "Lada is using every advantage she has. But she does not have many at her disposal. We have to find the weak points and press them as hard as she has pressed ours." He stared at the annotated map and the story it told. It was Wallachia, turned into a weapon. Lada was using their country the way she had always worshipped it: completely and viciously.

Aron threw down his pen with a splatter of ink. "What are her weaknesses, then?"

"People."

Hamza Pasha, the oldest man in the tent and leader of ten thousand spahi forces, snorted. "We have taken prisoners, and they are all mindlessly devoted to her, to the point of lunacy. We will find no weakness to exploit there."

"Not *those* people. Our people." Radu turned to Aron and Andrei. "She has killed many boyars. Those that remain are loyal to her, but they cannot truly trust her. Not after what she has done. She is giving land and power to whomever she chooses. They must know their titles—their lives—are not safe so long as she is prince. She has too little regard for tradition and blood."

Andrei lifted an eyebrow. "It seems to me she has tremendous regard for blood. She simply prefers it spilled on the ground."

Mehmed gave a small laugh from the corner, but continued to keep his eyes on his book as though he were not following the conversation.

Radu resisted the impulse to defend his sister. She did not deserve it, and she could defend herself. She had proved as much. "I have sent out men to find the remaining boyars. I will offer them an alternative to Lada's reign of terror, and they will betray her."

"How can you be sure?" Ali Bey's turban had come loose, revealing silver streaks in his black hair. He had lived far past the average Janissary life expectancy. Perhaps that was why he was leader—because of his experience, and his knack for not dying.

"They are boyars," Aron said with a wry smile. "It is what they do. They betrayed Radu's father in favor of mine. They betray the memory of my father in favor of a prince they hate. If we offer them security and power, they will betray her. And, eventually, they will betray me."

Radu placed a hand on Aron's shoulder. "We will see you on the throne. We will fix this." Radu hoped that Aron could restore some of the balance Lada had upset. Although the more

Radu saw of the country, the more he questioned how long it would take to return things to the way they had been. Lada had done so much in such a little time. Not only the destruction of the land—though that would take time to repair—she had also introduced her rebellious ferocity into a people long accustomed to accepting what was offered them and never demanding more. That infection of ideas would be far harder to recover from.

And, perhaps, it should not be recovered from. Radu would suggest to Aron that he should capitalize on the new social structures, rather than immediately dismantling them. Lada focused only on common Wallachians, not the nobility. It was her weakness. But the nobility had proved their own weakness in so long ignoring the potential of their own people. If anything, Lada had proved Wallachians could do great things under the right leader.

"Radu?" Andrei prodded.

"Sorry, yes?" The conversation had continued, leaving him behind.

"We have had outbreaks of sickness," Hamza Pasha said. Even now he hung back, fanning his face though the tent was not overly warm. At these strategy meetings he was often quiet. Not out of reticence, but because he apparently thought himself above discussing strategy with three outsiders and a Janissary. The Janissary-spahi rivalry was maintained for a couple of reasons—so that neither group got too powerful, and so that they never banded together against the sultan—but it was deeply inconvenient at times like this.

"And I should . . ." Radu trailed off, unsure what Hamza Pasha thought he should do about it.

"It is *your* country making them ill. Perhaps you know something about it."

Radu recognized a power play when he saw it. Hamza Pasha knew Mehmed was listening, and wanted to remind them all that Radu, though a bey, was not and would never be one of them. That it was Radu's country costing them so much. And that he was intimately tied to the person doing it all.

Radu smiled sweetly. His handsome face earned him no advantage here, but old habits were difficult to shake off. "It made me sick having to live here, too. I was not whole until I found my home at our sultan's side." Certain that his own point had been made—he had more of the sultan's ear than the pasha did—Radu stood. "But I will go see what needs to be done. Do tell me if this map reveals any secrets while you continue staring at it."

Radu walked from the tent, his steps light and confident. But his shoulders fell along with the flap behind him. Why was he still playing this game? What did he care about a stupid pasha questioning his value and his place in the empire?

Mehmed had said nothing when Hamza Pasha challenged Radu. Radu understood on an academic level the need for a sultan to hold himself separate. But Mehmed had had no problem commenting when Lada was the topic. Radu was tired of his place in all of this. He had been making these same desperately calculated plays for power all his life.

It came easily to him now, but that did not mean he enjoyed it.

He made his way past the borders of the camp, where they kept those who were sick. There were a startling number of them. Mehmed's insistence on sanitary methods of camp order usually kept sickness to a minimum. Maybe there *was* something about Wallachia that made people ill.

Radu covered his mouth with his cape, walking slowly. A feverish man lay on the ground on a worn bedroll, covered in sweat and mumbling to himself. Radu paused, listening. The man was mumbling to himself not in Turkish, but in Wallachian.

Radu grabbed one of the attendants. "This man. Where did he come from? Is he a Janissary?"

The attendant shook his head. "No, just a worker. Most of the sick are not soldiers."

"That is good," Radu said.

The attendant gave him a witheringly dismissive look. "It is good until you need support for sixty thousand soldiers. And then it is devastating."

Embarrassed at the rebuke, Radu crouched closer to the sick man. The language had given Radu a terrible suspicion he needed to disprove. "What did the prince promise you?" he asked in Wallachian.

The man had his eyes closed, but his mouth twitched in a smile. "My family. Land for my family."

Radu stood, dizzy. He had not expected to be right. He strode back to camp and found Kiril, the Janissary he used most among his group of four thousand. "Get me your whole unit. We have to go through the camp and interview everyone who is not a soldier."

"Why?" Kiril asked, but with curiosity, not judgment.

"Because my sister is full of surprises. None of them pleasant. Look for Wallachians. And look for anyone who is ill."

There was no telling how many Wallachians had slipped in among the chaos of the massive camp. They had to check the cooks, the servants, the—oh, God's wounds, the women who followed the camp to service any *needs* the men had.

They had been dragging Lada's weapons along with themselves the entire time.

She really was clever. Radu could not blame Mehmed for admiring her still. He could, however, wish that cleverness did not create so much extra work for himself and suffering and death for everyone else.

23

One Day South of Tirgoviste

LADA ADJUSTED HER STOLEN Janissary cap. She had not worn one in years. It was like revisiting a favorite story from childhood and realizing that while the details were the same, the entire meaning had changed. She looked over the group of twenty handpicked men, checking any last details. But they knew what they were doing. Other than Bogdan, they were her last remaining Janissaries.

She realized with an unexpected pang that someday soon these twenty would die, too, and she would be left without any Wallachians trained by the Ottomans. An unexpected urge to leave them behind and out of harm's way was pushed down as she cleared her throat.

"All we are after tonight is information. How the camp is laid out. Where the pack animals are kept. Where the food and especially where the weapon stores are. How many men. Pay attention to everything, but do not be conspicuous. Tomorrow night, each of you will lead men back into camp." Lada smiled, her teeth white as bones in the moonlight. "Tomorrow night is the fun. Tonight is the work so our fun will be fruitful."

Bogdan grabbed her arm as everyone scattered to enter the camp at different points. He stood too close, letting in little darkness between them. "I want to be with you."

"And I told you," Lada said, pulling away, "I need you out here to signal if anything goes wrong. We can still send enough men down from the hills to create a distraction and get out. But only if you are waiting to give them the signal. Otherwise we will all be dead if any of us are caught."

Bogdan moved in front of her, blocking her path. "Are you going after him?"

Lada did not have to ask whom Bogdan was referring to, but she wanted to punish him for daring to demand an answer. "No. Radu can stay there for his betrayal. I have no use for him."

"That is not who I meant."

Lada pushed forward and past Bogdan. "I am going to find where the sultan is sleeping. Perhaps I will murder him in his bed. Perhaps I will do the same to you later."

"Be careful," Bogdan said, puncturing her meanness with his constant care.

She kept walking.

The benefit of such a massive force was that there were any number of entry points into camp, and no way for anyone to know she did not belong there. They were prepared to fend off hundreds or thousands. Not one. She slipped in among the tents, then walked with purpose. Just another Janissary who knew exactly where to go and had a job to do. The camp was well lit with torches and campfires. There was less activity than she had counted on, though. All the soldiers were, as far as she could tell, confined to their tents unless actively on patrol. And the service portion of the camp she skirted was even quieter. Perhaps they had discovered her contributions to Mehmed's forces.

She had a sudden image of Radu falling ill. Mehmed joined him in her imagination, both wasting away with sickness.

No. It was not how any of them were supposed to die. So they could not. She physically shook away the image and turned sharply to go deeper into the camp.

The lack of activity made her job slightly more difficult but also gave her some advantages. With only minimal men out and about, it would take more time for them to muster a response to any attack. Soldiers in tents were sleeping soldiers. On a campaign like this, a man never passed up an opportunity for sleep.

She kept going, noting locations and positions of any importance. The camp was set against the hills with broad open plains on three sides. They had cut down any trees that might offer hiding places. No army could approach on horseback without being seen from a great distance. And the hills were too barren and rough for an entire army to reach under short notice. It was a smart, defensible position.

A position that all the devastation in the countryside— too many pits in one direction, too marshy in another, rotting animal carcasses left all over another option—had subtly but surely directed them to.

She smiled happily to herself. It *would* be impossible to set an army up in those hills if the army were coming now.

But not if the army had already been there for weeks.

She nodded companionably to a passing Janissary, then turned a corner around a cluster of tents and stopped cold.

He never learned. In front of her was a glorious tent, taller and grander than any others in the camp. Mehmed's name was actually written on it in the form of his flags and banners hanging slack in the still night air.

Lada walked around back, past the Janissaries standing guard at the tent's entrance. With a spinning sense of history repeating itself, she pulled out a knife and slit the silken material to create her own door. Then she slipped inside.

Mehmed was sitting at a desk with his back to her. A few steps. Her knife. The end of the Ottoman campaign in Wallachia. Perhaps the end of Ottoman dominance entirely as they were plunged into a question of succession.

"You never learn," she said. "I have killed you again."

Mehmed tensed. Then he turned with a smile. He held a dagger, too. "You are late. I have been expecting you every night since I crossed the Danube."

For a few moments Lada stood, poised on the brink of violence. Then she stepped past Mehmed and sank down onto one of his red silk pillows, stretching out her legs on the floor. Her boots got mud on his rich carpet. "I have been rather busy. Things to do. Empires to fight. Summer holidays to plan."

"Am I such a low priority, then? That hurts my pride."

He finally stood, his movements slow and measured as though she would spook—or attack—and sat across from her. He grabbed one of her boots and tugged it off. He tapped the knife she wore hidden at her ankle, then tugged the other boot off. He shook his head, tracing that ankle sheath, too. "Both sides?"

"I like to be prepared."

"I know." Mehmed removed her wool socks, knitted for her

by Oana, and began kneading her feet. She could not imagine him doing this with—for—anyone else. Certainly not any of the women in his harem. *They* existed to serve *him*.

"I want you out of my country," Lada said, not taking her eyes off him.

He smiled, as dark and secret as the night. "Then why did you invite me here?"

"I did no such thing."

"Lada." He moved past her feet, rubbing her tight calves. "You sent me men in boxes and an entire vassal state in turmoil. From you, that is practically courtship."

Lada laughed. She did not want to. She had not come here to be *with* him. But in spite of their history, in spite of his betrayals, he was ... Mehmed. Her Mehmed. She had known as soon as she entered the tent she would not kill him. Even though she really should have, if she believed in what she had set out to do.

She lifted a foot and put it against his chest, shoving him away. "You idiot. I should kill you."

He leaned back on his elbows. "Probably. And I should call my men in here and have you arrested. But I do not want to do that." His gaze on her was far more tender and intimate than his fingers had ever been. Lada felt it through her whole body. "I want you to come back with me."

"I never will."

Mehmed sighed. "I know. But I keep pretending to myself there is a way. To get you back. To be together. I have only ever wanted you."

"You have wanted a tremendous amount more than me."

Mehmed's grin was sharp and wicked like her knives, and just as familiar. "That is true. But I also want you."

"Yes, now that you have everything *else* you set out to gain." Lada pulled her legs beneath her, scooting closer to him. "Is it what you hoped? Constantinople?"

"It is more." Mehmed paused, his expression turning wistful and forlorn. "And less, at the same time."

Lada touched a corner of Mehmed's mouth. "I understand." It was a hard thing, setting a lofty goal and achieving it, only to realize on the other side that the work had just begun.

"I think only you could understand me. And you? You have your country."

"Says the man with an army camped in reach of my capital."

"You know I had no other choice."

Lada traced one finger over Mehmed's bottom lip, then down his chin and neck to his chest. She jabbed it there, hard enough to hurt. "You always have other choices. And you never choose my side."

Mehmed grabbed her finger, clutching her hand. "Because I want your side to be at my side."

"That will never happen."

"Then we are at an impasse. I cannot let your aggression stand. It sets a dangerous precedent for the other vassal states."

"Then give up Wallachia as a vassal state."

"I cannot."

Lada withdrew her hand, lifting a single eyebrow and letting disdain drip from her voice like grapes on a vine. "Here I thought you were the sultan. Emperor of Rome. Hand of God on Earth, or so all your missives have informed me. Were the titles lies along with everything else?"

"If I give up ground anywhere, I risk losing it everywhere. You of all people know how tenuous power is. Can we not compromise?"

Lada narrowed her eyes. Nicolae had told her she could and *should* negotiate. He whispered still, ghostly, in her ear. For once, she listened. "How would we compromise?"

"I will agree to forgive past debts in exchange for a renewed treaty."

"Never."

Mehmed sighed, lifting his eyes to the ceiling of the tent. "I will agree to forgive past debts in return for Bucharest and new terms of vassalage."

"You can have no land."

"Ah, but you did not say no outright!" He smiled slyly at her. "You sign new terms of vassalage, I do not meddle in your country, you do not harass my borders or the borders of any of my vassal states."

"I will never give you boys for your Janissaries again. And I have no money—and if I did, I would spend it fighting you."

Mehmed laughed. "I did not ever say you had to *actually* give me anything. All I ask is that you sign the terms. Just sign them, allow me to leave with a treaty that is respectable and shows Europe we have an understanding, and that is the end of it."

"Really?" Lada leaned even closer, as though she could read him like a battle plan. Radu would have known if he was sincere. Lada did not. But she found herself hoping. "You would give up the taxes, the soldiers, everything my land has to offer?"

"Right now all your land is offering me is swamps, poisoned wells, and the plague." He paused. "Thank you for that one, by the way."

Lada grinned, elation coursing through her. "I know how much you value a clean camp. I wanted to make things interesting for you."

"So you agree?"

Lada knew Mehmed would be a fool to follow through on such a disadvantageous agreement. And Mehmed was no fool. But if he left, it would give her time to organize. To muster more support. To rise to enough power to truly challenge him. Maybe he would never come back. Maybe their agreement would stand, and she would have saved her country from decades of conflict. She doubted it. But Nicolae pushed from the grave not to pass up this opportunity.

Lada leaned close, studying Mehmed's dark eyes, his full lips. Remembering the taste of him. "I will come back tomorrow night to sign it. And then you will take your men and leave my country."

"We are agreed." Mehmed took off her Janissary cap, sighing as her hair fell free. "You know, the last time I was here, you told me you would kill me if I set foot on your soil again."

"Fortunately for you, you have proved useful."

He lowered his face to her neck, brushed his teeth along the skin there. "Let me show you how useful I can be."

Their actions held all the tenderness of a battle, and twice the passion. Lada had pretended what Bogdan offered was enough, but this, with someone who was truly her equal, who understood her as no one else ever could, lit her body on fire in a way she could not experience elsewhere.

Mehmed put a hand over her mouth to keep her from crying

out. She bit him, and he shuddered before collapsing beside her on the rug.

"Marry me," he whispered, an arm thrown over his eyes, his chest still heaving.

Lada yanked her clothes back on, replacing her boots and shoving her hair under the Janissary cap. Then she leaned down and put her lips against Mehmed's ear. "I would sooner kill you."

She left the way she had entered. But this time she was the one leaving him betrayed, not the one broken by betrayal. Because there was another reason she had agreed to his terms. It meant the Ottomans would stay in this camp, in this position, for one more night.

And she had options if Mehmed reneged on their agreement.

She walked through camp as though in a dream, happier and more relaxed than she had felt in months. Perhaps years. Nicolae would be proud of her. She had made the smart decision. The decision that bought her time to build, to get stronger. To continue to create the Wallachia her people deserved.

Voices speaking in Wallachian caught her ear. She stopped. One of the voices pulled on her heart. It was a voice of her childhood, of hiding in barns, of venturing onto thin ice. Of tears and then of cold distance. A voice she had needed on her side.

She found the tent and paused outside, leaning close to listen.

"The Basarabs—those who are left—will support us," said a man she did not know.

"I suspect the Hungarian king will as well," Radu said.

"Perhaps not outright, but when Aron is on the throne, Matthias will not be a problem."

Lada's hands went to her wrist daggers. But Radu's words had already cut deep. After all this time, he was back in Wallachia. But he was here aiding her enemies. Not only Mehmed—that she had expected—but also the treacherous boyars. The ones who had killed their father. The ones who had let them be traded to the Ottomans. He had willfully become *everything* she stood against.

She staggered from the physical pain of hearing him conspiring against her. Then she steeled herself, listening more carefully.

Aron. Aron. Who was Aron? She knew the name.

Danesti. He was the son of the Danesti prince Lada had overthrown.

And he was in Mehmed's camp. Even as Mehmed was offering her peace, he had a replacement ready to go.

See, Nicolae? she thought. *I am always right.*

Lada would still be coming back the following night. And she knew Mehmed would be waiting in anticipation. This time, his hopes would be met with her blade.

24

One Day South of Tirgoviste

RADU WISHED THE TENT were larger so he could pace. Anything to keep himself awake during this endless discussion of probable futures with Aron and Andrei Danesti.

"Will you stay and help us, after we retake the throne?" Aron asked.

Radu wanted to return to his tent and sleep. He did not want to contemplate a longer tenure in this country. They had spoken of him staying to ease the transition, but he hoped it would not be necessary. Now that he was here, all he wanted was to be elsewhere.

"I do not know," he said. "To be perfectly honest, I do not like Wallachia. I have no wish to remain beyond what is necessary to aid the sultan."

Andrei grunted. "Like it or not, it is your heritage."

Radu smiled tightly. "I decided long ago not to let my past dictate my future."

Aron met Radu's smile with one of his own. "That is a very nice luxury."

Radu could not bear the judgment in the other man's tone. He owed nothing to this country, nothing to its people. They had traded him for a few years' peace. It was not the Danesti's place to imply that Radu was being selfish.

Radu nodded and, without bidding them farewell, left the tent.

A Janissary was standing nearby, posture stiff. He was short and stocky. Radu turned to go back to his own tent, but ... something ...

Something—

He whipped around and watched the Janissary walk away. The gait was aggressive, the movements predatory. Radu had never realized how well he knew his sister's walk, but it was unmistakable.

"Lada," he said.

She did not stop walking. He was not sure she had heard him. He could still catch up to her. Grab her arm and force her to stop. Send up an alarm and have her captured, ending this entire campaign. Once again he was faced with an opportunity to betray someone he cared about and force a quick end to violent struggle.

Instead, he watched her leave.

What had she been doing here? And where—

Mehmed.

Terror cutting a path before him, Radu raced through the camp to Mehmed's tent. The two Janissary guards moved to bar him until they saw who he was and let him pass.

Radu burst in to find Mehmed lying unmoving on the floor.

And then his eyes took in all the extra information. Unmoving and *completely naked*. And very much alive.

"So my sister has been here." Radu stayed on the edge of the rug and kept his eyes on the chandelier overhead.

Mehmed laughed sleepily. "Do not look so scandalized, Radu. We negotiated a new agreement."

"Negotiated. That is a use of the word I have never heard before."

This time Mehmed's laugh was bright and sharp. "Radu! I did not know you could speak so."

Radu squeezed his eyes shut and pinched the bridge of his nose. "She could have killed you."

"And yet, here I am. I figured out a solution. We give her what she wants, for now. She cannot sustain herself. That much is obvious. She has a few months, maybe a year, before she is driven out by Hungary or Transylvania or her own boyars. But *we* leave her on good terms so that when she loses it all, she will come back to us."

"I saw her outside. She heard me talking with Aron and Andrei."

"That does not matter."

"Imagine you were in her place. We have proved ourselves repeatedly to be against her. We are sitting on her capital's doorstep with an entire army. Of course she will agree to something. And then she will find the next opportunity to retain power, and the next, and the next. She is never coming back to us."

"She already has. I am not dead after all."

"For now." Radu opened his eyes. The chandelier dazzled his sight, making bright white spots where the flames imprinted on his vision.

"Radu Bey," one of the Janissaries outside called. "There

is someone to see you. He claims he represents the Basarab family."

"It can wait," Mehmed told Radu. "I am happy. Lada is happy. You should be happy. Radu." His voice was low and insistent, demanding Radu's attention. Radu dragged his eyes away from the light. White points of flame still danced, surrounding Mehmed.

Mehmed narrowed his eyes thoughtfully, his smile tentative but devious. Radu remembered that smile well from their days in Amasya, sneaking out of the castle in the middle of the night. Stealing apples. Swimming in their secret pool.

Mehmed patted the rug next to himself. "Come. Spend the night with me."

It was not a question, but it sounded as though Mehmed were trying on the words to see how they fit. Radu did not know what would happen if he crossed the endless, impossible space between them.

In that moment, his certainty was proved: he did not want this. He did not want to accept whatever love Mehmed decided to gift to him. His time with Cyprian—knowing that if their love had been possible, it would have been one of equals, hearts given completely and without reservation—had either broken him forever or finally healed him.

He loved Mehmed—he would always love and care for him as a friend and as his childhood savior—but he no longer needed or wanted something between them that would never be enough.

"Thank you, my friend." Radu's smile was the release of years of yearning and pain and the desperation to be loved.

"But I have work to do." Radu bowed his head, then left before he could see Mehmed's reaction.

Outside, the night was clear. The stars shone cold and constant above him. Once, long ago, Mehmed had told them the story of two lovers, Ferhat and Shirin. Ferhat had carved through to the heart of a mountain to bring water to the other side and win Shirin's hand in marriage. Ferhat had died inside that mountain, his heart broken. At the time, Radu had thought it the most romantic thing he had ever heard. What a noble end, to die for love.

Perhaps Radu would never know complete love in his life. But all these years of digging desperately had opened up the path to his *own* heart. He no longer lived in fear that it would break if exposed. A heart did not have to be stone to be strong.

"Radu Dracul?" a tentative voice asked.

Radu turned. Radu Dracul. Radu the Handsome. Radu Bey. All names bestowed on him by those with power over him.

"Just Radu, please," he said with a smile. "Now, tell me how I can help you."

25

One Day South of Tirgoviste

LADA HAD THIRTY MINUTES to topple an empire.

She doubted she would need that long. She walked confidently through the dark camp along the same path she had taken the night before. She still wore the uniform of a Janissary. Perhaps that was fitting. She would use everything the Ottomans had given her, right down to their own clothes, to destroy them.

Only outside Mehmed's tent did she pause. The weight of history, everything they had been and done together, slowed her steps. She felt it, accepted it, let it settle.

Could she do what she had set out to? It was one thing to plan murder and another to follow through. And tonight she would not act out of rage or instinct. This had to be a choice.

She would walk into that tent, and she would stab her first friend, her first lover, her only true equal through the heart.

She did not want to, she found. But she would do it anyway. It was what Wallachia needed, what it demanded, and Wallachia came before Mehmed. It always would. It had to.

Her heartbeat even, her breathing calm, Lada used the cut she had made the night before and entered Mehmed's tent for the last time.

"Hello, Lada," her brother said.

Lada scanned the tent quickly, her heartbeat finally picking up.

"He is not here," Radu said, leaning against Mehmed's desk. "But I can oversee the signing of the new treaty." He spoke in Turkish.

Lada's lip curled in distaste around the language she, too, had spoken for years of her life. "I am not here to sign a treaty."

Radu smiled. Truly looking at him for the first time, Lada saw in that smile how much her brother had aged since they had been apart. He was taller. Still lean, but with a hollowness to his face that threw his jawline and cheekbones into sharper relief. The too-large eyes were still just as striking. He was beautiful. And he was a stranger. The boy she had known, the boy she had loved and protected, was gone.

"What happened to you?" she asked.

"Too many things." Radu sat on one of the cushions, gesturing for Lada to join him.

She remained standing. "I told him he should not have sent you to Constantinople. I cannot believe he put you in harm's way."

"You would have done the same."

"I would not have! You always needed protection, and I protected you."

Radu tilted his head, a puzzled look on his face. She was reminded again how much he looked like their mother. And, with the weary sadness pulling at his mouth, she saw how life and its cruelty would break him. She had seen a glimpse into his future when she visited their own ruined mother.

"I think," he said, "you and I remember our childhood much differently. You protected me from Mircea, but only because you liked him even less than you liked me."

Lada snorted. "That is certainly true. But what about in Edirne?"

"I recall you refusing to do your studies even when I was beaten for your insolence."

"Are you that stupid?" When Radu looked hurt instead of understanding, Lada sat in a huff across from him. "They used everything they could against us. And they used us against our father. If I had stopped that tutor, if I had let them see they could use you to control me, you never would have been safe again. I let you be beaten to keep you from being used as leverage against me."

A dozen emotions flitted across Radu's face, none of which Lada understood. He settled on amused and sad. "We do have very different definitions of protection, then."

Lada searched her brother's eyes, trying to find the little boy he had always been to her. Even after his refusals to help her, even after all this time, he had not changed in her mind. But reality presented her with the truth. He was not her delicate, weak baby brother anymore.

"You look upset," he said, his voice soft.

"I have lost something." Even though Lada should have known it, she had never let herself believe it. But now the truth was undeniable. She had completely lost her brother to the Ottomans. "Where is Mehmed?"

"Why?"

"He has much to answer for."

"We all do, I suspect." Radu drew his legs up, wrapping his arms around them and resting his chin atop his knees. There! A fleeting glimpse, but Lada saw her Radu.

"Tell me what has happened to you. And why are you in Mehmed's tent? Are you—do you stay here now?" Lada kept her voice as even as she could to avoid betraying anything. But Radu was always better at emotion, better at reading people than she could ever be.

He laughed. She stood, bristling. Radu waved one hand, gesturing for her to sit back down. "No, I do not stay here now. I am in Mehmed's tent because you came here tonight to kill him, did you not?"

"Of course I did," Lada snapped.

Radu sighed, stretching his legs out again. "He did not believe me."

"He is a fool. Surely after all these years of studying him you have discovered that." Lada felt the pressure of time pushing down on her. She had spent too long here already. Her task should have been finished by now.

"Do you think it was him that came between us? Or were we destined to end up on opposite sides?"

Lada felt an unfamiliar heaviness behind her eyes. "We had to survive. We just figured out different ways to do it." It struck her, then, how they had lived the exact same childhood. How had the same circumstances shaped them in such divergent ways?

"So you do not blame Mehmed?"

"Of course I do! I blame him for a great many things." She

kicked a pillow in exasperation. "Why, tonight of all nights, do I finally find someone who has beaten me at my game of 'Kill the Sultan'? Tell me where he is and then flee the camp. I will send word that you are not to be killed."

"I had a chance, once," Radu said, slowly standing. "In Constantinople. Emperor Constantine trusted me. And I watched as good people on both sides were dying, smashed in blood and bone and terror against each other by immovable forces. Mehmed on one side of the wall, Constantine on the other. And I liked them both." Radu smiled wryly. "Though of course we both know where my heart was. There was one moment, one perfect chance to end it all. To take a life and spare thousands, tens of thousands, by making that choice."

Lada did not know what this story had to do with her. "Well?" she prompted, impatient.

"I made no choice. And because of it, Constantine still died, but countless others died alongside him who might have been spared had I made a choice. You would have made the choice."

Lada *would* have. It was a simple scenario. But she had a nagging feeling she did not like where this story was leading. "You could have killed Mehmed instead, you know."

"Do not pretend like that was ever an option."

But something tired and worn down in Radu's face suggested otherwise. There was potential there. An opportunity. To get him back—and to end this. Lada crossed the space to him and took his shoulders in her hands. "Tonight. Tonight, it is an option. We can kill him. For Wallachia. We can finally be free of the cage our father crafted for us, once and for all. Make the right choice tonight."

Radu, so much taller, so much fairer, looked down on her. He stepped forward, folded her into a hug. She stood stiff, unsure how to respond.

"I hope I already have," he said. Then, raising his voice, "Come in."

He held Lada tighter, pinning her arms to her sides and smashing her face against his chest so she could not see what was happening. "I do not want to see you ended," he said. "I could not bear it. I am sorry."

Lada stomped on his foot and shoved her way free. Ten Janissaries had entered, swords drawn. And from behind a flap where he had heard everything, Mehmed stepped free with cold murder on his face.

26

One Day South of Tirgoviste

"YOU CHOSE HIM AGAIN," Lada said.

Radu expected fury, rage, the Lada who had been the terrifying center of his childhood, ruling everything with her temper and her fists. Instead, his sister looked resigned. Tired, even. She spoke in Wallachian, changing from the Turkish they had been conversing in.

Radu answered back in the tongue of their shared history. "I did not choose *him*. I chose what I felt would create the best, most fertile ground for lives and faith. Look at your country, Lada. Do you really think you are growing a future here?"

"You know nothing about it! In the time since I have taken the throne, crime has disappeared. My people need not lock their doors, need not sleep beside their livestock for fear they will be gone in the morning. They no longer require an armed guard just to travel from village to village. My country is prospering like *never* before!"

"You turned an entire plain into marshes. You poisoned

wells and burned bridges. You have cut a swath of destruction across the countryside."

"Because he was coming!" Lada gestured sharply in Mehmed's direction. Radu did not look at Mehmed, certain Mehmed would signal him to speak in a language he could understand. The Janissaries edged closer. Radu was surprised to find he wished he had not called them so soon. This conversation with Lada felt like it might—like it would—be their last. And he did not want it to end.

She might have found him changed, but he found her more precisely, more powerfully herself than she had ever been. He was . . . proud. In spite of everything. And it made him devastatingly sad. She had worked so hard and fought so long for this. They were going to take it all away.

This was the first time the three of them—once inseparable—had been in the same room since Lada left. Everything had changed. And nothing had. She was still choosing Wallachia over them. Radu was still supporting Mehmed. And Mehmed was still demanding they both be his. The stakes had just gotten higher.

Radu sighed. It could have been such a different reunion. Well, no. Not with Lada. But it *should* have been different. "We came because you forced us to. We did not want this."

Lada shook her head, but there was something evasive in her expression that hinted to Radu she knew he was right. "I only sped up the inevitable. He was never going to let me have this."

"All you had to do was make concessions. We would have given you—"

"It is not his to give me! Wallachia is *mine,* and I owe nothing to him or anyone else!"

"That is why you will lose it!" Radu shouted. "Because of your refusal to bend. Because of your damnable pride! We offered you peace."

"And came armed with usurpers to betray and replace me!"

Radu threw up his hands in exasperation. "You cannot accuse us of betrayal. Not when you agreed to sign a treaty and came here to assassinate Mehmed."

Lada opened her mouth to argue, then stopped. A shocking giggle escaped her mouth. It made her almost girlish. "I suppose that is true."

Caught off guard, Radu found himself returning her smile. "We always have contingency plans, you and me. That has not changed."

Lada's smile deepened and darkened. "You have no idea what is coming."

"Are you certain about that?"

Unease crept into Lada's face. Her deep-set, hooded eyes narrowed, and her full lips pressed together. Radu had a shameful thrill that she now respected him enough to question herself. He would have given anything for a moment like this as a child, even more for a moment where she looked on him with pride for besting her. But he would never get that.

"Enough," Mehmed said. "I am taking you prisoner." His face was etched with anger, something cold and hard growing beneath the softness of his cheeks. "I should kill you right here for this."

Lada tilted her head, gazing up at him through her thick lashes. "You really should." She gave him a banal, blank smile as though she were the woman she should have been, a woman like their mother. "Make Radu do it."

Radu balked, stepping back. He glanced at Mehmed, seized with a sudden fear that Mehmed might be angry enough to demand that. But his friend shook his head. "I would never ask that of him."

Lada's smile turned coy. Radu saw a hint of himself there, as though she were imitating him. "You would, if you thought it was your best option. Do not pretend to put his feelings ahead of your own. You never have. You cannot."

"Just as you cannot release your insane fixation on this country!" Mehmed took a deep breath, trying to get his anger under control. The men around them shifted uncomfortably. This was not the aloof, self-possessed sultan they were used to serving under. "I offered you the throne."

"You offered me nothing I do not already have." Her upper lip curled in defiance, returning her to the Lada that Radu knew. "And you have given me nothing I cannot find elsewhere with far less hassle and far more pleasure."

Mehmed's eyes widened in shock and hurt. Then he shifted from Mehmed to sultan with a lift of his chin and a firming of his jaw. "Bind her and take her to the wagons. We will make quick work of the rest of this campaign while she is sent ahead to Constantinople."

Lada smiled at Radu, showing all her sharp little teeth. "Tell the Danesti boyars their kind does not live long in my Wallachia."

Radu wanted this to be over. He wanted to sleep. He knew he would not be able to, not tonight. He would change his plans and request to escort Lada back to Constantinople. Knowing her, she would goad the guards into killing her. She would never admit it or even realize it, but she needed his protection now. He would see her to prison—safe, at last, once and for all—and then he would be finished. "Lada, I am—"

"How long would you say I have been in here?" she asked, her expression thoughtful.

Radu gestured for the Janissaries to take her. "Be careful."

"We will not hurt her," Kiril said, nodding respectfully.

Lada widened her stance and bent her knees. "That is not what he is afraid of."

"I—" A deafening explosion rocked through camp, cutting Radu off. The tent shook, several panels detaching from their stakes and blowing inward. Radu ducked, covering his head as the chandelier came crashing to the ground. By the time he straightened, the two Janissaries closest to Lada were already dead.

"Protect the sultan!" he shouted, pushing Kiril toward Mehmed instead of toward the fight with Lada. "All of you, around the sultan!"

Radu drew his sword. Lada paused, two bloody daggers in her hands, three bodies on the floor. The other Janissaries had rushed Mehmed out of the tent.

"Will you really fight me?" she asked, pointing one red blade at his sword. Then she ran right for him. Radu twisted to the side, holding his sword to block her blades, not to strike her.

She stopped just short of him, giving Radu a look that made him feel like the child he had been, crying himself to sleep at night and never measuring up. "I thought not," she said. Then she darted out of the tent and into the night.

Radu dropped to his knees, hanging his head. He had a

sword to her daggers. He could have won. Again, he had had a chance to end things. Again, he had not made the choice Lada or Mehmed would have in his place. How many lives would pay the price this time?

Struggling to his feet, he followed Lada into the burning night.

27

LADA KNEW IT WOULD be impossible to find Mehmed in the dark and the chaos. Though there *was* significantly less chaos than she had been counting on. Nearly all Mehmed's men were staying in their tents rather than rushing out into the fight. It made things harder. She should have known better than to count on a lack of discipline in Mehmed's men, though. He always controlled everything. Why would his men be any different?

The gunpowder stores had already been attacked—the explosion was good timing, too, as it allowed her to escape. She knew she would find a large group of her men attacking the pack animals and wagons. There were five thousand already here or on their way, every soul she could muster streaming out of the hills and attacking from the darkness. She heard their shouts, their music playing, using the Janissary's own tactics against them. As soon as there was enough chaos in camp, Lada would send up the signal for the rest of her troops in the hills to attack. Five thousand more. It was only ten thousand against fifty thousand, but it could work. If everything fell into place, Wallachia could defeat the most powerful army in the world.

She could beat Mehmed.

Of course, things were already off schedule. The biggest tipping point into mayhem and despair was supposed to be the death of their sultan and leader. She had not accomplished that. She ground her teeth in frustration. Radu had beaten her.

Then again . . .

"The sultan is dead!" Lada grabbed a torch and set the nearest tent on fire. "The sultan has been murdered!" She continued thus, running through camp screaming about the death of the sultan while ensuring as many men as possible could not stay in their tents.

There was more activity around her—more and more men entered the mayhem. "Hey!" one shouted, grabbing her arm. She stabbed him in the side and kept on toward the animal pens.

Toward the back of the camp, the fighting was happening in earnest. She had hoped to draw the bulk of Mehmed's men here with her initial five thousand, mire them in fighting, and then hit them from behind with the reserve. From her vantage point, it looked like the Ottomans had several thousand engaged in combat. Not enough yet. Crossbow bolts, fired by her men in the hills, sang through the air, claiming Ottomans running around her. She risked being claimed by one herself if she did not hurry.

Women screamed as they ran through the main section of tents. Seeing them, Lada wanted to laugh. They were not Ottoman camp women, but Wallachian women, armed to the teeth, pretending to flee while cutting down as many Janissaries as they could. When they reached the far end of camp, they would circle back and meet up with the forces coming down from the hills.

Everywhere was confusion. Chaos. Blood and fire.

For once in her life, Lada longed to join the women. They were doing exactly what she wanted to. But she was needed elsewhere. She was not here as a soldier, but as a prince.

She skirted the tents, then ran into the hills, where she found her rendezvous point with Bogdan and her other leaders. They were waiting, anxiously watching the progress of the assault.

Lada shouted as she ran up, "Anyone with a Janissary uniform, go into camp to take up the cry that the sultan has been murdered!" Several dozen men took off. Bogdan raised his eyebrows hopefully.

Lada hated to admit defeat. She shook her head. "They were waiting."

He looked concerned, but he nodded and moved on. "Are we ready, then?"

Lada bit her lip. She wanted more time for order in Mehmed's troops to break down, but she also knew if they waited much longer they risked the opposite. The Ottomans could organize and form ranks. The fighting had intensified on the supply end of camp. It was a full battle now, one her men would not be able to sustain for long.

"Do it," she said.

Bogdan gestured to the trumpeters. The notes were brassy and clear over the tumult of noise in the camp. Lada watched the hills, waiting. Runners stood beside her, ready to take commands at a moment's notice. From here, she would direct everything. From here, she would watch Mehmed's army fall.

Something was wrong, though.

"Do it again," she said.

Again, the signal sounded. Lada's heart sank within her. The camp burned, but not bright or fast enough. Her men at the wagons fought, but not enough Ottomans had been committed there. Where were her boyars with the rest of her men? With the Hungarians Matthias had sent?

As the trumpets gave one final, trembling plea, Lada remembered Radu's response when she said he had no idea what she had planned.

He *had.*

He had known all along.

Her eyes desperately combed the hills for some hint, some sign she was wrong. That they were coming. That they could end it all tonight. If they had but trusted her, if they had followed her plan. The faithlessness of men, to take whatever false advantage Radu offered instead of choosing the valiant course. The course of blood and victory, the course of struggle and triumph for Wallachia.

No one ever chose Wallachia.

Lada dropped to her knees, throwing her head back to the smoke-choked stars. She screamed her rage and despair. Then she stood and drew her sword. If no one would help her, she would do it herself.

She took two steps forward when someone grabbed her around the waist.

"Let me go!" she shrieked.

"Sound the retreat," Bogdan said, his voice soft.

Lada twisted, snarling like a feral thing. Bogdan held tight, talking in an even, soothing voice. "They are forming ranks. No help is coming. But I count nearly fifteen thousand of theirs dead, countless pack animals slaughtered, their gunpowder stores destroyed. Now we run." He paused, then spoke again. "If we escape, we win."

"We did not win!" Lada kicked once more, then went limp, only Bogdan's arms holding her up. "We could have destroyed it all. We should have."

"Sound the retreat!" Bogdan shouted over his shoulder. He lifted Lada onto a horse and got on behind her, squeezing her leg in clumsy reassurance. "Your welcome awaits them at the capital. We run and fight again."

Lada heard in those words her entire future stretching out before her. She would never be able to stop fighting. Even victories that should be hers would be taken from her by faithless men. They would forever choose each other instead of her—choose treaties and tradition over a genuine chance for change.

It would always be a fight. Hunyadi had told her as much. Her dreams of decisive triumph drifted up like sparks, only to go dark and cold as ash.

28

Outside Tirgoviste

Hamza Pasha slammed his fist down on the table. "If the forces in the hills had followed her plan, we might have lost. She had *women* fighting! Women! I lost spahis because they were too shocked to raise a blade!"

Radu dreamed of lighting the table on fire, throwing it into the smoldering mess of their supply train. He loathed this table, and the map on it, and increasingly the people around it.

Ali Bey's smile was as pointed as the tip of a sword. "That is a failure on their part, then. My Janissaries overcame their shock quickly enough."

"Do not pretend your men turned the tide. We only triumphed because of Radu's deal with her allies," said Ishak Pasha, the most measured of the three.

Hamza Pasha blew air out between his lips with a dismissive noise, as though Radu's efforts in persuading the Basarab boyars to hold back was more of a lucky accident than a battle-winning triumph. "He cannot use the same trick at Tirgoviste. We cannot count on anyone else betraying her. The commoners worship her."

Radu glanced at the tent's door flap. Mehmed was not here. Radu had not seen him since the attack the night before. No one had, other than his guards. Kiril had reported back to Radu that Mehmed was unharmed and, apparently, perfectly capable of going right to sleep.

Radu rubbed his forehead. It ached from exhaustion and too much inhaled smoke. "We have the advantage with a siege."

"The advantage is always with the defenders! At Kruje——"

"I was *at* Kruje," Radu said, cutting Hamza Pasha off. He was tired of being dismissed by the old man. "Outside the walls. And I was at Constantinople, inside the walls. I am no stranger to sieges." He offered no smile to offset the harshness of his words. He knew what so many of these men still thought of him—that he only led his horsemen because of his beautiful face and favor with the sultan. But favor with the sultan was how *any* of them led. And Radu realized that despite his eighteen years, he truly did have as much experience as any man could be asked for.

He felt it thick and dark and choking in his dreams, a constant heaviness in his mind both awake and asleep.

Yes, he had far more experience than any man could be asked for.

Radu took a deep breath and spoke in a more measured tone. "Tirgoviste has none of the natural advantages of Kruje, and certainly none of the defenses of Constantinople. It is smaller than both. The walls are hardly formidable. They will be able to see us coming, but that is no secret. And as was clearly demonstrated last night, Lada does not have the loyalty of nobles or European support that Skanderberg or Constantine did. No one will come to her aid. She lost half her forces when the Basarabs abandoned her. We killed three thousand, which as far as we can tell leaves her with only a couple of thousand to command."

Hamza Pasha scowled. "We have lost *fifteen* thousand! And supplies and animals!"

"We can afford fifteen thousand with greater ease than she can fifteen hundred." Radu cringed at the callousness of treating men's lives as simple calculations. War made monsters of them all. "When we take Tirgoviste—and we will, no matter what she has planned—that will be the end of it. We will have the capital. We can install Aron and Andrei in their places and Wallachia will return to its vassal status."

Ishak Pasha tapped a finger against the table. "But the boyars and their men are not entirely off the map. If they were swayed to us so easily, they can be swayed back. They may already be behind the walls in Tirgoviste. What if she—"

"Her strength is not walls. It never has been. Doubtless she will have some plans, but she cannot fight the way she has up to now. This is where *our* training and skills matter. This is where she realizes she cannot keep the city in the face of the might of the Ottoman army. No matter how many men she can pull together."

The tent flap opened. Radu was shocked to see Mara Brankovic enter with a swish of layered skirts. "I had thought," she said, "to be catching up to a triumphant army already in control of the country." She pursed her lips in disapproval. "If I had known I would have to join the camp, I would have delayed my trip."

Radu pulled a chair over for her. She sat down primly, glancing over their plans. "Hungarian forces are here?"

"Yes, but they have not been in play. Yet." Radu had to admit Ishak Pasha was right. They could still decide to support Lada. In the end, the Basarab boyars who had led them were not in charge. The Hungarian king was, and if he sent word, they would do what he asked.

"Send Corvinus a gift," Mara said, opening her lace fan with a snap of her wrist.

"What?" Radu asked.

"Matthias Corvinus. Send him something. Luxurious. Beautiful. Oh, I know! Send him a jeweled velvet pillow for his crown. He will understand the meaning."

Ishak Pasha scowled, shifting his weight angrily from foot to foot. He had several old wounds that made travel painful and difficult. But such was his loyalty to the empire, he refused to let Mehmed campaign without him. "Why would we take time from war planning to send an enemy king a fancy gift?"

Mara leaned conspiratorially toward Radu. "I have just heard the most wonderful rumor. King Matthias was sent a rather large amount of gold from the pope to aid your sister in crusading. And, by a shocking coincidence, he somehow came into the funds to buy his crown back from Poland." Mara grew serious once again. "By using that gold for himself, he has stolen from the pope. It will not go over well among his European allies. We should make certain his loyalties remain firmly divided."

Radu toyed with a heavy ring. "And it would not hurt to include a note about how much we look forward to a long and peaceful relationship with Hungary's rightful king, whose crown we acknowledge and celebrate and whose borders we recognize and respect."

"With just the right amount of threat implied should he set foot over those borders into conflicts that do not concern him." Mara beamed. "I love playing this game with you, Radu. With one gift and one letter, we can take Matthias Corvinus off this map."

Hamza Pasha stood, stabbing a finger toward her. "This is not some game to play at like courtesans!"

Mara demurely covered her face with her fan. "It seems to me that whatever way *you* are playing it has not served you particularly well up to now."

Hamza Pasha stormed from the tent, followed by a less angry Ishak Pasha.

"Pay Hamza no mind," Mara said. "He is still sore that I rejected his offer of marriage."

"He wanted to marry you?" Radu asked, surprised. The other men around the table were leaving to begin the enormous task of repairing what could be salvaged and getting the camp on the road to Tirgoviste. Lada had done a tremendous amount of damage. They would limp all the rest of the way, but they would get there.

"Oh yes. Dear Hamza was madly in love with me." Mara paused. "Sorry. I mean, he was madly in love with my position as a favorite of the sultan." She smiled wickedly, touching her powdered hair as though there were ever a strand out of place. "It is my most attractive feature."

Radu held out a hand to help her stand. "I am quite certain your most attractive feature is your remarkable mind."

"If I ever found a man who wanted to marry me for that, I might just break my vow to never wed again."

"Really?"

She laughed. "No. But speaking of wives, I know a very pretty one who is only two days behind me. You should send word to delay her. This is no place for women."

Radu put a hand to his forehead in exasperation. In the madness of the campaign thus far, he had not even thought to warn Nazira to delay her journey. They had counted on being well settled in Tirgoviste by now.

Radu pulled out a sheet of parchment and cleared a place at the table to write his letter before something else demanded his attention. "Thank you, I will. If this is no place for women, though . . ."

"Never fear on my behalf. I volunteer to take Matthias Corvinus his gift in person. This country is simply awful, Radu. I do not understand how it produced you."

Radu finished his hasty note. "It also produced Lada."

"That makes far more sense."

As Radu offered his elbow to walk Mara out of the tent, his thoughts returned sickeningly to the callous way he had referred to his brothers who had lost their lives. He treated them as numbers. After all he had seen, after all the lives he had watched depart this world, he could not afford to think like that. Because once he started, how would he stop?

———•———

"God above." Kiril lifted one arm to cover his mouth and nose. "What is that smell?"

Radu smelled it, too, but he could not account for it. He

was with his men, riding in advance of the rest of the army. Their force was big enough to face any direct attack, and fast enough to get word back should something arise they were not prepared for.

Facing Lada, they could count on being unprepared.

In the distance Radu could just make out the dark smudge of the capital with a tree-lined road leading up to it. Aside from the skinny trees along the road, most of the forest around it had been cleared. It was smart—Lada had an unobstructed view of the land around the city—but it also meant she could hide nothing from them, either.

"Cautiously," Radu said, gesturing for them to keep moving forward. They had not seen a soul yet, though the sky was splattered with dark birds like drops of ink. The last time Radu had seen so many carrion birds had been in Constantinople. He could not quite catch his breath, their cries pulled straight from his worst memories.

They rode closer, everyone gradually slowing their pace. A sense of wrongness grew as steadily and strongly as the stench. Behind him, Radu heard men gagging. Kiril leaned over and heaved.

Still they had seen no one. Not a single soldier. Not one trap or ambush. Radu undid his turban and wrapped it around his nose and mouth, though he could still taste the putrid rot through it.

Then at last, like a landscape of nightmares, Radu was close enough to see the odd, skinny trees lining the road.

They were not trees.

Evenly spaced and planted with all the care of an orchard,

corpses were impaled on stakes. Some were newer, some so far decayed they had to be weeks dead. And all of them were Ottomans.

"Go tell the sultan," Radu said. He wanted to turn away. He could not. He rode forward into hell, the faces of the damned marking his progress with hollow, rotted eyes.

They were spaced so evenly it was easy to keep count. Tens. Then hundreds. A thousand. At five thousand, he had reached the houses on the outskirts of the city. The buildings were all cold, abandoned. Every door was open. He knew he should send men in to check for soldiers hiding inside, waiting to ambush them.

He could not manage to do anything but keep moving forward. The sheer overwhelming wrongness gave everything a dreamlike haze. He could not feel his limbs, could only see. Could only smell.

At ten thousand, he was finally close enough to make out the gates to the inner city. They were open. The stakes there were so close together that he could not see between the bodies. It was a solid wall of rotting flesh on either side, only the sky above visible as he passed directly into the city.

No sounds but the harsh cries of the birds, and the quieter but far more piercing noises of beaks tearing flesh and sinew from bone.

Radu knew his horse was making noise, but he could not hear it. He did not know if any of his men were still with him. He could not stop, could not look to either side. He was compelled forward as though, by making it through this tunnel of horror, he could wake up on the other side back in a world that made sense. A world where the gate was locked, the walls were manned, and there was something concrete and understandable and *human* to fight against.

He reached the castle. Twenty thousand stakes, as near as he could tell. Had it been just this morning he resolved to never again view men in terms of numbers?

There, in front of the gaping castle gates and doors, on a stake above all the others, a final corpse.

Radu knew that cloak, knew those clothes.

He was still sitting on his horse when Mehmed reached him. There were new noises now—retching and curses and a few quiet sobs. Of course there were more men here. Mehmed would not have come alone. Radu did not know how long he had been here.

"Is that . . . ?" Mehmed did not finish his sentence.

"Kumal," Radu whispered. The man who had given him Islam as a balm and protection for Radu's terrified young soul. The man who had become Radu's brother in spirit and in law. The man who had come here in Radu's place.

Kiril spoke. Radu had not seen him join them. He could not look away from where Kumal's kind eyes had once been. Did they rot out, or had they been eaten? It seemed important to know, but Radu had no way of finding out.

". . . all clear. There is no one here."

"How can we fight against this?" Mehmed asked. "How can we take a country when she simply walks away from the capital? How can we ever defeat someone willing to do this"— his voice broke as he swept his arm outward—"just to send a message?"

"How could a woman do this?" Ali Bey's voice was filled with equal parts wonder and disgust.

"She is not a woman," a soldier near Radu said, spitting. Normally a soldier would not dare speak in the presence of the sultan. But there was nothing normal here. "She is a demon."

"No." Radu closed his eyes against the forest of corpses grown from the indomitable will of his sister. "She is a dragon."

29

Outside Tirgoviste

IT HAD BEEN ALL Bogdan could do to persuade Lada not to dress as a Janissary and enter the city with Mehmed's men.

She wanted to be there.

She wanted to see it.

To revel in their shock at an unguarded capital. To see the looks on their faces when they realized they could not fight her. To see their despair when they were confronted with how far she would go to protect what was hers. They could have the city with her blessing. After all, Tirgoviste was not Wallachia.

Lada was Wallachia.

Instead, she sat in the hills and watched from a distance, imagining it. Relishing it. And looking on in astonishment and delight as Mehmed's army stopped, then turned around and headed back toward the Danube.

Finally Mehmed knew the truth. She would never be his. Her country would never be his. She had won. All it had taken was twenty thousand dead Ottomans on stakes.

And Mehmed thought she did not understand the power of poetic imagery.

30

Outside Tirgoviste

IT TOOK TWENTY THOUSAND stakes to make a single point:

Lada was not *ever* giving up.

Radu did not know which had shaken Mehmed more deeply: seeing so many of his men impaled in horrific defiance of Muslim burial traditions, or understanding that Lada truly had intended to kill him during the night attack.

Their retreat from the city had been necessary for both morale and health. At best, the tenor of the camp was one of unease. Radu heard a lot of rumblings about going home. They had to decide what to do before opinion shifted too far in one direction or the other and made the men unruly.

Mehmed had relocated to a far less ostentatious and more anonymous tent. They were there now, and had been for hours. Radu waited in silence next to Mehmed, who sat with his back straight, his eyes on the carpet. He picked mercilessly at the gold stitching on his robe.

"How can I fight this?" Mehmed finally asked. This was the first time since the night of Lada's first visit that they had been alone. Mehmed seemed a different man. Radu, too, felt different. Far older, again. How many lifetimes could he age over the course of a few years?

"How can I fight this?" Mehmed repeated, but Radu did not think Mehmed was asking him. Radu suspected that, until the double blow of Lada's true intentions and her horrific display, Mehmed had not actually taken any of this seriously. It had been more than a game to him, but far less than a war. He had faced Constantinople with religious determination. This had been all about getting Lada back.

And now Lada had made certain they could *never* forgive her. All hope Mehmed had held of reunion was as lifeless and rotten as the sentinels at Tirgoviste.

The camp had moved far enough away from the city that the smell was no longer making men sick. Radu had his own men—four thousand skilled and disciplined fighters—digging graves instead of riding into battle. But his men were not alone. Ali Bey, Ishak Pasha, Hamza Pasha, they had all spared as many as they could for the work of giving the Ottomans proper burials. Shifts were taken with solemn sadness. Some to dig, some to guard, and some to pray.

"We have Tirgoviste, but it does not matter." Mehmed's voice was as haunted as his eyes. "I do not know how to fight a war where tactics are useless, where numbers gain me no advantage, where gates are left open and cities are guarded only by the accusing dead of my people. Tell me how I can fight this." He looked up, pleading.

"You cannot." Radu knelt in front of Mehmed. His friend leaned forward, resting his head on Radu's legs and curling in around himself. Radu put a hand on Mehmed's turban. Radu's fierce desire was gone, his passion dulled by the long, heavy wear of time and disappointment. But his tender affection and deep respect for his friend, for the sultan, would not leave him without a fight.

"If we stay," Radu said, "we will have to chase her into the mountains. It will be months. Perhaps even years. She will wear down your men with time and starvation, sickness and frustration. We cannot fight on her terms and win."

"What should I do, then?"

The eyeless face of Kumal rose unbidden in Radu's mind. He closed his own eyes. It did not help.

Lada could not win this. Radu would not let her. "Go back to Constantinople. Burn the cities you pass, take whatever livestock is left, and, everywhere you can, exaggerate the numbers. Have Mara tell all her contacts what a great victory this was, how easily you restored Wallachia to its vassal status and put Aron on the throne."

"But Lada won!"

"And who will tell that story? Her peasants? Her hordes of landless, nameless people? How will they travel to the pope, to the Italians, to the rest of Europe to tell of her victory? Rumors will spread, certainly, but all evidence will be in our favor. Our man on the throne in the capital. Our triumphant march home."

"If we go, we leave Lada free to do it all again."

"No." Radu let out a heavy breath and smoothed the edge of Mehmed's turban. "I said we could not fight on her terms. We fight on mine, instead. With your permission, I will keep my men and stay behind to work. I can steal the country from my sister through the one thing she never could beat me at."

"Archery?" Mehmed said, his dark attempt at humor acknowledged by both men with wry smiles that faded as soon as they appeared.

"Sheer likability. I will defeat her through manipulation. Politics. Saying the right thing at the right time to the right people."

"She will fight you."

"She can try, but she will fail. She tried to dismantle the foundation of a building she was still living in. She tried to be prince while taking apart the entire system that supported the prince. I will find every enemy, every boyar who has lost a son or cousin or brother, every noble who rightly fears for their place in her new world. I will use Transylvania and Hungary and Moldavia. I will steal every stone of support she has until she is standing alone in the ruins of the new Wallachia she tried to build."

"And then?" Mehmed sat up, locking his eyes onto Radu's. "She will never stop. She does not have it in her. And what foolish hopes I nurtured that she could return to us are gone." Mehmed had been firmly against killing Lada. Radu saw that his position had changed. They had so much in common, his sister and his sultan. And now they hated with as much determination as ever they had loved.

The bodies were piling up because of it.

Radu knew he had faced this before, knew he had been too weak to make the right decision, knew he could not afford to do so again with so many lives at stake. It had been selfish of him, avoiding what had to be done. What Lada would do in his place. Radu could be strong for this one terrible task. It would destroy him, but he could no longer ask thousands to pay the price of his tender conscience. "Then I will do what must be done. I will finish it."

31

Poenari Fortress

LADA LEANED OVER THE stone wall where it jutted past the edge of the cliff. The Arges River curled distant and silver beneath her. Her fortress was finally complete. It would be her refuge, her sanctuary, her rallying point. Breathing deeply of the cold air still wet with morning mist, Lada fortified herself with the same unassailable strength as her fortress.

There was work to do.

Her men and women were scattered through these mountains in groups of two hundred. It was easier that way, both logistically with camps and strategically with remaining hidden from enemies. Even if one camp was discovered, they would not decimate Lada's reserves. She and her followers could hide here for months.

Not that she had plans to do that.

She turned to Bogdan and Grigore. She had promoted Grigore after his success in defending Bucharest, though he annoyed her. Everyone annoyed her for not being someone else she loved better. "Have word sent to the pope of our victory," she said. "Make certain he knows what we did. Fifteen thousand of their men dead, and the entire army turning tail and running. Perhaps with these kinds of results, he will send us more than praise. Praise neither feeds men nor kills enemies. I want money and soldiers."

Grigore shuffled his feet in obvious discomfort. "I cannot read. Or write."

"Where is Doru?" Lada asked with a sigh. "He can write."

Bogdan's blocky features twisted in awkward confusion. "He died. During the night attack."

Lada had not noticed. She waved, irritated with herself for not knowing and with Doru for dying. "Then you write it, or find someone who can. The pope *must* help us. I want real power behind us when we return to Tirgoviste. We have to plan for taking it back." She knew the bodies had been removed and that a small force had been left behind. But surely they did not think a few thousand Ottomans could stop her. Not now.

Lada's fingers tapped the sheathed sword at her side. "And I want all of the Basarab boyars' men." It had been the Basarabs, led by a man named Galesh—weak, faithless Galesh—who had held their forces back and cost her a true victory during the night attack. They were hiding somewhere in the mountains, too, using her same strategy. That would not work out as well for them. She had briefly considered killing them, but it was a waste of resources. She would just cut off the head and absorb the body. "I want *all* of the Basarabs' men. Along with Galesh's head. That is our first priority."

"Clean your own house before helping the neighbors," Oana said with a pleasant smile, passing Lada a steaming bowl of mush and a side of dried meat.

"Or, in our case, clean our own house before attacking the

neighbors for trying to steal our things. We also need to retake Chilia from my cousin to teach Moldavia that our borders are inviolable."

"Do you want to kill him?" Bogdan asked.

Lada frowned. She really was not certain. She could not blame King Stephen for his actions. She would have taken advantage of the same opportunity had their situations been reversed. There were several cities that passed between Moldavia and Wallachia every few decades that she would be happy to reclaim. And, in spite of his betrayal, she still liked her cousin. He reminded her of Nicolae.

She set down her bowl, her appetite gone. "We will deal with that when the time comes. Now, closer to home, do we have any allies in Transylvania?"

Grigore shifted, obviously uncomfortable with delivering bad news. "You are . . . not very popular there."

"Still? Even after I sent the Turks weeping back to their own lands?"

"We can send some men and see."

Lada nodded, then hesitated. "Perhaps do not send our best men. Pick some who are dispensable to go with you." Her own record with responding to envoys was less than friendly. She did not want to gamble anyone who would be hard to replace.

Grigore's eyes were wide and terrified. She could not understand why. "Oh," Lada said, remembering her words. She picked her bowl back up and shoved it at him. "Not that you are dispensable. I am certain you will be fine. Eat something."

She paced back and forth along the length of the wall overlooking the cliff's edge. "Is there any chance of getting Skanderberg to join us?"

Bogdan shrugged. "I do not have any Albanian contacts."

Lada waved a hand dismissively. Of course he did not. She wanted Stefan here. Where was he? Nicolae would—

She stopped pacing and rubbed the back of her neck. She needed her own Mara Brankovic. She even found herself missing Daciana. If Daciana had been raised with an education, she would be better than any of the men serving under Lada. It filled her with pulsing anger knowing how much potential was ignored among her people simply because of their sex. She tugged her hair off her neck and tied it back with a strip of leather. "Pick someone dependable and send him to Skanderberg. It is unlikely he can help—he is still fighting the Ottomans on his own land—but we may as well pursue every potential ally."

"Speaking of allies, what of Matthias Corvinus?" Oana reached up to redo Lada's hair, but Lada slapped her hands away.

"By his request, the men he sent were to be commanded only by Galesh Basarab. So I do not know whose cowardice and betrayal denied us our complete victory, that of the Basarab boyars alone, or Matthias's, too?"

"What does Matthias have to gain from your loss?" Oana shoved Grigore's untouched bowl back into Lada's hands. Lada wrinkled her nose and forced down a few bites. Eating and sleeping were chores. She wished she could assign them to someone stupid like Grigore so she could continue her work all hours of the day.

She feared if she stopped moving, if she stopped plotting and planning, then ...

She did not know. But the fear was constant and nagging, and the only way to outpace it was to never stop.

"What does Matthias gain? I do not know. A free Wallachia would only benefit him. It keeps his borders further buffered from Ottoman advance. But I cannot pretend to understand that man. If only his father were ruling." Lada allowed herself a moment to imagine what it would have been like had Hunyadi been waiting in the hills. How tremendous their victory, how complete the destruction of Mehmed's armies.

Everyone would have remembered that night, and their names, forever.

But then again, had Hunyadi been fighting with her, doubtless all credit for winning would have gone to him. Only he would have been remembered.

The guards presented a panting boy covered in a light sheen of sweat. It was no small task climbing up the mountain to the fortress. Most of her prisoners had died hauling stones up.

The boy bowed low, holding out a leather satchel. "Letters, my prince."

Lada took them. One, from Mara Brankovic, she tossed aside for later with a renewed surge of envy that she did not have her own Mara.

Radu. Radu would have been her Mara.

Her grip tightened, creasing various missives from people whose names she did not recognize. But at the bottom of the stack was a letter sealed with a coat of arms featuring a raven. Matthias. She sliced it open with her dagger.

Lada drew her eyebrows close, anticipating bad news. For once, she was surprised. "Matthias praises our victory. He claims to have been unaware of the Basarabs' cowardice, and gives us the last known location of the men Galesh was leading!" Had he merely claimed not to know of the betrayal, Lada would have continued to suspect. But if the location proved accurate . . . Lada could kill the remaining boyars and take both their Wallachians and the Hungarians into her own ranks. "He is surprised by how quickly Mehmed ran." Lada laughed. "Clearly Matthias does not know how deeply Mehmed cares about the cost of things. But Matthias is emboldened! He is willing to commit more men and money. He thinks we can retake the Danube, and deny Mehmed that passageway into Europe! With control of the Danube, we could damage his entire vassalage system. . . ."

Lada lowered the letter, her mind spinning with possibilities. She had longed for Hunyadi at her side, but perhaps Matthias would prove the more useful of the two after all. He brought European connections. She brought ferocity and the ability to lead men against Mehmed. Together, they stood a real chance of freeing not just Wallachia but also the rest of the European countries that Mehmed held under his thumb.

What a blow that would strike against Mehmed! Against his treasury, against his faith, against his pride. Lada could taste it. She wanted Wallachia free, yes, but if she could have even more?

She would take it. Gladly. Gleefully, even.

"Matthias wants me to ride to his court so we can plan, and then I will return with his men." If she left now, she could be there in a couple of days. It would give them time to come up with a strategy and track down allies. She had no doubt Matthias with his noble face and gilded tongue could do better than she. And she would be back in Wallachia before the remnants of Mehmed's men could set up a good defense in Tirgoviste unchallenged. Mehmed had left, but she was not naïve enough to trust that he was truly gone.

She tucked the letter into her tunic. "I will leave immediately."

Bogdan nodded. "I will come."

"No. I need you to go after Galesh and the Basarabs. This information might be a week old. You need to find them now. Send word when they are dead and the men are yours."

"I do not like you going alone. I do not trust Matthias."

"Neither do I, but for now our goals intersect. I will not let this opportunity fall."

"Grigore can handle going after Galesh so that—"

Lada grabbed Bogdan's arms, cutting him off. "I trust only you to do this." It was true. So many of her men were lost to her. But Bogdan remained. She knew that, of every man in the world, he would be true.

"I will attend to her," Oana said with a reassuring pat on Bogdan's arm. It made Lada realize how little they touched. Oana was far more demonstrative with Lada. So was Bogdan, for that matter. Whether it was because Lada had been Oana's charge, or because Bogdan had been taken from her at such a young age, Lada was the center of their mother-son relationship. She pushed away a pleased smile at the thought.

Oana threw her shawl over her shoulders and tied it in place. "A lady should not be alone, ever. Not in a foreign castle."

Lada snorted a laugh. "If someone threatens my honor, will you kill them with your knitting needles?"

Oana grinned, warm wrinkles around her eyes. "Do not doubt what I can do."

"I never would."

Bidding farewell to Bogdan, Lada and Oana climbed down the mountain with thirty guards. Horses awaited them at the nearby village, so remote the villagers had not bothered evacuating.

Lada sat straight and eager in her saddle. For the first time, going to Hungary did not feel like a punishment. It felt like victory.

32

Tirgoviste

RADU COULD NOT TELL if the stench of death lingered in Tirgoviste, or if his memory of it was so strong that he would never be able to walk through the city again without gagging.

The work of clearing the bodies—taking them down, burying them with their heads toward Mecca, and giving them the respect they deserved—was finished. It had been a week of nonstop, wearying work. Because they had no grave markers, and could not identify most of the bodies anyway, Radu had them buried in the sections of forest that had been cleared to make the stakes. They planted seeds and saplings between each grave. Someday, a forest would grow and hide his sister's abomination from the heavens.

Until then, they all carried it with them.

Radu paused at the castle gates, staring at where Kumal had been displayed. He would never tell Nazira. He would carry the memory himself; there was no reason to burden her. If Radu were still Christian, he would dedicate a church to his brother-in-law. As it was, whenever he prayed, he dedicated himself to Kumal's memory. It was not enough—it would never be enough—but it was all he had to offer.

"Sir," Kiril said, inclining his head smartly, then walking at Radu's side. Radu had promoted him to his second-in-command. "We have finished the last of the cleanup. What now?"

"We need to find my sister. Until we know where she is and what she is planning, we cannot accomplish anything here. No one will return to the capital if the threat of her wrath looms over it. But I cannot see any way for her to retake it with the numbers she has." Radu had been alert and waiting for attacks, but nothing had happened. Lada had vanished and taken with her everyone and everything they needed to fight. "Just because I cannot see it, though, does not mean she cannot find a way. More likely, though, is that she will try to draw us into the mountains where she will have the advantage. I do not particularly want to stumble into any more welcomes she has designed."

Radu avoided the castle door. He had no wish to go inside. Instead, he climbed a ladder to the wall that circled the castle. He leaned over the bulwark and looked out at the city. It was still nearly empty. It had been easy to house his men—they had an entire capital to choose from. "We should act less like Ottomans and more like Wallachians."

"How do Wallachians act?" Kiril was Bulgarian by birth, but did not remember anything of his homeland. He had been with the Ottomans since he was five. He often joined Radu for prayer and meals. They had the easy understanding of two people who had decided to claim the home that had claimed them.

Radu leaned on his elbows, looking back at the castle. In the center of the courtyard, as a child, he had once watched Aron and Andrei be whipped for a crime they did not commit. One he had framed them for. "Wallachians are desperate. Sneaky. Vicious. Or at least, that is how my family line has always behaved. Find a small group of men—those with frontier experience, not city experience. Send them into the mountains for scouting only. The smaller the groups, the more luck they will have in discovering without being discovered. We need to know where Lada is, and where she is hiding the bulk of her forces. Once we have that information, we will be able to move forward. In the meantime, we coronate the new prince of Wallachia, Aron Danesti."

"So we act as though the country is ours, when our enemies are still out there and everything is in turmoil?"

"Lada will be furious. She antagonized Mehmed—" Radu caught himself and corrected. "Antagonized the sultan to get him to meet her where she had the advantage. We will do the same. I do not count on her storming out of the mountains, but I also would not be surprised by it. She has a terrible temper when you take what she thinks is hers. And even if it does not bait her, it serves a purpose. Sometimes, the best way to achieve power is to pretend like you already have it. We coronate a new prince, and we begin ruling. The country will fall in line. Lada changed too much, too fast. Change is hard. It requires a tremendous amount of time and willingness to endure discomfort. Going with what one has always known is easy. Add that to the sheer destruction of Lada's tactics and the suffering that will cause? Wallachia will choose us, because we are the way to survive."

He hoped they would gladly accept a return to what had always been if it came with peace and stability. Even if, perhaps, they deserved more.

Much like he had returned to Mehmed again and again. He had finally decided that the lonely unknown was preferable to the lonely known. He would not go back to Mehmed. Not as he had before. He prayed that Wallachia had not been pushed so far that its citizens, too, would realize they deserved better than what they had always had.

Radu would do his best to improve the country for as long as he was here. But he could only do that if it was stable. And, for now, it could only be stable by resettling into its old shape.

Kiril nodded. "I think that is a good plan, sir. And—this may be out of place—but I am glad to serve under you. Doubtless you know the rumors of why you have command. But Mehmed does not give power out on whims or as favors. You deserve your place here, and I am honored to follow you. All your men are."

Radu laughed. "That compliment is a bit like a rose. It comes with a lot of barbs and thorns."

Kiril raised his hands, a flush of embarrassment covering his cheeks.

Radu put a hand on the other man's shoulder. "No, no, I understand. And thank you. Your confidence in me means more than you can know. I will always try to do right by my brothers."

Radu excused Kiril with one last warm smile. It was a good

plan. He would put on a show of power. Boyars would flock to him as the only safe option. And, if he was lucky, Lada would be so angry at being replaced as prince that she would come down to meet them where they had the advantage. Funny that after so many years of doing everything he could to avoid her ire, he was now in a position of using all that history against her.

Radu had to ride out of the city quite some distance to answer Aron's summons. He had wrongfully assumed the Danesti brothers had taken their family manor. He had been too busy to notice that they had not, in fact, settled in Tirgoviste.

Aron and Andrei had a few hundred men of their own that had been with them since the siege at Constantinople. The men's camp was disorderly, bordering on slovenly. Radu rode through it with a critical eye. He would not have tolerated such lack of discipline among his men. No one in the Ottoman Empire would.

Aron was waiting for him, pacing impatiently inside his tent. Andrei sat in a chair, leaning back with his arms crossed over his chest. "Here you are," Aron said. "It took you long enough to get here."

Radu opened his mouth to apologize, but cut the words off before they could escape. He owed them no such thing. "I was unaware you had not relocated to Tirgoviste. When will you?"

"We cannot live there!" Aron stopped pacing, horrified. "It is unhealthy. We would catch our deaths."

Radu lifted an eyebrow. "Do you think being impaled is contagious?"

Andrei gave him a darkly wry look. "Your sister is still free."

He had a point. "Fair enough. But it is important that we consolidate. You are vulnerable out here."

Aron had begun moving again. "We are going to our family's countryside estate. We need your men to go ahead and make certain it is safe."

They had not invited Radu to sit. He clasped his hands behind his back. "I do not think that is wise."

Aron stopped, frowning. "Why?"

"I doubt the Danesti family estate is fortified. If Lada found out you were there, you would be slaughtered."

"We will have your men as well."

"No." Radu spoke slowly and carefully. He was not certain how so little had been communicated. Had it been neglect on his part, or negligence on theirs? "My men are setting up to defend the capital. It is vital that we hold it as our seat of power as a signal to all of Europe who the true prince is."

Aron looked deeply suspicious. "The true prince?"

"You," Radu prodded. "Of course. You are to be crowned prince. But to be prince, you need to rule from the capital."

"I would not feel safe there."

"It is not about feeling safe. It is about appearing to be strong. If we cannot fool others that we are confident in your rule, why would they trust us enough to stand at our side? We pretend at strength until we have actual strength. It is a lie that will become truth."

"You seem an expert in these matters," Andrei said drily.

Radu was. He had pretended his way into Murad's favorites. He had pretended his way through enemy territory in

Constantinople. And he had pretended his way through a life-long friendship that he had wished was ever so much more.

And now? He would have to pretend in order to rebuild the country that never even so much as pretended to care whether he lived or died.

Aron shook his head. "I would still prefer to run things from my estate. You can divide your men."

"I will not."

Andrei sat up a bit straighter, and Aron stepped closer. He was smaller than Radu, though, and his attempt to loom fell short, literally. "I am here with the support of the sultan, am I not? What did he leave men for, if not to do my bidding?"

Radu smiled benignly. It was a good thing he had so much practice pretending, because if he were to be honest, he would laugh in Aron's face. "The sultan left his men here to provide stability. He left them under my command, and I will use them as I think wisest. Which, right now, is protecting Tirgoviste and reestablishing it as your capital."

"I am your prince," Aron said, lifting his chin proudly.

"Actually, you are Wallachia's prince. I am a bey of the Ottoman Empire, and am only here as a personal favor to you. I owe you no allegiance."

Aron and Andrei shared a look that was alarm on Aron's part and menace on Andrei's. "We want money," Andrei said. "We know the sultan left you with funds. As prince, my brother should be able to dictate where those funds go."

"The money is for fighting my sister."

"And by becoming prince, is my brother not fighting her? Therefore, he should be able to decide how best to put it to use."

"You can see," Aron said, holding out his hands in a placating gesture, "how it is concerning that, while I am prince, you seem to control all the men and all the gold."

Perhaps Radu had been wrong to assume these two had outgrown their childishly aggressive competitiveness. They had always been polite to him while among the Ottomans. But Radu had more power than they did there. Here, in Wallachia, they were determined to prove they mattered more. It was like the forest games they had been forced to play as children all over again. Only this time, Lada would not jump out of hiding to beat them for hitting Radu.

And this time, he did not need her to.

"I can understand that," Radu said. "The sultan has donated my men's time and resources. I have never seen him so generous with another vaivode prince. Our fathers certainly received no such level of support from Sultan Murad. I think that provided you follow the sultan's wishes by setting up in the capital and beginning your rule with absolute confidence, you can look forward to a beneficial lifelong relationship with the Ottoman Empire. And I can ask him to forgive the debts that Wallachia is several years behind on paying."

Radu did not voice what would happen should Aron decide he was not satisfied with Mehmed's generosity. But he could see in the shift from aggression to overly demonstrative smiles that he did not have to.

"Of course," Aron said. "We want the same things the sultan does. I am sure you will communicate that."

Radu had no desire to play politics with the Danesti brothers. He *wanted* them to have the country. But he had a job to do, too. Regardless of how he felt about Wallachia, about Lada, about Mehmed, he would discharge his duties here to the best of his ability. He owed that much.

Radu inclined his head. "Please let me know if there is anything we can do to ease your transition into the castle. It has been thoroughly cleaned. The whole city is clear and ready for life to resume its natural pace. While you are settling in, I will find the remaining boyars and bring them back as your support system, so that, with their help, you can begin reestablishing order. I know—as does the sultan—that you are the prince Wallachia needs."

Aron nodded as though everything Radu proposed had been his plan all along. "Very good. I will consider our return and send word when we are ready." He paused. "If we are going to pretend, though, I will need to put on a better show. I need new clothes more befitting my throne, as does my brother. We should also have livery for our servants with our family crest. And new horses, as well."

Radu could practically see Aron holding out his hand for gold. And if Radu agreed to this, he could only imagine the vital needs Aron would generate in the future. But he had to make some sort of concession, and it *did* play into the image they were trying to project. Aron was clever.

Radu was cleverer.

"It would be an honor to arrange that. I will have it waiting in your castle for your return." Radu bowed to cover the smile threatening to break free. He had missed playing court games a bit, after all.

33

Carpathian Mountains

THOUGH LADA WANTED TO get her business with Matthias done as quickly as possible, there was one stop she had to make on the way.

"Where are we going?" Oana asked.

"Detour." Lada directed them up a mountain pass that had been patiently carved by a tributary stream. The land was unforgiving, no clear path showing their way. But they had not made it very far before a woman emerged from behind a clump of trees, crossbow pointed right at Lada.

"My prince!" the woman said, lowering the crossbow.

Lada nodded to her. The guard went ahead of their company, alerting several other women posted on watch. Lada was pleased to see they had not relaxed their discipline in maintaining a lookout.

When they arrived at the camp, everything was clean and orderly. There were more than a thousand women here, those too old to fight or pregnant. They shared care of the children. It was one of three such camps, but Lada suspected it was the best one. Makeshift tents huddled between trees, each with a carefully cleared fire pit in front. A group of several hundred children sat in a meadow as women leaned over them, pointing to things.

Daciana smiled with unfeigned delight. "Lada! We did not expect you."

"It was on my way." Lada dismounted, peering past the nearest children to see what they were doing. Each child had a small stick and was scratching in the dirt with it. It was an odd game.

"We are learning how to read and write." Daciana pointed to the nearest woman. "Maria teaches us the letters at night, and then during the day we teach the children." Daciana's face glowed with pride. "I know the entire alphabet now. I am working on writing a letter to Stefan."

Lada was impressed. Though she should not have been particularly surprised. Of course the women would not be lounging about, idling away their hours. Wallachian women worked from birth until death. Even here, hiding in the mountains, they were finding ways to improve their children's lives.

"Walk with me." Lada turned and Daciana followed. She was beginning to show, starting to look more like when Lada had first met her, fierce and defiant, on the lands of the boyar who had impregnated her.

Lada looked up at the branches laced together. Though spring came later in the mountains, the trees were all budding. The spring green was almost gold. Little tufts of treasure on each of Lada's trees. Had any spring ever been this lovely anywhere else? Breathing deeply and feeling herself grow stronger for it, Lada spoke. "Tell me how things are here."

"Everything is going as well as can be expected. We have rationed the stores and should be able to stay for several more months if needed. We supplement everything with game we catch, though we are ranging farther to set traps. But the women in charge are careful and have not come across anyone else. How are things in the country?"

"We had a chance to win. But the Basarabs betrayed me."

Daciana spit. "Boyars."

"Yes. But the Ottomans left anyway."

Daciana's answering smile was as pointed and brutal as one of Lada's stakes. She had been one of the biggest supporters of Lada's Tirgoviste plans. A few of the men had balked at the idea of doing that to the bodies. But Daciana knew what it took to survive. And she had agreed with Lada. They were already dead—why not use them for a loftier purpose? "Mehmed did not like his welcome, then."

"Not at all." Lada stopped, turning to face Daciana. "Did you know Stefan is leaving me?"

Daciana had the grace not to pretend. She nodded, no fear or apology in her face. "It was not my idea."

"But you will go with him."

"I would follow that man to the ends of the earth."

Lada felt a stab of pain. Nicolae had once said something similar to her. And now he was in the earth, and she was losing her friends one by one. That missing feeling clutched her as hard and suddenly as she clutched her locket.

Daciana reached out for Lada's hand. Lada did not offer it. Daciana grasped her shoulder, instead. "I will miss being the lady's maid to the oddest lady I have ever known."

Lada turned to walk back to the camp. "I do not need one.

I will be fine." She hurried so Daciana would not be walking beside her. She had braced herself for a fight, or for anger if Daciana had tried to lie to her. She had not prepared herself to be so . . . sad.

She found her horse and rode away without bidding Daciana goodbye. Oana, slower to get her horse up the difficult path, had only just arrived at the camp. She grumbled about turning her horse around.

Lada still had her. She did not need Daciana.

But it was not quite the same. Daciana was a young woman, nearly Lada's own age. A companion of her own sex was something Lada had never had before Daciana. She had never realized she needed it—enjoyed it, even—until faced with its absence.

The ache inside her was aggravating. She had found strength in her friends, but the cost of losing them was increasingly high. How had she not learned this lesson yet? Between Radu and Mehmed, even starting as far back as her father, surely her heart should have known better than to allow anyone a place.

She would close her heart.

She did not realize she was again clutching her silver locket so tightly that the edges bit into her skin. She owed it to Wallachia to be whole and complete. Dedicated and clear-eyed. No one could break her heart if all it contained was her country.

—◆—

Unlike Lada's last visit to Hunedoara, where she had been invisible when she was not being ridiculed, this time she was treated with respect. One of Matthias's top advisors rode out to greet her at the outskirts of the city. He bowed to her as he would any male prince. There would be no dresses for her this time, no pretending to be something she was not. She entered the city as an equal.

"Your men can stay in the barracks," the advisor said as they were escorted to the castle. Last time, her men had had to sleep outside. Lada rode proud and tall across the bridge and through the gates that had felt suffocating just last year. Now, the castle rose around her like a promise.

"You," Lada said, selecting twenty of her men, "help see to the horses and the beds." The other ten she motioned to remain with her. Oana, too, stayed at her side. Oana's lessons about appearances had not failed entirely. Lada needed to make an impression. Fortunately, radiating power and authority came far more naturally to her than navigating crowded rooms in a bulky dress.

Lifting her chin proudly, Lada reentered the castle not as a nationless girl, but as a prince. A conquering prince, no less.

Matthias, as handsome and shrewd as she remembered, stood when she approached him in the throne room. He did not embrace her—it would have been inappropriate, and frankly Lada would not have welcomed it—but he did smile and incline his head respectfully. She did the same, as befitted their positions.

"You have surprised me," he said, studying her.

"That is because you never knew me. If you had, nothing I have done would surprise you."

Matthias laughed, gesturing to a servant. Wine was brought in on a tray. Lada took her goblet, raising it when Matthias raised his. He watched her over the rim, eyebrows drawn together thoughtfully. "I understand now why my father spent so much time on you. You know, I was a bit jealous. I did not see why you merited his attention when I could scarcely attract it all."

"Your father did what he thought was best by you. And it worked." Lada gestured to the room around them. "You are king." Lada lifted her goblet to his crown. Her hand froze midgesture. His *crown*. The crown he had not been able to afford. She lowered her wine, wariness settling over her like a cold draft. He wore a fur-trimmed vest with a high white collar that covered his neck. His dark hair was short and curling, his beard neatly trimmed. He looked exactly as he had the last time she had seen him; the crown had changed nothing. And everything.

Matthias sat back on the throne, tilting his head to one side. "You really are a remarkable creature. I still cannot believe what you managed to accomplish."

Lada held out her goblet for the servant to take. She tried to shake off the premonition of doom. It was just a crown. He had probably convinced Poland to give it to him. She could not risk losing his aid. She needed to leverage his newfound esteem into action. She cleared her throat. "Now imagine what we will accomplish together. For Europe. For Christianity. For our peoples."

"Yes." He smiled. "I have not forgotten the services you provided the last time. Please know how grateful I am for the service you provide me now. And accept my apologies, in advance."

Matthias gestured. Dozens of men swarmed into the throne

room, quickly overwhelming and killing Lada's. Lada drew her sword with a scream of rage, but already there were too many men between her and Matthias. She killed two, three, four before they had her on the floor, her face smashed against the tile as her hands were bound behind her back. She could hear Oana screaming curses in Wallachian, but none of her men cried out. None were alive to do so.

Matthias's voice rang through the room, bouncing off the floor she was smashed against and the ceiling she could not see. "You helped me to my throne, and now you will help me keep it. Such a little thing, to trade your freedom for my security. I know you may not think it, but I truly am grateful." Her last glimpse of him as she was dragged away was a warm smile and a goblet lifted in a toast.

34

Tirgoviste

RADU ONCE AGAIN FOUND himself hiding in the castle. It had been his main childhood occupation. Back then, he had hidden from his brother, Mircea, and, for a period of time, from the same men he avoided now. Though they had been boys back then, looking to hurt him.

Today they wanted money. At every opportunity, they pressed him for more. Radu struggled to remain civil and pleasant. He had stayed behind to help them. It was growing increasingly difficult.

He did his best to be impossible to find. He did not sleep in the castle, moving from manor house to manor house under the guise of making certain they were well maintained for when the boyars returned. He frequently patrolled with Kiril and Simion, and spent as much time on the outer walls as possible.

Today an argument between his Janissaries and Aron's men had forced him to return. Aron's men were insisting any horse stabled there necessarily belonged to the prince. The Janissaries were not as inclined to politeness as Radu was.

After firmly informing Aron's men that the sultan would not take kindly to his horses being stolen—and then arranging for Simion to transfer the horses to stables away from the castle, where they were apparently too great a temptation—Radu retreated to the castle wall to catch his breath. He leaned out, looking over the still-empty city.

A mounted procession making its way toward the castle caught his eye. Radu could not imagine who would be arriving this soon. Surely the boyars would wait until they knew things were safe, even after receiving Radu's invitations. Then he realized the guards all wore Ottoman-style clothing. One, riding in back, struck Radu as deeply familiar, though from this distance he could not identify why.

In the center rode two women. One dressed simply in dark blue robes, the other dressed like a flower in springtime.

Like the ghost of his father, a Wallachian curse came unbidden to his lips. "God's wounds," he whispered. Nazira must not have received his warning not to come!

Her route here would have taken them directly through the freshly covered graves. Radu cringed, thinking of the thousands of stakes that were piled on the sides of the road while they debated whether to burn them or use them to build another layer of defense around the city. The first was more respectful to the dead, the second more practical. Radu hated that these types of decisions fell on him.

He was grateful, at the very least, that Nazira had been delayed enough to miss the burials. He could not imagine what the original state of the city would have done to her. Or to sweet, delicate Fatima. They should not be here.

He raced down the wall, nearly bumping into Aron.

"I was looking for you. I would like to——"

Radu held up his hands. "So sorry, I cannot. My wife has just arrived."

Aron did little to hide his annoyance, though his words belied his tone. "Oh, by all means! Go and see to her comfort first. I can wait. But I would like a detailed update of all the efforts to fortify the city and find your sister."

Radu had neither the time nor the desire to pretend to involve Aron in the military business going on all around him. But if the country were to be Aron's, he would have to take over at some point.

"Yes, of course." Radu inclined his head respectfully, then ran.

He made it out of the gate just as the horses arrived. Radu was nearly knocked over by the flurry of yellow silk that threw itself at him.

"Radu!" Nazira hugged him tightly around the neck. "I am so glad you are well. We did not hear good reports of the fighting. We had to wait an extra two weeks at the Danube before they thought it was safe enough for us to continue. We even passed the whole army going the other way! Hamza Pasha said you remained to help."

Radu squeezed her back, holding her close, then pulled away so he could look her in the eyes. He wondered what else Hamza Pasha had told Nazira, and prayed that he had had the decency not to mention Kumal. "Why did you keep coming? You should have gone back with them!"

Nazira pursed her lips in a scold. "I told you, husband mine. We are not being separated again. We are a family."

Fatima dismounted daintily, smiling at Radu with her head ducked. "It was not such a bad trip." She was a terrible liar, and her efforts to make him feel better made him want to send her right back home. She deserved comfort and peace.

"Besides," Nazira continued, "I have always wanted to see where you came from." She smiled, an expression both generous and obviously false. "It is lovely!"

Radu laughed. "It is wretched. Lada left nothing unharmed. But someday I will take you into the countryside. Snagov is lovely, a little island monastery in the middle of a great green lake. And the mountains at the Arges will take your breath away." He eyed the castle warily. "Are you certain you do not want to go back to Edirne and wait until my work here is finished?"

"I am certain."

"*We* are certain," Fatima added.

Radu sighed. "Very well. Would *you* like to do my work for me, then, and allow *me* to return to Edirne right now?"

Nazira laughed, though it seemed a little quieter and more forced than normal. Then her face turned somber. "My brother? Did you find his body?"

Radu dropped his eyes to the ground. "He has been buried with all the love and respect he deserved. I washed and dressed his body myself, and saw to his burial. I can take you to his grave later."

"Thank you."

"I am so, so sorry that—"

Nazira put one hand on his face, forcing him to look at her. "I will receive no more apologies from you on the matter. All I ask is that you mourn the brother we both loved. And do so without guilt. I cannot have your guilt on top of my sadness."

Radu nodded, feeling selfish. It really did place a burden on Nazira. If she did not blame him, he had no right to force her to forgive him.

"Good." She brushed her hands as though wiping away the remnants of Radu's guilt. Then, her voice going oddly loud given the topic, she said, "I am going to settle into my rooms with Fatima. Please meet me on the north tower alone in an hour's time."

Radu frowned, puzzled. "I have not been staying in the castle."

"Well, that must change. You will need our help, as will the Danesti brothers. We will all stay here now."

Radu could not discuss the truth of the situation with her in public. Though, having her around would be an excellent buffer between himself and the Danesti demands. Nazira would probably have ideas on how to handle it, too. "Whatever you wish. I can show you to your—"

"Fatima and I are quite capable of settling ourselves in. Doubtless you have important work to see to. Just meet me in *that* tower"—she pointed to the tower where, as children, Lada and Radu had watched Hunyadi enter the city—"in an hour."

Radu bowed. "Whatever you wish."

Nazira went onto her tiptoes and patted his turbaned head. Her eyes shone with emotion; she smiled, though she looked on the verge of tears. "You deserve every happiness," she whispered, then turned and went into the castle with Fatima.

Radu really did not understand women.

He used the time Nazira had given him to find Aron and apprise him of the current plans, including the scouting groups he had sent into the mountains.

"I am sorry I do not have longer to speak," Radu said, though he was the opposite of sorry. "I am supposed to meet my wife. She had a very long journey here."

"Yes, of course. Will you be joining us for dinner? It would be nice to have someone to talk to besides Andrei. And Nazira is far more pleasant to look at than he is."

"At the risk of offending your brother, I quite agree. We should begin talking marital alliances for you. I will write to Mara Brankovic and see if she has any suggestions for how we can best use that to strengthen your power."

"Yes, I suppose that is the next step. It will be nice to have more company, too. I had forgotten how lonely this castle can be," Aron said, his eyes sad above the dark circles that never quite went away.

Some of Radu's resentment drifted away in a surge of sympathy. "I think our childhoods had more in common than we realized at the time," Radu answered.

Aron nodded, then smoothed the front of his new velvet waistcoat. "Perhaps there is a close relative of your cousin, Stephen of Moldavia."

It was a good idea. Stephen had been aggressive on the borders, and a marital alliance might smooth things over. "I will look into it immediately." The sooner things were settled here, the sooner Radu could leave.

He bid Aron farewell and made his way through the castle

and up the steps to the tower. He was a bit early. One of Nazira's guards was leaning out, looking over the landscape with his back to Radu. Radu did not know whether Nazira had a reason to request they meet alone. He would wait until she arrived to ask the man to leave, though. He closed the door behind himself loudly so the man would not be surprised.

"I am afraid the view is rather bleak right now," Radu said, with as much cheer as he could muster. The man was facing the direction of the graves. Thousands of dark patches of newly turned soil made a pattern like farmland with a tragic crop. "Did they give you food in the—"

Radu's words died on his lips as the man turned around to reveal eyes as gray as the water in the Great Horn of Constantinople.

"Cyprian," he whispered.

Cyprian held his hands out at either side in a stiff gesture. He smiled wryly; it was not the smile that had opened Radu's heart back when he'd thought it was closed to anyone but Mehmed. "I have no weapons."

"I—" Radu shook his head. He had not even considered that Cyprian might be here to harm him. Though the man had every right to hate him, to want him dead.

Cyprian's eyes flitted over Radu's face, and Radu did not know what to do with any part of himself. Every facial expression or posture that had ever come naturally abandoned him. He froze beneath Cyprian's gaze.

Cyprian nodded toward Radu's turban. "It suits you." He lifted his fingers to his own. "I am not used to mine yet."

"You—you came with Nazira." The man he had recognized from afar at the back of her guard. He had not looked closely at Nazira's guards when he went out because he had been so overwhelmed seeing her again. This was why she had given her meeting instructions so loudly. They were not for Radu. They were for Cyprian.

"I went back to Constantinople first," Cyprian said. "I will not lie: it hurt to see my city remade. But you were right. Mehmed has done incredible things with it already. It is vibrant and living in a way I have never known it to be. He has renewed its former vitality. But that only explained why you trusted Mehmed. I wanted to understand *you*, where you came from." He turned to the side and gestured out at the landscape, scarred and marked with the violence of twenty thousand desecrated men. "This explains a lot."

Radu was still too shocked to know what to say, or how to say it.

"I can see now, a little, why the Ottomans were your salvation. Why you love them. It is the same reason I loved my uncle. He took me from cruelty and gave me a place, a purpose."

Radu could not bear to look at Cyprian any longer. If being apart from him and knowing they would never be together had hurt, being here with him and knowing they would never be together was such agony Radu did not know if he would survive. He lifted his eyes to the cloudless blue sky. "I am sorry. I am so sorry. I cannot ever—"

Cyprian interrupted him. "I have thought through it all. I have thought of very little else, to be honest. And I have had a tremendous amount of time to think while stuck being cared for by our dear Nazira. I keep coming back to three details.

"The first: You never betrayed me or my trust personally. I gave you many chances to use me against my city, and you never did.

"The second: You saved my two little cousins when you did not have to. I saw them, in the city. I did not approach them. But they are alive, and happy. They would not have survived had you not gone back for them.

"The third: You had ample opportunities to assassinate my uncle, and you never made that choice."

"I thought about it," Radu whispered.

"But you could not do it."

"No."

"Because you are a good person."

"How can you say that after what I did?" Radu finally looked at Cyprian, searched his face for the trick or the lie. Because it was *not possible* that Cyprian could look on him with anything but hate.

"We were on different sides. I would have done the same, given the circumstances. I *did* do the same—I went into Edirne with the sole purpose of using you for information. But the sides we were on no longer exist." Cyprian took a step, closing the distance between them. Radu could touch him, if he could lift a hand. If he were not paralyzed and terrified by what he wanted.

"I told you once," Cyprian said. "Do you remember?"

"I remember every moment we spent together."

"I told you," Cyprian said, with a tentative smile so full of hope it was physically painful to see, "that I would forgive you. I meant it."

Radu let out a breath like a sob. This could not be real. It was too big, too great a gift, too powerful a mercy. He had never had anything like this in his cruel and punishing life. He did not know it was possible. Radu lifted one trembling hand and—still half expecting Cyprian to turn away—placed it against his cheek. Cyprian lifted his own hand, covering Radu's and twining their fingers together.

"I meant it," he whispered.

Radu leaned forward and Cyprian met him halfway, their lips touching in a movement as familiar, as sacred, as healing as prayer.

35

Hunedoara

"I THOUGHT SHE WAS GOING to be kept in a house," a man with a face like a turnip said, peering into Lada's dank cell. The door was solid wood with a square—too small to fit through, too high to reach the lock on the other side—cut out of it. A barred window was set high in the wall opposite the door. A pile of matted and mildewed fur lay on a low cot, beneath which a much-used and little-cleaned chamber pot resided.

"She is," another guard out of her view said. "But she needs a little time to calm down. She killed four guards."

"*Four* of them?"

Lada watched the first man's face make an expression no turnip ever could. She did not smile. She did not break eye contact. He looked away first, tugging at his collar.

A third man shouldered the others out of the way, carrying a metal tray with a bowl of porridge on it. "I know you prefer to eat your meals in the company of the dead." He leaned close to the opening. "Seen the woodcuts myself. No human flesh for you today." He jerked his chin toward the door. "Back up."

Lada did not move.

"Back away from the door!"

Lada still did not move.

He shrugged, turning the bowl sideways and shoving it through the hole. It clattered to the rough stone floor, spilling its contents in a mess. "Next time I can bring something to make you feel more at home." With a dead-eyed smile, he left. The other two settled into their chairs against the wall.

Lada stood in front of the door, watching them.

Hours later, her feet aching but her back still straight, someone she had never expected to see in a prison in Hunedoara came into view.

"Hello, Lada." Mara Brankovic smiled with bland formality as though this were a routine social call.

"What are—" Lada took a deep breath, steeling herself against showing emotion. "Mehmed bought Matthias."

"He does not come cheap, this replacement king." Mara wrinkled her nose, whether in distaste for Matthias or as a reaction to the odors of urine and despair that permeated the prison, Lada did not know. "I am sorry for this. You always insisted on taking the more difficult path. Think of how different your life would be if you had married Mehmed, as I advised long ago."

"*You* are not married, and here you are, free, while I am imprisoned," Lada accused.

"It took me many years and many sacrifices to get here. But I did it in an acceptable manner. I am sorry to see you like this. You may not believe me, but I sincerely hope this is the beginning of a new path for you. One that will not end in your death."

"All paths I take involve a tremendous amount of death."

Mara arched one elegant eyebrow. "I suppose you have only yourself to blame, then."

"I am perfectly capable of blaming you. And Mehmed. And my brother. And Matthias."

"Be that as it may, you were given opportunities. It did not have to end like this. It still does not." Mara leaned closer, her voice dropping lower. "Matthias cannot kill you outright. You still have goodwill in Europe for your success against Mehmed and for your willingness to fight. He is keeping your imprisonment a secret, so no aid will come. Only Mehmed knows that you are here. I am not to tell even your brother. As far as Wallachia is concerned, you disappeared into the mountains and abandoned them. Matthias will keep you for as long as he feels necessary. Play your part, be demure, at least pretend to be tamed, and eventually you may be able to arrange an advantageous marriage that will get you out of here. Not to Moldavian nobility—that would be viewed as a threat. Your odds of marrying *anyone* important in Transylvania are quite small. I assume you want no Hungarians. I can make inquiries among Serbian nobility."

"Is that what Mehmed wants for me?" Lada asked, incredulous.

"No, silly girl. That is what *I* want for you. It makes me sad to see you locked up. You are so young. You have an entire lifetime ahead of you. Do not waste it on this. Be good, marry. And then use that to secure more power. I am leaving this afternoon, but I will start looking for prospects and suggest to Matthias that an eventual arranged marriage for you is in his best interest. But you must do your part." She passed a tightly wrapped bundle through the hole. Lada took it, feeling its weight.

"No weapons," she said, disappointed.

"It is a dress, which is a subtle sort of weapon you will have to learn to use."

Lada tossed the bundle aside. "I have never been good at subtlety."

"I hope you will change your mind. Please know I wish only the best for you."

Lada opened her large eyes as wide as they went, tilted her head, and smiled. "Come in here and let me embrace you for your kindness."

Mara backed up a step, shaking her head. "Yes, you will certainly need to work on your acting skills. I have no desire to be anyone's hostage. Goodbye, Lada. Good luck."

Mara disappeared, and Lada stared at the empty space the other woman had so fully occupied. She had often imagined what she could do with Mehmed's resources. The money and the land, yes, but especially minds as clever and ruthless as Mara's at her disposal. Mehmed did not deserve Mara.

No man did, as Mara well knew. And still her advice was for Lada to marry. Did everything really come back to that?

———•———

Matthias waited an entire day before coming to see her. "Why have you not changed?" he asked, eyeing Lada's dirty, blood-stained tunic, which she still wore over her chain mail. The dress Mara had given her lay on the floor, half in the mess from the dumped porridge.

Lada did not answer. She had slept only a few hours,

preferring to let rage sustain her. The tapestry of power that she had spent so many years collecting threads for had once again been pulled apart by a man. A *stupid* man. He would pay.

"I cannot let you out looking like that. And you will get a chill wearing your chain mail in there."

Lada neither moved nor changed her expression, continuing to stare at Matthias with hooded eyes.

He shifted, shoulders twitching as though trying to shrug off some unseen irritant. "Did you consider I am doing this for your own benefit? Many people want you dead, little prince." He spat out the last word as a mockery. "You are safer here than you would be in Wallachia. Consider it my penance to the Dracul line. My father killed your father. I am keeping you alive." He waited. For what, Lada could not imagine. Gratitude? Weeping? He would get nothing from her.

"Change your clothes!" he snarled. "I have prepared a house for you, but you will not disrespect my hospitality by looking like an animal."

Lada finally let a hint of a smile break the flatness of her expression. But still she did not answer.

"Guards!" Matthias yelled. He turned back to her. "If you will not accept my generosity gracefully, we will help you."

Matthias moved out of her view. A lock clicked, and the bar to the door slid free. The guards were ready when they rushed her.

Lada was readier. She ducked under the arms of the first, kicked the knee of the second so hard that it popped. The third caught her wrist, but she twisted and threw her elbow into his nose. She was almost to the door when it was yanked shut. The lock clicked again.

"Now you cannot get out." The first guard, the one with the turnip face, held his arms out as though he expected her to run past him, to the other corner of her cell.

Lada bared her teeth at him in a smile. "Neither can you."

A flicker of uncertainty passed over his face. Then Lada launched herself at him. She knocked him to the stone floor. He wrapped his arms around her, pulling her down with him as he tried to pin her. Their faces smashed against each other's. She opened her mouth and bit down, hard, on his throat. He screamed, and her mouth filled with blood.

She was tackled from behind, her forehead bouncing hard off the floor. A knee dug into her back, then she was grabbed by her hair, and her head slammed into the floor twice more for good measure. Lights spun in her vision, and she did not know how much of the blood in her mouth was her own now.

"You stupid little bitch," the guard on top of her said, out of breath. He shifted to the side to get a grip on her clothes. Lada planted her palms on the floor and pushed with all her strength, knocking him off-balance. He fell to the floor. She stood and stomped with every scrap of strength she had.

His windpipe collapsed beneath her foot. As he grabbed at his throat, desperate for air that would never again fill his lungs, she turned to the remaining men.

Judging by the amount of blood on the floor from the turnip-faced man's torn throat, only one guard remained. He was pressed against the wall, balanced on one leg because of his damaged knee, banging on the door.

"Please! Please let me out!"

Lada looked past him at the door's viewing hole. Matthias

stared back at her, aghast. "If you would stop behaving like a rabid beast, I could *help* you," he said.

It had been years since Lada had killed a man without weapons. Her head swam from the blows, and she spat. She did not like the taste in her mouth. And she did not like the bodies on the floor. Why had they made her do this? "I have already had your version of help. I do not need any more. But he does. Open the door."

Matthias turned his head. "Get me more men!" he barked.

"They will not come soon enough." Lada spat blood again. The man next to the door had begun weeping. Matthias did not follow her order to open the door. She could show no weakness. She went far into herself, past the animal instincts that had propelled her to kill the other men. This one was more of a choice.

But there was no choice. She would do what must be done, as she always had.

Matthias, coward that he was, did not even watch as Lada broke his soldier's other knee, and then his neck.

———•———

Lada knew what Mara would have advised her. What Radu would have. What Nicolae would have. What even Daciana would have.

Play the part. Do as she was told. Survive.

But she was a prince. She had other methods of survival. She had cut through years and lives to get there. There were those in Europe who still believed in her, and those in Wallachia who would never give up on her.

She was prince. She did not have it in her to be anything else. And she would never give Matthias the satisfaction of thinking he had beaten her.

An hour later, the next attempt to dress her involved ten men. Lada did not stand a chance, and she knew it. But she did as much damage as she could in the meantime. After they had stripped her of her chain mail, leaving only her underclothes on, they kicked her and threw her in the corner. Then they grabbed the three bodies and hurried from her cell. That, at least, was gratifying.

Standing as carefully as she could to avoid showing how much she had been hurt over the course of the two attacks, Lada stalked to the door.

"At least now you look like a woman," Matthias said.

"And yet you still look nothing like a king." She smiled, her teeth bloody, her face covered in gore, until he turned with a poorly suppressed shudder and left.

Only when night had fallen and it was dark did she finally collapse onto the cot, curling around herself and feeling everything she had lost.

36

Tirgoviste

NAZIRA, TRUE TO HER word, had not only set herself and Fatima up in a room but had also secured the one next to it, for Radu. Radu was curled around Cyprian in the dark. He had thought he would never be happy in this castle.

He had been wrong.

He pressed his forehead against Cyprian's, relishing the tickle of the other man's breath on his face. It meant this was real. Radu would take all the evidence he could get.

They lay on top of Radu's bed, limbs tangled. Their discarded boots and turbans lay on the floor. Radu wrapped his fist in Cyprian's shirt, pulling him closer. "I cannot believe you are actually here."

Cyprian laughed, the sound as soft and intimate as the darkness around them. "You have no idea how long I have wanted this."

"You could . . . tell me?"

Radu felt the laughter in Cyprian's chest. He put his palm flat against it, relishing the beat of the other man's heart. His heart now, too.

"You know I wanted to know you from the first moment we met."

"I remember that, too. You made an impression when I thought I could not see anyone but . . ." Radu drifted off. There were still so many tender edges of their history that they would have to be careful around. It had been filled with terrible things. Which only made this miracle of connection feel even more precious and sacred.

"It was my smile, right?" Cyprian nuzzled his face against Radu's cheek, and Radu felt the smile there.

"No, that caught me our second meeting. The first, it was your eyes."

"Hmm," Cyprian said. "It was not your eyes that attracted me."

"What was it?"

"I do not know if anyone has ever told you, but you are quite a beautiful person."

This time it was Radu's turn to laugh, though his was sheepish. "I have heard that on occasion. Though the term more preferred is 'Radu the Handsome.'"

"Radu *cel Frumos*," Cyprian murmured, using the Wallachian words. His own language had never sounded so lovely to Radu. Even the name that had been used as a taunt sounded new and clean when Cyprian used it. It gave him hope that his past would not haunt him forever. He had not done or experienced anything he could not recover from—not with Cyprian at his side.

"It is such a relief to be able to touch you," Cyprian said, brushing his lips across Radu's throat. Radu's pulse strained with the effort of keeping up with his emotions. He had imagined how these things would feel, but he had never come close. Every part of his body was alive in a way he had felt only in battle. But instead of feeling disconnected and merely reacting to things around him, he felt completely and utterly connected to himself. Every touch, every move was deliberate.

"It was not easy in Constantinople," Radu said, "trying to hide how you affected me. And trying desperately not to be affected."

Cyprian laughed. "I am glad you suffered, too! Do you know how often I tried teasing some sort of reaction out of you?"

"That night in the forge . . ."

Cyprian slid his hand along Radu's waist, letting it rest where Radu's hip bone jutted out. "I would have leapt over the table at the slightest indication from you."

"There is a reason I kept the table between us! I was trying so hard not to love you."

Cyprian nodded, his face still against Radu's neck. "It was an impossible situation." Someday they would talk more about it; they had time. Right now what they needed was closeness.

"I always feared that *this*," Radu said, kissing Cyprian's forehead, "was an impossible situation."

Cyprian scooted back, taking Radu's face in his hands and peering at him in the dark. Radu could just make out the details of his expression. Cyprian looked worried. "Is it? For you? Orthodoxy is my religion the same way my father is my father. Distantly, and only because I was born to it. In Constantinople I saw too much damage done by people wielding the will of God like a weapon. But in Islam, can we . . . can you . . ."

Radu smiled. He had agonized over these things enough.

"I believe that God is merciful and great and beyond our comprehension. And Nazira always told me she feels closest to God when she feels love. I think she is right. In a way, love is the highest expression of faith—in ourselves, in others, in the world. I can expand my faith to allow myself happiness in this life, and trust in God's love and mercy *after* this life." He paused. "Though . . . I would like to follow as many rules as I can. The structure of Islam is important to me. It has been a scaffold of protection and comfort."

Teasingly, Cyprian lowered his hand, tracing his way down Radu's abdomen but stopping just shy of . . . where Radu would have liked him to continue toward.

"So what you are saying is that we need to be married very soon," Cyprian said, his lips right against Radu's ear.

"Yes," Radu gasped. "Very, very soon." His marriage to Nazira was legal. Her marriage to Fatima was spiritual, but even more binding. Radu would do the same with Cyprian.

Cyprian moved his hand back up, resting it over Radu's heart. It was both a relief and a disappointment. But as Cyprian moved closer and they breathed together, drifting toward sleep, Radu knew they had time to explore desire. There was no fear or desperation here. Only happiness and the incredible grace of loving and being loved.

All his life, it was the only thing he had ever truly wanted. He had found it in Islam. He had found it in his connection with Nazira. And now he had found the fullest form of it here. He rested his head on Cyprian's chest, falling asleep to the music of the heart that beat with everything Radu needed in this life.

37

Hunedoara

Two weeks into her captivity, Lada was fairly certain
Matthias was poisoning her. She could barely eat what
they gave her. As often as not, she threw it up. Though why he
was choosing poison, she did not know.

No, she did. It was a coward's way out. She only wished
he would increase the dosage and finish her off instead of this
lingering torment. Perhaps it was God's punishment. She had
given him the tools to take the throne, and he had poisoned
the sickly child prince to get there. Now she would die the
same way.

Though if God were interested in punishing her, she had a
great many sins worse than enabling Matthias. Had she reached
too far? Killed too many? Disregarded the advice of those who
truly cared about her?

Sometimes she felt them, here, with her. Nicolae in particular. He said nothing, but when she awoke from her dreams
of the bloody banquet when she had killed all the Danesti
boyars and begun the journey that led to this cell, she could

only remember the way he had looked at her. The way he had watched.

He had known, even then. And he had warned her. Radu had warned her, too. Everyone had warned her, and she had defied them. And she had won!

And now she was here.

All her rage had bled away, leaving her perpetually cold. She followed the small patch of sun that made it through to the floor. It was her only companion. She tried to move as much as she could, afraid of losing her strength and fighting ability, but a heavy lethargy of both body and soul pulled at her.

The eighteenth morning she lay on the floor, curled into a ball to fit as much of her body in the square of sunlight as was possible.

"Child, why are you in your underclothes?" Oana exclaimed.

Lada stood and rushed to the door. Oana stared back at her through the hole.

"You are alive!" Lada grabbed the bars. She had lost track of her nurse when they had been ambushed in the throne room. She had not allowed herself to dwell on that, but her relief at seeing Oana's wrinkled and worn face was almost overwhelming. Now that she knew Oana was not dead, she felt how deeply that death would have wounded her. She took a deep breath, pushing her fingers over her eyes, then reaching back to the window.

Oana put her hands over Lada's. "I am alive, yes. They tried to get information from me, but I am an old woman who knows nothing and can barely speak Wallachian, much less understand Hungarian. All I know how to do is sew. I have certainly never been privy to any of your plans."

Lada grinned, relieved that at least Oana was doing well in captivity.

"And now?"

"Now, at the insistence of Mara Brankovic, who has written several times, I have finally been permitted to bring you your food. Matthias says you are not eating much."

"He is poisoning me."

Oana peered down at whatever she carried. "I will eat some of it. Then we can know for certain."

Lada shook her head. "No reason for us both to die."

"Lada, my child, I have been with you since you were born and I do not want to live after you die." She leaned against the door and picked at Lada's food.

"Tastes fine," she said.

Lada wrinkled her nose in disgust. "Do you have any weapons? Those will serve me far better than food, poisoned or otherwise."

"They checked me very thoroughly. Actually, it is the most interested any man has been in my body for nearly twenty years now. I invited him back to my chambers, but he did not seem to understand."

Lada laughed, unable to help it. She was more profoundly grateful for Oana, here in the midst of her despair, than she had thought possible. She would even consent to having her hair combed if such a thing were possible through the door.

Oana glanced casually to the side. "Good. The guard does not speak Wallachian. He did not so much as flinch at my filthy implications." She began passing the food to Lada. "I feel fine. I will let you know immediately if I die, though." Oana stopped, staring into the dim cell. "What the devil is that?"

Lada followed Oana's gaze to the tableau she had built along the edge of her cot.

"Oh. The guards think it is funny to bring them to me. They say it will remind me of home and keep me from getting too sad." Several rats had been impaled on tiny stakes and pinned into grotesque positions. The stakes, unfortunately, were too small and flimsy to serve any practical purpose. "They are trying to upset me, so I display them instead."

Oana wrinkled her nose in disgust. "Pass them here. I will get rid of them."

Lada leaned against the door to rest. She needed to move more, to be active even in these confined conditions. "I will keep them. I can show no weakness to these worms. But enough about my cell. Tell me what is happening out there."

"You will not like it."

"Tell me."

"Radu is in Tirgoviste. He has put Aron Danesti on the throne."

Lada's jaw ached, but she could not unclench it. "Our men in the mountains?'

"We hear nothing of them, which is good. It means they have not been found or betrayed us."

"And what of the rest of Europe? How do they respond to Matthias's bold move in taking me prisoner?"

"No one knows."

Lada sighed. She had hoped that Mara would tell Radu, or someone who would spread the news. But Mara was Mehmed's, and would do what she was told because that was how she stayed free and powerful. How different the world would be if only merit and skill were rewarded, if only ambition created results. Instead, it was a tangled mess of threads. Lada had tried so hard to stay out of that web, to owe her power to no one. But the closer she got to transcending the strands that had bound her throughout her whole life, the more the web tightened around her.

Oana continued. "As far as everyone else knows, you are still hiding in the mountains. Or underneath the beds of small children who refuse to obey their parents. But at least Matthias cannot kill you and risk the ire of your fan the pope."

Lada pushed her head against the wood door, wishing the planks would part and allow her through. "Does the pope know where I am? Is there help there?"

"No. He thinks you are hiding as well."

"How do you know all this? Have you taken a lover here? Are you playing spy?" Lada could not imagine such a thing, but then again, Oana was always surprising her.

Oana laughed, a deep, guttural burst like Bogdan's. Lada was hit anew with longing to be anywhere but here. To be back in the mountains with Bogdan. At least she had made him stay there. He would have died, otherwise. She clutched the locket, which they had let her keep. It comforted her, knowing Wallachia was waiting. Bogdan was waiting.

Comforted and drove her mad in equal measures. What good was she to anyone here?

"I did not find any of this out myself." Oana shifted to the side, cocking her head subtly to the left. Lada leaned against the opening and looked at where a man was sweeping the floor under the dispassionate gaze of a guard. She did not spend much time looking out the window, feeling it made her appear weak, but she should have paid more attention to who was out there.

Unlike most people, Lada had trained herself to notice that bland, blank face.

Stefan.

"He began working here two weeks before you were captured. They suspect nothing. I should go now," Oana said with a smile. "You hold tight." She reached a hand through the opening and rested one dry palm against Lada's cheek. Lada watched her leave, careful to pay no further attention to Stefan.

For the first time since she had been locked up, hope fluttered in her chest. It was as small and fragile as the rodents twisted in macabre death by her bed.

38

Tirgoviste

WHILE RADU WAS GRATEFUL for Cyprian's help, having him sit in on meetings was distracting. Pleasantly so, but distracting nonetheless. With all the upheaval, no one had questioned Cyprian's presence. Radu had merely introduced him as a close friend and advisor. Radu's men had accepted Cyprian without question. And Aron and Andrei were too busy scheming to wonder where he had come from. Fortunately the meetings were conducted in Turkish: Radu's men did not speak Wallachian, and Aron and Andrei were fluent in Turkish.

"Radu!"

Radu tore his eyes from the teasing smile on Cyprian's lips. "What?"

Aron frowned. "I said, how many do you think we should plan on for the celebration?"

Radu leaned back in his chair, struggling to keep his expression neutral. "I thought we agreed paying for that much food and drink as well as furnishing all the guest rooms in the castle was not the best use of resources right now."

"We agreed on nothing," Andrei said. "You said we need to get the boyars on our side. How else can we prove to them that we are in control?"

Radu strained to keep the incredulity he felt off his face. "The best way we can show them the country is under control is to actually get the country under control. My men are still in the mountains hunting down Lada's forces. We have heard no word of her or her location for weeks, meaning any gathering of boyars is inherently risky. It is not like her to give us this much time to fortify. It makes me wonder what she has planned."

"Perhaps she is dead," Andrei said.

"She is not dead," Radu snapped.

"How can you be sure?"

He was not sure. Or at least there was no way for him to be sure. But he could not imagine that Lada would die alone and in secret. Or that she could be dead and he would not somehow know. Surely her death would be marked by something. A comet. A great hole opening in the earth. A tempest, a flood, a fire. A force such as Lada could not depart this world without leaving one last mark.

Radu rubbed his forehead. "Regardless, until we discover news of her, we must operate as though an attack is imminent. And if we want to avoid mass starvation in the coming year, we need to plant and rehabilitate the fields as soon as possible. People have started returning to the villages. Any resources not needed for protection should go toward rebuilding."

Aron smoothed his vest. "I think my brother is right. A show of strength is called for."

"Thus the forces in the mountains hunting down enemies," Cyprian muttered in Greek. Radu coughed to cover up his answering laugh.

"This is the way things are done," Aron said. "It is what my father would have done."

"Your father is dead, as are many of the boyars." Radu did not mean for it to be harsh, but Aron flinched. Andrei sat straighter, a protective glare sharpening his eyes. Radu held up his hands in placation. "What I am saying is, my sister has pushed things so far past what they were, we will have to be very careful in how we put them back together. If you had a horse that got free and lived wild for a year, you would not immediately saddle it and expect to safely ride. You would bring it back, feed it, make it feel safe, and remind it why you are a good master. Lada destroyed all the stables. We need to bring everything back to its place before we can expect a return to normalcy."

"You are the one who told us we need to act like things are normal in order for them to be so!" Aron again smoothed his vest, fixing a button that never seemed to stay fastened. "I am diverting funds for the celebration. I will repay the sultan by adding boys to the Janissary tribute. As vaivode of Wallachia, I do not need your permission." He held Radu's gaze firmly. "For anything," he added.

Radu opened his mouth to argue, then closed it and pasted a smile in place. "Whatever you feel is best. I will release the funds designated to you and then continue my work as directed by the sultan. Please let me know if you require anything further."

Radu stood, bowed stiffly, and walked from the room. He was followed by Kiril, his other lead men, and Cyprian.

"Aron is a fool," Cyprian said with a sigh.

Radu did not disagree, and it was disheartening. "I had hoped he would do better. He is pretending like he simply inherited the throne from his father. Everything is different, though. We cannot continue on as things were. And I do not think we should." As much as Radu had loved training with the Janissaries and valued the men he led, he also thought trading more Wallachian youth in order to throw parties was not the best footing for Aron to start on.

"How many people have come back to the city?" Radu asked Kiril.

"A hundred, perhaps? A few more come every day, but it is a trickle, not a flood."

Radu shook his head. "And Aron wants to celebrate. We cannot even be sure that some of the citizens are not working with Lada. She may be reviled by the boyars, but we should not underestimate how much she did for the peasants of this country. We will have to work hard to earn their support, or even just their complacency."

Kiril bid them farewell, and Radu and Cyprian walked alone toward their rooms.

"Do you think Aron is up to the task?" Cyprian asked as they joined Nazira and Fatima.

"I hope so." Radu could not help the fear that the cycle of bloodshed over the throne of Wallachia would continue indefinitely. Nothing ever changed.

No. Some things changed. Radu looked at his hand, his

fingers laced with Cyprian's. It did not seem possible that those were his fingers, that this was his life. How could something so simple as holding hands with another person feel like a miracle?

As though sensing his thoughts, Cyprian lifted their hands and put his lips against the back of Radu's hand, then rested his cheek there.

Nazira frowned as she listened to Radu's report of the situation, not looking up from playing with Fatima's hair. Fatima lay on the floor with her head in Nazira's lap. Cyprian and Radu were across from them in the sitting room that connected their two bedrooms. For the first time in his life, the castle felt like home. Not because of the place, but because of the people.

"I cannot believe he thinks a party is the solution. I have hinted very strongly he should focus on preparing marriage offers." Nazira sighed. "He only asks my advice on clothing styles."

"You should have heard him," Cyprian said. "He offers the boyars a dinner party as evidence of his right to be prince."

Nazira lifted her eyes to the ceiling in exasperation. "I do not think he is suited to this. He is not the type of leader capable of transitioning a country in so much turmoil."

"He is the only real choice." Radu closed his eyes, imagining them all back at home in Edirne, or, better yet, the country estate where Nazira and Fatima usually lived. It felt within grasp. He and Cyprian would marry soon, in the same way Fatima and Nazira had, and then ...

And then they would simply *be*. And it would be enough. More than enough.

"There is another heir far more suited to this work," Nazira said.

"Andrei worries me as well. I do not think—"

"Not him." The nagging tone of Nazira's voice forced Radu's eyes open. She was giving him a look full of meaning. "The Draculesti line has just as much claim to the throne."

Radu recoiled. "I do not want this throne. I never have."

"Which is why you are the right person." Nazira's gaze was intense with the confident assurance that carried her through life. "Not because you feel like it is owed you. You would take the throne as a true servant to your people. The prince they both desperately need and deserve. Not a violent warlord, and not a spineless noble. An *actual* prince."

Radu shrugged, but his smile was a challenge to her sentiments. "Alas! The position has already been filled. I will do what I can for him and for Wallachia. And then we are going home." He squeezed Cyprian's hand and felt the warm rush of reassurance as Cyprian squeezed back. "All of us. Permanently."

Nazira's full lips drew down at the corners. "Your people deserve better than Aron."

"You are my people. My people are the three people in this room with me right now."

Only Fatima looked pleased by the sentiment. Nazira's frown did not lift. And Cyprian made a noise in his chest that sounded unsure.

"We will get to Lada before anyone else does. We will send

her back to the empire where she will spend the rest of her days in a prison. And then Aron can find his way as prince without me." Radu spoke with all the authority and confidence he did not feel, willing it to be true. He did not want to have to shoulder the burden of Wallachia. Let it take care of itself as it had never taken care of him.

39

Hunedoara

LADA SAT ON THE floor, her back to the door. The cell that had been cold and dank was now oppressively warm and humid as spring shifted into summer. "I think I am dying."

"Nonsense," Oana chided from the other side. She rapped her knuckles against the wood. "You are not allowed to die. Besides, I have taken one of the cooks as a lover."

"You *what?*" Lada sat up straighter.

"The nights here are long. And it seemed an easy way to make certain your food was safe. He is definitely not poisoning you. First, because no one has told him to. And second, because if you died, I would have no reason to stay here. Poor fool adores me."

Lada did not know whether to laugh or to cut off her ears in an effort to remove the information she had just received.

Oana continued as though none of this was odd. "Now, to be quick. Stefan says there are always at least five guards. The key is kept upstairs in a locked room that also has several guards. He can probably kill the guards on this floor, but he is not certain he can get the key and then come down here and kill them all without raising an alarm. That would make it impossible for you to slip away once the door is opened."

It was still amazing to Lada that the greatest assassin she had ever known had been working as a cleaner for more than three months. He had made himself a fixture of the castle. No one noticed him; he could do whatever he needed to so long as he kept up his duties. She would never look at her own castle servants the same. Assuming she ever got a castle again.

Lada scratched her head, then stared at her filthy fingernails. "So I need to figure out a way to get the guards to open the door themselves."

"While Stefan is here. And he cleans this block only once a week."

Lada wrinkled her nose at the ever-present miasma. "I am aware. Unfortunately, ever since I killed three guards with my bare hands, they have not been willing to open the door." Lada had to pass her chamber pot out through the small hole in the door. That was also how she got water for drinking and washing, food—which after three eternal months still almost always made her throw up—and anything else they saw fit to send her. Usually more rats. She did not have the energy to bother displaying them anymore.

"You will think of something. When you do, we will be ready."

"What if this is it? What if I never get out? I will disappear just as he planned, and he will win. Mehmed will win. All the men will win. I cannot bear it, Oana."

"Who am I speaking to?" Oana reached a hand through the hole and blindly groped for Lada's head. She found it, tangling her fingers in Lada's hair. "It feels like my Lada, but it certainly does not sound like her. Will you really let this king with his fine clothes and his oiled beard and his gilded lies get the best of you? You are a dragon."

Lada nodded. But here, in this sweltering cell, far from her people and her land, she did not feel like a dragon.

For the first time in a long time, she felt like a girl. It terrified her. Because there was nothing in the world more vulnerable to be than a girl.

———◆———

These past three months Lada had spoken only to Oana, who was permitted to visit her once a day for a few minutes. She suspected Mara was behind that kindness. For a while she had wondered if Mehmed would send for her. But she had tried to kill him, and if he transported her all the way to Constantinople, word would get out, ruining Matthias's goal of having her fade from Europe's consciousness.

So when Matthias came to visit her the next day, Lada was happier to speak with him than she ought to have been.

"It pains me to see you like this," he said.

"Let me out and I will show you what pain is."

Matthias laughed. "You are very bad at negotiating. But it is no wonder that my father preferred you over me. You speak the same language. Did you know, he wanted me to marry you?"

"Yes. I knew."

"You did?" A flicker of confusion passed over his face. Lada assumed it was because he could not fathom any woman passing on the opportunity to wed him.

She yawned, stretching her arms over her head. "I felt it

would be disrespectful to your father to marry his son and then murder my husband in his sleep. Though I probably would have murdered you while you were awake, for the satisfaction of watching the look on your face as my knife cut your soul free from your loathsome body."

Matthias leaned closer, peering through the hole. "Why do you make your life so much more difficult than it has to be? You could have been in a house. With servants. With comforts. I would have taken excellent care of you out of respect for what you have accomplished. I am not a fool; I know you have done great things. But you made so many enemies along the way. Does it not trouble you that I have held you these last three *months* and no one has come looking for you? No one has inquired about your location." He twisted his face in mock sympathy. "No one cares that you are gone. You have been replaced on your throne without fanfare or struggle. You may have sent the Ottomans out of your land, but this is your reward." He sighed as though feeling actual pity for her. "I cannot kill you. I do not know if I want to, but even if I did, it would put me at odds with those who admire you. Besides, it is much easier to simply keep you. To let you stay here until everyone has forgotten you. Until your only legacy are the lurid woodcuts and terrifying nighttime stories of the Saxons. You will fade into a monster, a myth. And when that happens, I will be kind. When everything you accomplished has disappeared—and it will not take long—then I will take you out of this cell. And I will let you die."

He paused, considering. "Or I may let you live. I do not think it matters much, either way. The world was never going to permit you to continue. You should have made someone a repulsive wife, had an heir or two, and lived out your life in quiet misery."

Lada lifted an eyebrow coldly. "Your father would be ashamed of you."

Matthias nodded without emotion. "He probably would. I will have to live with that. And I *will* live. I have my crown. I will rule my people, and my reign will be long and fair and touched with glory. And you will be less than a notation in the triumphant history of my life. Who knows, maybe you will have a few lines in the sultan's history as well? You can always hope."

Lada wanted to find words that would do as much damage as she knew her fists could. She wanted to cut this small man to his very core.

But she knew that even though she was better, smarter, stronger, even though she had already done more for Europe than he ever would, even though she had worked and fought harder than he was capable of, he was probably right. He would be rewarded and remembered and respected.

He might even merit some of that, eventually.

"We could have done great things together," Lada said. "If you had but a portion of your father's courage, we could have changed the face of Europe forever."

"But only one of us wants things to change. How they are right now suits my people's needs. And be honest, my pearl. Did you really think the world would change enough to accept a woman as prince?" Matthias searched her face for an answer, genuinely curious. Then, with a shrug, he turned.

Lada watched the space go dark as Matthias walked out of view.

She knew perfectly well how to be a girl. She *was* a girl. People seemed to forget that, or assume she wanted to be something else because of her choices. Hearing Matthias lay out her future in such bleak terms might have sent her into a rage in the past, but she was older than she had been when she got here. She was weary.

She was ready.

The next time the cruel guard came by with a rodent, Lada smiled at him. She opened her eyes wide and smiled through her long, tangled hair. "I want bigger animals," she said. "Rats are not satisfying. Bring me rabbits. Larger animals. Men, if you have any to spare."

His look of gleeful horror confirmed to Lada that he would do as asked, if only to have a new account of her depravity to trade like currency among the other soldiers. She smiled bigger.

Lada lay in a pool of blood, her skin pale, her eyes closed. The blood was cold and congealed, an inelegantly written story of the end of her life spilled out onto stone floors.

"Devil take her," a guard at the door muttered. "Hey! Come look at this."

"Oh, God protect us. What a mess. Hey, you! Stay here. You have quite the cleanup job ahead of you tonight. Josef, go get the keys."

"Should I send word to the king?"

"No, not yet. We should check on her, make sure she is dead. Then move her out quietly so no one notices. After that we can figure out what to tell him. I better not get in trouble for this."

"I liked this job," the second guard said.

"Not me. Look at those animals! She was a monster. Lucifer is dancing happy in his flames tonight to get such a soul for hell."

After a few minutes, the door opened and two pairs of booted feet shuffled into the room.

"God save us, the smell!"

A boot nudged Lada's side. Then her wrist was lifted, held gingerly between two fingers as though the guard was worried her death—or perhaps just the smell—was contagious. "Where is the wound? Her wrists are not cut."

Lada twisted her hand, grabbing the guard's wrist. She yanked him to the floor. A cry went up but was cut short with the swift application of Stefan's blade. Lada's hands around the first guard's throat prevented him from shouting, and Stefan's blade silenced the other one.

"What took you so long?" Lada stood, shaking out her arms and legs to restore circulation. The animal blood made her dress sticky and stiff, but she had no replacements and no time to change.

Stefan wiped his knife on the tunic of one of the dead guards. He had slipped in after them. "I had to kill the ones in the hallway first."

He held out a length of brown cloth, and Lada wrapped

it around herself like a shawl. It hid most of the blood. She hesitated at the threshold, and then stepped into the hallway. It felt like a much bigger distance than it was. "Where is Oana? *She* was supposed to discover my body. I have been lying on the floor for hours!"

Stefan shook his head. "I do not know."

"We agreed that this was the day!"

"She does not always come when she is scheduled."

"We cannot leave without her. We will go to the kitchens, and—"

"Lada, we do not have time."

Lada tried to hurry down the hall. She wanted to feel triumphant, but a wave of dizziness washed over her. It had been so long since she had felt well, since she had been able to move enough. She leaned against the rough wall. Marveled that after so many weeks, it was a different wall than the four she had become accustomed to.

Stefan walked ahead of her, checking for other guards. "We do not have time, and you do not have the strength. If you want to get out, we need to leave now."

"You can go get Oana, then."

"If I leave you, you will not make it out."

Lada's heart raced in her chest. There had to be another way. A way to escape *with* Oana.

"If I go and pull her out of the kitchens, someone is bound to notice," Stefan said. "I cannot keep both of you secret."

"She would not leave me behind."

Stefan shook his head. "No, she would not."

Lada had to make a decision. And she had to make it now.

"She would not leave me behind, but she would tell me to leave her." If Oana was in the kitchen, she had witnesses and an alibi. No one could hold her accountable for the dead men in the cell. But they could hold her as prisoner. Forever.

Lada was trading her freedom for Oana's.

Accepting Stefan's elbow for support, she fled from the prison building and out of Hunedoara, hating herself with each step. Hating Matthias more. And hating the world most of all, for taking the people she cared about and making her choose between them and Wallachia every time. Oana had once told her at this very castle that no sacrifice was too great in the cause of their country. Lada prayed that Oana still felt the same, would still feel the same when she discovered their abandonment of her.

But another day in that prison might kill Lada. And she would not go back for anything.

40

Snagov Island Monastery

"TELL ME AGAIN WHY Aron sent you to an island monastery far from Tirgoviste on a seemingly unimportant task that could have been done by anyone else?" Nazira batted her eyelashes innocently. Fatima shushed her reproachfully. Cyprian laughed.

Radu sighed.

Their ride here had been peaceful. Too peaceful. The entire area between Tirgoviste and Snagov was still almost empty. Would the whole country hide in the mountains forever? It made Aron's task of ruling them far more difficult. How could he tax or command a populace he could not find?

Radu corrected his sturdy mare's direction, guiding her back in line with the others. In front and behind were Janissaries, but it was easy to feel like it was just the four of them. "Aron is sending me because Mehmed was not able to take Snagov—attacking the island was too logistically complicated and not worth the time. We need to make certain that the monks there are loyal to the throne, and also invite one of them to take over the cathedral in Tirgoviste. No one has been willing to so far."

"Yes, and that entire plan makes perfect sense. But the reasonable course of action would be to send someone to do it *other* than the man in charge of all the military forces currently in the country." Nazira shushed Fatima before Fatima could shush her this time.

Cyprian twisted his mouth to the side and drew his eyebrows together. Radu loved every single expression Cyprian's face was capable of, though his genuine smile was still—and always would be—his favorite. "I am inclined to agree with Nazira. Aron is trying to push you to the margins, decrease your visibility. You are already a threat."

Radu could not deny it. Things had become increasingly tense between himself and the Danesti brothers. Radu rubbed his forehead, gazing at the dock they were drawing closer to. "Aron has nothing I want. I wish he could see that. Still, we are close to being finished. By the time we return I should have all my scouts back. It has been over three months with no word of Lada. I cannot imagine anything she might plan that would require this much silence and inaction. I suspect something else has happened." He did not like thinking about what might have ended her aggressions. After everything she had done, he still did not want her to suffer. He only wanted her to fail. "Regardless, I am confident we can move forward very soon."

"Forward to where?" Fatima asked.

Radu dismounted and offered a hand to help her off her horse. "Somewhere out of Wallachia."

"I do not know," Cyprian said. "This area is quite nice."

He patted his horse and stretched his broad shoulders. Radu quickly looked away—and then remembered he did not have to. He let his eyes linger, drinking the other man in. Cyprian caught him staring. His answering smile was sharper than normal. Sharper, and more devious.

The Janissaries gathered and dismounted as well. Radu had left Kiril in charge in Tirgoviste, trusting him to keep an eye on things there. The guards who had accompanied them would cross over to the island with them, in case they encountered any hostility. In an effort to appear nonthreatening, Radu had dressed Wallachian-style. He had left his beloved turban at home and wore a rather absurd hat instead. He wanted to return to flowing robes and beautiful fabrics, leave behind these layers of breeches and vests and coats. Not only were they ugly, they were damnably hot in the heavy summer air.

Nazira and Fatima, too, had shifted their dress. They did not look quite Wallachian, but they did not look Turkish, either. As with everything, Nazira prettified whatever she wore simply by virtue of being in it. Radu suspected she could wear the dirty wool right off a lamb's back and make it look deliberate and fashionable. Fatima's clothes were serviceable and plain. Though Radu told her she did not need to play at being a servant here, she preferred to go unnoticed. Looking like a maid was an easy way to become invisible to anyone who had no use for you.

Cyprian at least was comfortable in Wallachian clothes, as they were similar to styles he had worn in Constantinople. He had stopped wearing the Janissary uniform—where Nazira had gotten one for him, Radu did not know, though he suspected somewhere was a Janissary still too charmed by her to bother being angry that he was walking about naked.

After issuing instructions to the guards, they walked to the rickety dock. It was apparent that the previous dock had been burned and dismantled. The replacement was just a few planks nailed together, but there was a boat waiting. With a queasy lurch, all Radu's thoughts twisted away.

"Oh, a boat! Radu loves boats," Nazira teased.

Radu climbed gingerly into the back, with Cyprian sitting at his side. Nazira and Fatima took a nearby bench, and the rest of the guards filled in where they could. They helped row, following the increasingly annoyed directions of the Wallachian-speaking ferryman. Radu translated as best he could in between trying not to vomit.

When they reached the island, Radu nearly fell over in his haste to rejoin firm ground. Cyprian leaned close and whispered, "Perhaps I was wrong. Perhaps the real reason you stayed behind in Constantinople was not out of altruistic duty to my little cousins, but because you knew you could not survive a boat ride."

Radu laughed weakly, and Cyprian joined him. That Cyprian could not only forgive his past but also find ways to joke about it was deeply reassuring. It would always be a tender spot—but as a scar, not an open wound.

After his stomach had settled, Radu finally took a look at the island. It was tiny, the borders marshy and overgrown. Insects droned, lending the humid and heavy air its own music. Short but dense trees offered the promise of shade, and a path led to carefully tended garden rows. The monastery rose in the distance, pale-red stone towers marking its place. Though the guards around them were on high alert, the monk ambling toward them seemed utterly unconcerned by the appearance of this many armed men.

"Hello," Radu said. "I am . . ." He paused, unsure whether Radu Bey or Radu Dracul would get a better reception. He had already dressed the part of Wallachian nobility, though. May as well continue to play it. "I am Radu Dracul, here on behalf of Prince Aron Danesti, vaivode of Wallachia."

The monk, his face lined and tanned with years of being outdoors, did not smile. But something in the lines around his eyes shifted with amusement. "Prince Aron? I was not aware we had a new one. Or that we needed one."

"Yes." Radu smiled, though he did not quite know where he stood with this man. "He sends his greetings and asks that a priest join him in Tirgoviste to take over the cathedral."

"Hmm. Well, come along with me to the monastery. We can offer you food and rest." The monk turned back down the path. Radu walked by his side, the others falling in behind.

"Have you been to our island before?" the monk asked. "You seem familiar."

"Not since I was a small boy."

"Ah yes. I remember now. Your sister told me."

"Lada has been here?"

"She came last autumn. In fact, look there—" The monk pointed to the spires of the church, nearly finished, with men on ropes clinging to the outside and hammering in shingles. "She donated the funds for the new building. She has been a good patron to us."

Radu frowned, puzzled. The church was functional and elegant with dusty stone that would age in beauty the way all churches here did.

"You seem surprised," the monk said.

"I never knew my sister to be particularly concerned with the welfare of her soul."

The monk smiled slyly. "Are we not all? Besides, as she put it, our church is Wallachian and thus deserves more glory and trappings than other gods."

"Ah, that makes more sense." If it was done for Wallachia in competition with other countries, then Radu could understand Lada's desire to improve the island. In fact, he was surprised she had not made the church much larger. And spikier. "What did you think of her?"

"She is singular. I have never encountered her like—though I have lived the last twenty years on this island, and we do not have many visitors. Still, while I was initially skeptical, reports from the countryside indicate that your sister is a leader of remarkable vision and strength."

"Was," Radu gently corrected.

"Oh?" The monk's face twisted playfully. "Mircea!" he called out. Radu cringed involuntarily, hearing his cruel older brother's name. But Mircea was dead, and his name common. One of the men working on the church turned his head. "Who is prince of Wallachia?" shouted the monk.

"Lada Dracul, may she spit ever in the faces of the Turks!"

The guards around Radu shifted uneasily, but none of the workers moved aggressively, or even paid them much mind.

"Does he not know a new prince has been crowned?" Radu

asked. Maybe people had not returned to their towns because they were unaware.

The monk opened the church's doors, the dim interior cool and inviting. "I think, my son, that he does not care."

Lunch was fish with summer vegetables and rough bread. The monks were polite and kind, patiently disinterested in anything Radu had to say. And even less interested in taking a position in the capital.

"Perhaps check in one of the village churches," the monk that had led him here suggested.

"Everyone is afraid to come to Tirgoviste," Radu confessed, staring up at a mural of Christ. "Most are still hiding in the mountains. Those that have come down are much like your man on the roof. They do not care about the new prince. We cannot even begin to collect taxes. We are mostly just praying they plant fields so we will have a harvest."

"It is a different country now. Your sister offered them change. They will not give it up easily."

"But she is not even here."

The monk lifted his hands as though offering evidence. "She is, though. As long as she is alive, so are the changes she wrought. The gates have been flung open, and the sheep have wandered. I suspect this Aron is not up to the task of shepherding them back in."

Radu could not argue with that. He said nothing, and studiously avoided Nazira's pointed look.

The monk stood. "Would you like us to do anything for you before you leave?"

Radu did not want to tell the monk that this religion had nothing he wanted any longer. They were good people—and he wished them all the best in living their faith—but it was only a childhood memory for him. He felt nothing for it, either good or ill. That, he supposed, was a blessing of sorts. It was nice to have something in Wallachia that he was neutral toward, something that caused no pain.

"Will you tell me if my sister visits again?" His own visit had given him the clarity that he was not only fighting his sister—he was fighting the very *idea* of her. And that was just as, if not more, elusive and difficult to target. Aron was not likely to inspire devotion or encourage a change of loyalties in anyone who had responded to his sister.

The monk gazed up at the same mural. "She did say she enjoyed being here. She found something as close to peace as a creature like her ever can, I think. I hope she will come again. And if she does, she will be welcomed, and none of her enemies will be warned." The monk looked at Radu, lifting an eyebrow. "Are you her enemy?"

Though Radu had no attachment to this religion, it was more than he had in him to lie to a man who had devoted his life to God. "I do not know. I think I might be."

The monk nodded, no reproach in his face. "You should spend the night. See if you can find some of the peace here as well."

No matter what he did, this country still belonged to Lada. He had never been able to take away something once she claimed it. Not their father, not Mehmed, and now not Wallachia. "Maybe," Radu said, but he knew there would be no peace for him here. Lada had seen to that.

41

Town of Arges

LADA HAD BEEN TOO miserable during their escape to think about much of anything. Stefan had gotten horses somewhere, and it had all been accomplished silently and swiftly. No one looked twice at a man riding next to a hunched-over, shawl-wrapped woman. Even if she was dirty and barefoot.

Once out of the city, it was all countryside and farmland. Summer had passed its zenith and was slipping from its muggy, warm haze toward autumn. Lada should have been overwhelmed with joy to be outside again, but she found herself aghast and resentful. How dare the seasons change, how dare nature continue its trek forward, when she had been so cruelly stalled? And how dare anything be so soul-nourishingly lovely when she had left behind her nurse in order to save herself?

She rejected the beauty of the Hungarian landscape, ignored the vibrant green warmth of Transylvania, and let herself take in only a little relief and happiness when they finally crossed into Wallachia. Even in this state, she could not resist loving her country. But she feared what she would find when she got there. Ahead of them loomed the mountains along the Arges, where she would return to her fortress. To Bogdan.

Without his mother.

Lada did not think Matthias would kill Oana. Or at least she hoped he would not. He seemed the type of person to think a servant woman inconsequential enough that he might not have truly noticed her. Besides, Oana had been nowhere near when Lada had escaped. Surely that would be in her favor. Still, Lada had to add one more name to the list of those who were not at her side.

Matei. Traitor, still missed as her first meaningful Janissary loss.

Petru. Murdered, avenged.

Nicolae. Died for her, which was perhaps why he haunted her most.

Oana. Sacrificed, which would doubtless haunt her.

And always, ever, the phantom presences at her right and her left: Mehmed and Radu. Someday she would grow old enough that she would no longer care about the two best companions of her childhood.

She hoped.

Both that she would no longer care, and that she would grow old. Neither seemed likely on that dazzling summer afternoon. Huddled and hunched in the saddle, Lada was bothered not only by what nature was flagrantly displaying but also by what it was not:

Farmland. They rode through acres and acres of unplanted land. Last fall, this very stretch had provided ample crops. This fall, there would be nothing. Which meant that the coming winter would be far deadlier than the previous spring. The Ottomans could be tricked, defeated, turned away. Starvation was the world's most patient and unrelenting foe. What had she done? How could she fix it?

Stefan drew his horse to a stop. "I am not going to Poenari."

Lada sighed. Another name to add to the list of those she had lost, and with him, Daciana. He had warned her; apparently that time was here. "Are you certain?"

He nodded gravely. "My debt to you is fully paid."

Lada lifted an eyebrow. "Well, not quite."

"Oh?"

"My debt for freeing you from the Ottomans, yes. But do not forget it was my choice to allow Daciana to remain with our company. If I had refused her, you would still be a shadow of a man, untethered, *mine.*" Lada scowled. "I should not have let her stay."

Stefan rewarded her with the barest of smiles, and she looked away so she would not get emotional. At least this one friend she was losing to *life*, not death.

Lada brushed off her heavy emotions and made her tone befitting that of a prince. "Do one more task for me, and then I will tell you where Daciana is."

"What task?"

"There are usurpers in my castle. Kill Aron and Andrei Danesti, so it is clear that I am the only prince Wallachia has or needs. It should not be too difficult for you."

"It will be done." He turned his horse away. "One last favor between friends."

"Do you not want to know where Daciana is?" Lada called.

Stefan looked over his shoulder, and, for the first time ever, Lada caught the full power of his smile. She understood what Daciana had seen, and why it might be worth having more than just the military loyalty of such a man. "I would not be a very good spy if I had not already figured it out on my own."

Lada laughed, undone by that smile. "Then why did you stay?"

"I told you: I am grateful. I wish you well, my prince. It has been an honor."

If Lada were not so weary and ill, she might have been angry at his departure. But the ghost of Nicolae was heavy at her side, reminding her it was not so bad to lose Stefan this way. There were worse things. "You had better raise your own little Lada to be a terror."

"I expect nothing less."

Lada watched as the last of the men she had trained with, the last of her core group of loyal allies and followers—friends—rode away. It was the end of an era. She did not know if she would be weaker for it. She decided she would not be. Each of them had, in one way or another, been sacrificed for the greater good of Wallachia. Had she not decided she would sacrifice everything it took?

Pulling the shawl tighter around her, she rode forward, toward her fortress and toward the last remaining friend of her youth. But what was she really riding toward?

She took account of her resources.

The only member of her inner circle left was Bogdan.

She had a few other men she knew to be good, but it was not the same. With Daciana and Oana lost from her household, she would never again trust anyone in the castle—assuming she got it back. After all, she had seen how easy it was for a servant to be someone else entirely.

Hungary was against her, though she knew Matthias would not fight her outright. She probably should have sent Stefan to kill *him*, but Wallachia always had to be her first priority. Regardless, there would be no conflict but also no aid from Hungary.

Moldavia was not against her, but her cousin King Stephen had taken land from her. That had to be answered with blood, so they would not be allies in the future. Maybe before then she could maneuver him into helping her. She could delay revenge for now.

Bulgaria, of course, hated her and would for some time. Albania and Serbia were firmly Ottoman vassals. She had no love for or from the Transylvanians or the Saxons.

The pope held her in esteem, but her country was not Catholic and he would only praise them, offering no real help. What help he had sent had gone through someone he trusted more—for all the good that did them. She would most certainly write of Matthias's deceit, though. Let him explain his crown to the papal treasury that bought it.

And even in her own country, her resources were sparse. Her brother had been helping the Danesti usurper. Tirgoviste would be fortified. Any boyars left would have flocked to him. Assuming Galesh Basarab and his men were dead—she hoped they were, but did not count on it considering the information had come from Matthias—Radu would not have gotten a huge influx of men from the remaining scattered boyars. But still, she did not relish the idea of besieging her own capital.

So: enemies within and without. All men in power set against her. Almost no one she could trust. A country in disarray. A fall without a harvest. A people hidden in the mountains. A capital filled with snakes.

There was only one solution.

She had been too kind, too gentle. She had tried keeping what she could intact, tried building on what was already there. But the entire foundation was rotten. She could not build a strong kingdom by removing only a few of the most decay-ridden stones. She would have to dismantle the entire thing.

She would have to burn it—all of it—to the ground. Only then could Wallachia rise anew from the ashes.

She sat straighter, eyes on the horizon. There was no room for kindness, no room for mercy. Matthias had proved that she could not play by any rules that already existed. She would have to become something altogether new.

The countryside around her was hushed, quiet, as though even the insects and wind recognized the passing of a great predator. She again imagined wings unfurling behind her, covering all the land in shadow and fire. There would be no more order, no more structure. She would kill the leaders of every country on her borders, and all their heirs. She would sow absolute chaos and destruction.

And she would be there, in the center, curled around her

own land. Wallachia would survive. It always survived. But with her there, and everything around them descended into deadly disorder, Wallachia would finally thrive.

After all, fire and blood and death were nothing to a country led by a dragon.

42

Tirgoviste

RADU STOOD AT THE top of the tower. This tower had heralded so much change in his life. First, when he and Lada watched Hunyadi ride into the city, signaling the end of their lives here as their father petitioned the Ottomans for support—and traded their lives as collateral. Though it had been terrifying at the time, it had been the best thing that could have happened to Radu. And now the tower had been the site of the most unexpected and joyful reunion of his life.

As though called by his thoughts, Cyprian joined him. The air was sharp with the first hints of impending autumn. Radu shivered, and Cyprian put an arm around him as they looked out over the dawn breaking soft and gentle through the mist. All the scars of the past few months had blended with the green, leaving everything muted and peaceful. The fields around Tirgoviste were full and almost ready for harvest. It had been an unconventional use of trained killers, but thanks to Radu's Janissaries working under the direction of a few grizzled farmers, there would be enough food to see Tirgoviste—and any refugees that joined them—safely through the winter. He had been stationed here to protect the city, after all.

Radu was proud of those fields. Aron had demanded Radu send his men into the mountains to hunt down Lada, but Radu had known there were more important things. And when Aron did not starve to death over the coming long winter, he would be grateful. Or if not grateful, at least resentful that Radu had, once again, been right.

A lone rider was leaving the city, heading toward the mountains. Radu did not begrudge him his freedom—but only because his own escape was fast approaching.

"We are leaving today," Radu said, turning from the landscape he could almost love now.

"Today?" Cyprian took Radu's hand in his own. Radu wondered when touching Cyprian would not feel like a shock, if he would ever get used to the thrill of it. He hoped he did not. He hoped they would have a lifetime to find out.

"Aron does not want me here anymore. I trust Kiril. He will do a good job leading the men we leave behind. And no one has heard a breath of news about Lada since the attack. That was four months ago. If she were going to strike, she would have done it by now. This waiting, biding her time—"

"It could be strategic."

"But it is not her style. She would not have wanted to lose momentum like this. I think—" Radu shook his head. "I suspect she is no longer in control."

"Do you think she is dead?" Cyprian asked gently.

"She is too mean to die. I am sure whatever has happened to her is not good, but I do not think she is dead." Radu put a hand over his heart, wondering if he would feel her death, if he would know. They had been separated for so long. She had looked at him that night in Mehmed's tent as though faced with a memory, not a man.

"Though," Radu said, thoughtfully, "if she is dead, that means I will live forever."

Cyprian gave him a puzzled smile. "I do not follow your reasoning."

Radu leaned forward and rested his forehead against Cyprian's. "A long time ago, Lada promised that no one would kill me but her. So if she cannot fulfill her end of the promise, it appears I will be immortal."

Cyprian wrapped his arms around Radu's waist. "I like that idea very much."

"You will have to live forever to match, though," Radu said.

"I will see what I can do." Cyprian pressed his lips against Radu's neck, and Radu shivered. No, he would never get used to this. Every moment spent with Cyprian would always feel like a miracle. There was something holy, something pure about the way he felt for Cyprian. There was no shame or anguish. None of the pain that had accompanied his feelings for so long.

"What are you thinking about?" Cyprian whispered.

"God," Radu answered.

Cyprian laughed. "I did not realize I was that good at kissing."

Radu laughed, too, and then their lips met again.

———◆———

They remembered to let go of each other's hands before reaching the bottom of the tower. Radu was floating, unable to release the smile from his lips as he had released Cyprian's fingers.

He did not understand how anyone seeing them could not know how they felt. But Nazira and Fatima had done this for years. People saw what they expected, as Nazira had told him they would.

"Radu Bey!"

Radu turned to see a Janissary guard running up to him, white-faced and wide-eyed. Radu's stomach dropped with fear. "What is it? Have they found my sister?"

The Janissary shook his head. "The prince."

Radu had been putting this off, but it was time to tell Aron that he planned on leaving. He wondered if that would help or hurt their relationship. It did not matter anymore. "Does he wish to see me?"

"No. He is dead."

Radu felt the words as though they had struck him. "Aron is *dead*?"

"So is Andrei."

In a daze, Radu stumbled past the Janissary toward the royal chambers. The castle was waking up, various servants moving about unaware that, once again, they were without a prince. Several Janissary guards stood watch outside Aron and Andrei's apartments. Kiril moved aside to let Radu by. The prince's body was on the bed. Radu moved as quietly as he could, as though worried that loud footsteps might disturb Aron. If only they could.

Aron was lying on his side, a tiny wound at the back of his neck where someone had slipped in a dagger and severed his spine at the base of the skull. It would have been a quick way to die. From the position of Aron's body, he had not even woken up.

"Andrei, too?" Radu asked, hushed.

Kiril answered in the same tone. "The same manner. Both in their sleep. The bodies are cool, but only just. It could not have been more than an hour or two ago."

"And no one saw anything?"

Kiril shook his head.

Radu stared down at Aron's body. He felt sorry for the other man, but a competing feeling of resentment churned beneath the surface. With Aron murdered in his own bed, in the middle of the castle, in the middle of the capital, how could Radu possibly convince any boyars they would be safe?

And who would be prince now?

———•———

Radu was too overwhelmed to pretend at decorum or tradition. Around the table he had Kiril, Cyprian, and Nazira.

"It was her, right?" Kiril asked.

Radu pulled off his turban. He felt trapped, constrained. "It had to be. Aron and Andrei have no enemies. They did not have enough time to make any. Bulgaria, Moldavia, Hungary, Transylvania—it is in all their best interest that Wallachia is stable and under control. No one would have sent an assassin for them."

"But why now? Why did she wait this long, doing nothing?" Nazira asked.

Radu shook his head. "I have no idea. Any word from the scouts?"

"A few have returned," Kiril said. "The rest I fear never will. Simion's men found bodies in a pit. They did not know who they were, but the clothing suggested boyars. There was some evidence of a large camp, but the trail was cold."

"The Basarabs," Radu said. "My guess is Lada found them."

"So, where do we go from here?"

Radu rubbed the back of his neck where a tension headache was building. He imagined a slender dagger sliding in. How precise, how surgical, how tiny a cut that separated one forever from life. "We need a prince. I do not think the remaining Basarabs have anyone of age, but I will look at the records. What few Danesti are left will likely be wary of coming anywhere near the country. They have all fled to distant relatives. Perhaps there is a good candidate for prince among the—"

"Why are you looking for a prince?" Nazira asked.

"We need someone on the throne."

Nazira's look somehow managed to be both hard and pitying at the same time. "Radu, my husband, we have an heir already. One we know is not afraid to come to Tirgoviste, or to face Lada."

Radu deflated. He had been hoping, pretending there was another option. "I do not want the throne."

"I know. We have spoken of it. But sometimes for the good of the people, we must do things we do not wish to."

"They are not my people!" Radu stood, surprised by the force of his declaration. He began pacing the room. "I do not want this. Any of this. I stayed as a favor to the empire. I cannot be prince."

"You have seen what state the country is in."

Radu laughed. "Precisely! Putting it back together will be the work of a lifetime."

"Hard work," Cyprian said, smiling sadly. "Important work."

Radu looked at the faces around the table, then collapsed back into his chair. "I want to go home," he said, knowing he sounded like a child, and not caring.

Nazira put a hand over his. "We have our family. We can make home anywhere. But I think we—you and I—carry a tremendous weight on our souls from what we have seen and done. We have participated in destruction. It will do our souls good to nurture and rebuild, instead."

Cyprian leaned close. "I know you want to retire, to live quietly and forget everything that has come before. But you could not turn your back on my cousins. Surely you cannot turn your back now on an entire country that so desperately needs you."

They were right. Radu knew he would carry the ghosts of Constantinople with him forever. Perhaps this was his punishment for everything he had done. But perhaps it could be his chance at redemption.

"Very well." The words tightened around his throat like a shackle. "I will be prince."

His friends nodded solemnly, knowing this was not a cause for joy or celebration. There was no triumph in Radu's ascension.

"Would you like to throw a party?" Nazira asked, in a generous attempt to ease the tension. "That was Aron's first order of business."

"No," Radu said. "We will coronate me immediately and send out word that I am prince. We will post guards around the city so it is perfectly defended. And then we are going into the mountains."

All the pieces of his life clicked together to form sharp stones of a brutal path. Everything led him here. Everything led him back to Lada. And he knew what he should do. What Mehmed would do. What Lada herself would do.

He had to end it, once and for all.

43

Poenari Fortress

Though she had maintained her filthy disguise this whole time, lest someone recognize her, she could not bring herself to hide any longer. She did not want to ride up to her fortress looking—and feeling—this weak. She arrived at the village closest to Poenari. It was tiny, clinging to a shallow stretch of land between the river and the mountains. She had visited it often and kept horses here. They knew her. As she dismounted, she pulled off her shawl and glanced around, hoping that at least this far in the mountains the land was still hers. If it was not, she was dead regardless.

"My prince," an old woman gasped, dropping the clothes she was washing at the bank of the river. She took in Lada's bloodstained dress, then stood. "Come with me." The woman dried her hands on her apron. Lada followed her to a humble home on the outskirts of the village. The woman pulled out a wooden tub and put a cauldron of water over the embers of her fire. She stoked it, humming to herself.

"I am sorry," she said. "I was not expecting to host the

prince. But you are a prince of the people." The woman smiled at Lada with more warmth than even the embers held, and Lada felt something inside herself break. She wanted to cry. She could not remember the last time she had *wanted* to cry, and could not fathom what it would accomplish now. Instead, she sat and accepted the bread and dried meat the woman offered her.

"How have things been here?" Lada asked. She did not want to specify in her absence—if Matthias had kept her imprisonment secret, she would certainly not be the one who let it be known.

"Quiet. Peaceful. A man came through a month ago asking for word of you." The woman smiled. "He did not leave again." The woman poured the scalding water into the tub, then excused herself. She returned with two buckets of cold water and dumped them in as well. "It would be the greatest honor of my life to wash my prince." The woman bowed her head.

Lada peeled away her clothes, throwing them into the fire. She set her locket carefully on a chair and then climbed into the tub, her knees against her chest. She sank as low as she could in the confines. The woman hummed a low sweet song to herself as she took a chunk of soap and a rough brush and began.

Though Lada had not been bathed by someone else since she was a child, she accepted the offering of this woman's kindness. Months of fear, of dirt, of caked blood came off into the water. Lada wished she could remove her skin to reveal something new and stronger beneath. Scales, or chain mail. But beneath the grime she was only soft and pink. Her body was unfamiliar to her. Her breasts still large, her stomach distended from months of poor nutrition. Her arms and legs thinner, weapon calluses on her hands gone.

When the water cooled, Lada climbed out. The woman wrapped her in a blanket worn soft with years of use. Lada sat by the fire and—in yet another inexcusable betrayal of Oana—allowed the woman to brush her hair.

"Why have you shown me this kindness?" Lada asked. It was one thing to serve the prince. But Lada had not demanded this, and it was clear she had nothing with her to pay for it.

The woman paused, then kept brushing, though more thoughtfully. "Because you are the only prince who has ever visited our village." Lada heard a smile shape the woman's voice. "Because you are the only prince who knows what it is to be a woman in this world. And because I am a little afraid that if I am not kind to you, you will kill me."

Lada laughed. "I do not kill my people. Only those who take from my people."

The woman laughed, too, the sound as worn and soft as the blanket around Lada. "Another reason you deserve my kindness. I have never much cared one way or the other about a prince. Never did me any good to. But the people here know and love you. Because of you, we get to keep more of our crops and earnings. And my grandson—smart, strong little boy—will never be sold to those godless infidels to fight their battles." She finished, patting Lada's shoulder. "Now, you wait here. I know you do not wear skirts. I will find some clothes for you."

Lada knew what a sacrifice that was. In a village this size, every person would probably have only one change of clothing.

The trousers and tunic the woman brought back were clean and well mended.

Lada dressed. When she was done, a little boy—probably the woman's grandson—peeked in. His eyes were wide with awe, or fear. Lada glared at him, then winked. He did not look any less terrified as he backed away and closed the door. The woman returned, smiling shyly, and held out a strip of red cloth. "My mother gave this to me when I got married." She stroked the material. It was simple cloth, but the color of dye was expensive. It was probably her greatest treasure. Lada turned her back, and let the woman tie the cloth around her head, securing her wet hair.

Standing straighter than she had when she arrived, Lada followed the woman out into the village. Everywhere, villagers had come out of their homes and back from the river or the fields. The woman's grandson was running from door to door, whispering and pointing to alert them to Lada's presence. They stood along the road, watching. Few smiled, but all regarded her with a fierce pride. Many of the women had their hands on the shoulders of young boys. Boys who would never be taken away. Boys who would grow up to serve their own country.

Lada lifted her chin. "For the kindness shown me here today, this village will never again pay taxes to any prince."

The people cheered, little girls waving flowers—one brandished a stick like a sword—as she passed. A man solemnly handed her his own boots, though replacing them would cost him dearly. Lada accepted them and mounted her horse. She nodded, proud and strong, before turning and riding toward her fortress.

No price was too high to pay for the good of Wallachia, and Wallachia—*true* Wallachia—knew and loved her for her sacrifices.

She met several of her soldiers at the base of the peak where Poenari loomed sentinel over the river. They seemed astonished at her appearance, but she invited no questions and offered no explanations. She handed them her horse's reins and then walked past them and up the winding switchback trail. By the time she got to the top she was winded and exhausted, but she did her best not to show it. She would project only strength.

Bogdan ran to the gate to meet her. She could see in his posture he wanted to throw his arms around her, but he restrained himself. She had trained him that well, at least. He looked past her.

He looked for his mother.

"She is not with me." Lada gestured for Bogdan to follow, knowing that this might be the last time he was ever willing to follow her anywhere. She managed to walk to her room at the back of the fortress, regally ignoring the men she passed. And then, at last, with the door shut behind Bogdan, she collapsed into a chair.

"What happened?" he asked. "Where have you been? I told everyone you were hunting Ottoman spies, but I did not know how much longer I could keep control of the men without you. I wanted to come after you. I knew you would want me here, though."

"It is good you did not come. You would have been killed. Matthias betrayed us. He took me prisoner."

Bogdan knelt in front of her, searching her face. "You have not been well."

"I think he was poisoning me."

"And my mother?"

Lada knew she should apologize. She knew Radu would, in her place. But she could not bear to. If she apologized, it meant she had done wrong, and if she admitted out loud she had done wrong in leaving Oana, she could never forgive herself.

"When I got there, Matthias killed all my men. I was in a cell smaller than this room for three months. Your mother was put to work in the kitchens, safe and healthy. I escaped with Stefan's help. We had to kill all the guards. Your mother was supposed to meet us, but she was in the castle when it happened. I could not go after her."

Bogdan's blocky features twisted, flickering through a host of emotions. Finally, swallowing hard, he nodded. "She would have wanted you to go."

Lada tried not to let her relief show, but she felt those traitorous tears from before pooling in her eyes. All she had now was Bogdan. If he had hated her for this, left her for this . . . she did not want to think about it. And she did not have to. She reached out and tugged on one of his stupid jug-handle ears, clearing her throat to try to dislodge some of the inconvenient emotion stuck there with all the tender aching of an old wound.

"Tell me what has happened in my absence."

Bogdan reported that Tirgoviste was fortified, but no major offenses had been made into the mountains. He had found and killed the Basarab boyars. The men under the boyars' command were scattered, hiding from scouts looking for them, but all were within half-a-day's ride and ready to reassemble as soon as she called for them.

"They remain loyal?"

"Most of them. The Hungarians left long before we got there."

It was as much as Lada could hope for. "How many do we have now?"

"Counting the women? Two thousand, maybe three. It is hard to know how many are still waiting and how many have fled. Are we going to kill King Matthias?" Bogdan's words were as rough and strong as his fists. He wanted it as much as she did.

Lada rested her head against the back of the chair and closed her eyes. "We are going to kill all of them."

"Good."

Lada smiled, reaching out a hand. Bogdan put his in it, hesitantly.

"Never leave me," she said.

"I never will."

As she slipped toward sleep, Lada finally felt safe again. She did not know what she would have done without Bogdan. She knew she should tell him how she felt—knew that he would treasure that knowledge more than the woman in the village had treasured this scrap of red cloth in her hair—but she could not bear to part with the words. He was no Mehmed. But perhaps he was something better. He would never challenge her, never demand she yield to what he wanted. He was *hers*.

Instead of thanking him, she decided that she would marry

him. It meant nothing to her, but it was a reward for his loyalty. And it served the double purpose of removing her marriage-ability from anyone else's political machinations.

She would tell him in the morning. They would marry, and then they would begin the work of destruction.

44

Carpathian Mountains

RADU HAD NO DESIRE for pageantry, for tradition, for celebration. And so his coronation took place in the middle of the twenty thousand graves that marked his sister's rule.

Amid the settling dirt and sprigs of trees growing around them, Radu knelt. He bowed his head, and a simple iron crown was placed there by the only priest who had returned to the capital. It felt far heavier and more restrictive than Radu's turbans ever had.

He thought of Mehmed's coronation. The weeks of celebration. The sense that it was the beginning of something truly great, of history on an unimaginable scale. Radu wondered what Mehmed would think of his new role. There had not been time for Mehmed to have received word and written back yet. Radu felt the distance between them keenly. But he also appreciated it. Because if he was being forced to do things he had no desire to, at least he could accomplish them however he saw fit.

Radu had but five witnesses: the priest, Nazira, Fatima, Cyprian, and Kiril. A few dozen citizens stood respectfully nearby, more out of curiosity than any sense of duty or excitement.

When the priest was finished, Radu stood. He was prince, like his sister and father before him. The grave dirt clung to his knees. He did not brush it off.

A week after the coronation, after making certain the city's defenses were set and the crops were well managed, Radu and Cyprian went into the mountains with Kiril and a select group of Janissaries. The sooner they finished this, the sooner Radu could lure back the boyars. Including someone—anyone—who could take over as vaivode. He was only prince because of Lada's violence. He considered it his singular princely duty to put a stop to that violence. And then his responsibilities would be fulfilled.

After two days of careful travel, they stopped to take stock. The mornings and evenings were growing chilly, but the afternoons still held the powerful, lingering heat of late summer. Radu and Cyprian sat in the shade of an enormous evergreen with Kiril, going over what they knew.

Kiril frowned, looking out over the steep ranges surrounding them. "We should find her hidden reserves of men. They are here somewhere."

They could wander for weeks and never find so much as a soul, much less carefully hidden people who knew this land like it was part of them. Radu shook his head. "We do not need to find them. Not if we find Lada. She has made certain that everything depends on her. Everyone owes their power and their hopes to her. If she falls, her entire system of government and leadership will, too. They will disband and drift back to their old lives."

Kiril scratched his clean-shaven cheek. Radu would not mind if he wanted to grow facial hair, but the Janissaries did not abandon their discipline for anything. "We still do not know where she is hiding, or if she is in these mountains at all. There are rumors of a hidden fortress, but there is no record of it being built, and no one can tell us where it is."

"Is it on a peak?" Radu asked, suspecting he knew his sister's exact location. How could he not have thought of this sooner?

Kiril raised his eyebrows, surprised by the question. "I heard that the mountain *was* her fortress. That is why it made no sense."

Radu felt more bleak dread than triumph. Some part of him had hoped they would never find her. That she would simply be gone. *Oh, Lada.* "Gather our men and the cannons. The lightest ones we have. It will not be an easy trek."

"You know where she is?"

"We share the same childhood. She forgets that, I think." Radu remembered the pouch his sister had carried all these years. She had filled it here. Held it like a talisman against the pain and distance they endured. And, when the pouch was ruined by blood, Radu had placed the dusty contents in a silver locket for her. She never took it off.

Lada's heart had always stayed here.

And it would stop here, too.

Radu had learned his lessons well. He had left Nazira and Fatima behind in Tirgoviste, in a small home on a side street, with nothing special to mark it as containing something truly precious. Radu did not know if Lada would try to kill his wife, but she had already killed his brother-in-law. He would never leave Nazira's life to chance.

Whatever happened here, Nazira and Fatima would be safe. And if Radu did not come back, he knew Mehmed would take care of them. Both to honor Radu's memory, and to honor Kumal's. All the pieces of his life had been settled. His friendship with Mehmed, finally released of pain and tension. His duty to Nazira and Fatima. With the exception of Cyprian at his side reminding him how desperately he wanted to live, Radu was as ready as he could be to face his sister.

As they rode deeper into the green and gray of the Carpathians, Radu felt the weight of the dead pressing closer than the looming peaks on either side.

Everyone with him thought he was the good Draculesti. The noble one. But did he not have as much to answer for as Lada? All the lives that had come into contact with them had, in one way or another, been forever tainted. Bloodied. Ended. And now they were on opposite sides, with so many more lives in the balance. For the sake of this country and all the countries around it, for stability and safety—not just for Mehmed, but for all the people protected under the empire's rule who would only prosper if the empire did—Radu *needed* to win.

He knew that.

But he did not know whether he deserved to win.

"What are you thinking of?" Cyprian asked, nudging his horse closer so the men's legs brushed.

"All the blood that has led me to this point."

Cyprian grimaced exaggeratedly. "I was thinking of what we might expect for dinner."

Radu tried to offer a smile, but with Cyprian he did not have to. He did not have to pretend or force pleasantness. Cyprian never demanded that he perform. Radu looked at him with all the tenderness he felt. And part of him whispered to cling to every glance, every moment, because an end was coming.

Radu swept his hand to encompass the ancient, towering mountains. Their horses clung to the path beside the river. The valley was so narrow that in certain places the sun shone only a few hours every day. One could climb halfway up the northern mountains and hit the southern peaks with an arrow, or perhaps even a well-thrown rock. "These are the paths of my childhood, but the boy I was then does not know the man I am now. And I think—I fear—this is the final step to becoming whatever I will be. I do not want to find out what that is."

Cyprian did not force a smile, either. He nodded resolutely. "We will find out together."

Radu crept up the side of the mountain across from Lada's fortress. The Arges was a black line beneath him, separating the two peaks. The two siblings. The night was as dark and thick as oil, heavy clouds cutting them off even from the stars. It felt portentous, as though all of nature knew what the future held.

Radu had spent a summer here. A happy summer, one of

the happiest of his childhood. And not long after, his father had sold him and Lada for the throne of Wallachia.

Lada had traded a life with Radu and Mehmed—a safe life, a life Radu still suspected could have been a happy one, somehow, at least for her—for blood and struggle and violence, had once again sold herself for the throne of Wallachia.

Radu, it seemed, was doomed to sacrifice for the same thing. Could no Dracul escape this cursed throne and what it asked of them? At least Lada and their father had been willing victims. Radu did not want to offer up what it would take to keep the throne.

He had no choice.

They made as little noise as possible, which was no small feat when one hundred men and ten small cannons made their way up the side of a mountain with no path. But Radu had been right about the location. A flicker of candle on Lada's peak guided them. On their side was a flat patch of rocky meadow about twenty feet above the fortress opposite them. From there they had a perfect vantage point—and point of attack.

Launching a siege against the fortress would be nearly impossible. Lada had made certain of that. It was as though the fortress had sprung from the very rocks of the peak, growing up around her.

Maybe it had. Maybe Wallachia loved his sister as much as she loved it.

But she made the same mistake everyone who went against Mehmed did. Because it did not matter how clever they were. Mehmed had the money, the men, and the weaponry to be cleverer. All they had to do was sit here, safe behind the cover of rock and trees, and fire cannonball after cannonball at his sister's fortress. Ten years ago, this attack would have been impossible. But Lada had not been at Constantinople. Had not seen an artillery designed by the deadly genius of Urbana.

A dozen men were making the trip back down to bring up even more cannonballs and gunpowder. Radu had several hundred more who would set up a position at the base of the peak once the bombardment began and the element of surprise was past.

Eventually the fortress would fall. Lada's men could not run without being picked off—just as Radu's men could not have attacked on foot without being picked off. The fortress's strengths were also its greatest weaknesses.

Just like the girl who built it.

"We watch and wait. We need to be certain she is there," Radu whispered. But he knew. Just as he had felt that she was not dead, he could feel her, heavier and darker than the night. She was there.

His men dispersed silently into the trees, the cannons covered with foliage so nothing could be seen. Radu lay on his stomach, only his head peering over the side of a large boulder on the edge of his mountain. Beneath him, only darkness.

Cyprian joined him, and they waited to see what the dawn would reveal.

"If she is there," Cyprian said, but then he paused, shifting to lie on his back and look straight up. Radu imitated him. In the silence and the night it was easy to pretend it was only the two of them. That they were not surrounded by men and machines made for killing. That his sister was not asleep only a small chasm away.

That last fact was harder to ignore. Lada was stubborn that way, always claiming space that did not belong to her, whether in reality or in Radu's mind.

"If she is there," Cyprian began again, "what will you do?"

"What I have to."

"And what do you have to do?"

Radu closed his eyes, the blackness behind his lids offering no more comfort than the night. "What she would do. What Mehmed would do. I have tried so hard to escape this, but my path was always leading here. I took every turn I could. I found faith and God. I found a new home and country, even new tongues and a new name. But I cannot escape becoming a Dracul. The cruelty, the willingness to destroy everything else in pursuit of a goal. I know what she would do. I know what I need to do. But I do not want to do it."

Radu felt Cyprian's long fingers reach for his, felt them link together. Felt the way they fit as though they were always meant for each other.

Cyprian lifted Radu's hand and pressed it to his lips. "Lada and Mehmed can only move forward. They have one path and cannot branch from it. But you underestimate yourself. You are not your sister, nor should you be. You have always had strengths she did not. If you want to go back down this mountain tonight and leave Wallachia forever, I will be at your side. And if you decide that killing your sister is the right decision, I will be at your side. But do not do something because she would, or because Mehmed would."

"But they were capable of greatness. Destined for it, even."

"Then do not aim for greatness. Aim for goodness. And however you get there will be the right path for you, my sweet Radu."

Radu felt warm tears track down his face. How could he find good in all of this? "She will never stop. She cannot. I cannot think of any way to save her *and* Wallachia."

"You survived a cruel childhood. You built a safe space for your heart and your soul. You navigated an enemy court and made it your own. You rose to power when you should have been a captive. You made friends with the most powerful man of our age. You went into an enemy city and helped turn the tide for your people—and managed to show tremendous mercy at the same time. If anyone can figure out a way, Radu, it is you."

———

At dawn, Radu prayed.

There were men in the fortress. They were small and insignificant from this distance, milling idly about. They had no idea they were being watched.

Radu had been right, had known they would find her here. Lada walked out onto the fortress wall and leaned over the edge. At her side was Bogdan. Though the distance was great, Radu would recognize that block of a man anywhere. He recognized none of the other men, a few of whom stood with Lada and Bogdan.

Bogdan tried to take Lada's hands, but she batted his away.

Radu knelt and reached for a longbow. Nocking an arrow onto the string, he breathed out, looking down the length of the shaft to his sister. He had always been a better shot than she was. It was the only physical thing he could beat her at.

Everything else about her had always been stronger. Including her heart.

Radu would break it. He took a deep breath, and aimed.

45

L ADA SLAPPED BOGDAN'S HAND away as he once again
reached for hers. "We are getting married. You are not a
child walking too close to the riverbank. I hardly think you
need me to hold your hand."

Bogdan smiled, joy softening his blocky features and turning him back into the boy she had shared a childhood with.
"Do you remember when you told my mother that I was your
brother, and Radu a worm? Now I will be your husband. This
is where we married the first time, too."

Lada rolled her eyes, but she remembered. And though she
did not feel the joy Bogdan so evidently did, it still felt right.
She had always wanted Bogdan at her side. It was a renewing of
that bond made in blood during their childhood.

A renewing of her bond both to Bogdan and her country.
She had not done enough yet. Had not pushed hard enough or
far enough. But she would. And Bogdan would support every
step, as he always had.

The crooked, gray priest from the village continued his part as though they were not talking over him. Lada wore chain mail and a tunic embroidered with her crest. She had left the red cloth in her hair. The old woman had worn it at her own wedding. It felt nice to honor her. It also felt disloyal, because the woman Lada should actually honor had been left behind in Hunedoara. Would Oana be happy about this official union? Lada hoped so.

The priest asked Bogdan a question. Lada was not paying much attention. She felt a flutter of nerves in her lower stomach. It made no sense. She was not nervous. She did not care enough about this ceremony to be worried or fearful.

The flutter came again. It was something new. Something foreign.

Lada put her hand on her stomach and looked up at Bogdan in horror. He was staring solemnly at the priest.

"Bogdan," Lada hissed.

He turned toward her, holding out his hands again. She reached up to take them, needing an anchor, needing something to hold on to against the sick dread that had opened like a pit inside of her. She needed her nurse. She needed Daciana.

But all she had now was Bogdan.

Concern erased his happiness like a cloud passing over the sun. "Oh," he said, frowning at the arrow that had appeared, embedded deep in his side.

He looked back up at Lada, then lurched heavily toward the wall. Lada reached out for him, but she was too late. His weight and momentum tipped him over the edge.

Lada watched as Bogdan spun through the air before finally

hitting stone, bouncing with a thick *snap* off and down the steep cliff face toward the river far beneath. His limbs moved without resistance, Bogdan already reduced to a mere body.

Bogdan was gone. And this time there would be no miraculous reunion, no finding each other again after years of separation. Bogdan was gone. Bogdan was not *allowed* to be gone. Bogdan could not be gone. He belonged to her.

Lada stared at where he had fallen. Around her men shouted, and someone tugged on her arm. If an arrow had found Bogdan, an arrow could find her, too. She looked up, searching the mountain opposite them.

There.

A lone figure, standing, a longbow at his side.

Radu lifted a hand and waved. Dazed and in shock, Lada lifted hers and waved back.

The first cannonball struck the fortress. The resounding crack of stone on stone jarred Lada from her dreamlike state. He was not waving. He was signaling his men.

"There!" Lada pointed. "Aim anything we have up there!" She ducked, jumping from the inside of the wall down to the floor. The landing was a shock she felt through her whole body. She needed it. She needed to focus.

Bogdan, spinning away from her forever.

"Cannons! Arrows! Crossbows! And watch the paths to make certain they are not sneaking up from our side, too!" Lada shouted directions at men. Men she did not know, men whose faces she barely recognized. They scurried around her, rushing into action, and she stood.

Alone.

Bogdan, the first man she had chosen. The last one to leave her.

A man screamed as an explosion blew tiny missiles of stones and debris into the air and sent Lada to her knees. She wiped away blood trailing into her eyes to see half the outer wall blown apart—the half that was one side of the room where their cannons and gunpowder were kept.

"God's wounds." She had always thought getting married would be the death of her. She had not expected that fear to be realized quite so literally.

One of the towers groaned, rocks raining down. The fortress had gone up fast, speed and secrecy being Lada's main goals. She had not designed it to withstand artillery, assuming no one would be able to haul massive, heavy cannons up mountains without being noticed. It had been a tremendous failure of imagination on her part.

Radu did not suffer the same lack.

Lada's men found openings wherever they could, firing off crossbows and arrows. She clutched her locket, a sensation that she was forgetting something, missing something vital plaguing her. But she knew what was missing, and he would never return. Then, another tiny flutter in her stomach. She felt as though she were the one tumbling down the mountain.

She had to focus. She ran to the other side of the fortress and climbed a ladder up the wall, peering down over the gate at the path that wound treacherously down.

"You!" She grabbed a man—Grigore—as he huddled next to the wall and whatever protection it offered. "I am sending you for help. They are not on this side of the mountain yet."

Lada threw a rope over the wall. She tied it off, then gestured to it.

"But—" He looked desperately around, hesitating.

"Would you rather be out there with them, or in here with me after disobeying my order?"

Grigore threw himself over the wall, scrambling down the rope. He was nearly to the bottom when a crossbow bolt sank into his belly and he dropped, screaming.

"Burn the bridge!" Lada shouted, ducking. The fortress was built on a jutting slab of peak, and a wooden bridge spanned the ravine between the peak and the rest of the mountain. It was another natural defense. For all the good it would do them under this barrage.

Lada climbed back down to the fortress floor as men dumped pitch over the wall onto the bridge, then lit arrows and fired them.

For all she knew, there was only a single Janissary on her mountain. If they all ran for it, they could possibly overwhelm whoever was out there. Many of them might make it. But Radu had more resources than she did. He could have ten thousand men waiting in the trees.

He could not bring down the entire fortress in one day. He could pick away at it, but it would be at least a week before the small cannons he could have hauled that far up the mountain would do enough damage to bring the whole thing down. He had been lucky with the shot taking out her gunpowder stores. The rest of the process would be slower.

Generously, Lada estimated they had one defensible week. They could fight their way down the mountain, but there was no way to do it in secret. So even if Radu did not have many men waiting, he would see them fleeing and have enough time to move his men to the bottom and wait.

If Lada waited out the slow cannon death of the fortress, the villagers would eventually notice. But they would have no idea who to go to for help. And she had not yet sent out any instructions to her men. As far as her soldiers hiding throughout these mountains knew, they were doing precisely what they were supposed to: waiting.

Thousands of willing fighters, and no one to help.

Bogdan was dead. Lada kept remembering that anew. But this time she felt a wash of relief that Oana had been abandoned. That she had not seen this. It had been a mercy, after all, leaving her behind. One good thing to come of Lada's betrayal.

She stood in the tiny courtyard, listening to men shouting, watching them running around her.

Seeing Bogdan fall, again, and again, and again.

She was alone. For the first time she could remember, she was well and truly alone. She had thought herself strong and apart, but that had been a lie.

As a child, she had had her nurse. Her Bogdan. Her worship of her father. And Radu.

Then she had had Radu and Mehmed.

Then she had had Nicolae and her men, and in her mind she had still had Radu and Mehmed, though she knew now that it was a lie and always had been.

She had even gotten her Bogdan and her nurse back, and built a small army of people around her. But one by one they had left, or been taken from her.

The fluttering sensation in her lower abdomen came back, and she could not catch her breath, could not stop her racing heart. She was not alone.

She was alone.

"Fire everything we have left, and then abandon the fortress!" she shouted. The men stopped, disbelief freezing them. And then, as they followed her orders, their actions became frenzied.

She walked, numb and heedless of the surrounding chaos, to the nearest door. Inside the room was an old well covered with planks of wood that they had built around. Lada picked up a length of rope against the wall and tied it to a metal loop fixed into the stones. Then she pushed aside the planks, dropped the rope inside, and climbed into the well.

The rope burned her hands and her arms trembled, weak from her time in prison. She went as slowly as she could, sliding down the last few feet and only just catching her toes on the footholds that led to the bottom of the well.

Last year she had found the cave at the bottom of the peak. During construction of the fortress, she discovered the well when bats flew out of it. It had to be the upper exit of the mountain's secret passage. But she had no idea if the handholds and footholds continued all the way to the bottom, or if time had worn them away.

If only they had found the well that summer they discovered the peak. She would have explored it. She would have forced Bogdan down. Or more likely Radu. Then she would know for certain whether it was possible to descend all the way to the secret passage. Her youthful exploration had failed her, as had everything from her childhood. Her mother. Her father. Bogdan. Radu. What use were memories if they could not save her now?

She was tormented by thoughts of Bogdan, of Radu. By the time the three of them had spent here. A summer of laughter and scraped knees, soaked in sunshine, the memory mocking her now that she was clinging blindly to cold, wet stone.

Radu had taken Bogdan from her.

Radu.

Who did she have now? Where was the strength and assurance that had sustained her? She should put her trust in her true mother, Wallachia, but she kept seeing Bogdan falling. Bouncing off her mountain. How could this, too, be taken from her?

The rocks were slick with moisture, portions caked with layers of bat droppings or moldy growths. She felt them beneath her fingernails, was glad she could not see their blackness clinging to her. It was completely dark now, the opening above her so far she could no longer see its light. Beneath her, her goal too far to even see a glimmer of hope.

Alone, stone pressing in, she knew: there was no heart in this mountain.

Wallachia was not her mother. Wallachia did not care what happened to her. And every single person who might have was either dead or trying to kill her.

Her feet slipped, and she hung by the tips of her fingers. Pain burned through them. "I am a dragon," she whispered. It echoed around her, her own words coming back haunted and empty of meaning or strength.

She fell.

46

Poenari Fortress

RADU SAT IN THE dim lantern light, his head leaning against the cold stone. In his hand he held one of Lada's knives. Wrist, wrist, waist, ankle, ankle. He had taken them all.

Lada's head rested in his lap, her eyes closed. Her breathing was even. Her arm had been bent at an impossible angle when he found her in a crumpled heap at the bottom of the long, dark tunnel leading to the fortress. She was not bleeding anywhere that he could see, but she had been sleeping for hours now.

He shifted, working circulation back into his legs.

Lada's eyelids fluttered. Radu stroked her forehead, brushing away one of her tangled curls. She sat up with a start, then cried out in pain, grabbing her shoulder and scooting away from him. She tried to stand but one of her ankles gave out. Dragging herself away, she hit the far wall only a few feet from Radu and stopped, leaning back against it and breathing heavily.

"Hello, Lada," Radu said.

With her good hand, Lada reached for her other wrist.

Radu held up the knife. In the lamp's golden flicker, Lada's black eyes looked dead, no reflection coming back to him. It was as though the light was sucked in, devoured whole, and disposed of.

"How did you know about this place?" Lada put her good hand on her ribs and grimaced.

"Did you think all I did that summer was cry because you and Bogdan would not let me play with you?"

Lada blinked, still dazed. "Actually, yes."

Radu laughed, the sound ringing brighter through the space than the lamp's light. "I did do a fair amount of that. But I also explored. I found this cave, and climbed all the way up to the fortress. As soon as I got out up there, I knew it was the secret you had been keeping. I did not dare climb back down, though. It took me until dark to hike back. You never noticed I was gone the whole day." Radu smiled.

"Father did not notice when I found the fortress ruins the first time, either. I was so excited to tell him. But all he wanted to do was leave us."

"That never changed." Radu sighed, a soft noise lost in the breeze that wound its way back to this part of the cavern. "When I heard rumors of your fortress in the mountains, I knew this was where I would find you."

Lada closed her eyes, another grimace passing over her face and then resolutely dismissed. "So you came down here after you missed."

"After I missed?"

"Your shot. With the arrow."

"I did not miss."

Lada opened her eyes, narrowing them at him. "And yet here I am, free from arrow holes."

"I hit my target."

Lada struggled for words. "You—you meant to kill Bogdan?"

It had not been an easy decision. Radu had sighted Lada first. But Cyprian's belief in him made him pause. If he had Cyprian at his side, he knew he could do anything. And if Lada had Bogdan at her side, he knew she would never give up. She would have to be stripped of everything she had claimed over the years. And so Radu had killed Lada's oldest friend. The son of their beloved nurse. Not an innocent man by any measure, but still, Radu would carry his murder with him until the end of his own days.

He had to break Lada before the end. And so Bogdan died. "I needed you to understand the cost of this. To feel loss."

"Or you simply hated Bogdan."

Radu rubbed his ear against his shoulder self-consciously. It was true. He had hated Bogdan. But hate had not motivated his actions. "You have to lose."

"You took him from me."

Radu's own anger flared at her accusations. "You murdered my brother-in-law!"

"*He* took you from me!" Lada lurched forward, then gasped in pain, collapsing back again. "I am not sorry."

Radu fought back his anger. She was trying to provoke him. "I know."

"You can tell Mehmed that. Tell him I was not sorry. Tell him my only regret was that he did not die under my knife."

Radu held up a hand and mimicked writing a letter. "Dear Mehmed," he said, his voice singsongy. "My sister sends her regards, and wants you to know how much she admires your blood and wishes she could have seen more of it. All of it, in fact."

Lada let out a shocked burst of laughter, holding her ribs and doubling over in pain. She panted, easing herself back up. "Finish it. I always said I would kill you. I never imagined you would kill me."

Radu did not take his eyes off his sister. "So you see, then. The result of your struggle. You are alone, in the dark, with no allies and no friends and no weapons."

Lada's face was as fierce and proud as it was drawn and pinched from pain.

"Was it worth it?" Radu whispered.

Lada lifted her chin. "Yes."

Radu scratched the knife against the damp stone beneath him. "Do you remember the story of Shirin and Ferhat?"

"We are in the center of my mountain, Radu, and I see no heart."

Radu smiled. "You are wrong. There are two. Yours, and mine."

Lada let out a deep, shaking breath, and some of her pride fell with her shoulders. On her face was an expression Radu had never seen before.

Sadness.

"I wish it was not you," she said. "I could take a blade happily from anyone but you."

"You will never stop, though. Even now. If there was a way to go on, alone, stripped of everything, you would do it."

Lada nodded, hand drifting up to the locket Radu had given her. "As long as I have breath, I will fight. Even when it feels like my own country does not want me to, I will fight. I cannot stop."

"That is what I thought." Radu stood, shaking out his legs, which were sore and numb from sitting so long. "You and Mehmed. I was always trying to protect you two, trying to shift your courses. I wish I had been able to. But if I had, you would not be the people you are, and I cannot begrudge you that." Radu closed the distance between them. Lada looked up at him with fierce defiance.

He tucked the knife into the waist of his breeches. "You really tried to protect me during our childhood. To make me stronger. Every time you let me be beaten. Every time you were the one beating me. It was because you could see no other way to protect me."

Lada lifted an eyebrow in confusion. "Yes."

"Then let me protect you in the way that I know how. I will not stay with you forever—I cannot, and I do not want to. But I can help you for a little while so that you can continue making Wallachia free. I think you deserve each other."

Lada frowned. "Is that an insult?"

Radu laughed. "I do not know. But you have seen what your methods have produced. Let me help you long enough to get you on stable ground. I can give you a throne without turmoil or threat so you can make your country healthy."

"And then?"

"And then I will leave."

"What about Mehmed?"

"Let me worry about him. Please. Let me worry about *all* the other leaders and nobles and boyars. I insist."

"I do not need——" Lada stopped, shaking her head. "I do need your help. I always did. But you were not here. You did not choose me."

Radu knelt in front of her, holding the knife out. Knowing that he had just killed her best friend. Knowing that he had stripped her of everything. Knowing that an injured, cornered wild thing was the most dangerous type.

Knowing that this was his choice. That it was not what Lada would do, or Mehmed. And that was why it was right.

Lada reached out, her fingers closing around the knife. She held it up, playing with the reflections of light. "You are mine again?"

"For a time."

"And then?"

"And then I am retiring to live out a happy, peaceful life far from thrones and rulers and impossible decisions." He paused. "Or we could do that now. Come with me. Leave it all behind."

Lada's hand tightened reflexively around the knife.

"I did not think so, but I had to try." Radu held out his hand. Lada sheathed her knife, and accepted his help.

"You do know," Radu said, his voice as gentle as his arm around her waist, "that this will be the death of you. Not today. Not tomorrow, if we have any luck. But eventually they will end you for daring to demand power."

"I know. But Wallachia is worth it." In his sister's voice,

Radu heard her acceptance of the end. There was no defiance. Her words were almost tender, as though spoken to a lover.

Together, they walked out of the dark cave and into the light.

"Also," Lada said, blinking as her eyes adjusted, "do you want a baby?"

47

Tirgoviste

LADA LAY ON HER back, staring up at the tree branches.
They were entwined like fingers, the blue of the sky
fighting through. Late autumn had left them bereft of their
leaves save for a few sad stragglers. It was cold enough that
their company was wrapped in furs, but no one had argued
with her when she suggested they meet in the forest. Nazira
avoided her, always finding somewhere else to be when Lada
was involved in meetings. Lada did not hold it against her.
Fatima the silent maid had come instead, along with Radu
and Cyprian.

Somewhere nearby Radu's men silently and invisibly guarded
the group. She often suspected their attention was turned more
toward her than toward other possible threats. Which proved
they were good men. When Radu had brought Lada out and
declared a treaty had been agreed upon, Radu's men had been
wary. But Radu still excelled at using his silver tongue to convince others that his way was the best.

He had written to Mehmed, too. Lada did not ask what

Radu said, or how Mehmed responded. All she knew was that Radu was on her side, which was worth more than she had imagined, and she would not jeopardize it.

"What about King Stephen?" Lada asked, continuing their conversation about threats and allies. "He still has the cities he took from me when he was supposed to be helping. I want to kill him."

Radu sighed, rubbing the side of his nose and leaving behind a trace of ink. Cyprian, the tall young Greek who was always at her brother's side, laughed and wiped it away. Cyprian was nothing like Mehmed. He was joyful and open, wearing his emotions so clearly even Lada could read him. Mehmed had always been so careful with what he showed the world. And where Mehmed was never satisfied with anything, always wanting more knowledge, more power, more control, Cyprian seemed deeply content as long as he was with Radu.

Lada had once questioned whether anyone could pull Radu's heart from Mehmed. She would not have thought someone so different from Mehmed would be the one to do it. She supposed she ought to be happy for Radu, but he was being very aggravating.

"You cannot kill the king of Moldavia," Radu said.

"I was not planning on doing it personally." Lada gestured down at her ever-expanding stomach. "Obviously I would send someone else."

"No, I mean, *we* cannot kill Stephen. He is still an ally. I have had good responses from my envoys to him. Besides, I thought you liked him?"

"I do. But that does not mean he should live after what he

did. What kind of example does it set if I allow him to keep the land he took?"

"We are not going to let him keep it. We are going to give it to him as a gift to thank him for being our ally, and as a gesture of future goodwill and cooperation."

Lada sat up with a grunt. "That is terrible."

"That is diplomacy. I cannot do much right now for our relations with Transylvania and Bulgaria, but we will not damage one of our only friendly borders."

Lada scowled, kneading her lower back with her knuckles.

"Let me." Fatima settled on the blanket next to her and rubbed Lada's sore muscles. Back in the castle, whether meeting with envoys or directing land management, Nazira wore a dress padded to imitate Lada's condition.

"You are only nice to me because you want this baby," Lada said.

Fatima did not pause or respond. She never did. She treated Lada with distant kindness that Lada knew she did not deserve, and it rankled her. Fatima should hate her, as Nazira rightfully did.

Sometimes Lada wondered if she should apologize to Nazira for murdering her brother. But she *was* giving her a baby, which apparently Nazira wanted very much. And Lada could not find the words—or the sentiment—to say she was sorry. She liked Nazira in spite of herself, though. Much as she had suspected and doubted the marriage, she saw now that Nazira was fierce in her own right, with a clever mind always looking for opportunities.

It seemed a loss to Lada that she and Nazira could not be

friends. But there was nothing she could do to fix what she had done. She would not try. Nazira still had far more than Lada did. Radu had managed to build a formidable family around himself. And, unlike Lada, he got to keep all of them.

A twig snapped, and she reached for a rock before realizing that Bogdan was not trying to sneak up on their lessons in the forest.

It was Oana, hiking through the forest toward them, lugging a large basket.

"We will kill Matthias, though," Lada said. The words hung in a frozen cloud of breath. She willed them to become a solid reality. "He betrayed me. Kept me locked in prison for three months. He also betrayed the pope and his European allies by taking the gold intended for our crusade against Mehmed and using it to buy his stupid crown back. He cannot be trusted. Besides, we cannot be sure he will not try to harm me again."

"We are not going to kill Matthias," Radu answered.

"He took me prisoner!"

"But he did not kill you. Or Oana. He even sent her back as a gift."

Oana grunted, unpacking their afternoon meal. "He could have sent something more valuable."

"There is nothing more valuable," Radu said, but he could not quite meet their nurse's eyes. Only he and Lada knew the source of his guilt. The closest Lada had come to apologizing for leaving her behind was not telling their nurse who it was that had killed Bogdan. As far as Oana knew—or would ever know—Bogdan went into the mountains to get help and never returned.

Oana should not have to live with the truth. It was enough that Lada and Radu did.

Oana's gaze shifted down to Lada's swollen stomach and her eyes misted with tears. Lada resisted the urge to growl. If she could remove the damned thing and have it over with, she would. It was like a parasite, foreign and intrusive. And Lada knew when others looked at her stomach, they saw what they wanted to.

Nazira and Fatima saw their futures as mothers. Radu, a secret to hide to protect Lada. Oana, her own flesh and blood mixed with her claimed daughter.

"Is it his?" Radu had asked one night as he helped Lada exercise her injured arm to get full movement back.

"You mean Bogdan's?" Lada had answered.

"We both know that is not who I meant."

Lada had not answered again. Nor would she ever. She knew that the child could be considered a legal heir—knew that in Mehmed's mind and in the eyes of Ottoman law, Lada was part of his harem. He would never have any of her again. Certainly not whatever beast was currently taking up residence over her bladder.

Radu was still talking. ". . . because we know what he wants, he is easy to deal with. And he is our connection to the pope and the rest of Europe. It is a fine line to walk, but I think we can manage to keep him on our side, or at the very least not directly against us."

"It would help if we had money to send Matthias," Lada said. "He is deeply loyal to money."

"A lot of things would be helped if we had money. First we need to survive this winter."

Lada knew that they would, and only because of Radu's foresight in employing his Janissaries as farmers. She had destroyed her own land. He had healed it.

Again, he was annoying her. "If you will not let me kill Stephen or Matthias, who can we kill?"

"I have made a comprehensive list." Radu shuffled through his sheaves of parchment. Most of them detailed funds, where they were, where they could go. Resources such as food and materials. Lists of men and where they were located, as well as people he felt they could trust or would be able to buy the trust of. In short, all the little details Lada had never wanted to deal with but that it took to run a country.

Radu made an excellent prince. She was not surprised. Nor was she even particularly angry. She had always wanted him at her side. Had always known that together, they could accomplish what neither could alone.

Perhaps if she had not broken so much to get him here, he would stay.

"Ah! Here it is." Radu lifted a piece of parchment and held it out to her.

Lada's eyes slitted to knife-thin lines. "This is blank."

"Exactly! We are building, not burning."

"I still think it would be easier to start over. Break down everything that existed and led to such weakness and rot."

Radu's jaw tightened reflexively. "I have seen what it costs to take something very old and make it new. Streets running with blood to clear out a falling empire and make way for the future. Children—"

Cyprian reached out and placed his hand over Radu's, which trembled so hard the parchment rustled.

Radu took a deep breath. "You do not want to pay that cost. I promise. Even you built Poenari Fortress on the stones of the past, the strength that was already there. We are doing the same."

Lada raised an eyebrow. "You knocked that fortress down."

A soft giggle from Fatima drew everyone's eyes to where she sat, curled up under a thick fur. "Well," she said, softly, "it was probably not the best example."

Lada leaned back and let them talk, listened to Cyprian and Radu discuss and strategize and plan. Radu was trying to give her the most stable throne he could manage, and she did not doubt he would do a good job. They had yet to discuss the biggest problem, the one they shared an entire history with. Neither of them had been willing to broach that topic yet. Lada's hands rested on her stomach.

She moved them away.

Fatima gently rubbed Lada's forehead and neck, where she had constant tension. Here in the forest, in her trees, in her country, Lada listened to the family her brother had built and desperately missed her own.

"He wants to meet," Radu said, staring out from the tower. Lada did not want to be up here. Neither of them liked the castle, but he seemed fond of the tower. It held only ghosts for Lada. Another night, another time, other men she loved. Lada looked down at Tirgoviste, trying to forget. Everything was frozen. Calm. War slept during the winter, curled up like a bear in a cave.

And so Tirgoviste was filling up again. Thanks to Radu's stores of food and Lada's presence, the people of Wallachia had slowly returned. And, again thanks to Radu, several of the large manors once again held boyars. Radu visited them daily, making social calls with his charming flower of a wife. But he also met with the people Lada had picked, the ones she had given land to. She could see in his actions that he respected what she had tried to do, what she was still hoping to do. He just wanted to be nicer about the whole thing, which was typical of him.

"We work well together," he said, as though reading her mind.

"You mean I do all the work and then you come in and smile at people to make them like you?"

Radu laughed. "Yes." Then he sighed and his face got serious again. "Mehmed wants to meet. He is sending envoys, all of whom will survive and leave healthy and well, and I am working on new terms that I think—I hope—he will accept. He owes me, and I have never asked him for anything. I think he will allow you to remain on the throne. But he wants to meet in secret."

"The two of you?"

"The three of us."

The thing inside her jabbed her ribs, which were still sore from her fall those months before. She shoved it with her hand. She had shed her usual chain mail. She wore odd, bulky robes somewhere between a dress and the entari worn in the Ottoman Empire. Her body was naturally thick and had hidden her condition for some time, but these clothes were her only option now. It would not be long.

Lada shook her head. "I have nothing to say to him."

"Even after everything?"

"Especially after everything. Did I tell you I saw our mother?"

Radu tilted his head, frowning at the subject change. "When?"

"When you were in Constantinople. I was trying to find support. I thought maybe she could connect me with her father."

Radu's eyebrows rose, and he looked like the little boy she had saved so many times growing up. But she could not save him from this. "She did not care," Lada said. "About us. About what had happened to us. She did not even ask about you."

Radu blinked rapidly, then attempted to lift the corners of his mouth along with his shoulders as he shrugged. "I do not even remember her."

"She does not deserve any place in your memories. She let the world—our father—break her. And she left so the same could be done to us. I will not be broken. And I will never forgive or forget those who failed to stand by my side."

"Mehmed was our friend, Lada. More than that. To you, at least." Radu's smile was wistful but not bitter.

"He had all the power in the world, and he would extend none to help me. He did not want to see me succeed. He only cared about me in relation to himself." She knew it was true, because she had treated Bogdan the same way. She hated Mehmed for it, and she did her best not to think about Bogdan, lest she hate herself.

Radu sighed, nodding. "I do not want to see him, either."

"What happened between you two?" Lada had been jealous for so long, worried about Mehmed's affections. She should have worried more for Radu. But neither of them had been able to avoid Mehmed becoming the central star around which they spun.

"Nothing happened. He asked me to stay, and I chose to leave. He is alone."

Lada scoffed. "He has an empire."

"And he has to be over and above all of it. He loved us— he needed us—because we were the only people he could be a *person* with. The only ones for whom he was just Mehmed, not the sultan."

"That is the cost of power." Lada did not look at Radu, knowing he would leave her, too. She would be alone, just as Mehmed was. Only Radu had chosen people over power. Lada looked up at the sky, where a crescent moon was beginning to rise. "Do you remember the night the moon turned to blood?"

Radu nodded. "I was in Constantinople with Cyprian."

Lada had been right here with Bogdan. With Nicolae. With Stefan. With Petru. She had already been alone. She just had not realized it yet.

"Mehmed can live in a hell of his own making," Lada said. "Promise him money I will never send. Do not agree to give him any Wallachians. As long as I am prince, the Janissaries will not be given Wallachian blood to fill their ranks." If the princes before her had been as strong, she would never have met her friends.

She wished that were the case. If they had not been Janissaries, they would not have been *her* Janissaries. They would all still be alive. And she would never have known them, which meant she would not miss them.

"Mehmed was humiliated by the failure of his attack," Radu said. "I think he will agree as long as it means peace. And because it is me asking."

"I *am* going to take back the Danube, though."

"Right now you are going to come down to the throne room and settle some land disputes. And if in ten years your people are not in danger of starving, and you have a standing army and the support of your neighboring countries secured through years of peace, then by all means: take back the Danube."

Lada faked a casualness she did not feel. "We could do it together."

"You will be alone," Radu said, his voice sad but firm.

"I know," Lada said.

48

Snagov Island Monastery

R ADU'S WORRIED EXPRESSION MELTED away when the monk informed him his sister had given birth to a baby girl. The winter was so cold they had almost not made it to the monastery in time, struggling to cross both land and lake. But they had gotten here. And now the baby had arrived as well.

Oana came from the room carrying an armful of soiled linen. "She did well." Her voice was gruff with emotion.

Radu opened the door hesitantly, and found Nazira sitting on a chair, holding a cloth-wrapped bundle. She beamed at him with tears in her eyes. Fatima was by the bed, tucking blankets around Lada and wiping the sweat from her brow.

There was an odd squeaking noise, and Radu realized it was the baby. Radu went to Nazira and peered down. The baby had thick, dark hair, and though its face was red and swollen from its entrance into the world, Radu needed only one glance to see that this was a mix of the two people Radu would know anywhere.

This was not Bogdan's child.

"What should we name her?" Nazira said, looking up.

"Theodora," Lada said, her voice raw. "Who was born to nothing and grew to rule an empire."

"She is not born to nothing." Radu smiled down at the baby.

Fatima came over and took the baby from Nazira. She nuzzled the infant's head, breathing in deeply. "The name is strong and beautiful. She will be, too."

"I hope for her sake she is ugly. Now get out and let me rest," Lada snapped. Nazira and Fatima hurried from the room with the baby. Lada turned in her bed, facing away from Radu.

He put one hand on her shoulder, felt Lada's body contract with silent crying.

"Get out," she said again.

He climbed onto the narrow bed and curled around her, holding her until she slept.

"How do you feel?" Radu asked.

"Like I will stab the next person who asks me how I feel," Lada said through gritted teeth as she rode next to him.

It had been only a couple of weeks since the baby had arrived. Nazira and Fatima were still cocooned on Snagov, having found a wet nurse who was willing to stay with them as long as the baby needed. She was even willing to relocate to Edirne. Radu suspected some of her eagerness came from the handsome pay, and some from the fact that Nazira wanted her only to feed the baby and required no other work from her.

"So you will leave and have a happy home in the countryside?" Lada said.

"Yes. Cyprian will marry Fatima to make things easiest to explain."

Lada made a thoughtful noise. "I suppose marriages always have been business arrangements to make life easier. Yours are simply odder than most."

Radu laughed. "I still cannot quite believe we all found each other."

"I can. You were always ruthless about finding people to love you."

Radu opened his mouth to argue, hurt. But Lada was right. He had always been as focused and determined as she had. They simply had different goals.

"You could still come with us."

"You could still stay here and help me rule." She said it lightly, but there was a clipped quality to her voice that made Radu suspect the offer carried more weight than she wanted it to.

"No." Radu had loved Mehmed and he had loved his sister, but he had no desire to serve them. Not anymore. He did not want to pay the cost of their ambitions, or to watch as they paid it, too.

Lada nodded curtly. "How long?"

"Three months. We want to wait until the baby is a bit older before we travel."

"Well then, ride faster. I have a lot of work for you to do before you go." But she did not pick up her own pace. She seemed content, for once, to take her time.

"I will send Oana with you," she said, burrowing deeper into her fur-lined coat.

"Does she want to go?" Radu asked, knowing that only Lada's wishes were what would count.

"It does not matter what she wants. I do not wish her to stay. She can help with the baby."

Radu suspected Lada did, in fact, want Oana to stay. It was obvious in the deliberate and determined way Lada had been rejecting their nurse's help since Theodora was born. If Lada did not care so much, she would never have been so mean.

"She will stay in Tirgoviste if you ask her."

"I cannot have another death on my hands," Lada said. The words came out so quickly, Radu wondered if she had meant to say them aloud. "Do you want the baby?" she asked in a swift change of subject.

Radu frowned. "Why would you ask that?"

"I know Nazira wants the baby. She would have crawled up into my womb to get it if necessary. But do you want it?"

"I did not think I ever wanted a child," Radu said, searching his feelings. He had scarcely had an opportunity to see the baby, and held her only a few times. Fatima had turned out to be incredibly possessive. "If you recall, our own childhoods were less than pleasant."

"You mean you have not already thought of all the ways you could leverage the infant for your own personal gain?"

Radu flinched. "I would never."

Lada looked over at him, suddenly solemn. "I know. That is why I gave her to you. Mehmed would use her." She paused. "I would, too, eventually. Or get her killed. I want better for her than we had. I trust Nazira and Fatima with that. And I trust you."

Radu nodded, his chest swelling with emotions he had tried his hardest not to let surface. "I will raise her in love."

"And strength."

"And strength. Though I am certain we could not keep her from being strong if we tried."

Lada reached up and undid her necklace. She held it in her hand, looking down at it. Then she took one of her knives and wrapped the necklace around the handle. She held both out to Radu. "Her inheritance. I do not expect you to ever tell her the truth of where she came from. But I want her to have these."

Radu took them reverently, feeling the weight of Lada's soul in his hand. "I may wait a few years to give her the knife."

Lada waved dismissively. "I had one when I was three."

"And look how you turned out."

She cackled, looking at him with a smile that meant destruction, fire, or both. "First one back to Tirgoviste gets to decide whether we kill Matthias."

Lada spurred her horse, quickly outpacing him. Radu watched as she rode forward into her destiny, knowing that she would always outpace him, would beat him to every destination. He was finished trying to catch up. It was a resignation both melancholy and peaceful.

49

Tirgoviste

LADA WATCHED LONG AFTER Radu and his party had disappeared down the road. Spring was reclaiming the land, everything soft and green with new growth. It was a time of renewal, rebuilding. And they were leaving.

It was good that he was gone. She would no longer have to pretend, have to fake happiness or calm when she felt neither. And it would be nice to no longer have him peering over her shoulder, telling her whom she could and could not kill.

He had done a good job, though. Better than she could have done. She had treaties in place with every border that mattered. The boyars Radu worked with seemed dependable, though she would watch them closely. Her country was running the way she wanted it to. With order. With strength. With justice and fairness. If it was slower change than she wanted, she hoped Radu's promise that it would be like a tree with deep roots, growing for decades, was true.

Lada drifted to the throne room. She sat, looking out where her father had looked out before her. Where the Danesti princes had as well.

The throne was a death sentence. She was not foolish. It would claim her eventually, as it had claimed all who came before her. All except Radu cel Frumos, the prince who had walked away. Who had chosen life and love over country.

Lada would not walk away.

Once, she had sat here with the eyes of her friends on her. Now, and forevermore, she sat here alone.

She had dug through the mountain to reach her heart's desire, and found the mountain had a heart after all: the beating pulse required of all those who would not stop, would not accept what the world offered, would not bow.

She drummed her fingers on the arms of the throne, looking out at the empty room. She was not stupid enough to think men would stop trying to take it from her. They would always be there, waiting for weakness, waiting for her to fall. They wanted what she had *because* she had it. And one day, eventually, someone would defeat her. But until that day she would fight with tooth and nail, with all the fire and blood that had formed her into who she was.

She was a dragon.

She was a prince.

She was a woman.

It was the last that scared them most of all. She smiled, tapping her fingers on the throne in a beat like her heart.

"Mine," she said.

Hers. And hers alone.

50

Three Years Later, Outside Amasya

RADU FINISHED PRAYING, THEN sat back on his heels, enjoying the particular quiet peace of the space. A thump and a laugh roused him. He stretched, glancing over the letters awaiting him on his desk. Most were regional issues—minor disputes, tax claims, all the little matters of keeping his bey running smoothly.

One was from Mara Brankovic, though. He carried it with him out to the dizzyingly colorful garden, where Oana was setting up an afternoon picnic while Fatima sewed in the shade. Nazira sat on the swing that had hung from the old tree on Kumal's country estate. They had brought it with them. Brought him with them, in spirit, in every way they could.

"It is from Mara," Radu said, handing Nazira the letter.

Nazira read it, smiling and shaking her head. "Mara says Urbana sends her love."

"She has to know we know she is lying."

"I suspect she does it to amuse herself. She thanks us for sending our respects when her mother died. Mehmed's eastern borders are giving him trouble, so he has not been in the capital much lately. Oh, and yes, here is the real reason for the letter, and it took her only three pages to get to it: she wants to know if you would be willing to remind Lada of her tax obligations. 'Such things are always so much more pleasant coming from a family member.'" Nazira laughed. "She is trying to delegate."

Radu lowered himself to the ground, sitting next to Fatima and peering over her shoulder at the tunic she was sewing. "That is beautiful."

She smiled, pleased. "It is for Theodora."

"So it will remain beautiful for three whole minutes after she puts it on."

Fatima's smile grew both softer and prouder. She stroked the cloth. "Yes."

With a roar, Cyprian ran into the garden, Theodora riding on his shoulders. He did several circles around the tree before collapsing onto the grass. Theodora jumped on his stomach, laughing, but Cyprian pretended to be dead.

Scowling, Theodora wandered back to the house, her long black hair already undone from the careful braids Fatima had put in just that morning.

Radu stretched out, resting his head on Cyprian's torso. The day was warm, lovely and soft, the best season. This evening, he would answer Mara and write his report on the status of his bey for Mehmed. But this afternoon?

This afternoon was for happiness.

Oana finished laying out the food, grumbling about not being able to find the right ingredients here. She had done well adjusting to a new life, though she refused to learn Turkish. It was good for Theodora, though, to understand Wallachian. It felt right. "Theodora!" Oana shouted. "It is time to eat!"

Radu sat up, passing the food and listening to Nazira make plans for a holiday to Bursa to see the sea. Someday they would make the pilgrimage to Mecca, but that could wait until Theodora was older. They would also visit Cyprus to see where Cyprian's mother had come from. But Bursa was far enough for now.

"As long as I do not have to ride on any boats," Radu said.

"Oddly enough, Cyprian and I have had a lifetime's worth of experience on boats as well," Nazira replied.

"And deserted islands," Cyprian said with a laugh, lacing his fingers through Radu's.

It had never stopped feeling like a miracle.

"I had to fight a mountain," Theodora said, plopping down in the middle of the blanket and knocking over several bowls of food. "It was mad. I screamed at it, and it had fire eyes. But then I got it with my knife." She held up a knife clutched in her still-dimpled hand.

Radu reached out and plucked it away.

"Where is she always finding knives?" Nazira said, frowning as she pulled Theodora into her lap and fussed over her hair. Theodora nuzzled against Nazira, reaching up and patting her cheek.

Radu knew he should be cross, but he could not help laughing.

Later that evening, as Radu tucked Theodora into bed, he reached beneath her pillow and retrieved a knife she had hidden there.

Her lips stuck out in a pout. He kissed her forehead.

"I will save it for when you are older. And if you have to fight a mountain, come get me. I will fight it with you."

Her three-year-old body could hold neither rage nor consciousness for long. Radu stayed, hours after she fell asleep, gazing at her face. Lada and Mehmed had combined in a softening of both their features. Mehmed's full lips with Lada's large eyes, Mehmed's dark lashes with Lada's hooked nose.

He had loved them both so very much, and it had not been enough to keep them. But he could make certain this little creature they made had all the love the world held.

"Be strong," he whispered. "Be kind. Be hopeful." He bent down and kissed her forehead.

"And be fierce."

EPILOGUE

RADU WATCHED THE APPROACHING boat grow larger. He was grateful he had arrived first so that he did not get out on the shore heaving for their first greeting in ten years.

Theodora fidgeted impatiently beside him. She wore clothes suited to travel, but with Fatima's excellent sewing and Nazira's love of color. And she always wore knives, too, her favorite being the one she had inherited.

Theodora was not elegant, but she was strong and undeniably lovely. She had adopted Nazira's clever optimism, Fatima's kindness, and, unfortunately, Cyprian's sense of humor. At twenty, she was still the brilliant center of their lives. Radu was grateful that she had demanded to accompany him. Making this trip alone would have left him with too many ghosts. Theodora was so brash and delightful, there was no room for melancholy.

She was also impatient. They had been waiting nearly an hour. As Mehmed disembarked, helped by a retinue, Theodora carefully reworked her face into something acceptable. Not demure, by any means, but at least respectful.

Mehmed did not appear to suffer any ill effects from the voyage. Radu smiled, but did not rush to greet his old friend as once he might have. Age had been hard on Mehmed. He was heavier and walked with a pronounced limp. A full beard obscured the lines on his face, but his eyes were as sharp and intelligent as they had ever been.

Mehmed waved away his attending guards.

"No stool carrier?" Radu said with a smile, unable to help himself.

Mehmed let out an exhalation that might have been a laugh. "He participated in an assassination plot. I had to have him killed."

"Really?" Radu said, his eyebrows rising in horror.

Mehmed's face split in a mischievous grin, taking him from forty to fifteen in a single expression. "No."

Radu laughed, shaking his head. "You remember my daughter, Theodora."

Mehmed smiled warmly at her. "Rumors of your beauty reach us even in Constantinople. I am glad to see you again. Last time you were far shorter than me."

Radu felt a spike of anxiety. Radu could not look at her without seeing Lada and Mehmed. But if Mehmed suspected it, he said nothing. He patted Theodora's hand, slipping her a pouch that sounded suspiciously heavy with coins.

"For all the birthdays I have missed, little one," he said.

Theodora's eyes twitched. "Thank you."

"I wish we were reuniting under happier circumstances," Mehmed said. "Though Lada did not excel at creating happy circumstances."

Theodora looked at Radu. "I wish I had known her. Instead

of only through stories." She grinned then, something a bit wicked there. "Though the stories are *quite* good. Lada Tepes, the Lady Impaler. No one else has such a remarkable aunt."

Mehmed and Radu laughed, but it was uncomfortable. Theodora had never been told the worst stories. Including how that aunt had killed her uncle.

"I will give you two a few moments alone before I pay my respects." She bowed her head. The silver locket she always wore around her neck fell forward. Mehmed stared at it as though seeing a ghost. He turned to Radu, but Radu did not show any emotion.

"Thank you," Radu said. "We will not be long."

"Of course." She spun with her arms wide, breathing in deeply. "Take as long as you want. There is something special here. I like the way Wallachia feels—warm and welcoming. Like a mother, is it not?" She walked away down the path, her steps assured and confident. She did not stomp and prowl as Lada had, but moved as though she owned whatever land she was on.

Radu felt his purpose here with a keener pain than he had before. They walked slowly toward the church.

Mehmed was still frowning. "Theodora is not Nazira's, is she?"

Radu's only answer was a sigh.

"I suspected. For years. But just now, the way her eyes narrowed in annoyance at my patronizing gift! I could scarcely breathe. It was like looking at the past. I see why you have avoided the capital all these years. Kept her away."

Radu paused with his hand on the door. "She is my daughter."

Mehmed's smile was both kind and sad. "I am glad. Would that we all had had fathers such as you." Mehmed's adult life had been tumultuous, filled with tragedy and violence, even in his own family. He turned and looked at the gardens, apparently unwilling to go inside just yet. Radu did not begrudge him the delay. "How is Nazira?"

"She is well. She is having more difficulty with her vision, but she manages it with grace." They were homebound now, but Fatima did not mind. The only place they had ever wanted to be was with each other, after all.

"And Cyprian?"

Radu's heart ached. He hated being away from him, even now. "We finally made it to Cyprus two years ago. It was lovely. But I think our traveling days are over. His ankle bothers him now from his old injury."

"You know, I thought of having him arrested."

"What?"

Mehmed leaned against the doorway, putting his hand on the stones as though admiring the work. Radu realized he was tracing the name carved there. Lada Dracul, the patron of this particular church.

Mehmed grinned, Radu's childhood friend once again peering through the beard and wrinkles. "Oh, it was years ago. And I was only going to hold Cyprian as a political prisoner. Just to make him stay in the capital so you would come back."

"You and my sister always had such odd ways of expressing affection. She used to hit me and let others beat me. You considered kidnapping my loved ones to spend more quality time together."

Mehmed smiled, but it was strained. "It was not the same once you left. There has never been anyone quite like you."

"Or her."

Mehmed's expression was pained. "Or her. Which is probably for the best." His gaze grew far away and misty. "I would have made her empress. You would think for a woman with her ambition . . ."

"She got exactly what she wanted."

Mehmed pulled at his thick beard. "She did."

And, in the end, she had gotten exactly what Radu predicted.

"Whose head was it?" Radu asked. "That you had brought to the capital and displayed on the wall? I have been wondering."

"I have no idea. It did not much matter. A severed head is a severed head." Mehmed had been fighting battles since he was twelve; Radu felt a little differently about severed heads, but they had lived very separate lives in the past twenty years.

Finally, with nothing else between them to delay the reason for their visit, they entered the main room of the chapel. Statues of saints stood sentry, and elaborate paintings told stories from the Bible. Radu noted the paintings were all especially violent ones, which was fitting, as this was the chapel Lada had paid for.

A monk stood, inclining his head. He led them to a portion of the floor with newer flagstones. A small marker at the top said simply PRINCE.

"No name?" Mehmed asked.

"I was afraid someone would desecrate it," Radu said. Even in death, Lada had many enemies. They stared down in silence at where his sister slept, forever entombed.

"Was it your men?" Radu asked. There was no accusation in his tone, merely curiosity. Lada had been killed as she stood on a field ready to meet Mehmed and his men in battle, their first direct conflict since those horrible days outside Tirgoviste.

Mehmed shook his head. "I have tried to find out who it was. Some suspect Matthias sent an assassin. Most think it was one of her own guards. No one knows for certain."

"The killing blow?"

"A knife to the back. They brought her body to me on the field. I think they expected a reward." Mehmed shifted, an abashed expression. "I killed those poor men on the spot. It was foolish, considering I was there to fight her myself."

Radu put a hand on Mehmed's shoulder. "Thank you for sending her body here."

Mehmed nodded, then eased himself down to his knees, resting a hand against the stones over Lada's body. "Even after all these years, I cannot quite believe she is gone."

"I cannot quite believe she managed to stay alive so long." Radu knelt next to Mehmed. "But you are right. It feels wrong to be in Wallachia, knowing she is not here anymore."

"She was a strong prince."

Strong and terrible and fair. "I suspect the name Dracul will not soon be forgotten."

"I am sorry for how things ended with us. All three of us. I wish it had turned out differently. That we had stayed together."

Once, Radu would have wanted nothing more. But his joyful life had worn away the sharp edges of the past's pain. In its place was something like Lada's silver locket: smooth, cold, filled with the much-loved dust of history.

"The two of you never had any choice but to conquer and lead."

"And you?"

Radu smiled, kissing his fingers and laying them against the stones. He had wanted so much less than they had—and so much more. They had chosen the hard paths, the lonely paths, the paths of blood and struggle.

"I am returning home to my family." He moved to stand, then, thinking better of it, took out a knife and carefully scratched two additions onto Lada's marker.

PRINCE

SISTER

DRAGON

It was enough.

DRAMATIS PERSONAE

Draculesti Family, Wallachian Nobility

Lada Dracul: Prince of Wallachia

Radu Bey: Also known as Radu Dracul and Radu cel Frumos, advisor to Sultan Mehmed

Vlad Dracul: Deceased father of Lada, Radu, and Mircea

Vasilissa: Mother of Lada and Radu, princess of Moldavia

Mircea: Deceased oldest son of Vlad Dracul and his first, deceased wife

Wallachian Court and Countryside Figures

Oana: Mother of Bogdan, childhood nurse of Lada and Radu, current aide to Lada

Bogdan: Childhood best friend of Lada

Andrei: Boyar from rival Danesti family, son of the previous prince

Aron: Brother of Andrei, in line for Wallachian throne

Danesti family: Rival family for the Wallachian throne

Daciana: Wife of Stefan, friend and servant to Lada

Lucien Basarab: Boyar from Basarab family

Galesh Basarab: Ally of Lada's, in charge of soldiers

Ottoman Court Figures

Mehmed: Ottoman sultan

Murad: Mehmed's deceased father

Mara Brankovic: Murad's widow, Serbian royalty now advising Mehmed

Halil Vizier: Formerly Halil Pasha, executed for treason

Kumal: Devout pasha in Mehmed's inner circles, brother of Nazira, brother-in-law and friend to Radu

Nazira: Radu's wife in name only, Kumal's sister

Fatima: Nazira's maid in name only

Cyprian: Emperor Constantine's nephew, missing after fleeing Constantinople

Valentin: Cyprian's servant, missing after fleeing Constantinople

Mesih: Emperor Constantine's heir and nephew, renamed and made part of the court

Murad: Emperor Constantine's heir and nephew, renamed after Mehmed's father and made part of the court

Ishak Pasha: Powerful pasha in charge of military forces

Mahmoud Pasha: Powerful pasha in charge of military forces

Ali Bey: Leader of the Janissary troops

Kiril: Janissary under Radu in charge of 4,000 mounted soldiers

Urbana of Transylvania: Expert in cannons and artillery

Lada Dracul's Inner Military Circle

Matei: Dead

Nicolae: Lada's closest friend

Petru: Dead

Stefan: Lada's best spy

Grigore: Wallachian soldier under Lada's command

Doru: Wallachian soldier under Lada's command

Allies of Lada

Matthias Corvinas: King of Hungary

King Stephen: King of Moldavia, Lada's cousin

GLOSSARY

bey: Governors of Ottoman provinces

boyars: Wallachian nobility

concubine: Woman who belongs to the sultan and is not a legal wife but could produce legal heirs

dracul: Dragon, also devil, as the terms were interchangeable

Hagia Sophia: Cathedral built at the height of the Byzantine era, the jewel of the Christian world

harem: Group of women consisting of wives, concubines, and servants that belongs to the sultan

infidels: Term used for anyone who does not practice the religion of the speaker

irregulars: Soldiers in the Ottoman Empire who are not part of officially organized troops, oftentimes mercenaries or men looking for spoils

Janissary: Member of an elite force of military professionals, taken as boys from other countries, converted to Islam, educated, and trained to be loyal to the sultan

GLOSSARY

Moldavia: Neighboring country and ally of Wallachia

Order of the Dragon: Order of Crusaders anointed by the pope

pasha: Noble in the Ottoman Empire, appointed by the sultan

spahi: Military commander in charge of local Ottoman soldiers called up during war

Transylvania: Small country bordering Wallachia and Hungary; includes the cities of Brasov and Sibiu

vaivode: Warlord prince

vassal state: Country allowed to retain rulership but subject to the Ottoman Empire, with taxes of both money and slaves for the army

Wallachia: Vassal state of the Ottoman Empire, bordered by Transylvania, Hungary, and Moldavia

AUTHOR'S NOTE

Please see the author's note in *And I Darken* for more information on resources for further study on the fascinating lives of Vlad Tepes, Mehmed II, and Radu cel Frumos. In the end, this series is a work of fiction. I have tried to incorporate as much history as respectfully as I can, and encourage anyone intrigued to further study this time period and region.

The characters in the series all interact with religion, and more specifically Islam, in various ways. I have nothing but respect for the rich history and beautiful legacy of that gospel of peace. Individual characters' opinions on the complexities of faith, both Islamic and Christian, do not reflect my own.

Spelling varies between languages and over time, as do place names. Any errors or inconsistencies are my own. Though the main characters speak a variety of languages, I made an editorial decision to present all common terms in English.

ACKNOWLEDGMENTS

Normally I save the best for last, but in this, the last book, I'm thanking the best first: Noah, you're the best person I know, and I'm so lucky to have a life with you. These books wouldn't exist without you.

Thank you to Michelle Wolfson, my savvy and insightful agent. I don't ever want to do this job without you. That might read as a little threatening, given that we've just spent several hundred pages with Lada . . . but it's meant to be a *lot* threatening. Never stop being an agent.

Thank you to Wendy Loggia, my incredible editor, who has shepherded this trilogy from the very beginning. I've benefitted from your contagious enthusiasm at every stage. You are a joy to work with, and I look forward to many more books together.

Thank you to Beverly Horowitz and Audrey Ingerson at Delacorte Press for the editorial and career guidance. To my stalwart copyeditors, Colleen Fellingham and Heather Lockwood Hughes, we lift boxes and raise eyebrows, I know, but I'll make the same mistakes in the next book. I'm glad you'll be there to fix it. To the First In Line and Get Underlined teams, thank you for coming up with new and exciting ways to find readers so that I can sit alone on my couch hanging out in the fifteenth century instead. To Aisha Cloud, I promise to never eat at an IHOP again as long as you keep being my delightful publicist. To John Adamo, Adrienne Waintraub, and everyone in marketing for executing such brilliant plans and sending our dragons to readers across the country. To Felicia Frazier and the sales team for such passionate and unwavering support.

The incredible covers of this series were painted by Sam Weber and consistently exceeded my wildest dreams. Isaac Stewart, thank you for the amazing maps, and Alison Impey, thank you for the stunning design work.

To Barbara Marcus and everyone at Delacorte Press and Random House Children's Books, there's a reason you were my dream house. It is a tremendous privilege to make books with you.

Thank you to Penguin Random House worldwide and Ruth Knowles for taking care of Lada in the UK and Australia. I wish I could join her there.

As always, an acknowledgments section cannot go by without including my two best writing friends. Natalie Whipple, you're always there for me, even when your own journey is bumpy. If I were Lada, I'd totally pick you for my inner circle. (But then you'd probably die, so let's have me be Radu instead.) Stephanie Perkins, you make everything better—my books and my life. I'm so lucky to have you as my friend.

Thank you to my three beautiful children for your patience and encouragement. The daily question "Are you all caught up yet?" really helped. (Seriously, though, you three are amazing and delightful and creatively nourishing.)

ACKNOWLEDGMENTS

Finally, to my readers. You've come so far with Lada and Radu. Thank you for embracing this fictional family of mine, for proving that no idea is too weird, no girl is too brutal, and no boy is too tender for readers of YA. You are going to change the world, and I can't wait to see how you do it.

ABOUT THE AUTHOR

KIERSTEN WHITE is the *New York Times* bestselling author of *And I Darken* and *Now I Rise*. She lives with her family near the ocean in San Diego, which, in spite of its perfection, spurs her to dream of faraway places and even further away times.

Visit her at kierstenwhite.com and follow @kierstenwhite on